# Murders In Time.

The story of Jake Rutter, a man, who can 'Time-Scape,' into the past.

## A work of fiction by Raymond Leonard Jones.

\*\*\*

*List of Contents.*
*Introduction.*
*A murder in Time.*
*The Diary.*
*About Quantum Time.*
*A First Meeting.*
*Back to Exeter in real time.*
*A Time Vortex.*
*The Reading Room.*
*The Next Day.*
*A Treasure Trove.*
*A Marriage of Convenience.*
*The Murder of a King.*
*A Danish Wedding.*
*Gytha.*
*The Romany People.*
*The Green Man.*
*The Test.*
*The Story of Gytha Godwinson.*
*Bishop Leofric of Exeter.*

*The Invitations.*

*Canute.*

*At Exeter.*

*Mandy Jones.*

*Back to Jelling.*

*The Fires of Hell.*

*A New Understanding.*

*Jake Rutter.*

*Hastings.*

*The Memory Stick.*

*Cern.*

*A Rift in Time.*

*Afterwards.*

*The End.*

*Epilogue.*

*Introduction...*

"Dr Robinson Sir, There is a young woman here to see you. I am sorry to interrupt you Sir, and she does not have an appointment, but from what she has told me I think you will wish to see her. She Is the Wife of Jake Rutter. And she has told me that he is dying, and she needs your help?"

*

You should know that My name is Dr Simon Robinson, I am one of the senior consultants, and the head of the Psychiatric department, at the Royal and Devon hospital in Exeter.

*And, on hearing what Jane had said over the speaker phone I felt my heart miss a beat as I heard that name from the past. As Jake had become so much more to me since he was my patient. and now, I had come to think of him thought of him as the son, we had lost in the war in Afghanistan.*

I knew I had to see his wife , and not keep her waiting if Jake, was in trouble. As Jake Rutter had been the person who was both a good friend and the young man who had set me on course to achieve the fame and fortune, that had followed my work with him.

*So, when Mandy Rutter came to my surgery in Exeter with the letter and the diary. And of course, I had to see her for Jakes's sake, as Jake had become very dear to me, and I thought of him as a second son. I had never had, as we had formed such a strong bond and I had been his Doctor and then a close friend, since our first meeting.*

All this started for me, when I was asked to treat the young lad, Jake Rutter, who had tried to kill himself, because he could no longer cope with the voices in his head. And the vision dreams, he had about some of the people he was to encounter? As I am now seen as one of the foremost experts, on Dissociative Identity Disorder, syndrome.

*So, when this Mandy Rutter, was brought into my consulting room, I saw she had been crying and was more than a little distraught and afraid of something terrible.*

And I tried to get my own emotions in order, as Johnson had said to me on the intercom, that this woman Mrs Rutter, had told her that her Jake was dying!

*So, when she came into my consulting room, she had a plastic carrier bag, that held some documents and book. The bag she was hugging to her broad chest as if it was the most precious thing in the world.*

But, this Mandy Rutter, was not at all the type of women that would have thought Jake would find attractive? Or ever marry.

*But It was my fault that we had not met before this. I had tried hard to get myself free to go to his wedding , but I was abroad, and it was such a quick affair.*

As far as I knew, the women Jake had liked, were the tall Icelandic type. Not this brown-haired short lady, with her wide face and hips and her tanned face? But here was a woman from the Welsh valleys, I thought, when I heard her thank Johonson for her help.

*"Thank you kindly, My Jake said you have a kind heart, so he did. But I must see the doctor see!"*

However, here, was a dark-haired short woman, with shoulder brown hair. A wide-open face and ruddy complexion, and when she spoke, we heard her rich warm voice that had a trace of a Welsh accent. I saw her look away, from my searching gaze, and to look at the photo of and Jake and I that was fitted on the wall behind my chair, and It was Mandy Jones, who broke the ice, and brought me back to the business in hand.

As I also thanked Johnson for her help, and looked at Mrs Rutter, across my desk and pointed to the seat, I said to my departing Nurse and secretary.

*"Jane my dear, will you find some tea, I hope you like tea Mrs Rutter, or we could have coffee?"*

Mandy smiled such a wide-open smile that lit up her whole face as she spoke to me with her warm Welsh ascent. I saw then, what Jake had seen, in this strong woman, as here was no Welsh Milk Maid, as her brown eyes were alive with intelligence. As was her whole demeaner, as she said to me,

*"Tea would be wonderful and as strong as you like. Two sugars and a dash please if you would be so kind. Doctor. you see Ido need to calm me nerves before I can speak to you…About my Jake?"*

I saw a woman, who knew who she was. and that was a strong and well-dressed middle-aged woman, and determined to tell me herstory, no matter what. She was Sitting there looking at me so directly , I had to turn away, to geta better look at her. and what I saw how much this meeting meant to her, with her hair piled up on top of her head and wearing a brown business suit and dark stocking, on her feet was a pair of light brown low-heeled shoes.

As she smiled, so did her farmers tanned face lit up, at seeing the tea and cake. As she said this, she gave me such a wide smile, I saw thewoman who had stolen Jake heart with that smile. As I said.

*"Well then , your news must wait until you have had some tea. But I am a very busy man, Mrs Rutter, and you have said Jake is in trouble. So please tell me what I can do to help you both?"*

She looked at me over her teacup, realising she had not used the saucer, and as the tea was very hot ,she put her hand to catch the drips. I saw just how out of her depth she was with me, but she managed to say.

*"I know's you know all about my Jake, and his special abilities Doctor, an' that he sometimes goes into some sort of a fit or dream state. So, he does?*

Was that the problem he was in then, well I had helped hm once before to come back to this world, and perhaps I was needed to do so again as for this Mandy, the woman he had married?

*I also knew that she worked in the History department at Exeter university with Jake, and I could not understand what the cause of this wreck of a woman was, who was sitting in my office.*

Then, as she decided to tell me all of it, she put the cup down with a thud, as if she had decided to let it all out ,she said.

*Well, the trouble is that he has been helping us in the University, to read some old books, you see. An' yus will not believe what he can do! But now he has left us and he canna' come back, see."*

Her Welsh accent was now coming out as her emotions took hold of her words.

*"Look Sir, it is all here in me bag, So it is, an' his letter. And now I need to use your facilities if you do not mind? So perhaps you can read his letter and then we can talk. What say you me boyo. I mean Sir?"*

I rang for Jane, and she took Mandy to our rest room and the toilets, I opened the bag inside. In it was his diary, and a paper manuscript, of A4 typed pages, which said this was a book he called.

## A Study of Murder. in Time?

There was a letter, which said.

*Well Professor, I am sending you these documents, because I need your help again. You see ,I may have time slipped back into the past, and I cannot return!*

Not without your help. I have also left a letter with Mandy, which tells her to find you, should the worst happen, and I am trapped in one of my vision dreams, for any long period.

And before you decide I am mad to think I am stupid enough to think I am a **TIME TRAVELLER!**

And before you think I have gone stark raving mad.

I ask you to read my diary and these typed pages that are a transcript of what the Bishop of Exeter who lived in the year one thousand.

It was Bishop Leofric, wrote about the Godwinson family so long-ago in the Tenth century.

But you will see they are incomplete, and tell his story, and not the official histories, we have come to believe to be our history?

And now I know you will think I have relapsed again, but the truth is even more amazing.

You see I read these pages in a series of books, that were hidden in the History department of Exeter university.

But in a secret codex that only I could read.

But that is not all, as with the help of my abilities, I was able to help the people the to read and record these pages, which as you will see, concern the life and times of the Godwinsons, including, King Harold Godwinson!

But I do not expect you to believe all this without proof, and once you have read my diary, and these pages?

I ask you to visit Exeter and ask for the head of the History department there who is Susan Simonson.

*And she will explain why we need your help in all this, as you, Professor, may have the key to bring my mind back to our time.*

*Jake Rutter.*

So now, and while Mandy was not here, I knew that I must at least read his diary, and then, I was so caught up in this incredible story, I looked at my old notes, on Jake Rutter. And study up on the possibilities of Time travel?

But first I must take care of his wife, and I knew that this was going to take the rest of my morning now. So, I went to find Jane, and ask her to look after Mandy.

*"Jane my dear, I fear that we are going to have to clear my diary for the rest of this day. And I need you to take care of Mrs Rutter for me. I expect she has not had lunch. Perhaps you could take her to the Royal Clarance for me? and buy her a room there. Tell her to comeback in the morning and then we will see what can be done. She will not want to leave us. But you must Insist, she goes with you, with a promise that I will see her again in the morning. Cancel my first appointment. Can you do that?*

So now, and before looking at what Mrs Rutter had given me, I went to my files to read my notes on the man that is that was Jake Rutter.

*So was My mind was sent back to our first meeting, When he was forced to set down so that he could make some sense of his life, after terrible the car crash, which was to change his life so dramatically As all Jakes problems was caused, by the crash he had been involved in. A crash by another car coming around a Devon corner, and his car was hit by a young man in a sports car.*

A gift from his wealthy father, as a prize, for the young man having passed his driving test. But he was driving too fast, he had run out of road, on the hairpin bend near Sidbury, Exeter Devon

Moreover, Exeter city was the place he, and his parents, had chosen to move to because of the school for the deaf, which was located there. As it transpired that Jake has been born with an enlarged head, and that needed the use of forceps to bring him out of his mother's womb.

*And soon they were to discover his hearing defect, and as he got older, it was become much worse. So, the Rutters moved to from London, to Exeter, so that Jake, could attend one of the best teaching schools for the deaf. A well respected residential and teaching School, for the hard of hearing. which was located there.*

Now and after some time, the school had found out the main cause of his problems, that were because of another birth defect, as his brain had not stopped growing. They said, he needed a series of electrical treatment to help stop his brain swelling. Or an invasive operation to enlarge his skull?

But after speaking to his doctors, they agreed that before this drastic surgery, I could try to help him using my new electronic shock treatments, and some hypnotherapy?

*But now and learning of his vision dreams and While it worked, I now believe it was these electronic shock treatment that were the cause of his troubles in later life.*

But the result was he was left without any hair on his head, and body. A fact which he hid from sight with a wig, and a hat, when he went out into the world. And he was totally deaf.

It was after the car accident that Jake was put under my care, and eventually, I was able to treat him for his illness, which we discovered, was some sort of a dual personality disorder.

An ability to see into a person's mind and look into their past lives. To be able to delve their minds and souls, and to dream about these multiple personalities and their past and current lives?

*Jake could Time slip? Or that was what he called it?*

We called it, a Dissociative Identity Disorder, is a mental health disorder in which a patient develops one or more distinct identities or alter egos.

And, in some cases, these alternately personas, take control of one's perceptions of space and time, held within the same person.

What makes it more interesting is that each personality is completely unaware of the others' existence.

So it was, that I was able to study Jake Rutter in depth, and to bring out all these problems under hypnosis, these dual personality symptoms and what causes the condition?

And now, I am considered to be one of the foremost experts, in the treatment of people with dual personalities disorders.

*Such cases are often the result of severe psychological trauma such as sexual or physical abuse at an early age by a close relative. Or in Rutters case, the loss of a loved one, that you cannot accept, and invent a different life, to avoid confronting this reality?*

The schism affecting the main personality is often a coping mechanism, which allows the patient to deal with this abuse, or trauma and the disorder is more commonly seen in females.

*As, this Dual personality disorder, and its symptoms, will vary in severity between different patients. In mild cases, the symptoms might only occur when the person is under great mental and emotional stress, but in more chronic cases, multiple personalities can continuously appear and take control. Resulting in a mental breakdown and even madness!*

Typical indicators of a multiple personality disorder include At least two distinct personalities within the same person, each of which relates to the world in a completely different way.

*For example, one personality might be passive and quiet, whereas another might be aggressive and demanding. However, these changes over from one personality to another can happen in the space of a few seconds.*

The patient will then seemingly become another person who exhibits completely different characteristics to the main personality.

*At least two of the personalities assume control of the person's behaviour at separate times, usually dependant on the circumstances at the time. Although it is not uncommon for as many as ten different personalities, to inhabit the same body. And in the worst documented cases, there have been cases where patients have exhibited hundreds of personalities.*

In most of these cases, the patient is unable to remember personal information when asked. Each personality assumes a different identity including name, age, personal history, and family details. These can include a different gender and nationality from the main identity, and, in some rare cases, a completely different species.

*However, Patients suffering from dual personality disorder, often lose large chunks of memory, as a result of flitting between different personalities. Patients might lose their childhood memories or forget about extended periods of their life.*

Another symptom of multiple personality disorder is "Complete Depersonalisation" *A patient will describe an out of body sensation in which they have no control over their physical self. They might describe seeing their body change shape or colour, or even dissolving into nothing.*

This can also affect external objects, which is known as *"derealisation".*

*Then, The patient might feel as if the world around them is no longer* **"real"**, *or it is constantly* **changing**, *in some way.*

*Other symptoms of multiple personality disorder, include depression, panic and anxiety attacks, unexplained phobias, paranoia, unexplained headaches, aches and pains, and flashbacks of abuse and psychological trauma.*

But the Diagnosis of dual personality disorder, is not always straightforward, as symptoms are not dissimilar to other conditions, such as borderline personality disorder, epilepsy, post-traumatic stress disorder, mood disorders, anxiety disorders, and schizophrenia.

Putting down Jakes file, I knew that all this began for me and Mr Rutter, when he was put under my care when his body had recovered from the car accident, but he had started having fits and he would drop into a coma?

*It was when Jake told me about the car accident, and that it had been his fault! My first thought these black outs, was his way of escaping from his guilt. As he had been driving and his parents had died that day!*

But then when I hypnotised him, so did we meet the real cause of his problem. and how he was able to make contact with people, in some sort of a vision dream?

*I saw this, as his mind trying to hide from his grief and loss of his parents, as he was blaming himself for their deaths.*

*So, with hypnosis treatments and some special drugs, he was able to tell me about the guilt he felt, and we were able to stop the headaches nightmares. So did the dreams stop coming. And he was eventually discharged from my care.*

That was on the day, he was discharged back into the world on his twenty first birthday…

\*

Having finished with my Typed notes And then I took up the diary which is headed Murders in time? And look up the latest thinking about the possibility of Time travel and |the field of Quantum physics! As far as I knew

Time travel was all nonsense, and science fiction.

*But I was to be proven wrong as the deeper I looked into this phenomenon.*

I was taught that your past, will always be your past as far as your own memories are concerned.

I had read somewhere, that It must not be possible to change it, as to do so, any time traveller find themselves ensnared in the problems of the Novikov self-Con is tansy PRINCIPLE. and also, the BOOTSTRAP PARADOX

Law, that say's that one cannot go back in time to charge your post or the events in your time personal timeline.

As to do would destroy your future.

And this is also seen as the Novikov's Principle. that says any action by a tone alerting on the past will lead to a time paradox.

And the matte of the universe as self-correcting. As it will only allow time to flow, in a constant streams or loop. and prevents the forming of such a paradox?

This the BOOTSTRAP PARADOX, which prevents, such a temporal entanglement. It says that if one could alter an event in your timeline , one would risk changing our future self, and erase the very information in the future, that will allow one, To travel to the past and create a temporal rift, where the events of the post change and can no longer align with their own time.

So, one's timeline, will no longer align with one future and their timeline where they came from, the person will not exist there? So, ensuring that the post remains locked in the past.

*But now Jake has said that he can reach into the past. Just how this can be possible, I could not imagine, but I also knew that his multiple personality disorder. di d allows him to think he can meet with people in his past. I thought I had given him away to tell the difference between reality, and these so-called vision dreams. So, what are these documents and what will they say or prove.*

*What if there is such a thing as Quantum space and time, as Einstein has said. My Goodness what was I getting into now?*

*What to do next. First, I will need some time to study these documents and then show them to some experts in History, and Quantum physics! As for Mrs Rutter I will tell her that I need sometime to decide if I can help them. Yes, that is a plan, a way to go! I will send her away, and start on the diary...*

\*\*\*

*The Diary.*

*Jake,*

So, diary, we come to the day I tried to kill myself! It was after the car accident, and when I knew I had caused the death of my parents in the car crash!

 But now after so many hospital treatments, I had been discharged fit and expected to live my life. as a normal young man should?

*The problem was that while they had healed my body, my mind, was a mess!*

And whilst I was still a young man, and quite well off, thanks to the large insurance pay out that my father had set up, and his trust fund. And because, he had also managed to buy some Shell oil shares, just before the War!

*And while I was a well-educated and fairly wealthy young man. The truth is, I am an emotional wreck! Not only because of my hearing defects, that was why I had spent my youth alone with my books and kept away from the real world by my loving parents.*

But that was behind me now, and thanks to the help I had received from Doctor. Simon Robinson, and at the school for the hard of hearing in Exeter. I now knew how to hand sign, and had a reasonable modern hearing aid, that allowed me to live normal life.

*So, when I was told there was nothing more, they could do for me, and I was told to leave the school that had been my home for five years. I am now twenty-one and lost again! Because I knew nothing of the real world of the opposite sex having spent my teenage years in a hospital of some sort, for most of my life?*

*So, when we came to Devon and the sale of the large house in Exeter, I knew I would not need to work. unless I wanted to spend my inheritance, but that was held in a trust fund, and I was given an allowance from it. So, I knew I had to be able to do something with my time, other than hiding away in the library, reading doing crosswords, and going to the cinemas, three times a week.*

It was when I saw an advertisement for people to be trained as computer programmers, and that they were asking for people who liked to do the Times crossword puzzle with little difficulty , they were invited to take their test, and join this new field of electronic computing...

*I applied and passed with flying colours, and became a good computer programmer, trained at St loyes a retraining establishment located, at St loyes college in Exeter.*

It was there, that I was qualified in general office skills, typing, as well as data input, a boring skill, for some? But I loved to see how a computer could solve so many of our day-to-day boring routine tasks.

*As, I found that loved the order of the numbers where everyone else, only saw as just rows of data.*

So, after gaining a degree in Computer science, at Exeter college. I was looking for employment, and eventually I was working for the Devon and Cornwall police. As a civilian office worker in the civil section, working in their computer department imputing their data and reports. In that way I was to learn all their methods and routines.

*But as it turned out the truth of it was that it was a safe bolt hole, and I was hiding from life there, and whilst I was now only twenty-five, I was healed in body, but scarred in my soul.*

If I went to the bathroom, and to look into the long mirror, there, *An act I tried to avoid as much as possible?*

I would see a strong and well-muscled young man with a strong body and who stood six feet tall.

But this visage was spoilt by my large bald head, and my sticky out ears. As for the white face, that looked back at me, it could never be seen as handsome, as my head been damaged at birth. *And from one direction, my nose would seem to be a little lop sided?*

Aswell as a bald head, I had no eyelashes and used false eyelashes, and eyebrows, when In public? As I could never grow a beard. But then I saw my startling blue eyes, and my strong straight nose, my wide generous mouth, and full lips I had from my mother. And her, generous smile.

*A smile that would fill her blue eyes and make then sparkle with life!* A gift I came to treasure When *I was amused enough to do so. A man with such little confidence and esteem, who was still a virgin, and a social outcast.*

As for the rest of my long body and leg as and arms I had from my father and his height. As I was to find useful, in his job as a Policeman. Along with his big feet!

So then if I was in the mood not to be so critical about my head? I could see that I had a good bone structure and fathers' firm chin, and his long neck. *A feature that made my stupid head, to seemed to me to look like a lolly pop stuck onto my body. And as I was quite slim, this made it worse, as I tried to keep in shape by constant exercise. By using the gym, I had installed in my home. I found that I could drive myself to exhaustion and try to forget the dreams and nightmares.*

I did not know it then, but it was because of the many electrical treatments on my head and brain. And while they had solved the problems that were killing me?

*They had left me with a strange new ability that allowed me to see what lay behind the eye's and to be able to look into their mind and souls, of the people I would meet. Especially anyone I wanted to get to know or befriends with. But any of these relationships would never last, as I would and know if they were lying to me, or trying to hide who they really were.*

Then I saw their true nature and that they saw me as a bloody freak. So, one can see how this would make his life extremely difficult at times. Especially with the opposite sex, or anyone who saw me as a computer geek, and nothing more.

*A man who was to be avoided at all costs just in case people thought you were one.*

But there was another reason I was a loner, a freak with an oversized bald head, and no body hair. As well as my long body and my hairless body, which had been damaged by radiotherapy. So, what I saw in the mirror, was a man and a freak!

*A man with a very white skin as I would burn and become a lobster in the sunlight? A man to avoid in the staff room, a man with no social graces or small talk.*

But there was another reason I needed to avoid close contact with people and that was my strange ability to see into the minds of some people who were not who they pretended to be? Or someone who had committed a crime or was going to?

At first, I could do this not by choice, and not every time But it was triggered by simply touching them, or an object they used. ,sometimes I saw into their eyes a glimpse of how theywere killed.

*A terrible ability and a curse! Or I saw their hatred for their lives, and yes fears, that they had hidden away for so long And yes also kindness and goodwill.*

But the result was that I would concentrate on my work and escape into the new digital world of Computers and the new virtual world of gaming.

*That was why I had given up trying to make contact with people, as I lived a lonely life listening to classical music, reading, and going to the cinema at least three times a week.*

*But my life was now caught up in the many new exciting computer games that were available. I began to think I did not need anyone in my life.* As I became a recluse, and lost myself in the worlds of computer games, and would read the books I could download.

*As for going out, I developed a series disguises to hide my white eyes and baldness with a hat or as hoodie?`*

One of my favourite set of Novels before the accident, had been the Saint stories, written by Leslie Charteris about his hero Simon Templer, who was the opposite of my life.

I saw how and James Bond, were so cool, and elegant, with his fine clothes and his smooth persona and the avatar as the Saint, a man who would sometimes help the police to solve the fictional crimes or frustrate inspector Eustace as he tried to trap his nemesis!

*Perhaps It was then, I read the novel, written about The Scarlet Pimpernel, by Broness Orczy!*

Her books were `which was a novel set in the eighteenth century, a time, where an English nobleman used his time and money to defeat, the evil regime, that had gripped France. I became Sir Percy Blakney, as he would find a way to save the people he saw In France. As then and he could help the hated Aristo's, escape the Guillotine.

So now I had a new hero, someone, who with guile and cunning, he managed by using so many disguises and ruses to bring the French nobles to England, with his faithful band of followers,

*So then as I became involved in that world of computer fantasy! I saw a way I could change myself into something like and someone I was not! .It started by reading some of the data I was collating and the police retorts about a serious crime. Usually, an unsolved murder or serious crimes.*

Then I would go to that place dressed in my new persona, of a crime reporter for a newspaper.

It was three years later and now I was a little more confident of myself and not quite so introspective. As, I was managing my life a little better and I had even had sex. And I had built myself into what the world saw as a confident man of Twenty-five.

*One day, all this was to change my life in a very special way. I was at the Exeter Racecourse, the place there had been a murder in broad daylight with hundreds of people there, as a man was pushed to his death under some racing horses. But no one could say who did this?*

It was that day, I saw a punter, or a Bookie, dressed in bright clothes, and a loud brown and red striped double breasted checked Suite, over a canary yellow waistcoat and red cravat. *So, I decided to use him as my first trial Public outing, in a big crowd?*

It was there that day I had a very strong vision , as when he brushed past me, I was caught up in a whirl of emotions, as he pushed me against the wall, I hit my head and was unconscious for a very brief moment?

*It was then I saw the man pushed down the stairs by the Bookies runner. I later found out that this attack, was pr-determined, so that this winning punter could not go to claim his winnings, But he was killed on the steps! Just to avoid his master having to pay out a one hundred to one winning bet that would have ruined him. But then it happened before I could do or say anything!*

*But what should I do about this murder?*

But later, It had been a simple matter to send a note to the police Inspector who was in charge of the investigation. I gave an accurate the report of this incident, describing what I had seen. And the culprit was later questioned and confessed!

So, here then, was a new outlet for my skills, and after that I bought a police officer scanner, I could listen in on their channels, hoping to be able to learn how to use my skills, and curse, to help society in a very useful way As my curse would be used for good?

*How stupid was that! and soon, I could no longer control my dreams! And, Although, I had promised myself to stop listening to the police channels', or to scan their radio messages. This was my only contact with the real world, and this work became my drug.*

Then there were so many more instances where the police were to be helped by another letter from me, that would provide the police with an incredible lead?

*I knew eventually, this was going to become too much for my mind to bear, as the nightmares returned, and I had to take sleeping pills to get to sleep.*

And then they no longer worked, as I began to fall apart. So did my work at the office of Jones and Jones, a firm of solicitors, began suffering, and Was told my work was no longer up to standard, And I was to leave at the end of this month. and until then, I was put on sick leave…

However, It was a policeman, John Barton, who was a part of the Canine unit, who had saved me from committing suicide, when it had all seemed to me that the only way to stop these terrible headaches and vision dreams was to end my life. *As no one would miss me or care.*

That day, I had bought a half bottle of whisky, and a length of large rubber hose, which I could fit to the car exhaust, and I was going to park up  going to use to kill myself in the Stoke woods. A place where there were so many parking places deep in the woods, and my car would not be found for days? I would go to sleep and hide from the voices once and for all.

*But I had not counted on dog walkers, and just as I was dosing off in a haze of whisky infused sleep, and the poison exhaust fumes. There was a knocking on the car windows and then someone opened the unlocked back door, and the fresh air cleared the fumes away, I was pulled out of the car nearly unconscious.*

I heard a Voice say.

*"There you are laddie, Come Rover! I think we have found him just in time. Come man this is no way to try to kill yourself. Surely things cannot be so bad you would do such a stupid thing. Suicide is an evil thing, so it is?"*

Rover was his cocker spaniel, has trained police dog, who could smell out death, or blood, and John Barton was my saviour, *Just walking his dog.*

*I awoke, held in a strait jacket but in a mental hospital room*

But the man who really saved me, and my sanity was one of the Psychiatrist at the mental hospital. He is Dr Simon Robinson, he was one am one of the senior consultants, and the head of the Psychiatric department, at the Royal and Devon hospital in Exeter.

It was he who realised that I was suffering from what he called a Dissociative Identity Disorder. But he said It was a treatable illness, is a mental health disorder brought on by the electrical treatments I had been given?

They had brought about dysfunction in my brain, and some sort of schism ,where a patient develops one or more distinct identities or alter egos, that alternately take control within the same person.

*And so it was that, with his help, I was cured of headaches and visions. For a time anyway!*

\*\*\*

It was a month later at the funeral of a friend I had met in the hospital, I met up with John Barton again, I was to learn he was a dog handler, who worked in the Canine unit based at Exeter police headquarters, and this unit was a part of the police force police.

That these dog handlers, and their trained dogs were used on all sorts of duties, crowd control, and were trained to be sniffers. After training they could specialise to search buildings and vehicles for any sign of drugs, or blood. And that he would be able to go places no human or machine could do, and in that way, they were used for search and rescue after any disaster? Such as an earthquake or explosion, then to send them searching for any survivors? *And then I realised that was something I could do, once Barton told me that. He told me that I should also apply to join this police unit, as detective Roger Short, had also said I would be suitable candidate.*

So, after my basic training at Hendon, and when my abilities had been tested and found to be so special, I was then trained to use a dog as part of their everyday duties, as my dog was to be my constant companion, on and off duty. As we were both trained to look for people by following their scent once they had been set on the trail?

*Moreover, they also were used to sniff out drugs, and explosives, when needed?*

And that is how the meeting with Barton was to change my life once again, I was trained to become a dog handler, and partnered up with Jasper, a one-year-old German shepherd, a male dog, who was now my saviour in so many ways. As now I could see myself reborn as a confident young man who had a job to do, and I could use my abilities to do good deeded.

As I soon managed to bond with Jasper who was my sniffer, we were inseparable after that. As we both became one of the top three teams at Exeter compound. And we were able to form such an incredible bond and a new life together, and the event that was to change my life so drastically. When I met Mandy Jones…

***

So that's why I, and John Barton, were sent to Exeter university that day to investigate the suspicious death of Professor Higgins, the head of the history department there. He had been found dead in a locked research room. With no windows and the doors had been locked from inside. However, detective Roger Short, was the officer who attended the report, sent in by the police Sargent, of a suspicious death of a man, who was found dead in a locked room? And to send someone to look into this, was the normal routine in such circumstances, for a healthy man.

*However, It had been the Inspector, who warned us about what we would find there, as the Chancellor and his Vice principle, was not going to be very co-operative, as he hated the adverse publicity, our visit would bring.*

So, when we came with our dogs, and before we were allowed to see the body or the room, the Principal of the University, said he needed to speak with us. As he thought this was just a normal death and a heart attack and he needed to make sure we did not say otherwise. As he then told us that he had been forced to allow our dogs on the premises.

*And we could not speak to the press about this investigation, as our presence would alert the media to the Professor's demise, and they would be sure to be looking to exploit any bad publicity, especially as the funding of the University was currently up for a review? And the Archaeological and History departments would be the first to go, if we found theywere lacking in any way?*

Perhaps that was why were given a brief by one of the other professors, the Vice chancellor. Rupert Heading.

I had been warned that Heading, was not at all pleased to have the police come forcing their way into his domain! But this was an unexplained death, and he had no option to cooperate with us, but once again he tried to insist that his was a case of an unfortunate heart attack, as Professor Higgins, was known to live a heavy smoker, with very unhealthy lifestyle, and living on campus, he had an eye for the ladies, and was very overweight.

*Not the report that Short had filed Mentioned this, But as he had no history of heart problems, the coroner would not certify that as the cause of death!*

*And now to cap it all, the police were bringing dogs into his beloved Halls.*

Not wanting them to bring our hairy animals into his study, he met us in the public lobby, that is outside the History department, where his secretary Mary Frost, was trying to stop us entering his domain. But She had list of who his staff were, and Mary Canning , a secretary receptionist, was pinning on our visitor badges, which would allow us through the electronic security doors, which led into the Staff sections, and the Research department.

*The inner sanctum, where Higgins had been working on the newly discovered Leofric files and books.*

The badges on our uniforms identified us as Sargent John Barton, of the police Dog handling department, and me as Inspector, J Rutter!

*As I had recently been promoted over John, but he had been pleased and we managed to remain fiends and colleges.*

I realised that Heading, did not want this to take any longer than necessary, so he tried to do as little as he could manage. but I saw the look in his eyes that said, he was not going to do anything to help us this day.

"Well then officers, we are at your disposal this afternoon ,and I have told my staff to make themselves available to you this afternoon, and we have closed the department for as long as this unfortunate visit is necessary?

 But I have taken the time to look into this unfortunate matter myself. You see we have some security footage for you to see, and it shows that poor Richard was alone *when he had a heart attack. But I must leave you to make your own conclusions, I am told!*

*And I have a meeting of the Governors. So, Mary here, will take you and these...these dogs, to meet with Miss Susan Simonson, is our senior History lecturer, and Richard's right arm. Or was. I bid you good day gentlemen, and pray that we can soon get back to our proper business, officers?"*

Then to Mary .

*"Pease send for the cleaners will you there is dog hair and paw prints all along our hallway?"*

So then, as we were we passed through the corridors that led to the History department, and then, onto the section storerooms, and into their inner sanctum that was their record rooms, that also held the university treasures.

And then into a long reading room, which was set out with the normal lined bookshelves, some study tables with angled tops, and Anglepoise lamps, where they could rest their precious books and such like along with the normal set up of office desks and some computer terminals.

We were greeted by Susan Simonson, a very tall an extremely striking young woman, who I thought was in her mid-thirties, and she looked at us with some annoyance on her face and in her eyes? She was wearing a long white laboratory coat, that hid her slim figure, and a badge that said, she was the senior science technician at the History department. To show that she was on duty today.

But It was her assistant Mandy Jones, who broke the ice, As she smiled when she saw us, and then her face was lit up with a wide smile when she saw the dogs. Her tanned wide face lit up, with joy at seeing the boys.

*So here then, was another dog lover and were straining to go to her, as she knelt down to greet them, her arm brushed mine, I was able to unintentionally delve her, and what I saw was her dark brown hair and how short she was. I looked again at her badge, which said she was Mandy Ruth Jones.*

Here was a woman from the Welsh hills then? possibly a farmer's daughter, who had escaped the farm, to get a science degree?

*But I told Jasper to stay, as I did not want his nose to be contaminated by her strong body smells, As Ruth was someone who would produce sweat just by moving. But I knew then that here was a good and fine woman who would not hurt a fly!*

Or the strong perfume Susan Simonson used to hide the chemical smells, that came from her lab coat. I knew that perfume, I thought was honeysuckle.

The secretary used another type, there was a bottle on her desk. It was Black poison, not a foretelling I had to hope! As that smell wafted towards us and before the dogs were contaminated by it, I had to intervene and speak to them with some urgency.

*"Please Stay away from us and the dogs ladies. You must leave us to do our job, Can you go outside if you will, as we must be able to do our work here this day, We will use the dogs to sweep the room before we can talk! Is there another room you could go to, and we will talk later?"*

I saw Susan Simonson, stiffen at this admonition, and my abrupt words, but I knew the dogs would be contaminated by their scent, and almost useless, for their task. Which was to smell out any drugs, or foul presence, such as violence and any blood still here?

It was Jones who spoke, and she was the opposite to Simonson, a dark-haired short woman, with shoulder brown hair, held in a hair-nett, to keep it tidy, she had wide open face and ruddy complexion, and when she spoke, we heard her rich warm voice that had a trace of a Welsh accent.

*"Well, as to that officers, we have been told what you need to do, so we were! And we will wait in the office over there. So, we shall. But please be quick about it as we have some tests to finish in here, so we do.*

*And if you must be about your business, I will put the kettle on, shall I? Coffee or tea? And water for your wonderful dogs if it be allowed?"*

As she said this, she gave us such a wide smile, she could not have deemed much different from the pompous vice Chancellor, or her boss. Susan Simonson,
Indeed, even in her long white laboratory coat, pulled over a black lace bra, that was showing the top of her ample breasts, and matching body, I saw Mandy, was someone I was going to warm to.

As for her boss Susan, here was truly beautiful woman, who could be from her Viking heritage, as she was so tall, and fair headed? With her long fine hair held in a hair net which had been platted, and tied up in two long braids, ending in a silver clasp and also held in a laboratory hair nett. She also wore thin rubber gloves, presumably to stop any contamination, when they needed to handle the books, and the objects laid out for our inspection.

*What were the tests I wondered?*

I had already seen there was a velvet bag of some sort, and a long-handled sword, as well as four books, as |Susan said in a very firm tone, Intended to tell us she was in charge here.

*"Ruth my dear, that is very kind of you my dear! But we should not keep these officers here any longer than necessary!"* Then to me. *"But it is our coffee break officers, and you both are willing to share it? But I am so sorry, officers, you see, we cannot allow these dogs into the common room. With our food. Can they stay outside In the yard when they have done what they need to do?"*

It was then, I realised she was afraid of them. And us? and I had to wonder why as the look she gave me was one that said she was hiding a secret.

*And one that she did not want to share? With that demand, I looked more deeply into her face and tried to delve her, but her gloves prevent any handshake , and what I saw was her long neck, her high cheek bones, and pointed nose, small mouth.*

What I felt in my mind, was here was a throwback to the Viking age? As, with her fair hair. And her startling blue eyes, a tight thin smile, a false smile, which did not reach her eyes? And when she came to leave us, she stood up she was so tall, and quite beautiful. As I managed to say.

*"Black Coffee for me if you please and Officer Barton, will stay with the dogs, if that is allowed? He is a tea drinker and likes it as strong as you like. Then we must talk about these books of yours, and these objects, but I*

*must warn you both, that I need to be able to handle and to be allowed to touch them?"*

Susan, on seeing, and hearing, that our two dogs were not going to touch her, she gave a gasp of obvious relief, but did not try to touch them, as she said.

*"Ho' how lovely officers, but I was told not to say anything to you about Richard! So, if you will excuse me, I will be in the office over there, and we will talk when you are ready?"*

However, I was not surprised to see that this beautiful woman was not intending to be such a help in this investigation, and it was true, that I was more than a little confused.

But the truth was that I now saw she was not being completely honest with us? And her loathing of dogs was not the half of it, as I saw her eyes close when she looked at me, and become as hard as diamonds, when I said I needed to touch the books and artifacts?

*And even more upset, at my own reactions to think that this Woman and even Mandy Jones were possibly involved with the death of the man Higgins, in some way?*

As now I was very interested in what these women were going to do, and tell us about their relationship with Higgins? As for Mandy, I had felt my heart take a leap in my chest, to see how warm and welcoming she had been, and I thought she had returned my admiring gaze when she invited us to have some coffee?

*As I felt her warmth and realised that she liked me then. A feeling I had also and one we could build on.*

As for Susan, my first reaction was that she was an Ice princess.

Trying to pretend she had nothing to do with \Higgins, but I saw her eyes change, whenever his name was mentioned? Trying to stand so tall with her blonde hair, and to realise that here was a stunning, and incredibly intelligent woman. Someone, who would not look at me twice, seeing only as an ugly policeman and not the man I had become. An officer of the law

*Why then, did I want her to come to like me then? But now I knew and prayed, for the first time, I was wrong about a perp, and that these two women, were not involved in the death here?*

As for Jones, I had not yet managed to fully delve her, but I already could see the warm arura that surrounded her, and here was a warm and generous woman, and a woman with not an evil thought in her soul, or mind?

*But I was about to find out that first impressions could not always be trusted, As my mind was caught up with what Susan Simonson had said, and their secrets, Unsaid? Because when she stood up to leave the room, it*

*seemed to me. that she took the sunlight with her? as I saw just how tall she was, as her now and long slim legs once again I looked into her startling blue eyes.*

To see her intelligence shining in them, and with her long-pointed nose, her small thin wide mouth, her high cheek bones, that matches her slim trim body and pale skin, this woman could pass for a native of Denmark, or Norway? But it was John who brought me back to the task in hand.

"Come Jake when you have finished goggling at that woman? Perhaps we should make a start here? What are your first impressions, the dogs seem to be happy. But we should let them have a sniff?

"Yes, let them loose but there was murder done here, or I know nothing. There is an evil smell to this room. I will take the table.

We began, by starting on the last book on the right, and as Jasper, bent forward to sniff it, we were linked, and I felt just how much he disliked what he had found. As when Jasper rose on his fore legs, to put his paws on the table so that he could sniff its contents. And despite my urging, he was reluctant to move on, and I had to pull him away as now he was drooling with delight, as if this book was one of his favourite treats? So, I said, *"leave it Jasper come away lad, see here, come to this next book?* I had to pull him away, before his silva would spoil its leather cover. But now I knew that it was not this book, which was the cause of this problem with Higgins, as he had never touched it? But when we went to the next book, the third in line, this time Jasper, simply sniffed it, and gave the soft bark, that was our normal signal that this item, was not any part of this problem!

But the at the first book, Jasper pulled away from the table and he let out a low growl, and then a snarl. And I knew that this was the source of some evil deed. Then we came to the book that Higgins had touched

*This was the book which Higgin's had opened, and was reading in the video?*

began to whine, as he managed to pull away, and refused to touch it , but I pulled him back to it saying.

*"Come lad what is wrong with this; what can you feel?"* I realised then that he would have used his paw, to take it down from the table, if I had not stopped him.

But now, we came to the velvet bag, and before I could stop him, he had it in his mouth, and he had jumped down, and he was holding it in his paws, guarding it, as if it was one of his precious play toys. As he sniffed at the blue velvets bag, and its golden tie, spilling its contents on the ground, he lay protecting them, with his head and open jaw. Our sign that I was not to touch it!

*He had closed his eyes and was wagging his tail so much I thought he wasin some sort of ecstatic state.*

Barton had seen all this, as he said.

*"Goodness me Jake what is going on here. But one thing I know is that the next thing we need to do it to take a butchers at the security footage again To see How could we have missed that bag? perhaps that will give us a clue to what Jasper has found here?*

*Isaid, " I am sure it was not in the video, that is why? And I need speak to Miss Simonson, perhaps I could do that while you deal with our sniffers? I think we must take them back to the cages before Susan Simonson, has a fewking fit."*

John smiled as he let both the dogs lose , They began searching the room looking for any more problems in this room, or to find any other sort of some sort of an unusual scent. I went to speak with Simonson, knocking on her half-glazed office door, she called out to say it was open.

*"Finished already officer, then, what can I do for you now? "*

"Well Miss Simonson, I do not think our dogs will be of much more help, here today, but we cannot leave until we have seen the security footage again. can you put that up for us here?"

It was Jones who said.

"Yes of course, does your Sargent need to see it and I would like to give your lovely dogs drink, and a biscuit, if that is allowed."

"A biscuit , no sorry, they would be contaminated by you… By Your personal smells, you see. Look we will take them back to the van, and then we must ask you and your people some questions I am sorry, but I have a feeling that you are all hiding something about his death, and we cannot leave until we know what!"

I saw how shocked, and upset, she seemed at my words, and then her expression changed to one of surprised and then anger, as she said.

"Hiding something how dare you say that officer, when we have all bent over backwards to help you all? You should know that we all thought the world of Richard, and I happen to know he would not harm a fly and he was such a kind and generous man. I will not hear you say such terrible thigs. I can assure you; we all want you to get to the bottom of his death. Look inspector Rutter, what I am hiding is a personal matter. But if it will help *you see the truth, I loved him you see. But I could never tell him so. As he is happily married. Or was! So, you can put that in your report if you must!"*

So that was her secret, and nothing to do with the death?

And next we watched the security footage on her computer in her office. It just showed Higgins sitting at the reading table with four large books, placed on them, from left to right, all about the same size. He was peering at some open pages of the second, leaning forward to put his finger on a particular page and text.

Then, he just slumped forward to hit his head on the desk lamp, a blow that would not have killed him, I was sure of that!

But did not move again. Nothing more was shown next, until Mandy came into the room with a cup of coffee, and found Higgins was not breathing, and then she called for help, and Susan came to help Mandy to lay the professor down on the floor, and tried Susan tried to resuscitate him. *But, out of the corner of my eye, I saw Jones, take a slip of paper from his inside pocked, and hide it in the pocket on her overalls?*

Then they sent for the Vice principle and the ambulance men came, to say he was dead, and they would take him to hospital so that a doctor could examine him and certify the time of his death?

And that is what happened , but the coroner could not say conclusively w3hatwas the cause of death. So then were the police involved.

And when the video was finished, I asked Simonson what they were working on ,what were these books about.

*"Well officer, they are a very exciting new finds for us, and the whole of the Historical world, as they were written by Bishop Leofric at the time of the Norman invasion in 1066. We believe that they are his secret accounts of what really happened then, and not the lies William of Normandy set down, for our, and his benefit.*

*You see Leofric was deeply involved with the Godwinson family, for most of his adult life, and he became their Confessor. So, what he has written in these four books, may be of great Historical significance. As they may throw a very different light, on those incredible times? We think they may explain so much we still cannot understand about how William managed to overthrow the Saxon way of life so quickly.*

*And with so few men? But they are written in old English and some sort of a code, A code, that only our professor Higgins was able to understand. And now we are at a loss, as to what we should do next?"*

I asked her how she thought they were a motive for murder?

*"So, you think these books can tell you all that, if they would be worth a fortune. Worth killing for perhaps? How many people know of their existence?"*

These questions, seemed to bring Simonson up short, as she also realised how important, and valuable these books were! And who would wish to have them?

*"Well, we did tell the whole facility about them, and there was a local newspaper man, who came to do a report, and he took some pictures, I know that they were printed a few days ago. And then, the nationals took the story up. So, officer, the answer to that question is a lot of people now know of their existence. But no one was ever allowed to be left alone with the books, as far as I know?"*

I said,

*"That is not quite correct, is it? according to this tape Higgins was alone for thirty minutes. While you had coffee?"*

Here then is motive, and opportunity?

I asked them if he could he have stopped the recording machine, and have time to stop or copy the books do you think? That question brought a ghastly silence. And Mandy Jones, had gone deathly white? As I said to them both.

*"Well now, we have a motive and perhaps someone who wanted the originals, had managed to get to Higgins or*

*his family? Did he leave a letter explain why he was alone that day?"*

I saw Mandy blanch at that question as I knew he had done something like that, and she had taken it? So gave her a let out.

*"You see, Miss Jones, I saw a brief moment on the video, when you took something from his pocket when you found him. You said you were in love with him? And love is sometimes seen as the death of Duty? Perhaps he was asking you to help him copy or steal them. Where are they now where being they kept at night? In a safe, I hope. Was it you who stopped the recording?"*

Mandy had also gone a little white around the gills at this question, and she flushed and looked away, trying to get her thoughts and feelings in check. And now Susan was now looking daggers, at her assistant. As Susan said to us.

*"Well, as to that they are still where Richard could have stopped the recording as he would need to compose his thoughts. But he would have to get up from the table to so? But as we saw, he was sitting at the reading desk, when he had the heart attack. As for these books, we were told not to move anything, until your detectives said we could do so. But this place is locked and patrolled at night officer. Surely, they are safe here.*

"What would they be worth on the open market?" I asked.

"Ho I do not know; you see, they are almost priceless!"

"Priceless indeed, Well then have you checked they are the origional books you found, as it has been weeks since they were found. Have you checked they are genuine?"

Susan gasped with the horror on her face at that possibility. As I asked them.

"What if Higgins replaced them without anyone knowing, and the guilt that now the media were alerted to their existence, he realised what he had done, and was sure to be found out was so hard, he could not bear it? No reaction?

"What can you tell me about the page he touched, or checked Perhaps guilt was the trigger."

Then before Jones could think about her answer, I turned to Mandy Jones to ask.

*What was on that piece of paper you stole from the Professors jacked Miss Jones?*

They both were biting their lips now, and now Jones face, was flushed with fear, at what I had asked them? Her hands had gone as white as a sheet, twisting in her grip, and her eyes flashed at me, with both her anger and then fear? As she turned to get up, as she said.

*"It was nothing really, just a note that Richard had asked me to keep safe. I knew he needed it kept a secret for a short time. He said that it was harmless and to be our secret. He said...*

Then she paused and turned her head away so that I would not see her tears that had flooded into in her eyes?

*"You see I was our secret. He said that he loved me, and that we were to meet him at my cottage that night! and afterwards, I knew that paper had my name on it, and then I would be seen as being involved in all this.*

Now Susan Simonson, turned to hit out at Jones, as she almost snarled at her assistant, she said to her, her voice full of hate!

*"You bitch you slept with him. How could you when you know I was saving myself for him. You are fucking whore!"*

To hear their secrets was no surprise then but we needed to know what was on that paper. I asked them.

*"Well, what a fine lot you are, with your high and mighty attitudes. I see you both now as who you really are now. Two bitches in heat!"*

I had spoken so harshly, intending to get them angry and then I could delve them for the truth. As I went on to say.

"Well perhaps that is no surprise as he was a very handsome married man. I thought that you scholars are people of high mind and morals. I saw how you lot were looking down your sciolistic noses at us simple policemen like me! But you are no better than the rest of us! Perhaps, I was right to say Love is the cause of many evils. And now we must have that note Jones, and now if you please.

She went to take up a book on the shelf al that was adjacent to where the body had been found and produced the folded piece of paper. She handed to me and for a moment I caught up with them and their so-called romance , As when I held her hand, and touched the paper, I knew just how much Mandy had been deceived, and how Richard was using these women for his own needs. But here also, was a motive for murder! I spoke.

"So, you both were in love with Higgins, And despite the fact as he was also a married man with a devoted wife and children. Moreover, you must know that he was never going to risk being ruined, by a love affair.

Then I read the note, I now realised that Jones was a very sexy woman and she had been easy pickings.

*Dear Ruth, I hope you know how much I love you., And I hope we can go on meeting at the George.*

*But I want you to do something for me my darling. It concerns these books, and yes, I have managed to read a little of the text. And It turns out, I need the ring that is in the pouch to do so. So, Can you bring it to me?*

*But this must be our secret for a while, and until I, we can astound the world with our discoveries. Only then we will be so rich, we can run away together.*

*But need is the key to all this. So, hide the pouch my darling.*

*XXX*

*Your Richard.*

Now, Susan had also read the note, and she managed to slap her assistant across her wide brown face, sending her flying across the room, as once again she said.

"*Take that bitch, Richard was mine!* Then turning to me she said.

"What an evil world you live in officer, and yes, we must go and check these books again… But I would ask that *you come with me as I do not want you to think I am any part in this or your suspicious mind. At least I told him he would need to get a divorce before we could go away together!*

*But now, I see he was a lying bastard, but I had nothing to do with his death. But hearing that he was a vile cheat, I am sorry I was so stupid to believe his lies.*

*But enough of that, and him, Please follow me and bring your Sargent as well. I may need a witness to show you both I am innocent in all this?"*

As we walked back to the reading rooms, Susan tried to tell me how far they had got in the examination of these new histories.

*"As you know, and Before you came officers, We were asked to compile a list for you to use and to see if these Books.*

*As We think it can provide the answers to the many questions held been searching for about these Saxon people and their times? But these Books are in a code. An ancient version of the Irish language?*

*And now we know that Professor Higgins was able to resolve this code, just Before he was killed in the study hall. But, As yet we only have a list of the chapters in these books, but from what we can read in these new secret books that Leofric compiled.*

*I now think that they are written in an old use of the Gaelic tongue, And Richard was the only one we had who could do that.*

*So, the truth is that we cannot read them until we find another Galic expert. We have sent to Dublin, for someone, and they have a woman man who has done some work on this period. She is their Senior Language expert who is based at Dublin University,*

*Jacqueline Frost is her name. So apart from looking at these books we cannot touch them, until she arrives next week.?"*

Then she pulled herself up short, as she was remembering what Jones had said and the note. Need is the key and the ring.

*"But I hear from our head of department, that that you have such a skill, Inspector, an ability to touch the past? And perhaps you should take a look at the book Richard was using to see if you can feel anything that is harmful??*

Jones, was sitting on a chair holding her swollen eyes and face, being comforted by Barton who was holding a towel to her face. As I said.

*"They are written in Gaelic you say, But Higgins need the ring to do that. And now we have the ring now, and Perhaps I could use it to be able to make contact with them in some way. As you now know I have a special*

ability to be able to read and feel what has happened to people and the objects they have held. I can do that by holding an object they had and treasured. If Higgins used the ring to read these books, perhaps I should try to do that."

Barton was agreeing with me, as he said

"I told you that Inspector Rutter, here, well he has a very special ability that will tell us if these are the real books at least? I agree he should try to see if they are dangerous in anyway?".

Then to me

"but if there is something in them that is dangerous, we need to take precautions Jake?"?

At that, Susan tried to regain and enforce her authority here as she was not at all happy to hear this talk of mystic abilities! So, she said with as much authority as she could muster, and to let us think that this was her idea?

"Yes, we can do that, Officer Rutter. Come Mandy pull yourself together girl, we have work to do."

I said to John Barton.

*John, I see that. Look, and yes, I will try as I want to do what I can to help Mandy here, And she should know that she is in the clear, as we have no reason to think she was the cause of his death? I think it was a heart attack and a death by natural causes. And I will put that in my report. Unless I find otherwise when I touch these books."*

Then to help these women,

*."So, now I see that you both are innocent in all this, and Higgins, tricked you both into helping him to be alone with these books? And, if you really want to help us in all this, and you both have a good reason to get to the truth. You said you had a voice recorder we could use?*

At that, Mandy brought it out from a cupboard as she gave me such wide smile and a look of grateful thanks, I said."

*"If you can set it up, I will try to say what I find if anything ,as I will put my hand on the books and The ring. And then, you can record anything I say, even if it is in Gaelic? Does it have a translation facility?*

This time, it was Susan who said.

*"We can go one better, we have a dictation system, that we use to produce the student notes, It has a good microphone, that will hear what is said, and type it up as Text. Then we will have a hard copy! Will that do?"*

*"Wonderful" I said, "but we cannot know if this will work? and if it does, so, we must have safe way to stop this seance."*

I saw Susan look dubious at that strange word, that was outside the field of science. So, Isaid.

*" I am a medium and I can read people, but I do not have time to prove it to you now. What if I tell you your real name is not Simonson But Sifa Sorenson. That you changed that to be seen as more English. That is a fact only you can know, and one I saw in your mind the moment I thought to delve you. Will you believe me now?"*

I saw how confused she was and begin to believe I was telling the truth.

*"As for the danger in making contact with Higgins, that is a consideration, and yes it can be dangerous. You see once before; I made contact with dead man, and …Well I nearly died as I could not break the link with his dying mind. As one's brain can indeed hang on for a short time, once the heart stops working. But these books are not alive, and I should be safe?"*

Once again Susan's face, had gone even more white as she put her hand to her mouth, and I knew I had been right in what I had said. She said what was in her mind.

*"My goodness , it is all true then! But Officer Rutter, I must hope and pray that you are wrong about Richard officer, and that he had no ill intent here, other than his greed for fame and fortune? But if you think I'm going to*

*let you anywhere near these books and use magic to read them* **You a fewking mad.** *This place is place of science, and we do not believe in magic or any sort of spirituality. Well not anything that will involve a seance as you call it.*

It was then that I saw just how sceptical all this would sound to these two woman of science, and that theywere not going to believe me, without some proof? So, when we were all set up, I told them what I had decided to do next as I started with our first meeting with them and the books.

*"I told you that I and Jasper, saw the power in this first one, and I can feel it hold a great power that may be from an evil source If so, I dare not touch it because it has a binding spell of some sort. A spell from a powerful mystic. I saw a Name Wulfnoth Cild? Am I right in this?"*

Before these scientists could try to stop me telling them about the powers of white and black magic, I went on to say.

*"And then this next one that Higgins has open. There is another name equally as powerfully, it was Gytha. I think it was she, who used the black magic to gain her desires, or wealth and power?*

*But this was not the first time such power was to be used. I Think we need to look into this first book is named The Story of Wulfnoth Child.*

Mandy was looking at me, as if I had grown two heads now.

*"Yes, they do Jake if so, this first book is named The Story of Wulfnoth Child. But We know so little about him, except he was the Saxon father of the Earl Godwin of Wessex. And as we have found out Gytha, is also recorded as the Wife of Godwin of Wessex and the mother of nine children who were to rule Engand including King Harold Godwinson. My goodness what have we found here?"*

*"Yes, indeed it would seem they are the origional books at least as far As Leofric believed them to be? And now perhaps I can help you to solve the mystery of how Higgins died here. As these books contain what we would call the essence of some sort of black magic?"*

Once again, I saw the women were about to want to argue and say there was no such thing as magic in science. But I went on regardless.

*"You must have heard of Black magic, That is the evil spirit I sense in this room. I heard it called a **fylgia** whatever that is. And if there is such a thing as the power*

*of Good, and White magic, that only good people can use to heal and speak of love and the works of Jesus Christ, and the miracles.*

*You must see that Black magic must also be possible. Or another evil power that is Blood magic, that is even more powerful?*

At that word, I saw Mandy Jones, utter a grasp of fear, and she crossed herself, I now saw she was now holding her hand, a silver cross at her neck? I saw her lips move to supress a word. *A Fletch I thought?* But I need to get their help now, so, I went on to say.

*"But before we can go any further, I will need your help in all this. As for you Susan, I feel that you may have the Viking gene, Or at least you come from the Norse blood line. I guess someone changed your family name over time, Did they not? I think a fylgia is something from Norse law is it not?"*

I saw her blush, and her eyes flash, as she said,

*"Yes, you are correct Jake, I was once Sorenson, we came from a place called Headley in Denmark I believe."*

Mandy was also thinking hard now as she said,

*"Well then, I believe, as I am half Welsh and we do not dismiss such things as Black magic quite so easily, as in*

all things there is both good and evil. So, tell us more officer."

"Well then and if you are willing, I am going to take you on a journey into the past. You see, it may be a dangerous thing we do, if I touch these books, I fear I shall be caught up in what I shall name to be a time vortex.

Susan gave out a suppressed laugh.

"No please do not close your mind to what I am going to tell you both, as it may seem incredible and impossible to you scientists. But Now that You can at least try to believe That I can timeslip, I am going to try to give you an explanation about **Quantum Time** and what it can do.

I expect you have heard of what we now call the Dark Matter that makes up most of the universe and hold all of space together and binds it in what we see as a matrix.

We now know that Einstein has proved that he was wrong to think that the speed of light was an unchangeable constant as time and light can be bent and slowed down when it reaches a black Hole. It is matrix which holds the matrix of space together ,well it can also span time and space. It is also the powers of this dark matter and how it can fill space and time. But that is not all as we now think that there is such a force as Quantum space, and alternative dimensions that exist simultaneously as ours?"

Susan said

*"You speak of Dark matter, Jake and Yes of course, That is now seen as good science, I have been reading about it, and some very important people, are trying to find a way of registering its effects.*

*"Are they, well I can tell you that they can also have an effect on time. You see I know that Time is not the fixed thing, we think it is! Because there is something called Quantum time, where space and time can be experienced by someone like me.*

It was Mandy, who said /

*"My gran said she could read the past, but never the future, is that what you mean."*

*"Yes and no. I will give you an example if I can. Imagine, we are all three, standing on a beach .Standing at a pole in the sand, at a set point in time, as far as we are concerned. This is our present?"*

They were nodding their understanding now.

*"And now we can look across to see our footprints in the wet sand. That is our past then, Yes? But as for the future what then?"*

It was Susan, who had realised what I was getting at.

*"The future is not yet set until we decide to act. Is that what you mean. Like Schroders cat in the box. it is alive*

and dead at the same time. Alive until it moves and releases the poison gas!"

"In a way ,but in my example, we can go to the water or the bank .Choose to go to the water, and that becomes our present, and out chosen future? But the choice to go to the bank was available to us, until we made a positive action.

But in another space time continuum. This alternative choice still exists for us to reach across the beach, in the quantum world.

At least for a moment in time. And both outcomes are possible futures! Some think that these alternative choices are spun away into another dimension of time. And they will have different outcomes?".

"Yes, I see that but how can you go into the past? Mandy asked me, her tone no longer sceptical, but interested.

"Well, the truth ,,is I do not know, but I can do so, until the alternative timeline fades away. And then I can see what happened in that moment."

"Pah! that is all nonsense. "Susan said .

"It is Not nonsense, and I will try to prove it to you? But to do that I must send my consciousness into this quantum realm.

*All I know now is that it works or not. It only works twenty-five times out of a hundred, and the most recent vision dream is the best and true one. Let me try here and now with these books and perhaps we can make contact with this bishop of yours?*

*As now I know that need is the key to any answers you seek. And with this ring, I think I can be reached back in time I did just that when I was unconscious, and I CAN PROVE IT. You said there was a record of my dream, where is it?"*

I put my hand on Book Four…

\*\*\*

It was here that I Dr Simon Robinson, had to stop my reading of the diary and Jakes account of what he had found at Exeter, as no my mind was boggling at what had been said and set down and I knew then, that I must look deeper into the science of the Quantum world and fine someone who could explain it to me .But for now I was going to bed, with a large brandy.

And it was the next week that I found the right man to help me with the prospect of Time Travel!

*Monday,*

Professor Paul Foster was waiting in my study, and I was glad to see he was one of the younger professors, who worked in the physics department.

He was a short man with blond hair and a wide-open face and had a firm handshake. He wore a checked cream and brown stripped shirt with a large brown bow Tie, at his neck, and under, a white laboratory coat that would denote him as a scientist. but he also wore bright yellow socks, that said he was not going to conform to any dress code? And holding out his large hand, he gave me a warm welcome.

He had some diagrams, and charts under one arm as he said to us. There was a laptop open on the bench. It was displaying clock of some sort.

*"Well Simon Robinson, I have been sent here to try to tell you something about the Multiverse and Quantum time. As I hope you have an open mind Simon, as what I have to tell you may seem to be science fiction, to a Doctor of medicine like you."*

I grinned, handing him a large brandy as we sat down beside the fire, to discuss this new science. As this Professor Paul Foster, opened the discussion.

*"Well as to that Simon, I have read your paper in the Lancet Paul and I like what little I can understand, about*

*the power of the human mind, and I can hope that you will be able to grasp the basics of the Quantum universe?*

*Well as to that, I have reads some of your papers Paul, and yes, I need to understand it all if \i am to try to help Jake |Rutter again?"*

*"Yes, I see that, and if you have the time, excuse the pun, I will try to answer your questions. I have also brought some notes for you to read at your leisure.*

*But I was told you think you have found a new time traveller. I have read the papers and some of Rutters diary so we could start with that. What do you think, can Rutter time slip?*

*Time slip, that is not how I see what he has done. But before I can explain what I think he has done we must understand what quantum space is, and the multiverse theories.*

*So, Simon, I must first tell you what I know about Quantum time? And what I think about the possibility of the Multiverse. I see you have managed to do some research into these incredible claims you make about Jake's ability to Time-slip! To feel the recent past as any medium can do.*

*Moreover, I have been able listen to the recording they made of the conversations Rutter had with the people in these books! So, I will begin with my investigations about time. Will you start the new recording, Simon, as we can play them back if needed?"*

I did so, and Paul began his lecture.

*"As you have been sable to prove Dr Robinson, Some of our brightest minds, now think that time might be a construct, the human mind is it a tantalising idea we all hope to exist in our own timeline.*

*and Jake has told us of how he looks at time, the now ,the past and the future.?*

And he is right in that, but the truth is even stranger, as it is also a paranormal world, that exists along with our golden timeline. Our very existence comprises of the now, and our memories of the past.

In that way we see as our dimension of Space and Quantum time.

*It's a subjective nature of time and space which is to most of us an unseen world, which records our experiences and records our decisions, which must transcend into the quantum world and there to form an alternative reality.*

*As to this question of an alternative reality of dimension in space time. For a long time, we were to discover that only those special people who can feel and see these paradoxes of time travel*

*But now with our knowledge of Quantum physics we are able to measure this phenonium and speak with those who people who mind has adapted to be able to reach into this quantum space, either by aa natural ability, or with the aid of some mind-altering drugs.*

*"Is that Like Jake can do with is mind. And why is he so he is special and what he has seen, is not a creation of sick mind?"* I asked fearing the answer.

Well yes in a way, I think that Jake They can timeslip into the past and even their own future. So, I also believe we are wrong, in dismissing the possibility of traversing these alternative branches of our timeline.

*You see, Quantum time itself is such a paradox. and we also fear to think it would be possible and they say that the grandfather paradox, will prevent us changing the past as to do so would unravel our timeline. And that is why time travel to the past is not possible.*

But if we could change the past Rutter here is right, we would never know of it, as then that would be our true memory of the past.

*As you know, this theory goes against what we see as the Causality paradox. That any changes we make become set in stone, and the matrix changes to absorb these changes , or form another reality in which these changes can exist? To cope with a potential contradictions that arise when altering it Challenges our understanding of* the Causality question of time.

That says what we do must be seen as correct to our minds. to relativity of time, and our understanding of time, with his theories of special and general relativity

*And now, even these absolute ideas about by speed of light and time can be changed and diluted. It was Einstein who introduced the idea of the time dilation and opened the doors to the possibility of time dilation, and the concept of Quantum time. The integrating time is the dimension intertwined with the three special dimensions.*

And now even the nature of time quantum mechanics complicates our understanding of time particles.

*As now we think they exist in state of probability of observation! it's probably the nature of quantum mechanics, and the questions we seek about the deterministic view of time.*

These Introduces The Concept Of Superposition For Particles Can Exist In Multiple Stage Time Dilation A Reality.

*To exist beyond science fiction, so does time dilation exterior special relativity experimentally contract time differently in the Quantum world. This compression different rights under different conditions, such as high*

*speed, or strong gravitational fields, such as a Black Hole!*

We Now think That This Phenomenon On Brings The Concept Of Time Travel Closer To Reality and to be able to Travel To The Past, The Possibility Of Potentially Allowing For Time Travel To The Past!

To be able to provide concrete evidence of time and entropy. this area of time, describes the unit directional flow of time future direction making events appear in reversible and flowing in One Direction.

*The implications and what Rutter here can do and experience, is only one of the most intriguing and subjective experiences I have found to date.*

*and with his help perhaps we can continue to explore, our understanding of time travel?*

*You see Simon, what we know is so little, and it is far from complete each new discovery and comprehension inviting us to ponder and question scientific inquiry."*

`With these words and question, Paul had stopped his long monologue, to take a drink from the brandy glass, as I realised that all this had gone right over my head and mind, as I asked him.

*"Come now Professor, If I read you correctly What you have said is that Time is a variable construct, and it is*

*possible to timeslip? Is that right Professor, If that is so I can have some hope that I am not mad, or going to be lost in time? But what can you tell us about the Multiverse ideas?*

"Mad. no Susan, I can promise you that you are not mad, to tell us of Rutters abilities, far from it! As for The multiverse, well, I am sorry but to do that justice will take two or three days, But here is what I, and so many believe to be the case…

However, I have brought you a paper I have written on the subject, and perhaps you all should read this first, and then, when we meet again.

But I will try to explain it all in plain English. However. I must warn you as I give you this information, it is only a draft paper. And you must promise me not to reveal it to anyone else, as I have yet to finalise it, or forward it to my superiors.

 I will leave it with you as my time here is up, and I fear you will find it is hard to read and understand? But, if you find the concept of a Quantum world-hard to comprehend, then the ideal of the multiverse's will blow your minds.

Even so, I hope to be able to meet with this Jake Rutter when you bring him back from the past!"

Quantum Time,

So it was that the next day, I made the time to take a look at what Foster had written about the possibility of a multiverse.

*This is what we read in this draft paper Paul had printed* out for us…

It starts with the question of a life after death, and claims, that none of us really die after our physical death. And that our spirit can live on the matrix of space time that is seen as the multi verse whose dimensions are known to be possible now.

*Just how this was different from the religious concepts that the people of faith believe, I was yet to find out!*

Moreover, in some cultures as the world of the gods are no longer seen as anything but a way for us humans, to find a code to live by.

*Yes, I have always believed that to be the case. But Paul goes on to say,*

So have science opened so many doors that nature tried to hide from us. And, until now, not even our quantum physicists, are yet to prove that we all live for ever in the quantum world. But they show us a glimpse of the Holy Grail, the philosopher's stone that says our spirit can live after physical death? A false construct and an idea, that will be seen to promise the ideal of immortality. the question of eternal life and immortality, that is found in many cultures of this earth. And there are just as many answers to it in our western culture, which still hold to the belief in life after death.

So does the principle of a journey of the soul to death or if one was unlucky to hell is hardly present in people's minds anymore.

Except in eastern cultures on the other hand the idea that the soul travels on after death but it goes to dimensions where the gods normally dwell, and that our souls returned to earth in a new round an in a new life is quite normal.

And there are hundreds of people worldwide or close to death, or even claims have already crossed the threshold into the divine realms and there they met entities that appeared like angels and had been sent them back to earth.

Moreover, It is said that such people experience spontaneous healings or serious illnesses, or radically change their lives, because they realised who they really are in the realms after death. until now all these were pure ideologies fantasies unimprovable claims or religious ideas.

*I wish that was so, as two thirds of us humans worship a god of some sort, and despite all that science can show them the ruth of our beginnings. And our advances caused by the concept of natural selection, as the strong thrive, and the weak are lost in time. Surely, they cannot be blind to what the fossils we have discovered show us. But none are so blind as those who will not see!*

So, now our society, wants physics to have provided the proof we really are immortal what if you would never die! But, have you ever thought about what it would be like to live forever, or you leave your body and go on into another dimension as pure information capable of simply reversing the ageing process.

Indeed, this is demonstrated by a tiny jellyfish, and accomplishes this very feat for some reason the simple example shows what is possible in nature.

And that we must never say never imagine if science decodes that trick or is able to programme your genome and bring down the age line.

So then by cloning and such gene therapy, we see that soon, we will be able to live forever? And in a way, you would be immortal they could still be on this earth in 1000- or 10,000-years' time?

And now we have the evidence in quantum physics, as our scientists may now have found the key to eternal life.

This exists in the world of the smallest particles mechanics building block of matter and light particles are much tidier than an atom can be split again into many smaller particles, and at some point, only pure information an energy remains as the actual building blocks of the universe.

We see that energy can fluctuate in absolutely balanced state, and disappear physically with it, but the information is eternal.

So, what if the energy in your bodies is matter which finally consist of condensed light and information your death your information remains consequently

But as yet we have not managed to calculate just how this can be done, as it would require the power generated by a star to do this!

It was an Australian quantum physicists expressed it in such a way the forest burns down the trees the bushes and the animals that lived in it disappear into the physical world.

*So here then are Paul's analysis of the religious theories and his answer, which is no answer at all but what of the multiverse? And while I found all this very Star Trek science , it was not what I also need ed to find out  the lates theories about Quantum time and alternative realities? Here then is his theory…*

The **multiverse** is the hypothetical set of all universes. Together, these universes are presumed to comprise everything that exists in its entirety.

 It Comprises, Most Of The Dark Matter, Of Space, Time, Matter, Energy, Information, And The Physical Laws And Constants That Describe Them.

Within these different universes, and part of the multiverse are called "*parallel universes* There are *flat universes*", alternate universes that all exist in parallel.

Some believe that there are such things as a child universe", "many universes", or "*many worlds*". *multiple universes*", "*plane universes*", "A parent universe.

One common assumption is that the multiverse is a patchwork quilt of separate universes all bound by the same laws of physics.[

However,The concept of multiple universes, or a multiverse, has been discussed throughout history, including Greek philosophy.

It has evolved over time and has been debated in various fields, including cosmology, physics, and philosophy.

Some Physicists Argue That the Multiverse Is a Philosophical Notion, Rather Than a Scientific Hypothesis, As It Cannot Be Empirically Confirmed!

In recent years, there have been proponents and skeptics of multiverse theories within the physics community. Although some scientists have analyzed data in search of evidence for other universes, no statistically significant evidence has been found.

*These Critics argue that the multiverse concept lacks testability and falsifiability, which are essential for scientific inquiry, and that it raises unresolved metaphysical issues.*

Max Tegmark, and Brian Greene, have proposed different classification schemes for multiverses and universes.

Then there is the Tegmark's four-level classification consists of these Levels, as an extension of our universe.

Level II: universes with different physical constants,

Level III: many-worlds interpretation of quantum mechanics, and Level IV: ultimate ensemble.

However, Brian Greene's nine types of multiverses include quilted, inflationary, brane, cyclic, landscape, quantum, holographic, simulated, and ultimate.

These ideas explore various dimensions of space, physical laws, and mathematical structures to explain the existence and interactions of multiple universes.

Some other multiverse concepts include twin-world models, cyclic theories, M-theory, and cosmology.

The Anthropic Principle Suggests That The Existence Of A Multitude Of Universes, Each With Different Physical Laws, Could Explain The Fine-Tuning Of Our Own Universe For Conscious Life.

*The weak anthropic principle posits that we exist in one of the few universes that support life. Debates around **Occam's razor and the simplicity of the multiverse versus a single universe arise,** with proponents like Max Tegmark arguing that the multiverse is simpler and more elegant.*

The Many-Worlds Interpretation Of Quantum Mechanics And Modal Realism, The Belief That All Possible Worlds Exist, And Are As Real As Our World, Are Also Subjects Of Debate In The Context Of The Anthropic Principle.

**This Is what I Have Come to Think Is the Right Answer.**

According to some, the idea of infinite worlds was first suggested by the pre-Socratic Greek philosopher, *Anaximander,* in the sixth century BCE.

However, there is debate as to whether he believed in multiple worlds, and if he did, whether those worlds were co-existent or successive. The first to whom we can definitively attribute the concept of innumerable worlds are the Ancient Greek Atomists.

Beginning with *Leucippus and Democritus* in the 5th century BCE, followed by Epicurus (341–270 BCE) and Lucretius (1st century BCE). In the third century BCE

*The Philosopher Chrysopsis Suggested That the World Eternally Expired and Regenerated, Effectively Suggesting the Existence of Multiple Universes Across Time.* **This also conforms with my theories about the multiverse existence.**

The concept of multiple universes became more defined in the Middle Ages.

The American philosopher and psychologist *William James.* used the term "multiverse" in 1895, but in a different context.

*The concept first appeared in the modern scientific context, in the course of the debate, between Boltzmann, and Zermelo, in 1895.*

It was In Dublin in 1952, *Erwin Schrödinger* gave a lecture in which he jocularly warned his audience that what he was about to say might "seem lunatic"

*He said that when his equations seemed to describe several different histories, these were "**not alternatives, but all really happen simultaneously**".[1]*

*This Sort Of Duality Is Called "Superposition".*

In the 1990s, after works of fiction from the time about the concept gained popularity, scientific discussions about the multiverse and journal articles about it gained prominence.

In Around 2010, scientists such as *Stephen M. Feeney*, analyzed Wilkinson Microwave Anisotropy Probe (WMAP) data, and claimed to find evidence suggesting that this universe collided with her (parallel) universes in the distant past.

*However, a more thorough analysis of data from the WMAP and from the Planck satellite, which has a resolution three times higher than WMAP, did not reveal any statistically significant evidence of such a bubble universe collision.*

In addition, there was no evidence of any gravitational pull of other universes on ours.

However, In 2015, An Astrophysicist May Have Found Evidence Of Alternate Or Parallel Universes By Looking Back In Time To A Time Immediately After The Big Bang, Although It Is Still A Matter Of Debate Among Physicists.

*It was when Dr. Ranga-Ram Chary, after analyzing the cosmic radiation spectrum, found a signal 4,500 times brighter than it should have been, based on the number of protons and electrons scientists believe existed in the early universe, thus demonstrating signs of collisions with other universes.*

In his 2003 New York Times opinion piece, "A Brief History of the Multiverse", author and cosmologist, I offered a variety of arguments that multiverse hypotheses are non-scientific:

*For a start, how is the existence of the other universes to be tested? To be sure, all cosmologists accept that there are some regions of the universe that lie beyond the reach of our telescopes, but somewhere on the slippery slope between that and the idea that there is an infinite number of universes, credibility reaches a limit.*

*As one slips down that slope, more and more must be accepted on faith, and less and less is open to scientific verification.*

So Now The Extreme Multiverse Explanations Are Therefore Reminiscent Of Theological Discussions. *Indeed, invoking an infinity of unseen universes to explain the unusual features of the one we do see is just as ad hoc as invoking an unseen Creator.*

*The multiverse theory may be dressed up in scientific language, but in essence, it requires the same leap of faith.*

*It was* George Ellis, writing in August 2011, provided a criticism of the multiverse, and pointed out that it is not a traditional scientific theory.

He accepts that the multiverse is thought to exist far beyond the cosmological horizon. He emphasized that it is theorized to be so far away that it is unlikely any evidence will ever be found. Ellis also explained that some theorists do not believe the lack of **empirical testability and falsifiability** is a major concern, but he is opposed to that line of thinking:

*So, now Many physicists who talk about the multiverse, especially advocates of the string landscape, do not care much about parallel universes per se.*

*For them, objections to the multiverse as a concept are unimportant. Their theories live or die based on internal consistency and, one hopes, eventual laboratory testing.*

Ellis says that scientists have proposed the idea of the multiverse as a way of explaining the nature of existence. He points out that it ultimately leaves those questions unresolved because it is a metaphysical issue that cannot be resolved by empirical science.

He argues that observational testing is at the core of science and should not be abandoned:

End report...

*

As I put down this document, I knew then that Paul had hedged his bets and until we could find some physical evidence of this alternative dimension theory no one was going to find it a possibility!

*"As skeptical as I am, I think the contemplation of the multiverse is an excellent opportunity to reflect on the nature of science and on the ability of a mind to timeslip between them. **So, now Jake Rutter, we come to you and probability to read these books!***

*Have you traveled back in time, but to an alternative reality? And Paul here has given me some of the possible answers.*

*So, my next task was to go back to those pages and the diary, to see what I would find in them...*

\*\*\*

Jake Rutter,

So now diary I must set down what that you have been able to transcribe from the Leofric books. And whoever reading them could not be amazed and see the detail in them. A detail that no modern mind could invent. Susan has asked me if you should be allowed to continue with the project, and I say it would be a tragic if you should stop. And I for one, will endorse your findings as a Time traveler extraordinaire! And Need is the Key!"

\*.

*Flash, Flash...*

*I see you spirit; You ask about these books then. A. I am Leofric Of Exeter.*

I shall introduce myself as the Chronicler of this Saga as these are the Chronicles of the Godwinson's, A family of Saxon Shipbuilders, and tell of their life and times at the end of the First Century.

In Book One, my readers can read what transpires with WUlfnoth Cild, the Father of Godwin, who, in time, will become the Ealdorman of Wessex. And a friend to two Kings! In Book Two, Godwin of Comptene, we read about How WUlfnoth son Godwin came to marry Gytha of Denmark and serve King Canute and something of their lives and times. But unfortunately, that bookended with the Death Of the Earl Godwin of Wessex.

*So now, in Book Three, we shall learn of what transpired next with Gytha and her children. I Leofric, shall tell this incredible tale as he will tell of his son Godwin, and his wife, Gytha. To speak of Their children were the last of the Saxon Earls to rule Engaland. Of the true story of Harold Godwinson, who was the last of the Saxon Kings of Engaland, was written in secret ledgers by the bishops and the men who lived through those times…*

So here, I will try to let the people speak to you, my readers, as if you were a part of their lives, and set down what they told me about these events which will also cover the lives and times of the people who played such an essential part in these times.

So, I must be your guide to speak of their Incredible lives, and learn of all this incredible Godwinson family, who are destined to shape the fortunes of our land for so long.

*And now, in book One, as we have learnt of the early life of Wulfnoth Cild, and so that my readers can make some sense of these turbulent times and be able to know some of the backgrounds of this account of the life of the Godwinsons. So here I must also tell you what I have discovered about the events that occurred at the death of King Edward, in that year of Nine Hundred and Sixty-Six!*

It was a terrible time for our Saxon lands, and the church! and now that Edward has been named a Saint. I speak of him here, so that you will better understand how Harold Godwinson and not his rightful heir and one of his blood line, his nephew Edwin, was prevented from claiming the throne, as Edward had no legitimate heirs!

Let it be known now that the Duke William of Normandy has come to Steal their Crown and Kingdom? But as it is the victors of any war, who live to tell the story, of how they came to power, so is their version not always the truth.

*So, here is my Introduction to the four books that will comprise 'The Saga of the Godwin family.'*

However, by compiling these books, so must I investigate forbidden archives. To look into the histories that my predecessors made. And seek out their records and the accounts of these incredible events, which had to be hidden from sight, when the Normans came to our lands in the Year of our Lord, One Thousand and Hundred and sixty-Six!

*Moreover, if you have found these secret books, I should explain a few things about these times of history as we go on.*

One reason is that I am an avid student of History, and a Bishop of the Holy Church. So, I must set down the accurate records of the lives and times of these incredible people, that will fill these pages.

*And not the falsehoods that have been passed down from those who would change the truth to suit themselves, as I fear that William I have done?*

*I hear He has set the weavers in Bayeux busy making a great Tapestry of lies and half-truths, which will make him have a rightful claim to the Crown of our Saxon Engaland.*

But I was involved with William, and Harold, here and also in Engaland, and then in Normandy, So I can tell the true story of how both Harold and Duke William, were able to steal the crown of England when Edward teh Confessor died without a son.

However, you should also seek to find my other history, which is named Harold Godwinson King of the Saxons, for the full history of how Harold Godwinson, become our king.

But if my readers allow it, I shall also set down the details of my humble life? Of how Lady Gytha chose me to become her friend and Confessor.

*You may have heard of my first book of poems, which is now seen as the Great Book of Exeter? As the Archbishop of Exeter and Canterbury, in this year of our LORD 1069.*

I am here in the library in the newly finished Cathedral at Exeter Devon. First, however, this is my humble

Introduction to these Godwinson's records, which must remain secret until after my death.

*However, just re-reading these pages sends a shiver of fear and apprehension down my spine, as should King William ever see what is written here.*

William would have these pages destroyed, and my head would follow with it. Yet, these words accurately account for the times and lives of these incredible people who shaped this age of strife and the church's birth in our lands.

*Moreover, I have promised my God to set down the truth here and not be bound by any thoughts of redaction of what I have seen written and told of in Confession. If I am wrong, so shall I be judged in time before my God.*

But they are well hidden, along with some of my other precious books. And now Harold and I, are the only people apart from Gytha, who know of their existence. *I have also put aside, my bishops ring and that blasted cursed sword, that Wulfnoth used to such terrible effect.*

*But if you read this account, I am long dead, along with anyone who lived in these times; you will have decoded the* code that will allow you to find these documents and my Exeter Book of my humble poems…

First, however, so that my writings shall not bore you all to Death, and send you to an early grave, so shall I allow these people a voice here to share their lives, and perhaps understand a little of their tribulations, before we judge them.

*For, did not Jesus say- Let, he who is without sin, cast the first stone!*

But now, I wish to tell my story and the part I was to play in these momentous events. As I fear the death of our Saxon way of life, and our lands are about to be changed forever by This false King, the Duke William of Normandy.

*As I now know that William has his story set down in a poem by Bishop Guy of Amiens. The Carmen de Hastingae Proelio is composed by Guy Bishop of Amiens, his Triumpho Normannico.*

*It is supposed to be the accurate telling of the Norman Conquest of Engaland. A song that was commissioned to celebrate the Coronation of William the First of Engaland.*

But I fear that King William will only wish us to tell the future what he wants them to know. But I know some of it from my own time, so I can tell what I have seen of it is a twisted version of what happened before and after the year of our Lord 1066! But more of that later.

*So, my task is to tell the people of Engaland, those who wish to be still known as Saxons, and not Normans, that William will try to make us become. But you should also how our King Harold came to win a crown and lose a Kingdom. However, this is also Godwin's story, a low birth man, who became a vassal to King AEthelred.*

This is also the story of the life and times of Godwin the Son of Wulfnoth Cild, as given to Bishop Dunstan, so that it will not be lost and forgotten, for it is with him that the Godwinson Saga began!

*But if you have found these secret books, I hope you have read the first book, which will tell of how, and when, Godwin was born, of his struggle to maintain his honour and life against the people who were to become his bitter enemies. The members of the Streona clan.*

Therefore, I will start where the book that I have finished. However, to be able to read some more of the

Godwinson story my readers must see to find my other books.

When we meet them in this book, Godwin, and Harold, has been forced to leave England to live in Denmark, as a vasal, to king Canute.

And In Engaland, Edmund has been chosen by the Witan to be their king and he has had to fight for his kingdom, as the Danes under Cnut, have come to claim their birthright as descendants of Forkbeard. And now the Godwinsons must choose which side they must support, and Harold is torn between his oath to Cnut/Canute, and his love of Engaland, and the chosen English king Edmund.

It is with the help of the Godwinsons Edmund, was able to retain some of his kingdom and the country was split between the Danes and the Saxon Wessex.

But his reign was to be short lived as Edmund, was foully murdered, and now Canute is to be the king of all Engaland.

But all that you will read in the third book that is called, **Harold Godwinson, King of the Saxons.**

But now Harold he has gained some standing with the Danish king Cnut, having helped him in the fighting to gain the throne of Norway.

As I pick up the story of Harold and Gytha, I must speak of his time in Denmark. As Harold Godwinson is heading back to his wife Gytha and a Danish wedding! To Hedeby, which is in Schleswig-Holstein, Denmark.

*There To Tell Her That He Can no longer be fit to be her husband, as Has Committed A foul Murder!*

\*\*\*

*Flash, Flash*

**"Jake come back to us Jake."**

\*\*\*


*Back to Exeter…*

Then, and before Leofric could speak to me about that time, I found I was back in my own time.

Once again, I was drenched in my own sweat, and I had been sick over the table, and once again Mandy was there with a sponge, and spume towels and some fresh clothes.

And when I was recovered enough to stand, I was allowed to look at the printout, and we all were utterly astounded at what we saw.

Because what I saw was what Leofric had said to me but in English! on it, was what I had seen and heard in my dream! When we looked at this writing and print out, to realise then, that the ring had worked, and I had indeed, made contact with Leofric? and what the machine had typed up, had been a voice from the past.

*Although these were my words on the recording machine ? and the typed text was the answer to our question? What are these books?*

It had taken some time for all this to sink in, and as I was so exhausted, we all agreed to stop this experiment for now. And to give us all a chance to process what we had read about this incredible book!

*However, and despite my reservations, it was agreed that we would try again in the afternoon, and Susan, was going to compile a list of questions, we should ask Leofric.*

So, when I was sufficiently refreshed, we were all to meet that afternoon, in the reading room. But this time, and to avoid any mishaps, I was to sit up in a chair to prevent the repeat of the mornings problems, and I had not eaten much at lunch time.

*But as I did not want to be sick again, not in front of these two women anyway! Indeed, they are giving me so many feelings of the past they carry such power. I have a fear I will become trapped withing the emanations, as they are a direct link to the past and their authors."*

I saw the two woman were still looking incredulous at my words, as now but they had seen what I had gathered from the note, and how right I had been about them having secrets! And I saw I needed Barton's and their help to carry on with this investigation and the reading of these books. I now know now that Need was the key, to understanding these books, and the ring**.** As I said.

*"I told you that I and Jasper, saw the power in this first one, and I can feel it hold a great power that may be from an evil source If so, I dare not touch it because it has a binding spell of some sort. A spell from a powerful mystic. I saw a Name Wulfnoth Cild? Am I right in this?"*

Before these scientists could try to stop me telling them about the powers of white and black magic, I went on to say.

"And then this next one that Higgins has open. There is another name equally as powerfully, it was Gytha. Do these names mean anything to you Susan?"

Mandy was looking at me, as if I had grown two heads now.

"Yes, they do Officer. This first book is named The Story of Wulfnoth Child.

We know so little about him, except he was the Saxon father of the Earl Godwin of Wessex. And the name Gytha, is also recorded as the Wife of Godwin of Wessex and the mother of nine children who were to rule Engand including King Harold Godwinson. My goodness what have we found here?"

"Yes, indeed it would seem they are the origional books at least. And now perhaps I can help you to solve the mystery of how Higgins died here. As these books contain what we would call the essence of some sort of black magic?"

Once again, I saw the women were about to want to argue and say there was no such thing as magic in science. But I went on regardless.

"You must have heard of Black magic, That is the evil spirit I sense in this room. I heard it called a **fylgia** whatever that is. And if there is such a thing as the power of good and White magic, that only good people can use *to heal and speak of love and the works of Jesus Christ, and the miracles.*

*You must see that Black magic must also be possible. Or another evil power that is Blood magic, that is even more powerful?*

At that word, I saw Mandy Jones, utter a grasp of fear, and she crossed herself, I now saw she was now holding her hand to a silver cross her neck? I saw her lips move to supress a word. *A Fletch I thought?* But I need to get their help now, so, I went on to say.

*"But before we can go any further, I will need your help in all this. As for you Susan, I feel that you may have the Viking gene, Or at least you come from the Norse blood line. I guess someone changed your family name over time, Did they not? I think a fylgia is something from Norse law is it not?"*

I saw her blush, and her eyes flash, as she said,

*"Yes, you are correct Jake, I was once Sorenson, we came from a place called Headley in Denmark I believe."*

Mandy was also thinking hard now as she said,

*"Well then, I believe, as I am half Welsh and we do not dismiss such things as Black magic quite so easily, as in all things there is both good and evil. So, tell us more officer."*

"Well then and if you are willing, I am going to take you on a journey into the past. You see, it may be a dangerous thing we do, if I touch these books, I fear I shall be caught up in what I shall name to be a time vortex.

Susan gave out a suppressed laugh.

"No please do not close your mind to what I am going to tell you both, as it may seem incredible and impossible to you scientists. But I am going to try to give you an explanation about **Quantum Time** and what it can do.

I expect you have heard of what we now call the Dark Matter, that makes up most of the universe and hold all of space together and binds it in what we see as a matrix.

 We now know that Einstein has proved that he was wrong to think that the speed of light was an unchangeable constant as time and light can be bent and slowed down when it reaches a black Hole. It is matrix which holds the matrix of space together ,well it can also span time and space. It is also the powers of this dark matter and how it can fill space and time.

 But that is not all as we now think that there is such a force as Quantum space, and alternative dimensions that exist simultaneously as ours?"

Susan said

"You speak of Dark matter, Jake and Yes of course, That is now seen as good science, I have been reading about it, and some very important people, are trying to find a way of registering its effects.

"Are they, well I can tell you that they can also have an effect on time. You see I know that Time is not the fixed thing, we think it is! Because there is something called Quantum time, where space and time can be experienced by someone like me.

It was Mandy, who said /

"My gran said she could read the past, but never the future, is that what you mean."

"Yes and no. I will give you an example if I can. Imagine, we are all three, standing on a beach .Standing at a pole in the sand, at a set point in time, as far as we are concerned. This is our present?"

They were nodding their understanding now.

"And now we can look across to see our footprints in the wet sand. That is our past then, Yes? But as for the future what then?"

It was Susan, who had realised what I was getting at.

"The future is not yet set until we decide to act. Is that what you mean. Like Schroders cat in the box. it is alive and dead at the same time. Alive until it moves and releases the poison gas!"

"In a way ,but in my example, we can go to the water or the bank .Choose to go to the water, and that becomes our present, and out chosen future? But the choice to go to the bank was available to us, until we made a positive action.

But in another space time continuum. This alternative choice still exists for us to leave the beach, in the quantum world.

At least for a moment in time. And both outcomes are possible futures! Some think that these alternative choices are spun away into another dimension of time. And they will have different outcomes?".

"Yes, I see that but how can you go into the past?

Mandy asked me, her tone no longer sceptical, but interested.

"Well, the truth ,,is I do not know, but I can do so, until the alternative timeline fades away. And then I can see what happened in that moment."

"Pah! that is all nonsense.

"Susan said .

"It is not nonsense, and I will try to prove it to you? But to do that I must send my consciousness into this quantum *realm. All I know now is that it works or not. It only works twenty-five times out of a hundred, and the most recent vision dream is the best and true one. Let me try here and now with these books and perhaps we can make contact with this bishop of yours?*

Now I saw Susan was beginning to think that I was telling the truth as I saw it, but then she shut her mind again, as she said.

*"You speak of a Quantum world ,we as it happens, we have someone her who can also tell us something about what you say , and that you can* **timeslip,** *as you called it?*

*So, we will have to send For our professor Peter Scott, and you can tell him what you have told us and then and only then if he thinks you are genuine, will we let you touch the books. So, Inspector, we should leave this for now and start again on Monday morning at Nine Inspector Rutter. Is that okay with you.?"*

*I said,*

"Yes, Monday will be fine, and it will give me time to get my thoughts in order and file my report to my superiors about all this.*"*

\*

\*

With that endorsement, The professor left us to decide what we were going to do next, and Susan the sceptic, came to take my hand to look into my face, and for the first time I saw that she was now willing to listen to what I had to tell her, As she said.

*"I am sorry I doubled that you were genuine Inspector, and I would apologise for my comments. as I see now that we must trust you to do what you can with our treasured books. And I see we must let you do your work, Officer! How can we help?"*

I said,

*"There are two things you can do, I need an escape route or word, one that will tell you all that I am in trouble, and need immediate extraction from the , from… this Time-slip, dream."*

As, now I saw theywere all willing to do anything I asked of them. And without further question!

*Then you must take the ring away from me. If that does not work, Barton here has a medical kit. In it there is a very strong bottle of smelling-salts .And as a last resort, a syringe that will renderer me unconscious, and end the link."*

Then Mandy Jones said, with some alarm

"Bloody hells bells then officer what I know of the spirit world is what my grannie told me, and she said it was bloody dangerous and an evil thing to try to summon the dead, so she did!

And I will have nothing to do with it so there. I see what you mean about it being dangerous to try to contact the dead. I am Welsh and know something of that world. My grandmother was a Gypsy you see."

I said,

"Yes, I see that, and we must speak of that if this process works. You see Mandy I am not going to try to contact the professor , as his spirit is long gone from here. I will try to translate these books that are over a thousand years old.

But if your grannie, had the Fey gene, well, I see you can help us when the time comes. Perhaps you should stay and help my quest, and then we can try to discover what this Bishop had to tell us, about these ancient times?"

Mandy thought long and hard and said to us.

 Yes, I will try to do that Officer, Andi see why you need recall code Vardo! Use that in the text and we will know you want to come back. It is a name from the present, the name of my perfume, and a name from the past.

I asked Suesan to check it.

"*Miss* Simonson, *can you look it up on the computer data base?*". See did so and said with some regret.

"*I am sorry Ruth, Thought it sounder familiar. It is the Roman name for some sort of a wagon.*" Isaid,

"*Then we must invent a word or phrase? But it cannot be long!*"

"*Vario then?*"

They checked that and found it was a person's name, but it was short, and rememberable, so it was unlikely to have any other connotations? I asked them,

"*I have it what about the word Television, surly that could not have been used in the past? Will that serve?*"

They looked it and to report, lots of types of vision references

"*But no Television, officer Rutter. When do you wish to start?*"

"*Well ladies, I do not know about your lot, but this has been a very long day, and we must return the boys to the kennels. And write up our report of what we have found so far.*

*What say you we meet here at Ten tomorrow. Then We will all be refreshed, and you will have time to set up your equipment. But I see that this may take quite a long*

*time and I will need a proper place to rest up between my attempts to read these four books.*

*Besides that, We will need a bunk bed for me that I can lie on, and still touch these books and artefacts and some chairs, some soluble food as well as some sort of sweet drink."*

*You see, we have done this before, and we have no way of knowing how long I will be out. But Barton here will know what to do to keep me safe and alive. But this time will not be in uniform, and you must promise me not to speak to anyone about us or this seance. And I will know if you do! As I see how hard it has been to get you to go along with this experiment, and the University will not want to be associated with my methods?"*

"Susan smiled and said, her voice almost a whisper.

"Yes, I see that officer. And we shall make sure everything is ready in the morning. God help us all!"
*

*The next day!*

So it was that we four and a police nurse we could trust to administer the injection if needed, were assembled in the room, and the books were set out on a small low table, and where I could touch them.

Barton sat on a chair beside me, and he had the ring in his hand. The two woman were at the computer and printer set out with a desk and three chairs. A rubber mat under my body.

After we exchanged pleasantries, we shook hands so that I could delve them to know they had said nothing untoward, about this day and we were ready once I had been to the toilet. And there was a rubber matt placed to catch and sick, and portable pot there just in case.

As one time before, looking into a death I had lost the contents of my guts! Before they could awake me?

So, when we were all in the room, I Placed my hand that was holding the ring and Thought about what Higgins had written on the note…

*Use the ring need is the key Ask your question.* Was my thought.

*In my mind I thought.*

*Who are you Leofric, what are these books?*

*Caught in A Time Vortex And almost immediately, I was overwhelmed with the feelings of powerful vibes that were filling the room. And the time vortex that was swirling around these four books! And the items in the velvet bag.*

\*\*\*

## Flash, flash, Flash...

My mind was spinning out of control, down a shining tube, that I now knew was a wormhole in time.

I was still holding the ring in my hand, as the time vortex began to swirl around me, I felt sick and dizzy from the disruption of space and time, but somehow, I managed to grip the ring and think of what Higgins had said.

### Need is the key

When I needed to feel what any object wanted to show me in the past, I had a simple feeling in my guts, and my mind told me what I need to know, **but not today.**

Today I was going to have a full-on vision dream where would think I was in the mind of the object's owner hearing what he or she, had seen and done in their time

.To feel it ds power and this day, I thought about this ring owner, who was Leofric.

It was then that I was spun out of the wormhole, into another time and place. Into a small dark room, lit by candles and a big fire in the hearth.

\*\*\*

*Flash, flash, Flash...*

*A very old man was sitting at a table that held the books he has written; he was writing in one. It guessed was Leofric, as he wore the ring, to my surprise and no little consternation he looked up at me, as if I was really there with him? He mumbled something in his beard.*

*"I see you spirit, are you my fylgia, have you come to find me again, and do you bring my death at your heels.?*

*If so, you are welcome, come spirit, I am ready, and my task is finished with this last book.*

*But then, as I looked around the room, I knew that this was no ordinary vision dream and somehow my mind had been transported in time and space to appear her as a ghostly entity to Leofric, in his time and space?*

If this was the library of Leofric ,the Bishop of Exeter, and a secret room he had built in the Cathedral of St Peter. The new church, he had built in Exeter, to honour his God.

*Moreover, I had seen a drawing of this book that he was using, and now that lay beside him. It was a large, illustrated book, that I had last seen displayed in the foyer of the University, held safe under toughen glass., was also to hold his* **Great Book of Exeter.**

And there set out decide this important book, and also set out on a large wooden table of Saxon design, were the four books we had found in the Twentieth century!

*His secret accounts of his life and times that were laid out on this dark oak table. But he looked at me then as if he needed to say something to death?*

*"I see your dark shadow, my dear friend. But first I need to tell you spirit Are you one of the* **fylgia** *come to take my soul . I hear your question spirit , ask it again!*

*You ask for the key to these books but only those of pure heart and mind may be able to read these secret books and* they will need my ring So begone I say and leave me to die in peace this last day.

So, must I make my peace with my God, and ask his forgiveness for my sins. Begone, I say!

In My Mind I Thought. And Said, I Am A Seeker Of Knowledge Leofric, And I Have Found Your Books, And I Have Your Ring. So I Am Seen To Be Worthy Of Reading What You Have Written In These Holy Books. Who Are You Leofric, And What Are These Books, What Is This Key You Speak Of?

'If that is so then you are a welcome ghost, my friend, and yes, I will help you And when you need to read my books so must you hide them away from those men who would try to steal our Saxon way of life.

And to read them you must have my ring, or else they will seem to be gibberish.

*But my race is run, spirit, I see you also must leave my side my fylgia friend, As this is my last day on this Gods earth, and we will not meet again.*

*Need is the key. and so, it is written so shall it be. Be gone I say.'*

And with those words his head fell onto the table and the ink was spilt from the bottle to stain the table, I felt his spirit depart from him, as once again, I was caught up in his passing, I was being pulled away from this place, And not before he had given me any further answers.

*"**Television.** You must come home, Jake. Come back, Jake Rutter!*

\*\*\*


## Television.

Then, I was lying on the wooden block floor of the university library reading room, and I had fallen off the bunk bed!

*So, I had been sick again and covered in what had been my last meal and my mouth tasted foul and dry I was choking on a wet rag and finding it hard to breath. Barton had the ring, and the Nurse was trying to get the rest of my sick out of my mouth, as I had been about to choke to death on my vomit!?*

It was then that I realised that John and Mandy, had also come to my bedside. Mandy was holding my hand, and she was praying for me, under her breath while John had managed to place a cloth in my mouth, our routine method, to stop me biting my tongue, when I had a bad fit?

I was on my back, and I told the women to get me up, and sit on a chair as Barton, said.

*"Well Jake, my old friend, We thought you are a goner this time, You were gone so long! I was worried that we had lost you for good this time.*

*Come please drink this, it is some brandy and water. No do not try to speak yet, as we need to look at the record we have made, as now we can all see just what the printer has typed up and then, you must tell us about what you have seen?"*

*"So, it fewkin worked? There is a record, how Wonderful! I was not sure it was going to work. And you will not believe what I saw!!! How long was I out?"* thinking it must be moments?

*"Four hours Jake, that is the longest time you have been out of it, for a long time. But Susan found the smelling salts and this Brandy.*

*"Where am I?"*

*"You ,we are in the rest room of this Building , we were here with these books to find out why Professor Higgins killed... But you know that?"*

John asked me to make sure I was back in my own mind. As, I realised that Barton was holding the ring now, having removed it from my grasp and that was what had broken the time link? I turned to Barton and Simonson to say almost in a whisper.

*"I was away for a time you say, but to me it was only moments. I had an out of body experience. Shall we say. You see, I actually met this Bishop Leofric, on his death bed! He said Need is the key!"*

The two woman were looking utterly puzzled, but they knew now what they had been told, that this was a normal procedure, and a skill that we used on a crime scene, if we needed, to learn what had really happened there.

So, I had told them it was a form of self- hypnosis, that I could use to send my mind away into another dimension of space time, To seek a golden timeline... And now, after what the professor , had told us, theywere willing to believe it was possible.

*"Well now what can I tell you, not much and not yet! but one thing I found out was that we need have no fear that these books are guanine.*

But I still realised just how difficult all this talk of time travel would still sound to these two woman of science, and that theywere not going to believe me, without some proof?

And I still need their help to make sure I was not trapped in the past. So, I told them what they must do to prevent that.

*"Well ladies there is a way you can help me to return from my dreaming ,you see Indeed, these books hold some sort of a powerful protection. So much so that they are giving me so many feelings of the past, as they carry such power that was given to them by the Bishop Leofric.*

*It is A protective device, that prevents anyone reading them who he feared would wish to destroy them.*

*So, you see, I have a fear I will become trapped withing the emanations, as they are a direct link to the past and their authors."*

I saw the two woman, and even John Barton, were still looking incredulous at my words, as now but they had seen what I had gathered from the note, and how right I had been about them having secrets! And I saw I needed Barton's and their help, to carry on with this investigation and the reading of these books. But I now knew that Need was the key, to understanding these books, and the ring. As I said.

"Well now ladies we have heard The Professor say, that he believes that I can timeslip into the past. then is what was to read about Quantum time, and what a multi-Universe entails. But after Reading all this, I am still as confused as I was reading all these strange theories. but one of the explanations about quantum time has stuck acord with me.

And now I have come to think that Leofric was on a different timeline to us.

 And to think that the Golden line of the Godwinsons, and their history timeline, seems to have been changed, when Gytha came into Godwin and Harold lives?

As for these books that detail their life, and while he has set down, and what he saw and was told to be true may not be the same as our timelines.

No, Jake, we dare not do anything of the sort, you must not try to change anything.

You speak of the laws of time and one I know is about the Grandfather paradox. It says if you go back in time to change anything no matter how small the knock-on effect could change all of time and we would never be born. Did you not hear what Professor Scott said?"

Well as to that so called bootstrap paradox, we must see that there have been so many critical moments in time *when a single action could have changed the outcome of our timelines.*

*And Yes Susan, I see that, and as an historian I have often wondered about those pivotal moments, and even in our time, the World War 2, would not have happened if Hitler had been killed at Munich, and before he came to power? Or in the USA when one man decided to use the atomic bomb against Japan. Or in our time, what if Kennady had listened to his generals, and used their atomic weapons when Khrushchev was in power.*

*So yes, there are a few moments when out future hangs on one single moment in time that could have killed so many or caused the deaths of Millions. Or saved them from the Holocaust!*

Susan was thinking hard now trying to think what I was getting at. As she said.

"Yes Jake Rutter, I see that but that is all wishful thinking, So what we cannot do anything about that? Isaid.

"Can we not, surely, we stand at just such a moment when Harold Godwinson is at such a crossroads.

What would have happened if he had won the battle of Hastings and defeated the Normans. From what we know it was a close-run thing until he was killed, and the

*Saxons broke their shield wall. What If as Leofric believes he was not killed then?*

*Surly that is such a moment in time and England will remain a Saxon kingdoms. And If I can make a small intervention using the ring of power what then?"*

Susan was silent for a long time and then she said.

*"How can you do that? It is one thing to be a silent witness to what Leofric, has told us about the at battle. But we have no way of acting there. And we cannot be sure that it will invoke the grandfather's paradox?"*

*" Yes Susan, I suppose you are right? But even so, I am going to read that part of his book and see for myself. And the professor, also told us about the constant causality idea, that says the matrix of Quantum time, will self-adjust to preserve any golden timeline. But you are right I should not risk doing anything of that sort. But we must get back to the readings."*

But it was then that a small germ had begun to grow in my mind that should the time come when I could influence Leofric as I had done at our first encounter, well I was going to see if I could make a difference, and save the Godwinsons, on Senlac Hill! Moreover, it was a possibility that these books were not a part of my, our, Golden timeline, as having spoken to Susan, there were some small a*nd large differences in what we had seen so far.*

One such concerns the battle of Hastings. Leofric has said that King Harold was not killed at Hastings and that he and Gytha and their surviving sons escaped to Devon and Exeter.

*And then, Where over the next five years and with the aid of an Irish and Cornwall army, they came to fight Duke William and stopped him becoming their king.*

 So, here does Leofric say that instead of going on to conquer all of Britain, the Norman army was he sent back to Normandy, and England remained a Saxon nation with all that would mean for our country and history?

*"So, Jake, you think these books are not a true description of our Timelines, as they tell of a different time and a very different outcome to our Saxon Story."* Mandy realised?

 *"If that is so  what should we do now. I ask this because we have a chance to try to change  the outcome of the Godwinson story lines, if I can speak to the King at Hastings? As I think I can speak to Leofric, if he was there?  I could save the Godwins and the Saxons and Engaland, from Duke William!"*

Moreover, and If I was to be able find out what was the cause of the evil in these books, I realised that I would have to try to read of the Four books, and that was going to be a mammoth task and take an age, at the speed I could manage. *And time I did not have.*

But as all this ran through my mind Susan was looking aghast at this news, as was Mandy but she was also seeing the possibilities of such an action as she said.

*"All this talk of changing the past is all very well, ,but the truth is that we still do not know what Killed poor Richard. I think we need to see what happened at the Danish christening, and that curse, before we try to do anything more that will harm anyone or alter time.*

I saw she was right of course, and I said,

*"Yes, Susan I was stupid to think that, and you are right of course. We will make a new start in the morning.*

\*

### *The next day…*

But to everyone's surprise and delight, we were to find that when I went to touch the book in the afternoon session, wearing the ring, I could now read every word that was written and reading them aloud in modern English as the pages turned into text. *Need was the key then!*

### *And what I read then, was the life story of Bishop Leofric!*

***

## *Flash, Flash, Flash...*

*I am the Leofric Archbishop of Exeter, and in truth, my life began in Cornwall, where I was born in the year of our Lord, One Thousand One Hundred and Sixteen, and brought up with my Cornish family.*

However, to my eternal relief, my elder brother 'Ordmaer,' was content to manage the farm and the estate. Moreover, it was soon evident that my parents saw that I was far more interest in learning about our histories and spent a great time with the local Priest Patrick.

It was Patrick, who said I would never become a farmer with my thirst for knowledge and my love of reading.

My Family name was **Brytonicus,** and it was my mother Rita, who said Patrick was correct to say that I was born so small. *I would not survive their hard life, and I should be given up serving God, and I must be sent away to train as a priest.*

And so, and with much to the disgust of the men in our family, when I was old enough, I was sent with a letter to the bishop at *Lotharingia,* and my education began at the church of St *Stephen's in Toul.* It transpired that my mother had a cousin who knew one of the cannons there, a confident the holy priest *Leo.* And so began my rise in the clergy ranks, as I managed to make friends with Leo.

*But I did not know then that Leo who was such A scholarly man, and to be Gods servant who was destined to become Pope Leo IX's in the future years!*

But with Leo's help, and once I became ordained, I was lucky enough to meet with the English atheling Prince Edward, the seventh son of Æthelred the Unready. We met at a Synod held in Bruges. When I was studying in Flanders, in the year of our Lord One Thousand and Thirty-Nine.

Even so, and then I was still considered to be a young man of Twenty-three. But If I was to look in one of those polished mirrors, one could find it in the Kings' palace, One would see a man from Cornwall stock, but where they are tall and broad-shouldered. I am short and slim with fair hair and blue eyes, not the brown of my father. A white skin that would burn in the sunlight and never go brown.

*My people would say I came from a Welsh stock. But I did not have their build either, as I stayed small and slim no matter how much food I consumed, and I had found it hard to grow a beard or become a strong, well-built man like my brother?*

*So, I was content to hide from the world, by serving God as best I can and doing his work among the people and the sick and poor.*

But it was then that fate decided to intervene in my life and not for the first time!

*As That was when Prince Edward came for me that day at Bruges. So then was my destiny to be changed beyond anything I could have imagined as in Bruges, I was then to meet the future King AEdward, who was to be known as the Confessor?*

So then was my destiny to change as I met a great and pious man in Bruges at the time of his exile from England.

When he found out I could read and write so well, in five languages, so then did I became his Chaplin, and he was to become my benefactor and friend when he could return to Engaland to claim his birthright.

*So, I went with him to Engaland the year Nine hundred and Forty-Two and became his priest and confident and then a good friend. I was only twenty-four, having been born in the year 1015. And now I am an old man of Fifty-seven, and at the end of my long life in the year of our lord 1072.*

*But as I write these last chapters, It is the month of February, and I can no longer use my hands to write, and soon Bishop Walkeln will come to hear my confession as I am near the end of my days, and I see the shadow of the angel of death in my dreams!*

And what can I tell him, about my incredible life, and the people who were to come to know and serve all these years, as well as my God?

*Today he will see a bent and crippled man with arthritis and as bald as a coot.* But once I was a fine and strong man, when God made me his servant to be involved with the momentous events of state.

*As in time, I came to serve three kings and be a friend to the love of my life Gytha Godwinson.*

But this was an unrequited love as I managed to maintain my vows of chastity that I had given to God. Then, and even now, my heart will beat faster at her memory.

*For, she was a wife to Godwin Earl of Wessex, and I must hope that she would never know of my love for her.*

We met in the year 1035 when Godwin and Gytha and her family came to Winchester to the funeral of King Canute. It was then that She came to me to ask me to become her confessor, and to hear her story that I have now set down in my secret journals.

As for Edward, perhaps it was because of our friendship at this time of strife, and our shared love of books and learning, that King Edward offered me the post that was now vacant in my homeland?

*To become the successor of Bishop Lyfing to the Sees of Crediton and St. Germans in my beloved Cornwall. And then, I was then called the "king's priest", but I was determined even then to try to be my own man under God? So it was that*

*Edward was to find that he had appointed a new kind of Bishop, but one he could trust.*

And because of his need for a man of honour, I was also to be his Chancellor, the Keeper of the King's purse, and the treasure house, like Bishop Lyfing before me. *and later to become his Confessor and his secretary, and I like to think his only true friend!*

But now, as the "king's high chancellor," I was soon to find out that this was a poisoned chalice. I was someone of influence and someone who could be bribed or asked and given favours! But they soon found out that I was seen to have reflected the Royal Confessor's earnest piety.

*So, while I managed to keep the king's secrets and take care of his treasury, so did I make many enemies in this difficult time. The task I was given in that year of One Hundred and Forty-Seven, when the Conflict with the Godwin family was soon to come to a head?*

So it was, that in the year 1050, it had become evident that maintaining the church at Crediton was no longer fit for my purposes. I was then determined to move my seat of office because Crediton was too poor and rural.

Moreover, Exeter was a city with protective walls and an abandoned church that could be used as the new Cathedral I intended to build there one day. But then, I was told that prince Athelstan AEthelred's first born. had some land there, and built a small church, which would suit him? But that had been in the year 928; the Aetherling Athelstan was long dead.

*May God bless his soul.*

So it was that when I went to inspect this church of St Peter at Exeter, and to see for myself just how lacking in episcopal vestments and the other items that are required for church services. *A poor church indeed in both ways.*

But, nevertheless, a list of gifts to the church gave vestments, crosses, chalices, censers, altar coverings, and other furnishings, which I could take to the new Cathedral.

The histories will say a monastery had been founded in Exeter by King Athelstan, in the year of our Lord, Nine hundred and Twenty Eight. And that it was dedicated to St. Mary & St. Peter.

*But as we shall see, as it was in the year 1050, Along with its possessions, this monastery was now solemnly assigned to me as the Bishop Leofric, as the principal place of my See.*

But when I was installed in the episcopal chair by Edward himself, who *"supported his right arm at the blessing! and Queen Edith his left."*

So, the ceremony took place in the two archbishops and many other bishops and nobles. Then, however, there was somewhat more security within Exeter's walls after what we had found at Crediton. A fortified Roman built town that we thought was safe from the Danish raiders! However, I was to find that the monastery of St. Peter had been despoiled by the Northmen. It was so poor the only land it had was at Ide, where only two Hydes of Land remained in its possession, and only seven head of cattle were upon these. the monastery itself was not much better furnished.

But now I have half-a-dozen books of little value, and *"one worthless priest's dress"* was all the library and wardrobe that, according to his statement, I was to find found in it when I took possession.

But, on the other hand, along with the vestments, articles of church furniture, and sacred vessels bestowed on it, I had managed to acquire fifty-five books, both in English and Latin.

*So, did a few monks who remained in the Convent at my accession must be found another place to live and worship? Some others were sent to serve King Edward, sometimes called the Confessor, due to his obvious piety, and served at Westminster's Abbey.*

But, as I worked to increase the diocese's endowment, especially the cathedral library, which I had found almost empty upon my arrival. There were only five books owned by the cathedral chapter when I became its Bishop.

*However, I am pleased to say that my work, the "great English book with everything wrought poetry-wise", remains famous among the Cathedral treasures.*

But I was careful to make sure that the Monks of St Peters, were not left without a roof over their heads, and they were given a large Building at Cowick Barton, on the other side of the river and outside of the city.

As I had replaced them at Exeter with a body of prebendaries, or regular canons, who, according to

English custom, *but instead following that of Lotharingia,"* they lived together, eating at a shared table, and sleeping in a shared dormitory. But during as all this, I had managed to remain on good terms with the King, for I was present at Edward's Christmas court in 1065.

*A wonderful day that saw the consecration of Edward's Westminster Abbey church there. But that is yet to come to pass.*

So did my life become ever grander and more complicated as with my donation to the monastery of St. Peter at Exeter, for my hope is that one day it shall become a cathedral.

The letter from the Archbishop describes me as a man *"of modest life and conversation who, when he succeeded to his See, went about his diocese studiously preaching the Word of God to the people committed to him and instructing the clergy in learning.*

*But why have I told you, my readers, about all this history and life?*

One reason is to establish my authority as the Chronicler of these books, including the life and times of the Kings of England and how the Godwinson family played such an important part then.

*And to let you see, and learn, how I came to live through these turbulent times and to be able to say what I have written is done so under a holy oath by all who have contributed to these chronicles.*

*That is why I and the other bishops who set down these words for the people in the future to know and read what we have written.*

That is the truth as to whether they are the authentic records of these times and testaments of these people; perhaps my future readers will be able to judge.

*But I fear I have bored you long enough, with my own story, which I have added so that you can know these dates and times.*

So, for now, In this year 1072, I am an old man of fifty-seven and near the end of my life, and it has been hard Looking at what has transpired in them? And how I was to become involved in these momentous events!

*But looking at what I have set down about my early life, I can see just how a reader will think of me as a vain person and a glory-seeking man.*

*But that is not who I am, and as these chapters unfold, that tells the story of Lady Gytha and her husband Earl Godwin and his family. I can only hope and pray that God will show me a way to come to the right path to give them some resolution. I will be able to also provide them with absolution for all that they have done.*

*So, help me, God!*

\*\*\*

## 𝓕lash, 𝓕lash.

Television.

It is here, that Jake had stopped reading ,both, to take a drink, and some refreshment and to look at the typed pages and to discuss them with the others.

*"Flipping heck! what a treasure trove we have here, and I can see how and why Higgins wanted to keep them secret as they would have made him famous."*

Barton said.

*But we still have no clue as to why he died and what should we do now? Now that you have managed to use the ring to open these books, I wonder if we could use it to do likewise, as it would allow you to get some rest?"*

That was a good idea, so he and the women tried in turn and failed to see or feel anything, as Barton said.

*"Well, I see that you are stuck with this task Jake. but one of us must return to my normal duties. But it would seem we still are no further forward with the death of Higgins; I think he died of a heart attack and unless you can say otherwise our work is done here Sarge?*

I took Barton to one side and out of earshot of the women.

*"Yes, I am prepared to think that, but we have untangled a love triangle here. And it is possible the Professor was poisoned somehow? Although the autopsy will show that. So, I need to dig a little deeper here and look into these two women. And, if they think we have given up on that part of the investigation , and you should leave, and perhaps they will let their guard down and I will catch them out? And besides I think I must carry on with these readings while you go back to report to the office.*

*"Then that is a plan Sarge, and I will leave you in the care of these ladies, and the nurse, shall I sarge?"*

John was nodding to indicate he agreed with this, and it was a sensible plan. I also was thinking It would allow me sometime to finalise my plan for Hastings. As I could see that John was right to say that, and I agreed that he should return to the station, and we would keep in touch ,sending the Inspector, and the detective, any relevant information by email and fax. As, I also knew they would want me back on my normal duties and not here helping to read these books. And it would seem that Higgins had died of a heart attack.

Once Barton had left and during coffee, we had to decide what we were going to do about the books. I said to the women.

*"Well then it seems that you must wait for the woman who can read Gaelic, or I could go on reading this book as it is set down by the Bishop, even if it is not on our timeline?*

*And now we know now that need is the key to finding the information we need? We should go to your list and the open pages, that Higgins was reading?"*

Susan said,

*"Yes, we should do that, and perhaps it will throw some light on his death? He was looking into how and why Godwin was to go to Denmark and become a vassal to Canute?"*

So, I put my hand with the ring on the book ,and to ask it our question and the dictation machine began typing. It was headed A marriage of Convenience.

***

*Flash, Flash.*

*The book opens to The chapter heading said, A Marriage of Convenience.*

The year was December 1039, and this is a momentous year in Engaland, Denmark and Norway. It is the year that Canute the Great ,shall die from a heart attack, and the wounds he had encountered at his last battler with the Norwegians.

And now Godwin and his widow Emma must decide who they will support to be the new King, As so many shall come forth to claim his three kingdoms. When both the rebellious Danes and Normans from Normandy and Saxons and the Norse countries, saw the time was ripe for them to try to overthrow the rule of the Danes while Cnut was away in Engaland.

But Godwin is now a man of Thirty-Six years, and he also has been through so many battles and trials in the service of Canute, that he also feels his age and the injuries he has sustained. *But now, he is the Earl of Wessex. And one of the most powerful men in the land!*

So, Godwin and Gytha have decided to find a way that the church will accept their danish wedding and hand fisting ceremony. They must do that because they have lost the protection of Canute and their enemies, will seek to bring the down here in Denmark, and England.

*To do that, they must seek Leofric out at Winchester, One aim was to ask him to come to Denmark and to be a witness at their christening ceremony at Jelling. and to officiate at the blessing of their son.*

But Harold another agenda, and that was to ask Leofric, to hear his confessions as Godwine wants to tell me of the events that were to transpire after his Danish Marriage to Gytha, and perhaps clear his conscience about his treatment of his eldest Sons — and speaking of the blinding and Death of Prince Alfred who was England rightful heir when Aethelstan died.

*But I was not yet ready to forgive Godwin, for his part in that terrible act. So, he and Gytha came to find me and then passed this task to me. However, it is now that I can come into this story as a witness to what was said and written.*

So, must I go to Winchester for the funeral of Canute, so shall I meet Godwin, and Gytha, again, and for the first time since Godwin had fled their after being exiled by Aethelred. So must I obey my conscience, as I listen and set down this part of the Godwin and Gytha's story. Their story that ` shall it be added to the secret manuscripts that I Leofric can read and use to compile this third volume that you have discovered. I must also go to Denmark as an ambassador for Edward, and to be his eyes and ears.

    *

This is what Harold, was to tell me in his *confession.*

*"I see you, Leofric, and I am pleased to meet you and see that you have an open mind and are willing to listen to me. As I hope that you can listen to my story without too many interruptions. But I and the lady Gytha will be here in Winchester for the funeral, and we will find the time to talk with you. If that will not suffice, you must come to Lundune or Comptene.?"*

I was so amazed I said nothing!

*"Look, Priest, If you do not wish to do this, speak now, or we will find someone else? But I like you, and my wife says she has spoken to you about her life and fears? So, I am willing to do the same. So that we can both speak to you from time to time, what we say to you must be written down each session, and we shall read it then to ensure you have not misheard us? As You see, I have good reason to know how words can be twisted and the truth lost. And lies become the truth. This was what happened to my father, and I wish to avoid this trap. I want an accurate record to set down in our Saxon words, and not your Latin, of what we have done. A true record not to be tampered with by your bishops and our King's men! Both good and bad things we have done over the years, As we have done some evil things, in order to do a great good. Can you do this, Bishop and not speak of it?"*

*So, far, I saw that these meetings were not going to be given under the confessional as to write down a confession was forbidden and great sin? But why was Godwin making such a fuss about this meeting? I saw he was not going to change his mind or these conditions. I spoke out.*

"So, my son, these words are not to be given under god, but you should know that what you say to me will be judge one day, when you come before him!? He will know of any lies or half-truths, But I will do as you wish, my Lord. So, help me, God."

"Then I choose you, Leofric, and I know you to be a good Saxon, and an honest man of your word, as Gytha has said I can tell you anything I need to explain my actions. I see now that you are a Godly man and serve your Lord Christ and also king Edward in such earthy matters. And when we are finished, you must decide if you can give us absolution. Or a penance and tell Edward my story?"

I nodded my understanding and said what was in my heart.

"I am true that I am a man from Cornwall lord, but in a way, we are all Saxons now, and under one king, so you have my word that what I hear will be our secret. But is it wise to have it written down?"

"Yes, as I see now that one day soon Bishop, my enemies will try to spread their filthy lies about me and mine. And to have your writings given here, may be my salvation? Here on this earth or in the afterlife? So, I will provide you with everything you need as well as ...As well as an escort and a guard, as you will not *mind if your writings are kept secret and locked away after our talks."*

"Yes, that is a wise precaution." I said to him. He spoke.

"So, I see that , I can trust a scribe to help you do this. And they will also keep you safe. But know that all this is said under your honour and this oath. However, I expect you know we had a similar arrangement with Lyfing, and the spoke of us to his priest Godfrey, blast him to hell, as he is spreading his foul lies about me and Mine!"

I saw him grimace at that, and I crossed myself at this blasphemy. As he went on to say.

"But they are all dead now, and Gytha thinks you are our man. What says You, Leofric. I want to be able to call you by your name if you permit it?"

"Yes, my lord, I would like that. And we should make a start?"

"A start, but I also see that this may take a long time, so you must also commit to that. I see you are looking at these neck chains I wear that say that I am a pagan, and also a Christian. The truth of it is that I do have Odin in my heart, as did my father, *and I have learned Jesus Christ's words. I have come to see he is a messenger from your God.*

*I believe that he was a saintly man who was out of his time, and he came to show us the way of love and peace. So, I wear his cross in the hope that one day the way of peace and forgiveness shall come to pass. But it is not this day, as today, I am with Thor and Odin as well as Jesus the Christ children's. But I have tried to be faithful to both concepts and doctrine. But I have had to make some hard choices and killed my fellow man in battle and anger.*

*However, I have tried to live by my father's code of Honour and do what my heart and honour demanded of me. I have tried to be a good man to those I love and those who serve me. And to grant mercy to my enemies. Who are many.*

*So, It will be for the Gods and you, Leofric, to be my judge, and jury when we are finished with this life. However, I see that you are worried about what I will tell you? so I will give you the rest of this day and a night, to decide if you can help us in the matter of a Christian Marriage, and perform the christening?*

*However, should you agree to do this, I and Gytha, will be forever in your debt, and you will be well rewarded. I will not be ungrateful, as I will build you a fine church at Exeter if that is your wish?"*

So, I spent the night in prayer, and it was then that I went to find the secret bishop's records for the first time. It was then that I knew that the story Godwinson story had to be told.

*As It was also a History of these times when we could have a New Engaland at last?*

But, as I also believed that Canute had been a good King, in his own way, and he had given our lands some stability at least. *So that she was a Dane, as Gytha is also a pagan.* But was this the task God wanted me to perform, to bring them both into the church and the true faith?

*If so, how could I refuse them? Moreover, as Canute had shown us the way to unite his lands, , and now is story also deserved to be told. So, I had my answer and a few conditions of my own.*

\*

The next day, we were all five seated in a small room in a side room at Winchester

Cathedral. And once we had made sure, we could not be disturbed, or overheard, I said a blessing for us all, and now we could set the date for the christening.

*However, I would need to find a bigger room for our next meeting, as this Sola was now more than a little overcrowded. As It would soon become hot and uncomfortable as there was me and the scribe provided by Godwin, an older man who I knew was one of Godwin's trusted men, Thomas of Comptene.*

Gytha was sitting in an alcove looking out of the window, presumably, she also wanted to hear what her husband would say, And perhaps she was going to speak here as well. But Godwin had said that they both wanted to have their say, here this summer's day?

We were sitting at a table that held a golden cross that seemed alive in the morning sun, coming from the one window.

*A good sign, I thought!*

There was some food and drink and a slop bucket behind a screen. I had a bottle of holy water to sprinkle around the door and window and seal the room. But I had not expected to see that Godwin had brought a guard and a scribe who had a chest for the writing materials, and just in case, some candles.

There was a jug of Ale, some cheese, biscuits, a bottle of red wine, and Roman made glasses brought From Comptene. On seeing all this, I knew this could be a very long session, as Godwin said.

"So, Leofric, I was glad to get your letter, and the Archbishop has told me what you have said to him, and I agree with your terms. So let us begin!"

My terms were that my word as a man of God must suffice as to what I was to set down And as to my keeping their secrets, my word would have to be given and I was in the hand of my god, and I needed no guards. Not here or at Exeter.

But I see that Godwin and his Gytha needed some physical protection so I said that I would only allow two guards to be their escort when I am with Godwin. As for any other time, I was under the king's protection as one of his principal advisors *and no one was going to attempt anything against me.as I did not wish to be watched night and day.*

*Another was that we would only have my own scribe who I would teach to use my secret cypher to use, and they could be sure that no one else could read what was written in these meetings as this was for my protection as much as Godwin's!*

They had agreed to this, providing I showed my cypher to Thomas of Comptene, as he was someone Godwin could trust with his life. And I was going to show him and Thomas how to write it all in a Gaelic dialect I had learned in Ireland, and when I had time, theywere to be transcribed using my codex...

And it was The next day, we were ready to begin this monumental task. The day I was to go to Denmark as both a friend to the Godwinson and the envoy of Edward, at this wedding.

That day I was with Godwin on his ship as he came to find me to ask me to hear his confession!

*

"So Leofric, You ask us to tell you about our life in Denmark, and how we became to have a Danish wedding? but first, you should know that I am no longer in a state of Grace.

You see I have killed a man with my bear hands, but in the service of my king and my task to find the killer of our beloved king Edmund, may his soul rest in peace.

But you know I have been to war in the service of my kings. And that any war is an evil thing in itself. In a war the innocent is the first to suffer and be killed. But they died for a good cause, and I do not consider that to be a murderous act.

But you should know that I have done murder.

And this is known to Gytha. I have told her and my King about my crime. I had decided to do so , before I was to ask his permission for a Christian wedding. So, it was when I came back from Engaland, when our King Edmund was murdered.

But you should know that I have told Gytha of what had transpired in Lundune, and I have received her forgiveness, but not your Gods.

So here then Leofric, is my first Confession...

I will tell you of that terrible day in the year of 1018, that I was to return home from Engaland and with news of the killing of King Edmund....I will send my mind back to the day of my return to Denmark this day.

If you remember that you were so seasick, you had yur head in sick bucket. I was standing on the ship named for her The Gytha, and. I am trying to decide what to tell you about my time in Lundune. It was a new year, and now I must tell both you and Canute the truth concerning the Death of King Edmund. And not the foul lies, that Lyfing and Godfrey were spreading, that it was at my order It was said that he was to be murdered in his privy! But I know that this was how his murderers were able to use the Garde-Loo, to gain entry to his rooms. And that he was killed in his bedchamber! Not That I Was Involved In That Deed. Which I will swear to on my honour, and any hope of resurrection, to be true!

But now Canute has become our King of all Engaland, because of the agreement at Gloucester that day.  An agreement between him and Edmund *that I had brought about that day, and at the King's Moot!*

*So now, I must speak the truth of Edmund's death, as many were saying that it was I who planned this evil deed, and it had been Canute, who had sent me to Engaland, to find the truth for him and myself, and him, as he had been so angry when he was told of Edmunds death! An even more so when I asked him if he had ordered this done? I had accused of bringing about this deed. But I was to discover I had been so wrong to accuse him of this foul deed. Moreover. Cnut had had been so angry at my accusations, that for a moment, I thought he would have struck me down there and then, a despite what I had one for him in the battles for the crown of Norway. The time I had saved his life and his longship, from being overrun in the dried upriver bed that had been the result of the battle for Haverford...*

*But that day it had been Ulf and his son who, had borne the brunt of his anger.*

*This day, he had sent me to Lundune with a mission to discover the truth of this murder*

*I was sent back to Engaland to find out who did this and bring them back to Canute and Denmark. So that Canute, can punish the murderers.*

*Moreover, I was also charged with ensuring that Edmund's body was well cared for and Edmond would have the Royal funeral he deserved!*

*First, however, and so that the people of Engaland would not make my mistake, I was also charged with making sure the Ealdorman should be told that Canute had nothing to do with Edmund's Death.*

*So then, now these murderers, must abide by their oaths to make Canute the undisputed King of all of Engaland! But ,when we had captured them as theywere foolish enough to use their blood money so freely, In a tavern so did my men manage to find them and make them our prisoners. And with some persuasion, barely stopping from torture, so did we learn of the horrible details of this murder. But it was Alain who killed Edmund, and I had been so angry at the men from the Circus.*

   *Yes, it was these Gypsy men were a part of a circus act, and it was these men, we found responsible for the foul murder of our king. And to avoid anyone seeing an open wound, they used a hot poker pushed up his arse, Alain did this using a copper, metal funnel, then to thrust in the hot poker, to puncture his gizzards, and stop his heart! You Alain boasted how clever this was to do a murder In that way there would be no sign of a wound!*

*I was then that I also was to discover they had had the acrobatic skills to enter the Castle by stealth. So it was that after some persuasion, the leader of this attack, Alain, of Lundune, told me about that day and how he did not know who he was to kill?*

*But when the full horror of Edmund's death, was told to my men, and then to me. It was then that I had decided he did not deserve a trial, or to be allowed to live another day! so I had used all my strength to crush his skull with my bare hands.*

*But I know now, and in the cold light of day, that Canute and the English Noblemen would have been condemned to an even more terrible fate, should they be brought to trial for the murder of a king?*

*As with the confessions, There could be no other verdict, but guilty of killing a king had only one punishment, and that was to be Hung and taken down while still alive to have your chest opened and see your guts spill out and be burnt before your still conscious eyes? Then while your mind still lives, to have your body cut up while your head is placed on a spike for all to see.*

*You know that is the law, and the horrible fate of these men who committed regicide!*

*However, my task was not yet complete, as I still had the Circus folk onto my ship. And the then take them all back to Denmark to face a trial under the hand of Canute.*

*And I knew then that these murderers, were going to say they said that Edmund's death was an accident, and that they had been paid to torture a jealous lover? And that they had no idea who their victim was. And that may well be the truth for the youngest of them ? But Alain had mentioned two names to me, that had may me kill him, One of these was Aelfric the Son of Eadric Streona, my sworn enemy. And a well-known traitor and turncoat. Another was the priest Oswald, who was to grant them absolution for this crime, as he believed that Edmund was no rightful king and his master, Eadric Streona should have been chosen at the Lundune Witan, as Streona had been already named to be the new King at the Southampton Witan.*

*And To My Horror, And Another Was Queen Emma? But as these names were spoken under questioning, I had no proof to share that they were not lies, or to get an answer, As to who had paid for the killing. So, you see Bishop, As for Alain, of Lundune, perhaps I had given him a quick death. A merciful Death?*

*As the rest must still face a trial in Denmark. And while it is also true that I have killed so many men in battle, the truth of it is that I was sorry to kill this man with my bear hands and in such a rage of hatred. But I would have killed Eadric Streona twice over, given a chance.*

*But I was never to be allowed to do this, because when we all came to Lundune, Canute had seen though Streona lies, and betrayals, and the head of the Earl of Mercia Eadric Streona had been cut from his body, on the orders of our Canute and the man who is now my King?*

*So now, you have heard it all, and as I think back to that month in December, I am trying to put my feelings of guilt behind me. I must say I regret that killing and will do any penance you set for me. But can your god forgive this act of Murder Bishop?"*

\*\*\*

The Murder Of Edmund Ironside!

Now it was my time, to re- read what was written, in this, his confession and how he has asked for absolution of this one crime?

I also realised that Godwin had told me the only the bare bones of this murder, and the tortures his men had used. I had read what Godwin and his people, had done in the service of his kings, first had been Aethelred, Then Cnut, and Edmund and now Canute. I had to see that all he had done to date, he had done with justice on his side and with as much honour and compassion, as he could in these warlike times.

I knew that all war is utterly evil, and we are taught to turn the other cheek? But I also know that for evil to win out, all a good man needs to do is too standby and do nothing.

But that was not Godwin of Wessex. And the few men who did so in our time, were now dead and buried and were soon to be named as Godly man and now Saints like St Stephen.

And, what of Godwins sins, and I knew that they were many and now he had added Murder to them. That I could not forget or forgive.

So, I was trapped by conscience. I could not grant him absolution. But what could I do.

And then God gave me the answer a I open the bible, to seek an answer I Read how Jesus had said that his people must give unto Ceaser what is due to Caesar. and to god what is his which are their love and souls. This was what Godwin must be allowed to do now!

*Here then was a possible solution.*

As here was an honourable, and a good man, with a great heart and a champion for the forces of good, I this evil world. A man who had been caught up in the events of these times, and in such a way that he had tried to stand up for what is right, I asked him.

*"So then, Godwin of Wessex, Do you regret this death then Earl Godwin, I see you acted with such anger of the moment. I see you would have*

*delivered him up to Canute ,and to his justice and not yours?"*

I had to hope he saw the let out, in my words, and he would repent so that could give him absolution on this death? He looked up then and his eyes were shining with hope.

*"Yes of course I do that, father, and every day since. You see, I tried to stop Canute taking his revenge on the others, but he saw this as a weakness. But yes, I still see his head in my hands in my nightmares! and I will do any penance you set for me?"*

I had already thought of a suitable penance.

*"If you build God a fine Cathedral, I think that will suffice! andyou are forgiven ,that sin this day, Earl Godwin. But what happen next, that you a Saxon, were allowed to marry danish princess?*

*"I do this as I must gain your absolution before I can be given a Christian wedding here in Demark.*

And that is what we were to agree would serve as a penance. And as we approached the place of Godwins new home, I saw that

*Canute had come to see him and me at Hedeby.*

*And now there was to be a reconning, for what Godwin had done in Engaland, as there were the banners of Ulf Gytha's eldest brother, flying on his longship. And now, Godwin, must tell the King and Ulf of his crime. And the gods and my King must decide all our fates now? As for Hedeby I knew that this is where Gytha grew up and where he is expected to stay with her as her bondman for five years. And that is an incredible story that she shall tell you. If she thinks it will help our cause. As it was, Gytha, who had to pay a high price to save my life that day in Gloucester. That and a shipload of Silver and some of the lands in Denmark.*

*Moreover, and as Godwin was her bondsman, the bargain was that and he was also going to show the Danes how to build a Norwegian built Frigate, Like the Urien, his father, had constructed and used to such terrible effect.*

I believe that You will find his story in the book that you have compiled that is called, The Story Of Wulfnoth Child. A sad story, Godwin had recounted to me while we were at sea.

"And You should know Bishop, that The ships were a part of the bargain that Canute and Edmund had struck at Gloucester, to divide the country again and stop the fighting destroying our land.

So here I am living with Gytha in Denmark, and soon there will be a Danish wedding between myself and my beloved wife. If we had time, I would speak more of our courtship and how we found that we were meant to be married and what had been a Marriage of convenience was to develop into so much more and even a deep love and respect.

Perhaps Gytha will have the words to tell that part of our story?

But I had only agreed to do this Danish ceremony and a christening for Sweyn, when Gytha told me she was pregnant again.

So, for my part, I was content to go along with this, but I had said it was enough that we had gone *through a Saxon hand-fisting wedding two years past now?*

But then Gytha had said our son would not be seen as a legitimate heir here in Demark unless we had a formal Denmark-style wedding. So, then I saw just how important this was to us both, and I agreed that my Gytha and her brothers would be there that day.

And that was why Canute come to Hedeby, along with his new Bride Emma. A queen in her own right and the widow to AEthelred. Also, a very determined and powerful woman who had given Aethelred children and she was someone Canute thought would help him with the English nobles?

As for our new home in Denmark, the nearest I have of its Norse name is Heioabyr not a Saxon name. Or Haithabu in Germania. Hedeby is a settlement on the southern end of the Jutland peninsula. It is a trading base at the head of a narrow inlet to the Baltic Sea.

It is the ancestral home of Gytha's family, but her father Thorgil has passed on. But she still had two her brothers, and as I had found to my cost, they are mighty men here in these lands.

*Of course, I had met and fought against Earl 'Ulf the strong when I served with Edmund. And we fought against the Danish raiders.*

*The histories will tell you of these battles and how we were forced to make peace with them and divide the county again*

*Ulf is one of Canute's Warlords and her other brother Eilaf is a man of high status.*

*But in time, and for Gytha's sake, I had come to see a man as a friend. And someone I liked not least as it had been she and her younger brother Eilaf, who also saved my neck at the trial in Gloucester! So now you know the worst of it Leofric, what say you can I be absolved of this death of the evil man?"*

As we docked at the Jetty, I looked across the water to see this Viking home. As for the Holdfast in the Haddebyer valley. The hills and mountains surround the village as the land on three sides.

But the Hall and the huts are protected from the sea by high banks and a stockade fence on the south side; there is another fence and ditch to protect it from the bay, with a lookout tower and drawbridge that will be a defence from any attack from the sea?

It is also surrounded by marshland, that is, the Haddebyer Moor. In earlier times.

*I knew that it was the base for the Viking Jarl Leif Erickson, but now Canute's elder brother King Harold. had brought it under Danish rule.*

So now my thoughts were still in turmoil, as I knew that I could no longer put off this meeting that would bring an end to my short-lived happiness that I had found here with Gytha?

*As I held her tight as she gave me her warning. As she said into my ear.*

"Remember what I said about my brothers Husband, They hate to speak in your English tongue, as they have had a pidgin husband. they know you have done something terrible in Lundune?

So, Take care as my brother is very angry with you, and if he is in a foul temper, as he has a toothache and has drunk a lot of brandy. He will wish to take it out on you!"

Then she hugged and kissed me for what seemed an age.

It was much later in the Sprakling Hall; I ordered my men to hand over to the Danish guards, the remaining murders now kneeling before Canute and the Sprakling brothers. I was flanked by two of Ulf's men and kneeling on one knee, waiting for Canute to ask me to speak. But it was Ulf who said.

*"I see you, Godwin! You were told to find out what happened to Edmund, were you not? and report back to our King and his council? I hope you can explain this act of cold-blooded murder. How can we question dead men, Hey?"*

As I listened to this tirade, I realised that Canute had asked Ulf to speak for him, in this hall, as he could listen and pass judgment on these men and me.

But now, the Earl had asked a question. I was free to stand and not look at Canute or Gytha,

Who was sitting with Eilaf and to the side of this inquisition? Gytha tried to smile at me and say aloud for all to hear?

*"Tell it true, husband, but I have spoken to Canute, and he will not harm you if what you have told me is true!"*

Ulf looked at his sister then, because he did not want me to be able to wiggle out of this judgment. And I knew that while he had been forced to agree to my Marriage to his sister, he was not at all happy to have a Saxon in his family! So, he was going to take every opportunity he could to stop it, and this was another stone he could throw at me?

But now I knew that Gytha had told Canute of this murder; I knew I was on firm ground. If he wanted to harm me, I would already be in a pit somewhere.

*"I see that you already know of what happened in Lundune, and I will not be judged for an act of mercy that was a mercy killing compared to what he would face here? But I have also been told that this killing was done in a moment of anger?*

*And Yes, my liege, I broke the man's neck in my rage at what he told me. But I have regretted that moment ever since, and now. And I have made my confession before this Bishp Leofric, the very man you have held in your Feast Hall. I have chosen him to stand up for me at my wedding Sire, should you decide to allow it?*

*However, I also I stand here to account for it to you and your Gods. And now, my masters, but you are a fair man , and someone who believes I should have let our Gods deal with this matter, and these evil deeds of recticide."*

I said this knowing how serious the murder of a king was in these lands. And then I told him what Leofric had told me.

 *"And if what the Christians have come to believe is true, we must hope and pray, that we will learn to turn the other cheek one day, But it is not this day.*

 *And yes, I was both judge and executioner as this man, who told me how he and the others had tortured and killed my Saxon king!*

*And that is the truth of it. But now you must hear it all, and then I will abide by your judgement of what was done that day?"*

I took out the silver amulet, which hung around my neck, that was the amulet of Thors hammer I was also invoking his presence, to this trial? As then as I looked at Canute, I had to hope that by appealing to Thor, I had to hope that the Norse Gods would understand this act of passion. A life for a life! As I said.

*"So is it said and so was it done and If you wish it, I will swear to you and the gods here and now It was an act of passion and true justice. And If I am aloud to live past this day, I will tell you about all that had occurred at Lundune.*

*And to speak of this tale of murder and horror. As I will also suggest that we ask more of Queen Emma, about what she knew of this day.*

I saw Canute start in his seat at the mention of that name. I also saw his demeanour change in a very strange way, and now, he was no longer smiling, and he was now very angry for some reason? I decided to risk one last throw of the dice.

" But I can prove none of my suspicions about who ordered this killing. And as I have done all you asked of me, I would ask a boon of you this day. To ask the hand of a woman who I love and even now bears my child.

I ask that Gytha Thorkling, is to become my Danish wife. Do that ,and I will build you a fleet of Ships that will make you the lord of all the seas."

I had stopped to take a drink, but I saw the anger in his eyes and the sorrow there as he remembered that dreadful day. I then spoilt it all by saying.

"I know Queen Emma is a very strong and powerful woman, Lord. But you must have proof of this before you say it to anyone, or it will be your life in danger. And yes, she will answer to God one day?"

Canute was on his feet now as were the earl Ulf and his kinsmen. Canute was almost shouting at me and the people in the hall, while looking daggers at the Earl Ulf.

"Indeed, she will Godwin of Wessex! Am I being not wrong, to see you as a friend and faithful Vassal, as we all must, this day.

But I have indeed spoken with your Bishop, and I choose to believe what he has told me of the true story, of what was done in Engaland that foul day. As he has given you a penance. so must I find you innocent of all the false charges that have been bright against you by your enemies in Engaland, and here in my court's shall they feel the full force of my justice.

So are You a free man, and free to ask Gytha to become your English wife. And I know to my cost, what that will mean for you Godwin my friend as she has a mind of her own and a Danish temper to go with it!

so, I do I wish you both well of the bargain and I expect to be able to dance at your wedding!"

*And from that day, Godwin was taken into the service of Canute in Engaland and made an earl for what he had done in Denmark.*

It was much later; I was allowed to speak to them of my Saxon marriage to Gytha. And to my surprise Canute had asked to be present that day? And I heard Gytha gasp then as I had only now decided that this is what I must do, and I knew she was heavy with child, and that this would not please her. But it was Canute who saved us.

*"You speak well of, Godwin, Bishop andyou are to be his best man as you say in Engaland? and yes, I also will have some questions for you Leofric, about the priest Oswald and a certain woman of Normandy. So, I will grant you a private audience, but it must wait until after our Danish wedding. And a Christening?"*

Canute had paused to look at Gytha as he said to us.

*"As for Emma of Normandy, as I mean to invite her to my court, if she will come? As for the problem of who was responsible for Edmund's death, it must wait, until your son is born. But I have heard enough of these matters to know that we cannot blame you for the Death of this assassin.*

Turning to Ulf, Gytha and then me, he said.

"Come, I see that we all need some fresh air after today's business. Is done with. Come Godwin, I am going hunting, and perhaps you Godwin will come with me? As we need to talk some more and as I have a boon to ask of yours, and a task that only you and Gytha can perform. but it is a secret that is not yet common knowledge.

As for you, Gytha dear. Thank you again for your wise counsel, and I will return here in five days, to stand for Godwin here at your wedding.

And before anyone could object Canute said in such a way it was an order to be obeyed.

*"As for the here and now, I need to kill something, a deer or a boar will be far better than your husband; hey!*

*So, now you should know that I ordered that these men of the Circus, were to be crucified as had the Stabbed King of the Christians that is Jesus Christ.*

Somehow, I managed to keep my thoughts to myself, knowing, if this were so, it would be a slow and painful death, and a spear in their side like Jesus would be a welcome relief, but I knew better than to argue about this with a Viking who saw Death every day...

So it was that that afternoon, Canute, and Godwin went hunting, and to my relief, Gytha said she was too far on with her child, to risk riding a horse.

*As the truth of it was that I was desperate to talk privately with her and ask her about Streona's son Aelfric being involved, I wanted his permission to go to Normandy and find how Emma could be involved in all this?*

Godwin had stopped speaking to look at Gytha, who was still sitting in the window seat and bathed in golden sunlight as he said to me; he smiled at her and, as he said.

"As for Gytha staying in the home, well. I have discovered that one could not order Gytha to do anything, as she will do the opposite. But she saw I *was right this day, as we both know she had lost her first baby this way?"*

At his words I saw Gytha was about to change her mind about the hunt, but she turned towards us to try to smile, but I thought she was still remembering those times, and I saw the pain in her eyes at this remembrance of a miscarriage?

But Godwin was speaking again, and Thomas took up his pen and afresh piece of parchment. I nodded for him to resume his writing.

"So, Canute and I went to find a boar and try to forget that we had just sent those men of the Circus to their deaths. But, moreover, had we known what the outcome of that act would be, we would have taken their heads in that Hall. But that is a story for another day? As it was during this hunt, I soon discovered the real reason Canute had asked me to go with him, and that was to ask me what I knew of Emma of Normandy?

We had not gone far, and we were now at the top of Haddebyer hill when Canute stopped his horse and got down from Prancer to look out across the bay. Then, he indicated to his guards and the *hunters that they should leave us as he turned to me so that I should stand with him. So, did I have a chance to get a good look at this Dane who was having such an effect on my life?*

*Moreover, Bishop, perhaps I should tell you that I had met him at Bruges in the year 1013 when he was only a youth of eighteen, and he had come from Engaland to help his father Forkbeard secure the loyalty of the earls of the North. To do this, Forkbeard had married Cnut off to the daughter of AElfhelm of York.*

*But he and his wife were much older than him at twenty-three years of age. Just what they both thought of this arranged Marriage, Canute had never said until this day!*

But I knew that this was no love match as his father had arranged it that Swyen could make sure he had control of Jorvik and hold the North, so his Marriage to AElfgifu of York was not a love match but a marriage of convenience?

And while Canute had changed a great deal since our first meeting, and now he was my Liege lord. I had seen Canute in Lundune and Brantford and later in Gloucester, and now as he stood staring out to sea, I saw the man for the first time and our

*King of Engaland. And what I saw was a man born to rule as time had taken its toll on that youth, who had to fight for his Kingdom and win against all Edmund and I could do to keep Engaland a Saxon land.*

*But now Canute is a full-grown man but still a noticeably young man to have done so much? Today are our birthdays, and he will only be Twenty-two years of age, while I am also considered incredibly young to be seen as the Victor of many battles? My father said I was born in the last decade of the last century in 995. So, in this year 1017, I can count my age as twenty-Two, and my age is the same as that of Canute? While my Gytha is now nineteen, coming on Twenty-three years when our child will be born?*

*We both have done so much, and we are trying to look a lot older now as I have grown to my full height as had Canute. But now that his body has filled out, and one can see how strong he is, and so handsome, some say? But his nose is thin and hooked, But he still had a fair complexion, if somewhat weather-beaten from fighting so many battles? And a fine set of blonde hair tied up in a que, with a silver headband that allowed his hair to fall to his waist and tied with a scarf and hair ring.*

*This day he was wearing his soft light brown leather jerking and matching leather trousers and a pair of knee-high hunting boots. But when he looked at one, I could see his startling blue eyes that never missed a thing, and he could have been a hunter with his keen mind and quick reflexes?*

*But then Canute caught me looking at him and pointing out to sea, he said to me now very seriously."*

"Come, Godwin, my friend, tell me what you see?" *I wondered and tried to guess what he wanted me to say?*

"I see the Lands of your people and the Islands of the Kattegat. Those were once where my mother lived as she was a Jute. I see far of Sweden and Norway and your lands of Denmark, Sire."

He was looking quite sad now.

"Yes, and that is so, but what do I see. I see the land in turmoil since my brother has died so young. Some say it was the plague, and Some say he was poisoned. And like Edmund, I fear that we have a mystery to solve, do we not?"

He looked at me then, and then he seemed to make a decision.

"Godwin, I want you to know that I am going to Trondheim to see if I can solve this mystery and arrange for his funeral. I want you to come with me, but first, I have a request for you and Gytha and a task you can perform, if you will?"

Any request from Canute was to be seen as an order, was my thought? As Canute said.

"You see, I fear that I have been away from Denmark for two long and some here still see me as a mere boy who can be manipulated, as they still hold to the Viking ways. Both here in Denmark and Norway? Now he was looking at the far horizon towards Engaland?

But I am now King of Engaland as well, and with the Death of Edmund, I must find a way to get you Saxons to accept me and my new ways. Do you remember our talks in Lundune when Edmund was chosen King, not me?

How could I forget what he had told me of his plans for Engaland had been astounding and the reason I had given him my allegiance! As I said.

"Yes, Sire, they are burned into my brain and my heart. And all I wish is to be allowed to help you bring them about. I said with all my heart and hopes in my words

"Yes, and Godwin I see you are indeed, a man of your word. and I see that now, But I must be hard with those who would defy me in Engaland, These Saxon lords and even the men of the Daneland? And Those who will see me as a Danish usurper. There will be those who will say I killed Edmund, will they not?

Now he was looking at me with those glaring eyes and as if I could name them to him here and now? What could I say to that question as I knew it would be so?

"If that is true, So now I have a problem, as I must make them see me as an English KING. And there is a way to do that, and I want your help in this and that of Gytha."

Again, Godwin had stopped speaking and turned to look at Gytha. And then he said to us all — his words were full of meaning.

"As you can imagine, with this mention of my wife's name, my heart skips a beat, and it was as if someone had spat on my grave? I knew that the Saxons would see her as only a Danish woman. So, what help could we be?"

But then Canute told me. What he wanted us to do for him, that was to concern Emma of Normandy! And I nearly fell to my knees in surprise as he said.

"Well now my Saxon friend, I believe Gytha was able to significantly help Queen Emma, as she also was with Queen Emma at the time of the hostages that were taken by Streona. That time? And that even now, they exchange messages as your Gytha is still seeking a way to help you with Emma, is she not? If that is so, I want to send Emma a secret message. And I want your wife to invite Emma to your wedding next month...."

I was still looking puzzled and confused as I had been told that Emma was somehow involved in the killing of Edmund. But, before I could say so, Canute said.

"You see, Godwin, to get the Saxons to accept me, I am going to marry AEthelred's Queen! If she agrees to my offer, I will marry an English Queen. I will put my Saxon wife aside and Marry Queen Emma in a church and before their Christian Gods. And I want you both to help me do this thing?"

The truth is that I had been, so God smacked at his words. After that, I could say nothing and just stood there with my mouth open, as Canute said.

"Well then, Godwin, as my vassal, I can ask you to keep this a secret, until we know more of what Emma will say. But you must also make sure she did not kill Edmund! I do not want to die like him with a hot poker, thrust up my Danish Arse! Come, we must return to speak to your wife on this plan?"

\*\*\*

At another session, I was to ask Godwin and Gytha about the birth of their Son Sweyn and their Danish wedding. But this time, we were at the Danish Church at Jetting...

*

## A Danish wedding and a Christening.

Here is a transcript of what was said that day... The year is now 1018, and I can tell you how Godwin was to become to fulfil the role of a Royal Pimp, and how he had to seek out Emma of Normandy for his king...

*

## Godwin's story,

"So, Leofric, when we returned from the hunt, my mind was buzzing with the news that Canute had told me this day, and any thought of the circus folk had been pushed away from my mind. However, when we returned to the Hall, we had to pass the place outside the hill where the men of the Circus had been tied and nailed to the crosses, as the punishment was to be crucified. And I knew this would be a long and painful death. But Canute did not turn his head to look at them as we rode by. So, I decided to ask him if they could be given a quick death. But I also knew I would have to choose my moment as this was the Viking way for king killers...

But that time did not come to pass, and it was later that day, and after our lovemaking that night, I did not immediately fall asleep as was my wont. But lay on the back wishing I had spoken to Canute about the men of the Circus and his verdict of the crucifixion. But now I had more pressing problems, and that was how to get two of the most influential people I know to come together without causing anger and resentment here in Hedeby and Denmark? But this was my new home. And to do resolve this difficulty, I had to betray my oath to Gytha and Canute, for I had promised Gytha that I would make no trouble here. And Canute was not pleased when I put these men to Death, to end their torment.

So, it was when I and Gytha had retired to our bed chamber that night I found that I could not sleep even after making love, and I lay awake looking at the chair and my day clothes that were piled there. I looked at my sword belt lying on a chair beside our bed. It was a habit I had adopted *since I had been marked for Death by Eadric Streona and one that I hoped would save me from an assassin? But in the morning, I was going to use it to end the lives of the circus people. I had given them my word that they would be given a quick death if Canute had found them guilty? And I hope that I can do this without anyone knowing.*

*Then, of course, I would have to deal with their two Guards, but I could knock them unconscious as they would not be warriors? So, with this resolve, I turned my mind to the problem of Emma and her complicity in the Death of Edmund. And if she were to bring her Confessor Godfrey with her, that would be a bonus of a kind as he will speak about this man Aelfric, who is said to be the son of Streona!"*

Godwin had stopped speaking now as I saw that he remembered that moment in his mind, and the look on his face was one of a man who was no longer in the room but lost in his memories and perhaps that was why he had forgotten that I was there, as he went on to speak of his time with Gytha…So did I put down my quill. As he said, what was on his mind and in his heart.

"I must have groaned aloud then as those thoughts became a plan and Gytha stirred and tried to turn to face me, but her bump was so big now she did not manage it. Indeed, all her body had grown with the pregnancy, but her ardour for the fulfilment of the sex acts had not, and she reached across my naked body seeking my member while putting my hand on her now enlarged breasts; as her throaty voice, heavy with desire she said.

"Still awake, my lion, then let me send you to sleep, but first I will want you to pleasure me with this mighty weapon of yours."

Usually, she only had to speak to me in that sultry voice, and my cock would stand to attention, and we would make love, but this moment, it decided not to perform? So, I sat up and looked at Gytha, who had also sat up with the aid of so many pillows now? And taking her hand away, she said.

"I know what is wrong, my husband; and this is my fault that you no longer want me! I felt it last night when I saw you looking at my fat body. Just look at me, will you? I am fat as a cow, and I would not blame you for hating me now. But if you think…."

I stopped her with a finger on her mouth and spoke.

"Ugly, never, my darling, how could you ever be Ugly? No, it is not you that keeps me awake at night, but what Canute has told me on the hunt."

She was about to get out of bed, but I wanted her beside me where She could not start a fight.

"Look, my love, There are two things I must do in the morning, and one concerns Emma of Normandy. But I see you must hear it all, and then we will make love if you still wish it?"

I saw the look in Gytha has green eyes sharpened to pinpricks, at the mention of Emma, and now, she was fully awake as she pulled the furs to her neck as if they were going to give her some protection now? As I waited for a moment to speak to her about what Canute had told me concerning Emma of Normandy, I waited for her, as the look on her face was fear, anger, and confusion?

"I said In a hurry of words, He wants you to invite her to our wedding, and it must be in ten days. We are to find a way to put her to the question about any involvement in *the death of Edmund? but not to anger her or harm her as he intends to have her as his wife.*

*I know you have wanted to wait until your brothers are here. But Canute wants her here, before returning from Engaland, where they plan for his Coronation. So, that is the end of it, WIFE."*

If I had hoped that being firm with her would serve to make her obey the king, but of course, Gytha could not be ordered to do anything! But then the waters broke as she was shouting now...

" Emma, What Of Emma. I Hate That Woman. I Forbid This Canute Can Shove His Big Prick Into His Big Mouth. Who does he think he is, interfering in my Marriage?"

Then she saw the look on my face at her crude words as she flopped down on the side of the bed.

"I see there is a lot you have not said, Husband, so tell me the rest, but first, I need a piss. By the gods, your son is kicking well now."

She went to the slop bucket to find it had not been emptied from the previous day and staggering with it in her hands, taking it to the window, she emptied it there! Muttering some dire threats against the servants. Then she came to sit on the bed and indicated that I should do the same, so in the darkness, we were two naked people holding hands…

So, I told her all about my meeting with Canute on the so-called hunt and finished with his command for her to send the invitation to Emma. Gytha was silent for a long time, then she said.

"So, now, do you see the husband of mine? Why we must have this wedding here in Denmark, my love. Because if Canute can put aside his Saxon wife and children just like that., So can my brothers say that we were never properly married and if anything should happen to me, they will blame you? But what will happen to lady Aefgifu? I will not see her harmed." I said in reply.

"Yes, she is a worry, but Canute gave me his word that she will still have a place at court. She will have her own Hall and servants. He said she will be regent in Norway and given money and titles as long as he lives?"

"Do you believe this is possible? From what I know of her, what of Emma? She will not rest while

AElfgifu lives and her children. What say you now, Godwin?"

"Well, that may be the situation, but it is beyond my understanding to resolve, as is how we can make Emma obey our king without knowing if she is a murderer?"

Gytha said.

" Godwin, the heart of my heart, How can you think I would even try to help him in this madness when he has those fine children and a wife, and now she is to be put aside and possibly kept in prison for the rest of her life, along with her children?

Do you not see that Emma will always see them as a threat to her?

Do you not remember how she tried to take me to Exeter and keep me there as her hostage. So no, Husband! I want nothing to do with this woman, Besides, she will never agree to come to our lands, as she was also involved with our Saxon wedding, and the hand-fisting, was she not."

I knew Gytha was obviously thinking of that time of the hostages when her friend Bridget had been raped and killed on the orders of Streona at Wareham? as she looked up at me to say.

*"I also know Emma to be a powerful and cruel woman, who would do anything to gain her ends, and perhaps she would see her Marriage to Canute as a marriage of convenience?*

*Or a way to get back into power and allow her sons to go to Engaland. And Suppose she was to have some more children by this Danish king. What then, my love?"*

"Yes, I see that may well happen! So, it seems to me that we are both caught up in this fishing net, and I can see no way we will be able to get out of it with our lives and honour intact."

I said,

*But if you cannot bear to have her to our christening, I will tell Canute that, and we must face his anger. I will take the blame, my love."*

Gytha smiled at that.

"No, my lion, I will tell him, as I know how to twist him around my little finger. So never fear you will not be blamed. It is my right to have the last say as to who can come to our sons christening. But

Leofric will be there, and she will not dare to cause us any trouble then. And as For Canute wish to have her as his queen, it would be far better to her in Engaland where we can keep an eye on her."

"Then we can make it seem that we at least tried to do his bidding, and then perhaps we can think of a way to broach the subject and tell her of the killing of Edmund?"

"I am very sure, Husband!" Gytha said her words were Ice.

"Then I am sorry, wife. I forbid you to risk your pretty neck in this way. I do not wish you to have anything to do with her of know about the spies you speak of.

But for my life, I cannot have this moment think of a way that will not anger the King and look like an insult to Emma of Normandy. So, then, we are agreed Gytha, we must send her an invitation to our wedding.

And God knows, we did not part on good terms, and she may refuse? But I know Canute's mind is set on this meeting, and if we fail him, We shall soon find that Canute can be ruthless as any Viking when he needs to be!"

"Yes, I do know that HUSBAND! So, what is the other matter you spoke of?"

I was about to deny my intent on the mercy killing of the circus men, when I felt a waft of air across my naked back, and a clink of metal on metal, and I knew that someone was trying to sneak into our room?

And before Gytha could speak, I was across the bed and leaping for the shadow at the doorway, and I had my blade at the throat of this tiny assassin who was dressed in black! A Ninja then, as I had been told that the circus people, had a way to reach this sect of deadly assassin.?

Then was a flash and spark, Gytha had managed to light a candle, and I saw this was a woman I held, and her blood was seeping from the tiny cut at her throat, as Gytha screamed at me.

"Stop, Godwin. That is Rosa. Rosa, what are you doing here, Girl?"

I realised then that his servant had been hiding in an alcove, and she was waiting for us to be asleep?

Here was no Ninja! As she held in her hand, a clean slop bucket, and now she let it fall to the ground, with a loud clanging of metal on the stone floor, which would have the guards come running to our room.

But all I could think was that she was a spy? As she had overheard all, I had said to Gytha about Emma. And she had she been there when we made love? So, I put my hand on her shoulder and forced her to her knees, as I said.

"Speak, woman and tell it true, as your life hangs on a spider's thread now."

"I am so sorry, my Lord, but I came here to change the slop bucket. That is all. But I know I do wrong, my Lord. So, I do. Please do not kill me, Lord?"

Now Gytha had come to the doorway dressed in a bearskin draped around her shoulders, and as it was opened by two of the guards who were posted outside, she said to them.

"I am sorry, Ragen, I dropped the slop bucket. Please Go back to your post as there is nothing to see here. Go back to your post, and we thank you for your diligence."

Then she shut the door And took the servant's arm to stop me from hurting her again. She asked her,

"Come girl tell me how you are here at this time of night?"

"I do be about to change the chamber pot when I heard you coming, my lady. I heard you say to the guards that you must not be disturbed this night, So I did. And I hid in that dark place to wait for you to leave. So, I did. But then your Lord came, and he looked to be so angry this night, I just froze, with fright so I did."

Gytha looked at the chamber pot that was now lying on the flagstones. Then she remembered the one she had emptied and used. Then, looking at Rosa, Gytha asked her.

"Do you usually do this at night? Why was the piss pot not emptying this morning? Come speak up, Girl, as no harm was done."

Then I said.

"No harm, but she has heard all that we said. She must be silenced. Perhaps, I should cut out her tongue out?

I knew that I would never do such a thing, but Rosa did not as she began whimpering and said, with as much courage as she could muster, as her eyes flashed her defiance in the candle's light.

"I know how to hold secrets, so I do! And so do all the servants here, Lord. So, please do not cut out my tongue Lord."

Now Gytha was smiling, and she said to her servant.

"Then you must promise to hold this tongue of yours and swear an oath never to repeat anything you may think you heard concerning our king and a certain lady? Or I will learn of it? I will put a hex on you, or worse. I will come into your dreams and send you mad."

Just how Gytha had thought to scare this servant this way was a surprise, but I saw Rosa clutch an amulet she wore at her neck. Gytha looked at it to say.

"What mischief is this then. I have seen these signs before; they are Chaldean symbols. See, half is a moon, and the other is a Sun. So, who are you really, Rosa?"

Then looking at us, I saw fear in her eyes as Gytha said,

"I think that these are some sort of spiritual protection similar to your Silver hammer that you have husband?" As Rosa said, now her voice was sure and strong.

"Are you from Romany blood than my lady? If you can know of the Chaldeans magic and say a Curse, I think I can help you with your …With Queen Emma so I can. And my mother is also a **Hedge witch,** and one of the most potent of the Chaldean Sorcerers, so she is. Rachel is her name, and he is one of the Drabarni, so she is. And she is a wise and cunning woman who tells fortunes and answers questions. She can do an Aura reading to perceive a person's spirit and soul and link them to places and things. If she wishes it, She can use the power of her potions to get a person to speak the truth. so, she can"

We were both astounded at her words, and we were looking at her swarthy features and the neck chain Gytha now had in her hands. At the end was a silver wheel with a tree in the middle and no spokes?  It was one of the like I had seen on a Romany beggar once before when I was with my father, and he had stopped to talk to her and give her money for food.

When I asked why he said it was necessary, he had said that it was a gift to avoid her hexing us for not buying her wares. Then I saw he had a sprig of heather at his buttonhole. I also knew just how dangerous it was to intentionally make a Gypsy angry or refuse to see one. Then she will hex you, and your luck will be the better for it.

Touching the sprig, I asked Rosa what she was doing here as a simple servant.

"It is my punishment, so it is! I am a Romany princess in our world, and  I thought I was above you... Cadjios people that I refused to go with my mother to the gathering.

Yus see, I refused to honour the Danish King Harald, when he came to ask that we tell him his fortune and help him in his war with Sweden. Instead, he came to honour us with a gift of silver and crystal. Ma' was so angry with me I was given this punishment.

So, I am sent here without any powers to empty bedpans until my mother allows me to return. But in a way, that is why I was not here this morning to do just that, So I was. I had gone to the woods where Rachel was camped to ask her forgiveness.

But she saw into my proud heart, So, she did, and I was forced to return, and now you know it all, so, you do."

I looked at Gytha and saw that she had believed every word of this, and then I remembered Grace and how she had healed my father from near-death at the wash and how I saw her do the blood magic. So, I let Rosa's arm go, as she said to Gytha.

"I see you, My lady. I am sorry to have come here this moment and hear of your problems. But I do know of a way to find out if someone is telling the truth, but I am fearful of speaking to you, and speak of the how of it, you will be angry with me for listening to what you have said. But I promise you that I can keep secrets and swear on my mother's life that I will never repeat anything you have said here."

"Go then," Gytha said, -but do not leave the Hall, as we may yet need you to speak to your mother?"

"Oh yes, I see that now; please give me back that charm and let me go about my duties. I will be in the kitchens if you need me." Then she was gone in the darkness.

I knew that someone had been helping my wife with the problems she was having with the birthing and that she was something of a healer, and she managed to get some potions from the gipsies that were her family. I had been angry to hear of this Romany magic. But, Martha, who was our Birth Nurse ,and a fine and experienced midwife, who Gytha trusted this Girl, and her potions had made all the difference in her pregnancy, and it was due to her help that her son what is to be born next month…

Then when we were alone and still naked, Gytha came to me and helped my hands in hers as she said.

"So, my sweet man, this may be a way out of our problems, my love? but you must know that to use this Romany magic is dangerous.

I only know of it from Old Martha; she helped my birthing and became my breast mother and Child nurse. The truth is that my mother did not live long after my birthing, and it was Martha who brought me up. I did not know it then, but she was a Romany woman. She is a Hedge witch of sorts.

But she still lives here at Hedeby, and I should have told you this, my love, as she has been giving me some potions that helped me keep this baby, and we both owe her for our son. But it seems that we need her to tell us if the Chaldean women can be trusted? What say you, husband, Will you come with me to speak to Martha about this fortune teller?"

*"I would be hard for me to do that for even you, my love. As I also have some knowledge about the blood magic that these people can use. And it concerns my father Wulfnoth. But I know to my cost that all magic comes at a*

*cost. For my father it was teh plague! And I must forbid you to have anything to do these gypsies, Gytha, my darling.*

*So, we must ask her if she will bring him here with here and when I return, I will agree to meet with the Fey woman. But it would be best if you took great care, and I fear becoming involved in magic again. I have good cause, to know that magic is real and dangerous.*

*You see, I was also involved with the Deep Magic, and I saw how the white witch Grace, who was to use her powers to beguile my father and she became his wife. But that is not the half of it as she used the Blood magic at the battle on the fens, and when Wulfnoth was drowned, she managed to bring him back from the lands of the dead!*

*So, you see, my love, I also know how dangerous it can be if used in the wrong way. One is the malicious use of compulsion, making people do terrible things against their will and nature. If I go with Canute to Norway, I want you to have my father's amulet as a remembrance of this warning. Wear it night and day."*

She took the round amulet, which was n the form of the Volva symbol, it was silver with a red ruby at its centre. A jewel, which would glow to warn one of any evil presence! I t was a gift from the sorcerer Urien, And in that way, I had been able to keep these evil spirits at bay. Grace had said it was cursed by Fycat and she would not have Wulfnoth wear it in her presence. but it was no coincidence, that they both had died of the plague when he had taken it and put it in a lead lined chest? And it had done for my father and then me. I had found it so many years ago now when I was dealing with his funeral at Bosham.

I have since discovered that was once a gift from my father and I knew that it would protect her against any evil powers, when he had been forced to confront the black magic of the witch Fycat. And it was an amulet of great power that had saved my life so many times when I had gone to stand against the foe, and any evil spells. So now I could leave Gytha knowing she would be safe from harm. But I still needed to tell her about my visit to Norway.

*"But Gytha my dear wife, the other matter I spoke of concerns Canute. So, you see that I am ordered to leave with him at first light to go to Trondheim. You see, we intend to find the true cause of how King Harald, died so young. And now that Canute has asked me to see if I can discover the real cause. He asks this, as he can be sure I can have no other allegiances in Norway, and I am a*

good and a good judge of men. And now when he asks this of me when he could command it you must see that is my duty, and I cannot avoid it.

But as for Emma, we must allow her to come here at least, as it would not hurt anyone to look into this idea of Rosa's? and it would be a way to find out if Emma can be trusted to be a suitable wife for Canute, without her knowing why she was being questioned? But that is all we will ask of her witch mother!"

Then, I saw the fear return to Gytha's eyes, and I took her into my arms to say.

"So, we must allow this invitation to be given then, as this is the only way we will be able to confront Emma with our suspicions concerning Edmund. And I want the chance to question her Confessor, the priest Godfrey!

Then I took off my amulet from around my neck, Keeping the silver medallion in the shape of Thor's hammer, and I gave Wulfnoth's amulet to her, to hold.

"This has saved me from any harm that the spirits can bring against me on many occasions. So, my dear Viking, I must ask you to take it and wear it around your neck should you decide to go to the camp of these gipsies.

*But I cannot go with you as We are to leave by ship in the morning and we will be away for a week at least. Moreover, the king has said that our wedding must take place when we return home, as he also what our son to be born here in Denmark and be a Dane at his birth. So, time is against us, and your letter to Emma and the invitation to our wedding go as soon as possible. And the meeting with the gipsies also must happen soon."*

Gytha was now on tiptoes, and she nuzzled her head into my hairy chest, I felt my ardour returning, and I picked her up in my arms to kiss her lips and whispered in her ear.

"But we still have a few hours to daylight…. *So, Husband, we need to find a bed.*"

Gytha was still asleep when I awoke, and I took my clothes and weapons away to get dressed in the other room; from here, I could see the crosses on the hill that were now lit by the rising sun.

Then I looked again to see that they were still there but empty of their grisly charges?

So now I was out of the Hall and running for the stable to find a horse to use, so was my mind in turmoil as the events of last night crowded into my mind as I rode on past the startled hustlers and the horses that were getting ready for our departure to Norway. I jumped onto the nearest, who was my Storm and then out of the enclosure and up the hill where I saw a scene of Death.

All the guards and the men posted there to protect this site were lying on the ground face down. I jumped from the horse to turn over the dead guard, and at first, I could find no wound; then, I saw his neck where there was a red circle that had bitten deep in his neck. So, he had been Garrotted and taken from behind without any warning being given?

Then it hit me. I only knew of one sect that could get close enough to take a man from behind. That was the Ninja! I went across to the crosses to see blood around the nails, but the ropes had been cut. So, the Circus people had been taken by this attack or was it a rescue. But who could afford to pay for their services or even know of them? Either way, I must warn Canute to be aware of this peril. And now, even Gytha, I was also at risk, and why must she seek to use such evil as the Blood magic to protect us all? And now we can ask her? To tell the truth of it Leofric?"

*So dear reader I may be that you have not yet found the previous books that will speak of Gytha Godwinson, and who she was, before she came to marry Godwin of Wessex. And here is what was set down in the official record books. But as you will discover, there is so much more to her story…*

\*\*\*

*Gytha Thorkelsdóttir (c. 995 – c. 1069), also called Githa, was a Danish noblewoman. She was the wife of Godwin, Earl of Wessex. and became the mother of King Harold Godwinson, and the mother of Edith of Wessex, who was the queen consort of King Edward the Confessor.*[1]

*Before she met Godwin, Gytha Thorkelsdóttir was the daughter of Danish chieftain Thorgil Sprakling (also called Thorkel).*

*Gytha was also the sister of the Danish Earl Ulf Thorgilsson, who was married to Estrid Svendsdatter, the sister of King Cnut the Great.*

*It was in Engaland She married the Anglo-Saxon nobleman Godwin of Wessex. In a Saxon hand fisting ceromancy,*

*They had a large family together, and one of her sons, Harold, became king of England.*

*Two of their sons, Harold and Tostig, faced each other at the Battle of Stamford Bridge, where Tostig was killed.*

*But, you should know that Less than a month later, three of her sons, Harold, Gyrth, and Leofwine, were killed at the Battle of Hastings.*

*Shortly after the Battle of Hastings, Gytha was living in Exeter, and may have been the cause of that city's rebellion against William the Conqueror in 1067, which resulted in his laying siege to the city.*

*She pleaded unsuccessfully with him for the return of the body of her slain son, king Harold.*

*But I was there and can tell you the truth of this. But, According to the Anglo-Saxon Chronicle, Gytha left England after the Norman conquest, together with the wives or widows and families of other prominent Anglo-Saxons, all the Godwin family estates having been confiscated by William.*

*Little else is written in the official records concerning much of Gytha's life after that time, although it is probable that she went to Scandinavia where she had relatives.*

*But if you read on you will learn the truth of this?*

*Her surviving (and youngest) son, Wulfnoth, lived nearly all his life in captivity in Normandy until the death of William the Conqueror in 1087. Only her eldest daughter, Queen Edith (d. 1075), still held some power (however nominal) as the widow of King Edward the Confessor.*

*So Now I Must Speak Of The Blood Magic.*

*I cannot say that I was at all pleased to have to stay silent, as Gytha told us of this part of her confession, and to learn that they both had been involved with the black arts from time to time. And that night, I prayed for guidance as to what I should do, and a voice in my heart said that there are many houses in my fathers' world.*

*So, give unto Caesar what Caesar must-have? And give my father what is his – your Soul.*

Then I remembered the miracles of Jesus, and I knew he had used the power of the Deep magic that was once known to the druids, And these Romany people. So, the next day, I sought all the books I could find that spoke of this Chaldean magic, and I was astounded to read that they also believed in a life after death and followed another way towards enlightenment. So, who was I, Leofric, a mortal, to deny Gytha their help?

*Here then, is what I set down about what Gytha told me about her time with the Romany people…*

So it was that Gytha went to find the old nurse Martha, who was well known to be one of the fey people from Wales, and to ask her if there was a way, they could make sure their first born, was to be a healthy boy?

So it was that, after Godwin and Canute had sailed away to Norway, she had managed to go down to the Jetty to wave them off, and She was proud to say she had not shed a tear.

Not in public, at least? But as Godwin took her hand and then Canute said to her, as he hugged her, into his chest he said.

"Never fear for him, Gytha. We will be back as soon as we can. I will make sure you are safe. But you my dead must remember that you are a Danish princess, and your child will be a bridge between Denmark and England.

And you must know that I have great plans for your son.

So, you must do all you can to make sure he is, born strong and healthy. You should know that I have sent for your woman Rachel, and her mother Rosa, she has told me that there is a way to bring this about.

No do not try to speak . But my last order to you is to listen to what she has to say about the Romany magic.

Do that we will talk when I return. If I do from this blasted war, with these rebels in Norway!"

I see you wear the Volva Amulet, that was given to Wulfnoth Cild?

*That is a good omen, and it will ensure that you Gytha, as you know our secret, and have kept it all these years. I know that I can trust you to obey me in this.*

*Go with the Gods. and that will protect you now."*

Then they boarded the ships, and it pushed off into the Kattegat sound and watched them go until they were a speck on the horizon and past Roskilde.

Then she shook herself and turned to Rosa.

*"Come by, dear, for we have many things to do besides mooning here."*

But when Godwin, had told her of his fears concerning the missing Circus men, and his suspicions concerning using the Ninja sect of ruthless assassins ? and now She said to herself that she would ask Rachel, for a way to detect them. as she was not going to spend her life chasing shadows. But the truth was that she was now looking into every shadow, half expecting to see an assassin there.

But she was not going to tell Godwin so!

So, with Rosa as her companion, she went to find the hut where Martha lived in her old age. But to do so and not be seen, they had to use a carriage this spring day. But they found that Matha was not alone, as she had a visitor. It was Rachel, Rosa's mother. And then she realised that Canute had ordered her here. And that he had asked Rosa to arrange this meeting somewhere outside her protection and the Romany camp.

*But Rachel had brought her own guards; it would seem?*

So as Rosa helped Gytha down from the coach, that she had used to come from the docks. So did, two of the Romany people, who came from the hut.

But these men were unlike any men Gytha had ever seen or imagined. Of course, these were not unlike the Samurai that Godwin had described to her that had served his father so faithfully, but these were Romany men and not from Japan. Their uniforms were, edged with a red and gold fringe, and upon their heads, they wore a bright metal skull cap edged with white fur. They also had thick black bushy eyebrows and brown eyes, high cheekbones and a hooked nose with a full mouth and shaved chin.

They were staring straight ahead, as a servant came to help Gytha demount from the carriage, but these warriors were seeing every movement at the same time. Gytha said, that while their arms were bare, and they wore some body armour on their chest, which stopped at their waist and on their torso. They also had an overshirt, held in place by a row of wooden toggles, which carried three sharpened throwing knives in their sheaths, three on each side of their enormous chests. They wore a red and gold sash around the waist with a sword belt, which supported what looked like a Sabre? However, their trousers were made from thick linen sailcloth that finished at their knees. *As far as Gytha could see, they were barefoot, presumably, so that no one would hear them coming. The truth was, they were a fearsome bunch, and no one in their right mind would think of tackling them. But they bowed to Rosa as the man who held the door said…*

"I see you, Rosalinda., and you, Gytha, Daughter of Thorgil Sprakling, Come Rosa, Your mother awaits your coming. But I see that this Cadjios woman has a hidden weapon. I am sorry, my lady, Gytha, but you cannot enter here with any weapon. Please give it to me and any other weapon , as the spirits will know of them, and they will be angry!"

It was true that I had another blade hidden in my shawl, and before I could move, the guard had moved so fast I was held as the other reached across my bulge to take the thin needle blade hidden in the body stocking. So, I would say that we needed it to fight the Ninja if they came? But Rosa said.

" We will not fear these black devils, as they fear my mother's power, and she will know of them coming. Come inside my lady. I promise you we will be safe here, my lady."

Rosa saw that I was never going to go anywhere unknown and unarmed, as I was about to return to the coach she said.

"You see, My mother is a Drabarni Queen, my lady. No one can come into her presence with a weapon. So come, we must not keep her waiting any longer. I can feel she is furious this day?"

Then I heard Martha say in a weak voice.

"Is that You, Gytha Sprakling, my child? Please let her in, Rachel, as we have much to tell her."

I had been to this hut many times to see Martha was well cared for, and get some of her potions, but this time, it was as if I had walked through the cold shower or a water cascade, when I entered the hut.

And then there was shift in the air, as I realised that I was no longer in the hut.

It was warm and so brightly [painted like Romany caravan I had seen at a fairground?

*If I was utterly stunned to see this transformation but, I was not going to let them see my fear as I realised a Chaldean spell, held here in this Caravan?*

We were Seated at a table in the centre of this incredible room, was the Romany Queen. There was no sign of Rosa or Martha... And as I felt another mind brush across my mind, it touches my soul —

*I realised to my horror that I was blind as darkness descended on my mind and something gripped my heart To hold it safe, or stop it?*

*But then, I felt another presence there, and as my sight returned, so did I see an older woman sitting at the table, which now held a glass crystal bowl at its centre, and the table held a cloth that depicted the sky and the oceans.*

*But. as I concentrated on it, I thought the clouds and seas moved, as did the waves and sea. I was so surprised I tried to step back, but my limbs would not obey my will, as the old woman said.*

*"Please do not be frightened of me, Gytha Godwinson. I have brought you to this place that is out of time and space to be tested. for I am now in your debt as you could have killed my stupid daughter last night but spared her useless life,*

*So, I have a blood debt,*

*So no, do not try to move or talk, as you will find you are tongue-tied until I need you to speak. So, listen carefully.*

*Firstly, you can ask me only three questions, but only if you pass the tests.*

  *I see you have then written some on the skins that Rosa gave you. That is good. And very wise as most people who seek their answers can often forget what theywere in this place! But I must warn you that in order to answer your questions, we must use Blood magic. And You must first, remove that amulet, And my powers will not work for you as it will prevent them speaking to you! And, as you can see, we are no longer in my home. Instead, we are in one of the three realms that are to be found in the fabled* **Wheel of Boleros!**

  But now, before I could think about this blood magic, or try to speak, even more of her guards were seen standing behind her, and I was sure they had not been there before? But I then knew that this was to stop me trying to get to their queen as she had now spoken of this forbidden black magic!

  I knew the last thing I should do was to take off the amulet, But I was still caught up with this magnificent spectacle, Which was this caravan and the warriors, who made in their uniforms and muscular physic. Each was had muscles to die for, and with their red and gold clothing, I could not but be impressed by this fearsome lot. If these were the Queen's guards, then she was well protected, it would seem.

And despite myself, I removed the amulet as it fell to the floor so was it lost from sight!

*I knew I was in mortal danger here as these warriors they would all die rather than be defeated.*

Each man had a shaved head, except for a long hairpiece platted and tied with red ribbon and fell down their backs; it was tied back with a part of the silver bangle. I could not help thinking that this would be something of a hindrance in any hand-to-hand fight, but what did I know! As for their faces, they were unlike any Romany pictures I had seen. If anything, they were from Persia that she had seen depicted in one of the kings' books.

They all wore a sarong and belt like the pictures of the Samurai Godwin had spoken of. They even had long and short swords to prove it. But now, they all looked to the front with expressionless faces, but once again, their eyes were taking everything in.

However, the insides of the cabin were even more brightly painted, and every surface and nook and cranny were decorated. The walls were painted pale yellow, with painted flowers and twisting vines on the bulkheads and ledges. There were side bunks that held silk cushions to match and a beautiful Persian carpet on the floor.

With So many nooks and crannies were necessary for storage, and four arches that led off to other rooms were protected by heavy damask curtains, which could be tied back if necessary? As well as numerous pots and jars stacked neatly on the shelves; hanging from hooks were some dried plants and herbs, which filled the air with the smell of Lavender. A smell I hated and as I began chocking until Rachel put her hand on mine.

As, once again some movement on the table caught my attention as my eyes were drawn to the glass globe which now also sat at there? And at this Romany Queen, who was leaning back into a highchair or throne, was also a sight to see.

As for their Queen, she also had changed from this person I had seen when I came in. And now with her touch, I was allowed to see the real woman. I had to think that I had passed the first test.

As, I could guess I would have never seen the real woman, if I failed this first testing? Now she seemed ageless as she had bronzed skin and black hair, brown eyes, a strong chin, and a beautiful young woman's body. With her deep brown eyes said she had done and seen so much, and her body was wrinkled and that of an older woman.

At least she was my Idea of a Romany woman. She had a headscarf tied across her forehead and jet-black hair. She wore a shawl across her forehead was some Tiara which held five jingling medallions, And with her ruddy complexion, a pair of propitious black eyebrows that she had never plucked, as they almost hid her brown eyes and Romanesque nose.

Across her shoulders was another white silk shawl with a red fringe. Her blouse was also white, but her skirt was the colour of fire. And when she moved, it seemed to flicker like one? But then she placed a long booted black boot foot on the rim of the chair, and she looked at me to say.

"What then are your questions. Speak up Girl, come now; I do not have all day?"

I smiled to hide my fear as I thought of Rosa's statement, and her warning about showing fear to her mother. Remember my warnings; say and do nothing until we are safe, and you are greeted as a guest here. You see, this is the second test, she will give you."

Then I turned back to face the Queen and to say.

"I see you are one of the Drabengro. Are you a Hedge Witch to speak so? How dare you speak to me as if I was a Gajio?

*As I know that it was King Canute, who has sent me here. It is him who will pay your price my Queen. He sent me here to ask you about the Queen Emma of Normandy. That is my first question.*

*And My husband Godwin would know if Emma can be trusted to be the wife of Canute ?and, did Emma have anything to do with the Death Of King Edmund of Engaland?*

*For my part, I would ask about the baby I bear. Will he be strong and healthy? And a boy? That is my second question.*

*My third is I need to know if the prophecy of my children are to be among the greatest in these lands will come to pass?"*

Then I remembered something Martha had said once about how the Romany people will try to twist and turn every bargain they ever made, so I said.

*"So, I ask that you shall not try your Haki tricks on me. These are not worthy of a follower of the Wheel of Boleros? I should box your ears for keeping me standing here. And Where are your manners, I am no Chovani woman? Are you a*

*Queen? then know that I am Danish Princess! I am from the Fey blood line of kings"*

Rachel hissed but said nothing as she looked at me so very hard and for a long time! I had to turn away from her prying eyes. Then she snorted, as I realised that this was another test and one of our willpower. And she had lost, the initiative, after that insult and challenge, the woman said something, and the guards parted to leave the Caravan.

So, were my eyes now wide open to the Queen's chamber, and what I saw was incredible, as I realised that I had passed this final test, which was to be brave enough to put off the amulet? as I was seeing the real cabin now. I also `saw that the Queen had been drinking from a golden chalice. And Rising from the chair, she went to sit at the table, and As she stroked the tablecloth, it immediately changed from white to green.

Now the things on the table shimmered, and then there was an empty glass bowl, which was both to be seen as frosted and opaque at the same time.

It seemed to me to hold some strange blue liquid or the shining water they had seen in the rock pools. But when Rachel poured the liquid from the goblet into it, it turned milky white. As the woman said in a high-pitched voice and in the Romany tongue that I could now understand.

"This is my Scrying dish; it is worth a King's ransom. So please do not try to speak, not yet. Not until it recognises us!"

Now my eyes had adjusted to the low light in the cabin, I could see the Queen up close, and despite her diminutive size, she was someone who could fill the room with her aura and presence. But, first, to see her long thick black hair hidden under a bright red headscarf, with a headband to hold it in place, studded with medallions, gold, and silver. Her brown eyes were partly hidden beneath her black eyebrows, and with her hooked Romanesque nose, and a very long pointed chin, she was the epitome of a Romany woman.

But perhaps her most striking feature, was her intense gaze and bright eyes, which seemed to stare right through me. But as she raised her head to inspect her surprise guests, I could see here, was a very powerful, seeress?

As I managed to tear my gaze from her face and look away at her fabulous dress. Her shawl was now a sheer silk and almost see-through, and I could see the dark roundness of her naked breasts beneath it.

I realised then that I was blushing with embarrassment at this display of her apparent charms. I quickly pulled my gaze away from her bosom and onto the back of her face and the Torc around her neck, which was carved with the various signs he had seen on the wall paintings.

Such Wonderful painting, that seemed to be alive ? as I recognised as the Wheel of time and what he took for as the Tree of life. Then Rachel said,

*"So Gytha, I see that you can see my true form. Not many can do that unless I permit it. So much for the tests. Gytha Godwinson!"*

And with a touch of her necklace, her clothes became more proper and expected. Now she also had a red and gold skirt and a golden belt at her tiny waist that held some sort of a chatelaine, on which is hung a range of golden ornaments.

But, when I looked again, these golden charms also seemed to change into different animals; one was a lion, and another a bear, others were the Wheel, and some assortment of gold lockets and keys.

I had seen similar charm bracelets on the pictures of these gipsy women. And with her bare arms, she had various tattoos in the shape of the runes I had seen painted on the cabin door. Another was a representation, of the tree of life !

*So, these are Some sort of magical protection, then? That was my thought.*

Then my gaze turned to the Queen's delicate hands; each finger had a ring encrusted with a collection of sparkling diamonds, rubies, and pearls. Her fingernails were long and painted bright red, as were her thin lips. A myriad of bangles played that same music at each wrist when she moved her hands. As again, all I wanted to do was close my eyes and listen to it. But, as she moved, they began to chime in unison and once again, I had to concentrate on avoiding her music, sending him to sleep.

But then I tried to remember what Martha had told him about their mind tricks, and so was her spell of compulsion, was broken.

As he did so, so did Rachel smile, as if she knew she had failed to steal my mind and bend it to her will? I jerked awake to hear her say.

"Goodness, you have a strong will, Girl, and you have passed the third test. So, now I must do what I can to help you. Then had looked up at me to say. For that, we shall use the scarifying bowel.

Then, at her question, she stepped forward to the shallow bowl in the centre of the table.

"I give all hail to you, who will come here this day and those who can answer the three questions that are placed before you. So, is it said, and so must you speak only the truth as I, the descendant of Danu, do command it? I greet you as one of the descendants of the first people, the great druids that were the Tuatha-De-Danann. We come here to ask a boon of you and your Chaldean magic."

Then I heard them answer from a white mist from the bowl?

"A command, you say. Can you pay the price I will ask; I wonder?" this said with a half-smile on its phantom lips.

"We will, for we come at the bidding of bidding of the great Drabengro, Washi Dai, He is a brother to our great earth mother, and he greets you as one of the Ten and the Weshui Dai. The mother and guardian of the Wheel. As for the price we offer, we come to bargain for three answers to our questions."

As Rachel said this dedication, I could see the Queen's eyes light up at the mention of this, and now she was almost glowing with pride.

"I see you, Gytha, daughter of Thorgil, and he will speak to us. As shall My sister, **Nineveh** spoke of an amulet, that this child wears as it is given by one of The Vola, who shall answer. also, who you must summon her this day.

*But they will want a life for a life? so be careful what you ask of them!"*

I was just about to blurt out that I was no child when Rachel kicked me hard. But then, I was able to remember the warning. *Do not speak until you are spoken to first? As Rachel said in the high Tounge.*

*"Well, you may wish to take care you do not offend their Chakra, since these Chovan children are all exceptional! Can you not see the fine golden hair that she has from Fryer and her green eyes? So, we see she has the fey gene; she must ask the first question. It will be concerning the nature of magic.* After that, came their answer.

*You may ask your questions, Gytha Sprakling.'*

At these words, the Queen came across to peer into my eyes and swept my blonde hair from my face to look at my eyes. Then she grunted.

*"So, they do have the Chakra, A boon, you say, well questions asked, and a bargain struck. I agree with your terms. We agree A life for a life!*

It was then, I managed to say to them that this was not the bargain I wanted as I realised the price they had demanded for my answer's. WHO's life Hot that of Godwin. I must ask them and Rachel.

"A life for a life? What is this you have agreed to now, Rachel? I do not agree with that price. Who will they take? Not my child or Godwin. No, I came here by my free will, and I will leave now if I may."

Rachel had taken my hand to look into my eyes and to say.

"A living sacrifice is required if you wish to know the future Girl. But It can be a chicken who *dies, not a human. But I see you need to know that we will not harm you here, and I must tell you more of our Chaldean magic so that you will know that all life is sacred to us. But that will take far longer than we have now. But there is a way I could put this knowledge into your mind if you allow it. We could mind-meld?"*

I had heard of this from Martha, and it was dangerous to do as the adept she would have control of your memory for the duration. But then it was as if Rachel was already reading my mind as she said.

*"To do this, I will speak into your mind, but not so deeply that you will lose control. If you hold this amulet during this melding, you will have complete control of your spirit, and the bond will be broken if you let it fall from your hand.*

*Look, Gytha, I have done this many times, and you and your child will be safe, I swear it. But you must trust me and do this if you want your answers? But we have gone to far for either of us to back out now and to so now, so shall we both w be lost in Meriben child.*

What could I say or do now? I had come so far with my stupid attempt to find out the answers to these important questions. However, I knew I could not give up now, so I said.

"Then let it be so. What must I do?"

"Shut your eyes and try to relax them; think of some pleasant memory that will open the door to me; I will hold your left hand like this and count to five.

One-Two-Three…"

## The Green Man,

"Well now, what have we here, a Danish Princess, who would have thought you would find my Tree? Gytha's it not. I am Cernunnos; some see me as a druid and some as the Green Man. Your people know me as Heimdall; why have you sought me out this fine day?"

But now, this Green Man was now part of the woodland, and he was sitting beneath a large Oak tree, and the air was full of the scent of spring flowers. Then he pointed to a seat beside him.

" Come sit, and I will tell you about the Chaldean people and their ways. I see you have the Amulet of Thor, so you must hold it tight if you want to hear my story. But, first, I will tell you of the separate realms that exist here in this world.

We are both here in Avalon is one, and that is our Celtic world; another is the world of the spirits you know of. The lands of the Norse gods and Vaettir, a place that holds the Tree of life: Yggdrasil, and where the Asir Vanir are revered. That like Avalon is nearby as we speak. As are the Norse Gods and their realm you know as Asgard. If you are found worthy, it is they who shall give you the other answers you seek?

Moreover, the third dimension is that of the magic of the Romany people, who some call the Romani.

This is called Elfame, and that also has A great Tree of Life and a great wheel of time that sees the movement of time and the seasons. So, I must tell you not to be afraid of them as they are a wonderful creation with so many gifts, as they try to follow the way of the great Wheel of life and are part of the Fey world.

*Their Cosmos is divided into the Upper World, The middle world, and the lower world.*

*They also have a dark underworld that holds the power of Meriben, where the shadow daemons reside; the gates of this world are guarded by the Dark Fey and the Dwarves, who have become their servants.*

*To find this murky world of Meriben, one must travel to the caves of* **'Scholmance,'**

*To travel the river to this lower world of the Dschuma, a place where fear and dark passions can be fulfilled. And there, one will find the bang, people, and the* **Bangesko demons.**

*Those spirits, Who must obey the Serpent people who live in the highest region of the Dark Fey realm?*

*Why do I speak of the* **black magic?** *It is because I foresee that you will soon have to deal with one of the* **Dark Fey!** *I cannot see his face, but he is someone close to you or Godwin.*

*However, it will be someone under the control of an evil witch, a man called a Borsako, and a Female would be a Boraski?*

*And I must speak of all those who can use magic among these Romany people are named Gadjo, or the Fey. But as there can be white and black witches in our lands, so are their good and malign ones in theirs.*

*But **Meriben** is a dimension out of time and beyond the Cosmos, to be seen as a dream world, a place where all the opposites are united, and everything has yet to be united in reality?*

*A place where everything still has a potential outcome. A place of Emergence and Transformation.*

*A place where even life and Death can be re-united here, as it is a source of both magic and paradox in the world of men.*

*The gates lie in the lowest and highest realms of the Cosmos, and sometimes its agents can be seen as any black and white creatures, such as a Magpie or the evil witch Macha and her ravens of Death*

*And if you are to be able to avoid them, you must know that there are four types of magical powers. The First is a Chovani woman, and a Chavano man, is a benign sorcerer who can work with nature and the elements. It is such a being of the Dark Fey who is your enemy, this day.*

*Then there is a higher level of power: the Drabengro man and a Patinengi woman.*

*They can use herbs, make potions, and be Kind and Wise men or women to heal and speak to the ancestors' spirits. Your Martha is one such, I believe?*

*However, the Chovana are even more powerful, and they can commune with the world of Dreams and enter,* **the Drom world***, to use the three keys to enter the Faerie lands with the help of a familiar or Spiridush animal? They also have several tools to do so? one such is a* **Vastengri,** *a musical instrument we would know as a Tambourine. Then there is a particular type of drum and all sorts of amulets and magical charms.*

*But among the most potent tools they use are their Crystal ball and their magic wand that they call a Bakterismasko- Ran.*

*A Ran wand holds great power in the hand of any Borsako adept. The Dramani Queen has given you another amulet, a ring of power. When you hold it to your skin, it will tell you that evil is near, and then you will be protected from their powers in the real world of Humans.*

*So, guard it well and keep it around your neck, or wear it on your finger at all times, and all will be well.*

*But you must not tell anyone of its purpose as they will see it as a simple jewel or speak of what I have told you. So, promise me that, or the protection spell will not work!*

**Do this only if you have passed the tests the pain of death or else, it will use its power to stop your heart.;"**

"I do promise you, Cernunnos, but I need…." Cern held up his hand…

So is was that when Gytha, on hearing this warning, I was able to meld with her thoughts then of how Grace had the powers of a white witch, and perhaps her brother Eadric Streona had used the black magic to rise to become such a powerful man Moreover, was her mind filled with the details of this Chaldean magic? And as she tried to remember what Cern had told her…

That A *Chovani* is a sorcerer who can use the elements and their energies to perform the deep magic of *Danu*, to transform objects; using the powers of Apportion, they could also move an object a short distance. They could find water by dowsing and performing levitation. Some could perform *Pyro-Kinesis,* and control fire.

*A Drabengro is a male sorcerer, and a Pertaining is usually a hedge witch, another white witch who works with potions and herbs.*

She can use the spirit, and life energy, of a person to do the healing we call faith healing. Sometimes, she can tap into the power of the great earth mother to do Psychic surgery. This power is the ability to remove sickness and illness or such disorders within the body via an energetic incision, which is invisible to the naked eye.

The third and most potent of the Chaldean Sorcerers are the *Drabarni;* she is a wise and cunning woman who tells fortunes and answers questions?

*I knew then that Rachel is one such, I just hope that she can do an Aura reading to perceive the spirit and soul of a person and link them to places and things.*

*If she could use her powers of Clairvoyance. and extrasensory perception, and if she has the potential of Divination, the ability to touch the Occult., perhaps she could tell me what I needed to know about the danger I am in?*

*But that is an devil thing, and frowned upon; since then, they also reach the powers of the evil blood magic and the Bangeske Demons who live with the serpent people, in the cavern of Doindanieil!*

*But, I know new with this new knowlage that Cern had given me, that a Drabarni; could summon up these spiritsand force them to anwer three questions. But there would be a terrible price asked?*

*So then could Rachel do thisthing, using the skills of Medium and the crystal globe, she can make contact with the spirit world, gain the ability to see the past and future, make a prophesy or give a reading, which is a premonition of bad luck to come. Some like the more powerful Kristin seeresses, who have the gift of second sight, and by Scrying, over water, can see what is happening in the world, as long as there is another crystal ball nearby.*

Then there are the evil ones, who we have been sent to fight for their freedom back into the world of men? *The Mages.* They are also called *Borsako,* for a man and *Boraski,* for a woman. We are more familiar with witches, as they make themselves known by their evil deeds and malign magic.

*But I know knew they are not welcome in any Romani society, and all Gajio users are evil in both action and thought.*

And one of the significant features of Romany magic is their connection to the great earth mother. And the Wheel of Time revolved through the three levels of existence.

*This is part of their soul is their Chakra, a symbol of how life is ever-changing, and they believe we must move forward when our time comes, and the Wheel of Boleros comes into our lives, we must move forward and go somewhere else; both physically, and mentally.*

But one can escape being crushed by the Wheel of life through immanence and transcendence. That is why the Romany culture is based on moving around in their caravans. And, To stay in one place too long will bring about the feeling of Puskaria, and they will feel as if they were in prison, and their heart Chakra will wither and die.

\*\*\*

*Gytha,*

*But now I can see that this power, and this magic which comes directly to their ability to feel the power of the dream world.*

as I am still held in this vision dream, with Leofric and Gytha, try to make some sense of all this talk about black magic?

As it is possible that as it would seem that it was possible the cause of Higgins death and it seems that Gytha is the key? So, Gytha had discovered that a Choana's power comes directly from their relationship with Fey and their contact with their ancestors and sometimes their demons. In the dream world, they receive this contact with their spirit and the Drom, which is one of the keys to the world of the Fey. They also believe this Drom, is the real road to accession and Nivernais… And back to the fourth book.

"So, there then, it is, what I have learnt about the Chaldean magic. So now, I must see that there is something in this deep magic. But now I knew all this did not mean he could use it or even understand much of it!"

For so much of it was still buzzing in my mind, and I could feel the world was spinning around me again, I was becoming giddy, and he felt as if he had been standing for hours, so he just let go and fell to the ground unconscious.

*It was dark as I awoke to find I was sitting in the Queen's chair again! There was no sign or smell of woodland. Then it was gone!*

"Are you awake, Gytha? I fear you fainted, and your reaction to the Ran, was indeed more powerful than I have seen for such a long time. And I see the quickening almost came to claim you.

But we cannot allow that; not yet! Come to get up, and we will re-join the others; it is time for your questions. However, while the answers you receive from the spirit world will be yours to keep. I cannot allow you to retain your knowledge of our Chaldean magic! So, when you return to Martha, it will be lost to you.

I am sorry, but you will be far too powerful if you have this knowledge in the physical world of men."

So did the Romany Queen, and once again Rachel was theseerees,as by useing her Ran wand, she used it to open the power of the scrying dish, say the words that would the enchantment to summon a water spirit, who would come to us?

, *So, do you know of the spells of Chakra? So have you past the testing, and we must honour our pledge to thee.*"

I was about to ask my questions, but Rachel put a hand over my mouth.

"No child does not try to speak; you must ask your questions now while you have the amulet. Come, we must summon the spirits to hear their answers? Come back to sit beside the scrying dish."

*"Pani, Pani Sivoka! Dik the upre, dik tele! Buti Pani Silove! Buti pal yakh the dikel Je akana mudarel."*

'Now I knew these words? Water, water hastens! Look up, look down! So much water hastens, May as much come into the eye, which looked evil on thee, May now perishes!'

The Queen stood back, her eyes alive with the magic of his words, and then the waters in the bowl began to swirl and turn milky white and form the sign of the Boler wheel of life. Once again, she took back the wand and turned to proclaim what she had been told by the spirits

" I see you now, Sweyn Godwinson, a child, not yet born. But you must be protected from this spirit world., and the Dark fey who will come to claim him!

I see Nine of Your children born Of the Viking blood that runs in your veins, Gytha. Those who are yet to be conceived, as you will always be a Viking in your heart and mind and seek to rule in the lands of the Norsemen.

I see Harold Godwinson, who shall win a crown and lose a Kingdom

Then shall Tostig, a true Viking who will seek to rule a Viking kingdoms. He also will be claimed as one who will serve the Bangesko that hold his soul. As shall your children who will try to change the world of men.

But your first-born Edith is the one who shall be a Queen, as so shall The Faithfull Gyrth who stands strong in the light, when needed.

As will Gunhilda and Leofwine and even Wulfnoth who shall try to save us all but only if you can pay the price asked of the great Wheel?

These are the answer you seek concerning your first question, Gytha Godwinson. **So, is it said, so shall it be?**

The second is that You ask about Queen Emma of Normandy, and yes, she is innocent of the charges laid against her, and it is foretold, she will be the next Queen of Engaland!

As for you and Godwin, this future is not yet set. But, if you can survive the evil Jagalo Manus sprit, that stalks you both all this will come to pass. But only then!

**So, you have your answers and can say no more, and you must let us go back to your world."**

*

Then the waters turned blood red as a voice said,

*"A life for a life so was it promised, so is it done."*

Then did Rachel fall to the table utterly exhausted as these words of Prophecy, had come from her mouth, but the effort had taken all her strength?

*Leofric,*

"I tell you now Bishop, For a moment, I thought she was dead, and I realised that she had not told me who was expected to pay the price. But we did not have long to wait as we came to the christening of Sweyn.

Then I was back in Martha's cottage with Rosa and Martha as the distant voice of Rachel said to me.

"I see you Gytha, but you must not speak of this foretelling, not yet. It is not safe here."

Then I went to Martha, who was slumped in her armchair. Her arms at her side were as white as fresh snow, and she had taken out her amulet across her chest!

And when I held it in my hand, I felt it grip my heart so strongly, I thought I was about to have a heart seizure of some sort.

Somehow, I managed to let the amulet fall to the ground. And then I knew who had paid the price for the answers I had been given. *Martha had done so and because of her love for me!*

It was later that I looked around for Rosa was no longer there. And she was not to be found in the hall, and I realised that she must have returned to her people.

*Nine children. Good grief, I was going to have Nine children! But both CERN and the Gods had said Godwin was in danger?*

\*\*\*

*As I Leofric, heard Gytha speak of her encounter with the Romany folk, it was proper to say that I was not to be both utterly confused, and a little frightened to hear Gytha speak of her encounter with the Chaldean witch and their blood magic! And also, more than a little afraid to hear what was said about her future.*

But we all were in for another surprise as once these words of magic were set down on the vellum, so did they begin to fade, and they were lost to us then?

As such black magic and its power cannot be written in this world of men for very long, without it tainting everyone who read it or believed in such things. Certainly not! For I am a man of God. But it would seem that this servant, had been convinced she was the one to pay the price asked of these Dark Fey?

And now Gytha has given me that very amulet to hideaway from those who would invoke its powers. And now, I realise, that I should put it in a holy place. just in case? But, even then, I retained some of it, and I told Thomas what he should put down for posterity to read. But Gytha never spoke again of this to me, and I do not know if she could remember this foretelling.

A foretelling, that Gytha had a message from her gods and these Dark angels, that said her children would be born healthy and that they would all shake the world in their long lifetimes. But I needed a long time to gather my thoughts about this part of her confession.

So then, later that year, we all met again at Winchester to hear what Godwin told us about his visit to Trondheim and the death of The Danish King Harald the Second.

*And now Canute will become King of Denmark, Norway And Engaland! And, Just how he was to be able to manage such a monumental task, we were yet to find out?*

\*\*\*

## This is Gytha's Story

Now shall I set down the events that Gytha was to tell me, when we were alone, as he had said she needed to remember the events that were to occur at the blessings!

*So, this is what Gytha has told me as her confessor about how she tried to have her newborn son Sweyn, brought into the church, and have him christened by the priest Godfrey had come to Denmark from his church at Winchester? So that he will be seen as both a Christian and a Dane.*

But, when Gytha told Godwin of this plan Godwin had told her was content with a blessing, and not as he wanted the boy to be able to choose which God he would serve. And this day, Gytha had to promise him that this ceremony, was not to be seen as a religious christening.

Moreover, Gytha had to agree that both king Canute and his new bride Emma could also come to this chapel, for a Saxon blessing on their future wedding.

So, one can see that this fateful day was doomed to go wrong, from the start. And If I had been there, I would have stopped it happening. As this should be better done in Engaland. But we were to lean that Godwin had his own reason, to want Emma and Godfrey there and in a place where he could ask his questions!

So now must I speak of The Blessing, and what Gytha had done that day to save us all, from the Man of Fire, who was the Jagalo Manus!

*


Gytha,

"So now, Leofric, I must I tell you about the priest Godfrey, and how he changed all our lives at the christening of my son Sweyn. And confess to the church why he has a Viking name?"

After all the worry and heartache, our wedding day, I can say, it went smoothly, despite everything the spirits had foretold. And thanks to some herbs Rachel had provided, my first child, who was a girl, did not come to term and twelve months later I was pregnant again.

However, we were to learn that someone started a foul rumour that this child was conceived when I was forced to sleep with Canute! A foul lie, and one I shall speak of now!

*But with some semblance of truth to it, as a drunken King had come to my bedroom to claim his rights as my liege lord. But I had wind of this, and I tricked him that night, as he slept with my maid.*

And then, Sweyn had been born, and to or delight and relief, he was indeed a strong boy who was full of life and as normal as possible.

So that day, he is to have a Saxon Christening, and a blessing performed by the priest Godfrey, in a new chapel that we have built here in my hometown, and despite my objections I had to agree that both Emma, and Canute, are to attend.

As it transpired that the crafty Emma, had told Canute that she would allow this blessing, as long as they could have a grand wedding in Engaland and in Winchester Cathedral! A place that would show the people of Engaland that she was back and in charge?

*As for the christening of Sweyn Godwinson, My cousin Tyra, was to be my Woman of Honour, and as my birthing was near, I had allowed Rosa and Rachel to attend me, just in case something went wrong, and we needed a midwife?*

So, Leofric you will see that this simple blessing had become a much grander affair than I or Godwin wanted. But, first, as Father Godfrey is to do the Saxon part.

As for our Danish blessing, Jarl Otis, was our Danish gothi, will bless all the Danes there?

*But you should know Leofric that Godwin had never been to the Holdfast where Canute had been born, and the holdfast of Jelling.*

So, Before Emma was due, I had told Godwin something about the Danish House of Jelling...

So, husband, to be, I fear it will not sit well with my family, on this our wedding day, if you cannot know anything about who they are and where they come from. Have you ever been to Jell? I asked him. He looked at me as if I had lost my wits?

'You know I have not! Apart from walking to the shipyards. I may be about to become your Danish husband? but in truth, I am your prisoner here at Hedeby. I do not want to see any more of your brothers than I have to. I am a virtual prisoner here, so you must tell me what I need to know?'

'Yes, my love, and I see that, and when Canute comes, we will ask him to change their orders, But at least you have your Saxon friends that are building our new ships, while I am sick and have to endure this son of our who will be born soon, I hope. But you have the freedom of my homeland while I am wrapped here a virtual prisoner. And now I cannot ride or sail to get a moment away from this bloody Hall!'

*Gytha had stopped speaking and looked out at the open yard and the open sky that was freedom? But went on to say.*

But the truth of it was Bishop was that I knew then, Leofric, that I was being stupid to want to risk my baby in that way. And That Godwin had made a prisoner here so that he could be my protector.

But I was sick of being pregnant and unfair as my confinement was necessary as I had already lost my first baby, a girl, by taking a stupid horse to ride that day!

*I said nothing as I knew she had been near death then. As Gytha came back to this moment in her mind and memories.*

"So, then, Bishop, I will tell you, what I told Godwin that day, about the family that you are marrying into; this is the House of Cnut's family. And that it is now the ruling royal house in Scandinavia and Engaland.

My house is that of my father and brothers, and we are the Sprakalägg clan.

A noble house here in Denmark as my father was the son of Tyra of Denmark. She was a member of the Jelling dynasty, and Those are descended from Gorm the great. So, in our own way we are equal to Canute's line!

As were Cnut's father, Sweyn Forkbeard, and his grandfather Harald Bluetooth, the House of Denmark, and the House of Gorm, all are part of the Jelling dynasty. But Gorm and his son, Harald I Bluetooth are one of the older clans.

Harald the First is the elder brother, to Canute and as you now know, Canute is the second son. However, as for Gorm, they have erected several monuments at Jelling, including a pair of enormous grave mounds, the largest in Denmark.

I was told that Gorm was buried in the larger one, although the second one is not thought to have been used as it was reserved for Harald and Canute.

Even so, you will see that there are also two runic stones at Jelling, and the larger one is thought to have been built by Harald and the smaller one by Gorm before him.

But I had to stop Godwin going there and to want to climb them, he said he wanted to just look out to sea!

As I yelled at him to stop the jarls who were nearby coming at him with their raised taxes.

"Stop you fool Godwin. do not move whatever you do, please do not touch these runic stones known as they are our most holy Jelling Stones. Come away you fool! Only a our Danish gothi, can do so. And they now stand before this Christian Church or ' this new Jelling Kirke as we shall call it once it had been blessed. But these sacred stones, are seen its equal, in our sight.'

Do you not realise just how close you came to having your head taken from that pretty neck of yours.

I told you that this the chapel that Godfrey will rededicate to his church, and the Christian God! And then we can use it for our wedding and the Blessing.

I was later to learn you how special this his Jelling Kirke was the third such church to have been built on the site, a former wooden version having been built by Harald, who converted to Christianity. This conversion is also evidenced by a figure of Jesus on one of the stones.

So now, you know we came to the blessing and why Emma and Canute were there. But do you also know that things did not go well for us that day…


Gytha,

But enough of Jelling, perhaps I should start with the arrival at Jelling by Emma, as she came with what she said was a small party!

But it took three *Knarr* merchant ships, to bring her and her people to the Jetty. Then, of course, Godwin wanted to know what he would face then, as Canute insisted that he be there along with all the nobles of our Island, to stand with me, to greet Emma of Normandy.

However, I last saw Emma these five years since, and I had managed to escape her grasp, as she intended to keep me a hostage at Exeter? It was then that I fled from her fishing nett, and with the aid of Carl Half Dane, and I escaped her trap, and returned to Denmark. Carl later told me that I was to be taken as a hostage to make Godwin do her bidding.

But events had moved on and now Emma was in exile and no longer the young Norman Queen of England. But she still had her sons. Born of The princes of Engaland to care for.

\*

Leofric,

*Perhaps I should add a note here, concerning Emma and her many children as they will come to play such an important part in these histories and the fist books that describe her life and times. The books I urge you to read.*

*I do this to clarify my reader mind as to who was who in this forth book.*

*As we have leant Emma was married to king AEthelred, until his death…Here are my notes.*

*Emma of Normandy (referred to as Ælfgifu in royal documents;*[3] *c. 984 – 6 March 1052) was a Norman-born.*

*A noblewoman who became the English, Danish, and Norwegian queen, through her marriages to the Anglo-Saxon king Æthelred sometimes called the Unready.*

*And later, as we will learn, to the Danish king Cnut the Great.*

*Emma was A daughter of the Norman ruler Richard the Fearless and Gunnor.*

*She was Queen of the English during her marriage to King Æthelred from 1002 to 1016, except during a brief interruption in 1013–14 when the Danish king Sweyn Forkbeard occupied the English throne!*

*Æthelred died in 1016, and Emma married Sweyn 'Forkbeard son Cnut.*

*As Cnut's wife, she was Queen of Engaland, from their marriage in 1017.*

*She was seen as the Queen of Denmark from 1018, and Queen of Norway from 1028 until Cnut died in 1035.*

*After Cnut's death, Emma continued to participate in politics during the reigns of her sons by each husband*

One such was Harthacnut, and Edward the Confessor.

In 1035, when her second husband Cnut, died and was succeeded by their son Harthacnut, who was in Denmark at the time.

So then was Emma designated to act as his regent, until his return, which she did in rivalry, with Harold Harefoot.

As for her Marriage to Æthelred II.

Upon their marriage, Emma was given the Anglo-Saxon name of Ælfgifu, which was used for formal and official matters, and became Queen of England. She received properties of her own in Winchester, Rutland, Devonshire, Suffolk and O xfordshire, as well as the city of Exeter.

Æthelred and Emma, had two sons, Edward the Confessor and Alfred Ætheling, and a daughter, Goda of England (or Godgifu).

Emma and Æthelred's marriage ended with Æthelred's death in London in 1016. Æthelred's oldest son from his first marriage, Æthelstan Ætheling, had been heir apparent until his death in June 1014.

*So then did Emma's sons had been ranked after all of the sons from Æthelred's first wife, the eldest surviving of whom was Edmund Ironside.*

*However, so did Emma, make an attempt to get her older son, Edward, recognised as heir. Although this movement was supported by Æthelred's chief advisor, Eadric Streona, it was opposed by Edmund Ironside. More of that later, when*

*Æthelred's third-oldest son, and his allies, who eventually revolted against his father.*

*So here then are Her children.*

*Edward the Confessor c. 1003 – 5 January 1066, died without issue*

*Goda of England c.1004 – c.1049*

*Alfred the Noble c. 1005–1036*

*Harthacnut End detail.*

\*

But Emma was now thirty-two years of age, and she was still a powerful and vivacious woman, and a beautiful one if the reports we had received were accurate.

And despite motherhood, she still had her trim figure; she was tall, standing at six feet tall with the long blond hair and clear white complexion with solid brown eyes that she had from her mother. But, When she had sent back her acceptance of our invitation, there had been a letter of thanks and a miniature painting of her standing holding a rose.

The note said…

*Falaise Normandy,*

*I must say how pleased I am to be invited to your second wedding, as In a way, I was instrumental in bringing about the first. So, I will be with you by the new moon.*

*I will bring a surprise or two, and a gift for your son. I know Goodwin will need a sword on this wonderful day. So, I will bring his father's sword that he gave to*

*Aethelred after the battle at The Isle of Wight!*

*She had signed it just,*

*Your friend Emma.*

Reading this, Godwin had said.

"By all the Gods in Asgard, if she has my father's first sword my love, that will be a wonderful gift. As was also that of my Grandfathers. You say I need a special sword to wear at our wedding, and it is an ancestors' sword that we can use! And then It will be as if he were here! Come my love, surely, we cannot refuse such a gift? That would be a wonderful gift indeed. and I thought I would have to ask Canute for one of his to use!

But as for Emma, well the truth is, I feel for her now. And I believe we should show this painting to Canute , for it is the work of a master. But she is quite young here?!"

And when Gytha was persuaded to look at the miniature she also saw that the artist had flattered her when it was painted ten year's past?

And now one must look at it with some appreciation of this woman that looked to be such a beauty, as the master had painted it with great skill.

But what would he look like now they wondered.

As she looked to be a woman of twenty and not thirty-two? That was their thought!

But if It, was an accurate representation, Emma had changed from the hard woman we had met before. As Godwin said that day, Gytha knew that he wanted her to be able to forgive her , mostly because as our new Queen she could do us great harm should she wish it.

*And as you know Bishop, that was to be a foretelling! As Godwin lied to me and say,*

"Is that so. Well, It is true that I hated her once? And she deserves to be taken down a notch or two, but now she will be a Queen again, and I am fearful of her and what she will do in Engaland?"

"Yes, Husband, I also see that, and she is a mighty woman in every way. But she also has been placed in a difficult position with the death of Aethelred and now Edmund. But I fear that she is a true Norman at heart, and she will not mourn the passing of their Saxon line? However, much as Emma disliked her husband, his death placed Emma in a very precarious position. Who would she turn to now, Her remaining stepchildren?"

Godwin was thinking the same as he said.

"No, you are right wife, I see now that we cannot help them, or even those innocent children of Eadgifu, However much she might have desired it, her children would not claim the crown.

So, I intend to do my best to ensure that AEthelred's son Edmund Ironside was sure of the succession?"

I said to Godwin with as much hope in my words, as |I could muster.

'So then, her only hope was to keep close to his side and try to keep control of her estates. But she had to make a hard choice when Cnut seemed poised to defeat Edmund, but with your help, they came to a settlement carving the country in two.'

Godwin was silent for a time as if he was remembering that war?

'So, I did my love, and you had to save my life then and so many times since. But Unfortunately, Edmund did not live to complete his part of that deal. And now that Canute is going to be crowned as our king .

At least he had brought an end to nearly four decades of Viking raids, and now we have Cnut who is poised to become an overlord of Engaland. And what of Emma? I see that She had not wanted to be kept under siege with me as her protector in the fiercely pro, Anglo Saxon Lundune. So, who could blame her for going back home?'

I said,

'Home, and soon she will be here, and now we are helping Canute use her to help him win all of our Saxon Engaland? At first, I thought she would be his trophy and link between the old regime and the new. But I fear she will never be content to stay silent for long! Husband.'

"Silent? No, never that, and If I know her, she will soon have a finger in every pie she can find. But I saw the look on Canute's face when he was told of her letter and when he saw the portrait, she gave us. Even now that she hoped he would show it to Canute, and now he keeps close to his heart, A heart that I fear she may well break as For on his part, this is a love match?'

I realised then that Godwin saw this, and how close Godwin and Canute had become, as he said.

"Well, my dear brave Gytha, You must become my watcher, my eyes and ears in this matter. At least her in Denmark your people will talk to you. But in time, I fear we can only see what will transpire when she comes here.

As for Emma, it at least gave her the prospect of a future for her and any children she might bear.

As for Her children by Aethelred were safely in Normandy at this point. Her decision to remain in Engaland during the period before Cnut's victory may seem odd, but in Engaland, she had estates; in Normandy, and the west country did, she did not"

"Yes, I said, they are in Devon and Exeter, the very city she hoped to hold me to ransom or as a hostage. And you must try to understand why I will never forget that! And the truth is, that She is a Norman, and so are her children; but at least her children were born here, and they know and understood the Anglo-Saxon people. Or we must hope so?"

Godwin had taken my hand to look at my angry face as he also was remembering that time when he had to fight our rightful King. And why he and his men ship, and his father had come to Denmark to escape his death and became an outlaw.

"Indeed, and some people were spreading a lie that she was willing to hand her sons over to the Danes, if her own life would be spared, and she could maintain her estates."

But this time, Emma was trying to pretend that she held no grudges, and she is certainly beginning to acquire something of a reputation for making tough decisions."

" Well, at least we have dealt with another thorn in the side of Emma's along with Emma's good fortune. What about the wife Cnut had taken in 1006 that is AElfgifu, daughter of the slaughtered AElfhelm, A man, whom Aethelred had seen fit to murder?'

Godwin said to me then, more in hope than expectation. but I saw a white lie on his lips. I asked him if his first marriage was legal?

'Indeed, that is going to be a problem, as one could see that our hand fisting wedding is not to be seen as binding here in Denmark and that I why we must go ahead with this Christian wedding. and I asked Canute about her. He said it was not a legal marriage ,and a hand fisting ceremony, done as a young man underage, who only did what his father wanted.

*And he promised me that when he married Emma, Cnut said he would not abandon her or their sons. He would send them away to live?'*

*" Yes, at least that is so. But, you see, I have learnt that Emma has now negotiated a deal in which Cnut swore he would support only their sons in a claim to his throne. Would he have agreed to such a deal? It seems unlikely.' I said more in hope than expectation.*

*'Well, wife as for that, I heard Canute talking to the Norwegians in Trondheim, and I thought he agreed to send back some of the troublemakers from Engaland. Or even put to death any that he considered might get in the way of his rule..."*

\*\*\*

But now, and once again I Leofric must set down what was said and done at the wedding and then the christening that took place a month later, of their first born Sweyn Godwinson But to my eyes the babe looked a lot more like his Viking mother or even Canute ? Then a Saxon baby?

And, I would add another note here, that will say that, So it was that Edmund Ironside, Cnut's

adversary to the throne, left behind a wife and two sons. But now they appear to have been whisked out of the country to appear in Hungary eventually. And we're safe for a time at least?
*

Here, Gytha, tells of the meeting with Canute and Emma.

"So, then Bishop The reception of Emma's party was held on the jetty at Jelling, the road to the King's Hall was laid with fresh straw and sawdust. And was lined each side, with Canute's men in his house livery and some of his soldiers to hold back the crowds that had gathered to see the expected spectacle, of the arrival of the Queen of Normandy."

Here is my record of her words that day as she described that scene...

There were some tall flagpoles and garlands that were heavy with the bunting, and entwined flowers of honeysuckle and vines. Around these flagpoles were the ribbons of Normandy, and an arch would provide a tunnel for Emma's coach to pass through to the king's hall, where a feast was waiting."

At least It was a fine summer's day without a cloud in the sky, as luck would have it. But just in case of rain, there was a fine coach waiting with white bedecked white and red roses, or Emma and me to use.

But It also would provide a secure way of getting to the feast Hall, from the Jetty.

However, Gytha, said that was not going to risk spoiling her new clothes by walking there and not in her condition.

So, it was when they were all at the jetty Godwin and his welcoming party, were waiting under an awning that held the flags of Denmark, Norway and Normandy, and the new symbol Canute was going to use in Engaland as the Red Cross of St Gorge, for all of his new Engaland.

As, He had told us that with Emma's help? His new kingdom could become a united Engaland!

*But he had some questions to ask her first and that was why he was not to be seen standing with Godwin, among his welcoming party.*

And now, as we all we waited in the hot sun, were all regretting the wearing of our thick undergarments as well as our finest clothes.

Canute was standing aside from us, and out of sight of the jetty. Godwin had told me that he was in disguise as he did not want Emma to see him there and appear so eager, to see her. And that it would suffice that they would meet at the Hall when he was to be seen as a king. So, now, he was dressed as a man from Bruges, in a brown doublet and trousers, and he looked like a wealthy merchant. He even had a stovepipe hat in his hands.

And with the blaring of Danish horns, and French trumpets, we knew that the barge bearing Emma and her retinue was here now, and what a sight they were, and put our meagre guard of honour, to shame.

Although, Godwin was dressed as a King's Thegn with his best uniform. Gytha said she was dressed in a tight-fitting dark green woollen dress that fitted at her shoulders, and was so loose it would cover her bulge, as it fell to the floor. But this overgarment was both cumbersome and warm. However at least she had made sure that she had three of the servants and Rosa to help her with it, and it would hide a small stool if needed.

And she said that despite how hard she tried to control her nerves, and anger at this meeting with Emma who was once her enemy.

Gytha said that she felt a shiver run It was supposed to keep me warm from the breeze always found at the Docks. Over this dress, she had a light green shawl, a mop hat and a white headscarf and neck coif. She had told Godwin, that she looked like a bush and not his wife. He had laughed to say

*'Well, Canute looks like a brown tree trunk, so we must hope there will be no dogs nearby who will cock a leg against these noble personages!'*

And they both fell about laughing.

And now the sun was up, and it was mid-day, and Gytha was beginning to feel uncomfortable. But, still, she was not going to show it to Godwin, or any of the Nobles that were assembled there.

They were the mayor of Jelling and his council members, and all the Guilds were here. But they had a separate roped off enclosure, which was also richly decorated with the yellow flowers of Normandy.

So, when Emma and her party stepped ashore from her ship, she was greeted by the Mayor and Alderman Thomas, was ushered forward to the front of the awning where we were waiting out of the sunlight.

As for Emma, she wore a large expansive white bridal gown made of Bruges lace, ? But no vail. And Gytha exclaimed quite loudly, that Godwin , turned to give her that look!

*"How dare she be so brazen, the Norman bitch, she is!- Gytha said top Rosa.- She is no virgin to wear white!"*

But at least Gytha said that her two attendants, were dressed in a matching gown of pale-yellow dress with a white coif to cover their heads and some of their faces. This head coif was held in place by a golden circlet that denoted their status as one of the noble families in Normandy. Around the shoulders, they also wore a white delicate shawl, that was white lace that would have cost a small fortune in Bruges. Their dresses were also very long and had a tail that would reach the ground Just.

Under this white over dress, Emma wore a dark blue long gown that shimmered with the light as it moved, and Gytha's thought, was made of this new satin or silk material, that everyone was talking about? She also wore a lace headscarf that hid he golden hair and was draped at her shoulders. In addition, she wore a tiny golden crown on her head to set off the purity of the Lace. The dress was fitted at her waist and fell to the ground with a trail that a page boy held.

Then Gytha said all this changed as she looked up at us all, and smiled at Godwin and then his retinue, just as the sun shone on her face, and the effect was magical!

*It was as if one of the angels had come to this reception.*

Her wide smile and strong face were indeed that of a very beautiful woman. But the sile did not reach her eyes, and Gytha saw her eyes change to blue steel, as she saw Gytha was there. And no sign of Canute! Then she was all the charming Ex-Queen again. But Gytha knew just how calculating the moment was, and that Emma was no angel, and the truth was that she was nervous about meeting her.

So, as the Burgomaster offered her his arm, and she was gracious enough to take it, she said that she was steeling myself to step forward and welcome her on Canute's behalf.

At least that was the plan, But before they got to the Dias and the awning shelter. Canute stepped forward, to take her other arm as Thomas the Mayor stepped away; Canute said to us all and looked at me, to take my arm.

'Let me have your arm my dear Gytha, I see you, are in need of a rest. We cannot allow you to tire yourself any further my lady.

So, Godwin, I ask that you Let me speak with this Queen. I thank you Gytha Sprakling, and soon to be a Bride to Jarl Godwin here, and a mother?"

Then to Emma with a deep bow, and a wave of his hat he pointed to the bedecked pathway.

So, my lady Emma, perhaps we will walk to the hall, and allow the lady Gytha to take the carriage to my hall. Perhaps the lady Gytha here, will be so gractime.to allow this indulgence, as you see she is near her time? I will introduce The Jarl Godwin here, and then we all meet at the Feast Hall.

As he, like all here, cannot take his eyes from the vision that is our Queen Emma.

Then Canute used his hat to point at the Queens retinue, who were about to follow them it would seem? He said to us all, not a request but an order.

"But if Queen Emma allows it, we will walk alone, Your ladies may come, but stay out of earshot. We shall walk together and take a stroll in the sunshine, as we have much to discuss this day?'

I saw Emma and her people and guards were now looking at Canute with utter astonishment and some fear as here was a merchant who had dared to speak out like this, and they could only think that he had come to ruin everything as I said in my loudest voice.

"Yes, my King, you do. Then to Emma, I am pleased to introduce you to our Liege lord Canute of Denmark, king of Norway, and now Engaland. So, my liege. We will wait for you at the hall then."

And by the time they had both walked along the aisle to the hall, the questions had been asked, and his proposal had been made and accepted.

And now, Emma would be A Queen consort, to both Denmark, and Norway, and soon to be crowned the actual Queen of Engaland as the wedding and coronation were going to take place in St Pauls' Cathedral In Lundune! As Gytha asked me.

*Were you there that day, Leofric?"*

"No, my lady, But if you allow it, I will hear more of your wedding day, and the birthing of your firstborn Sweyn Godwinson?"

"And so, you shall. And it was that morning, Godwin had found me alone for a change, and I saw he was still troubled about some problem concerning the blessings?

"What is it, my love? You must be pleased that Canute and Emma have hit it off so well. So please tell me you are not still troubled by our wedding plans?"

Godwin took my hand to say.

"Yes, in a way. You have taken such care to make them so unique and wonderful! But I am afraid I will not be able to live up to all this pomp and circumstance. I am just a simple Saxon seaman at heart, and I am afraid I *will do something that will spoil it all?"* Godwin asked me,

*"How can you say that husband? When have I seen you stand in your ships and command an army? This is nothing to what you have achieved."*

He smiled then and laughed at my jibe.

*"Yes, of course, I know that!* Godwin said, *But perhaps it will help me settle my mind if you go through it all again, as it will help clarify my role in all this?"*

*"Yes, I see that now; well then, you big oaf. I see you have nothing to worry about but sit and listen, and then we will drink a toast to ourselves. Because this is our day."*

And so Leofric, that is what we did, And this is what I said to Godwin…

On the wedding day, an archway is known as a "gate of honour" **a "æresport"**) is placed around the door to the bride's home or somewhere close to it. It is made of pine branches and various flowers. The gate of honour is made by the family members, friends, and neighbours. Some people put the gate of honour on the door to the place where wedding ceremonies or wedding reception are organized.

The "*gate of honour*" is made again on the 25th wedding anniversary. But the truth is that not many married couples would ever reach that target? This is what a Danish bride, traditionally wears at a white wedding dress and a veil. And now we see that why Emma was so wrong to wear white!

So, the female guests should not wear white clothes. The bride also has something red. Because this colour symbolizes love, some believe it wards off evil spirits. Finally, the groom buys the bridal bouquet.

Of course, I knew I would have to do this for Godwin, as he had no interest in flowers and had a terrible colour sense. The groom should not buy the wedding shoes for his bride, as She must get them by herself, and She should not sell them after the wedding, as this will bring bad luck and the marriage will not last? However, the Wedding ceremony, can be held in the church or outside in the open.

Traditionally, the bride and her father are those who arrive last. After the wedding ceremony, rice is thrown at the newlyweds to symbolise fertility. By Odin, if I had nine children, there could be no doubt about our fertility. But I had to thrust that prophecy away for now!`,

Usually, there are less than fifty guests present at the wedding and about one hundred at the reception. But as Canute and Emma were going to be there, I knew I would have to shorten my list! But when guests arrive at the wedding reception and find their seat, they stay standing until they are given a sign that everybody should take a seat. Taking a seat on your own is considered impolite.

But it is the toastmaster who manages the whole event. There are several speeches made during the wedding reception. The first one who is going to speak is the bride's father. But this was a worry for me as my father was long dead, and Eilaf, my Brother, would do this as I could not trust Ulf not to say something awful!

After that, there is a lot of singing. People often change the lyrics of a famous song to relate to the newlyweds. The music is provided by a Harp, a fiddle and a drum and a flute, and these minstrels travel all over the country performing at weddings, birthdays and religious festivals and the like.

But I had sent the first lot away. Much to the disgust of Godwin, he had chosen the cheapest! As he was tone-deaf, he would never know who the best set of musicians for our wedding was to be found in all of Denmark.

After the Dancing, the couple is surrounded by the guests, and then as they slowly get closer to the couple at the end of the dance, there will be no more free space. The bride and groom then kiss. Immediately after that, the male guests will take off the groom's shoes. The best man then cuts the tips of his socks. This is done to prevent the groom seduce another woman than his wife.

*Some say that the reason is entirely different. They say that the cut off sock tips , are given to the bride, who should repair the socks, and show that she will be a good wife. As the guests destroy the Bride's veil!*

*But I was never going to agree to that version!*

So, it is never to be seen as fine silk or lace, as It is done as it is believed that she will not need it anymore. *But I was to discover that Emma had come wearing the lace she had made for AEthelred? Was this a message?*

The happy couple cuts the traditional wedding cake called "crankcase" sometime around midnight. Each guest must get a slice. Otherwise, the couple will have a troubled marriage. The "Kransekage" is often decorated with small flags.

The wedding reception also includes another tradition. A guest starts stamping on the floor. Other guests join them, as the newlyweds then hide under a table and kiss. And yes, there can be a lot of kissing and in some cases a lot more friendly encounters!

But *I fear we will miss that part as Godwin, as nor I could get under a table to kiss!*

*However, the next tradition is, let us say, rather noisy, as our Guests shall take parts of the silverware and start striking glasses or plates.*

That is the sign that the bride and groom have to stand up on chairs and kiss, and declare their undying love for one and another, In public. this is the last change for a woman, to refuse her husband and the marriage. Then, there is even more kissing, by all and sundry? and I fear Godwin will never allow this?

And another such tradition is When the best man and bridesmaid, has to go to see them in their wedding bed. As the. Female guests rush to kiss the groom and escort him to the bridal bed... It is the same with the groom.

But, after the wedding, the couple must give the bridesmaid a special gift and send a "thank you card" to all guests, usually, it is a flower. As Gytha went on to say,

"So, Godwin, love of my heart, it is time I got dressed in my wedding dress, and you shall find your best man and tell him to be sure to have the rings and make sure that you both are on time at the chapel…

And then Gytha was silent for a time, and I was about to ask her what was troubling her, when she said to me.

"So, Bishop, we come to the blessing, and the day I had to tell Godwin, what Canute had insisted we do then and how we were all nearly burnt alive at the christening?

But Godwin had taken her face in his big hands, to say.

"Well wife, Emma is going to be our queen in Engaland and then she can be a friend or an enemy. Which would you choose , I said yes so that she would be in our dept!"

\*\*\*

Television

Flash, Flash It is time to come back to us Jake Rutter. Do it now.

So dear diary, that was when I was, I pulled away from the book four and forced to return to my life and times, and once I had recovered from this reading, we were back with the two women and able to read what was written on the latest pages.

*And what an incredible story it was*

*And now, I knew I would need some time to myself, and before I was ready to continue with the readings. But, as this hard task, and the concentration required, for the translations, it was becoming ever more draining. Both on my health and spirit. as I knew I had gone far too deep now, as I was so caught up with these histories, I knew I was close to another breakdown, unless I had a long break from these books.*

It was when I told all this Mandy Jones, a woman I had come to see and like, as someone I could talk to and tell her just how much these sessions were draining me, both mentally and physically! And it was Mandy Jones, who said she had solution.

She said that I was spending far too much time with the books, and I must make time to get out in the fresh air before each session. And she offered to show me the grounds of the University .

And it was in these walks, that I began to see there was so much more to this history student, as it turned out we were nearly of the same age, as shet old be of her lonely life on the farm and the Welsh hills At Brecon, And how she also found it hard to meet people being so tied to helping on the farm And she had an accident on their tractor, that put her in hospital for nine months, so that her father had to hire help and then she passed for grammar school and then university followed that and she never went back to the farm.

*And them she said how she loved our walks as she had never told anyone about the farm before.*

So then, I told her about something of my life and my mental troubles after the car accident, and about my deafness. and my need for my hearing aids and my shyness. So did we begin to open up to each other and I was to return to the Reading room, refreshed and eager to continue with the incredible task.

*A task I could now share with Mandy!*

As she began the normal routine, we had developed together, the help that would be needed, after each reading, and now, instead of the nurse, it had been Mandy, who was cleaning me up.

Because, when I was out for any length of time, sometimes, there was some dribble around my mouth, that needed cleaning up. Something I found horrible and degrading as I was now an adult, and had a serious job as a Police officer? I was ashamed that sometimes I managed to wet myself. Or worse!

But Mandy said that this was because of the vision dreams, and I had little control of my body functions. It was then she had made it her job to look after me with body wipes or take me to the showers that were part of this department, and for the technicians use.

And then I would drink large amounts of water and a small glass of Brandy, before I was ready to deal with what had been recorded or speak about it.

The next day we were back in the reading room and while the others were busy setting up the equipment and testing it was ready to record, Mandy Jones came to me and asked me if she could have a private word with me, so we went into my rest room.

I was waiting for the right moment to tell them my news about the books, when I saw she was looking at me as if she was trying to decide what she wanted to do next? And now my senses were on full alert, as they recognised her emotional turmoil? And whether she could say what was on her. mind and then she come to a decisions as she said all in a rush

*"Jake, even I, can see just how tiring these sessions are for you and you are right it is long past time for you to have a break from all this. After all these books are not going away any time now, and I have a question for you, that may or not be appropriate?"*

*"Ask away?" I said to her.*

*"Jake, Inspector Rutter, would it be possible for me to ask you to dinner, I expect that you are utterly fed up with this University corporate food, and sleeping on a Bunk Bed every night. So will you think me a stupid woman, and a fool if I if I tell you how much I have come to like you since we have begun working on the books. And I feel we have begun a friendship on our walks?*

*You see I know now just how shy and sensitive you are, and how you try to control your feelings and have to hide them from everyone. And I know that you may never speak to me about them. But it breaks my heart to see how you are so lonely and alone all the time. So, I want you to know I would like to become your friend. If you would like that."*

I was just about to tell her just how much I had come to look forward to our walks but as usual the words would not come in time as she went on to say.

"No, Jake Rutter, please do not say anything as it has taken all my courage to speak to you now. But perhaps we could find a way to get to know one and another. A little better? Just as good friends and comrades of course."

Somehow, I managed to say.

"Yes, Mandy Jones, I would like that very much, but I would like to take you out to dinner if you would like that?"

I saw her mind working at this formal invitation.

"Yes, *Jake* that would be very nice! but I am not good with eating in public. as find it hard to be stared at as a...Well never mind what.

You see I have something more private in mind. You see, I have a small cottage these grounds here. If you wish it, I could cook you a home cooked meal. And offer you a place to stay away from all this sterile place where you are not wanted?

It would be a place for you to fell at home and a place to relax and unwind? and I do have a spare bedroom. I am a good cook.

So, Inspector, I can offer you my spare so that you can get a good night's sleep and try to forget these Bloody Books for a time?

*But you should know that, is all I on offering to you. Jake, well not quite, I can make a good breakfast. With no strings attached. What say you? Jake Rutter. Will you come home with me later this day?"*

Go home with her! As she spoke to me, all I wanted for some time now was to go home with this sensuous women and make love to her! And now she was offering me a bed?

*And something in her eyes, told me that if I wanted more that was not impossible? But I also knew that to have a liaison with anyone on such an intermate and an emotional level, would be a disaster for my investigations.*

*As then I would no longer be able to maintain an unbiased assessment of them or the situation.*

But the truth was, that I had discovered that this woman was such a warm and generous soul, and during our walks, I had found that more than my feelings, had been caught up with her. And now my prayers had been answered in such an unexpected way!

*And if we could become friends at least, well that would be wonderful, and as for something more like sex, that would be something I had longed for since our first meeting.*

As for the sex act, I was not really a virgin, but so far, I had managed to keep this on a professional level, by paying for it with a recommended prostitute , by John *She was a mature woman, who had been very nice and discreet, and willing to show me what we were expected to do, and how. But my emotions had never been involved then. And now my emotions were running riot. But I heard myself say.*

*"Well Mandy, that would be just wonderful! And Yes please. But I will need to fetch some night things. But now we both need time to think about what this may mean and yes, I do like you. I like you a lot!*

*But we must get back to work, and If you still think this could work for us both. Then please ask me again, and if the offer still stands, I will be delighted to become your lodger!*

Once again, I inwardly cursed myself for these stupid words, and the delay. but I needed time to think about what I was getting myself into, now, there was still the question of her liaison with Higgings.

*So, all this must be put on hold, until I have told them what I have found out about Higgins."*

And when we were ready to start a new session, I told them my theory about the heart attack…

*"Well, then, you have all read the latest transcript of Book four, where the bishop is telling us how Godwin and Gytha, were to come to England with Canute from Denmark, and we have read a little, about their Christian marriage, and*

*how Gytha has consulted with a Romany seeress, to get some answers to her questions. And now we must decide for ourselves as to whether this is even possible, in our timeline?*

*But the point is, that they believe in their various gods, and their magic powers they had and used? And I think that the Godwinson, 'are all to be seen as a very special family indeed and are some of those people who are a part of their, Golden timelines."*

I stopped there, expecting the questions this statement would invoke. It was Susan who asked the first question.

*"So, some more mumbo Jumbo Mr Rutter. Is this more of your magical stories about time travel?*

I knew she was not yet ready to listen to my explanation about the quantum world, but I saw a way, to tell her about how the matrix must maintain the Golden Timelines, and who and why that was so?

*"Well as to that idea Susan, is it mumbo Jumble as you say? You have seen on this print out what I read from this book and how Lady Gytha Godwinson, and her people, believe in the power of their Gods. And how they believe that they control their destinies. As to whether They do so, rightly, or wrongly what matters is that they believe it to be so.*

*As do so many, in our world and timeline? now believe that our God, gave us a code to live by. Is that so different? As we believe in the divine spirit, the holy ghost, and the promise that Jesus gave us?"*

She sniffed at that and said, in a hard voice.

*"I do not believe in an afterlife. I did once, until I saw the light and the lies told in the name of any religion. I am now an atheist so there."*

I waited for more, but she was not about to enlarge on that, and I knew that most scientists, had found it hard to believe the bible stories concerning our creation, once Darwin had let the cat out of the bag. When then, Dawkins had proved his theory of how and why the humans became the dominant species but natural selection and the survival of the fittest! And now with the fossil records being discovered, and the advances in modern science were uncovering all the secrets that Science and Nature held.

*"But I need her to hear what I need to tell her now.*

*So now I ask that you both should come with me and hear what I must tell you about the Quantum world of space and time if you will. We should have a cup of coffee and try to put aside your doubts and use your scientific mind if you can.*

*As I ask you to see, that the Saxon people, and the Danes, will listen to what their priests and mystics tell them, so do they mostly do what they are told, and see in their hard lives, where lightening is so dangerous, as are floods and drought.*

*So, they seek an explanation for these things that will allow them to find away to live their lives. so do they believe that there are such things as the magic of the gos.to be true.*

*And If someone is cursed, they will believe it to be true. They also believe that some people are chosen by the gods, to be special people, who can commune with the spirits, and they are called priests, Shaman, or Druids.*

*So, then these people are a part of the Golden timeline as are the very powerful leaders and become their rulers. And to destroy any of their Gods and those people who serve them will have grave consequences. In their timeline, and the others. Dimensions, that exist in Quantum space. And yes, we now think that there are many such universes and multiple timelines. and now I must ask you to think differently about time and space.*

*You see and because of my strange ability to timeslip I have had to look for reasons and answers to all this and this is what I have discovered.*

*That we live on what is our GOLDEN Timeline. Well, that is going to be difficult to explain, as it is caught up* in the matrix of Dark Matter that hold all of this together.

In one way, One, can see it as large, sliced loaf of bread.

The crust is the matrix and the sliced different universes and time periods that all exist at once as do we.

I told you it is hard to get your mind around, but we do exist there and so do our choices change what happens . But not the Golden timeline s as should this be changed, so will that universe destiny also disintegrate and be m no more."

Susan was still looking sceptical as she said.

"Pah, you said this was science, but all I hear is just theories. Can you prove any of this rubbish you speak about this Time slipping?"

"No not in the way you will see and understand. But I can see and feel the recent past when I have a vision dream. but as for the future that is not set until we choose it to be so.

But I do not really understand it fully. I have told you I have special ability that allows me to go into a vision dream and though the recent past and present. To do this

*I must enters a dream state. then I can touch an object and feel what has occurred with it or them?*

*And then, I see our own portion of the matrix. And our time. but only in my own time period. I can tie the immediate past and present. Some people can slip between the Time Scapes to see into these alternative timelines and see or enter another a different slice of Bread. but each of these timelines, have a golden thread that holds the loaf together and seeps it falling apart.*

*I am sorry Susan, but that is the best way I can make sense of this. you see in each of these slices. Have some people who will make a difference to the destiny of everyone else.*

*And they can choose to do good or evil in their lives and so effect that of their timeline.Pleaese.do not ask me how this is possible because I do not know how this can be so.*

*But in our lifetimes meany such people have existed. Hitler was an evil example as was Stalin, but they are balanced by Mother Terasa, and Gandhi!*

*And you must see how Somehow, we have managed to avoid WW3, and find so many cures to the illnesses we would never survive. they follow a golden timeline that must not be draped or lost on ease the women sprit will be lost,*

*And now you both have my secret as I was told all this by Doctor Simon Robinson, the consultant who saved my life, when all I wanted was to end it.*

*But I see I am wasting my breath telling you all this. b ut you must have an Astro physicist here in this university Or someone who understands particle physics. So, you should ask him about Quantic World. A world that even Einstein spoke of?"*

I saw these thoughts, and arrows had struck home as I had touched on her world at last. But then, I needed to get back to the books.

*"And now ladies and having read how Gytha and Godwin are so central to this Saxon timeline so also can we see that they must be some of these Golden people.*

*How else, can they have such an influence on these year. As for Good or bad, we are yet to discover?*

*Godwin and all his family, are also here of these special people? And we must do our best to find out, how and why?"*

*You once asked me if I could change what I saw in my vision dreams, and the answer I am not sure? As So far, I am only a simple observer.*

*I once though that, I could try to change the past And present, to allow the future for the better outcome, or give* someone a warning. But that ended in a terrible outcome for me, and that person as she had a fit and died. As that was one of the Golden time threads, that I tried to change for the worse.

However, as you know, I have been able to help the police since then with their investigations by reading a crime scene, and to help the police in that way with information, but that also was a disaster, when I was nearly killed by a planted bomb. So now you can see that that would be such a bad idea as I could not know if I had destroyed one of these Golden people So to try to change our current history, that must remain a question we should try to answer now. As long as we take some simple precautions.

But As for our past and these books, it was so long ago and what is here in these books I think they must be set in stone.

    Mandy said.

"That is a shame Jake, as I would like to think we could do something to help King Harold save his Saxons at Hastings. And that day when Duke William came to steal our country and change our history so much. For when he came to give our lands to his Norman followers so did my people have to run away to live in Wales."

I said, *" Well as to that there is something called the boot strap paradox, or the Grandfather paradox. which says, if we could kill our grandfather in the past, we would not exist in the future, to try to change the past. so, I am sorry Mandy .You would not have been born in Wales and that would be a great shame."*

Mandy was smiling now and as she squeezed my hand; I was so embarrassed Isaid what was on my mind

*"Even so, ladies, I am having second thoughts about what we have revealed so far, and I am wondering if we should we publish what we have seen in these books?*

*You must see that these pages, may still have some cause and effect on our timeline What do you think? And what do our History books, tell us About Gytha Godwinson?*

It was Susan who answered my question, and Here is what I found online, but these are only the bare facts of her life and that of her children. And now thanks' to Leofric, we can read something of their true story. But these details make no mention of her terrible accident that was to occur at the time of the blessing of her newborn son Sweyn.

*"I was told of a story that is set in an ancient text at Jelling, that she was involved in a fire. A terrible fire that burnt down their new church. Gytha was badly burnt trying to rescue her husband Godwin.*

*She recovered, but her face was so badly burnt she had to wear a face mask, And some sort of a vail and retired from public life, to have her nine children in private. Ther is now pictures of her after that day. but there is a wonderful glass and lead window painting, of her as a young woman in a church somewhere. I will find us a copy.*

*There was a mention of a curse of some sort.*

*But we know from the Saxon chronicles, that she was there at Hastings, when Duke William, forced her to identify the body of her son Harold.*

*Otherwise, the histories not say she was to play an important part in the Godwinsons story?*

*It is believed that Gytha left England. She either entered the convent at St Omer or returned to Denmark. In the year 1072 (around) Gytha died in Flanders. So, I intend to make sure we must play special attention to what Leofric has to tell us next?"*

*I said, "Yes indeed we must and try to discover if there was a fire, and what caused your professor Higgins to have a heart attack, as he was reading that section. A curse you say?"*

It was Mandy who asked us why this was important?

*So, you think that Higgin was so caught up in this narrative he also had come to the part where Gytha was told not to use the amulet would be dangerous. And Not until she had been tested and found worthy by these strange Volva spirits?"*

Once again, Susan was about to debunk this theory, but I said.

'Indeed I do if like me he was so caught up in her story and was believing what he was reading. It is possible he had a seizure of some sort. Brought on by auto suggestion then the power within the amulet, would kill him? Or anyone who tried to use the magic it held. The Deep magic that could be used to protect or kill?"

I waited for this to sink in, as I saw Susan almost snort with derision, at my suggestion .But the fey hearted Mandy, was looking for a lot more thoughtful, as she said.

"I see what you are getting at Jake, we do know, and with your help, just how powerful the mind can be! and we know believe in the force of auto suggestion and a trance like state. It is during a trance, that some people can do incredible things that are far outside their normal abilities. But that is not magic?" I said,

*"Indeed, it is not seen as magic, but I have good reason to know that the mind can do incredible things, that will seem like magic to anyone who is able and willing to open their minds to such ideas, and powers!"*

Now Susan was ready to say.

*"So, you think it was a curse from this witch and her amulet that killed Richard. What Tosh. I know he was holding it when he was reading that some of book one that day?"*

*"If so, then you should have said so and not hidden it away Susan. But It is possible he was so caught up with this part of the book. As I also, felt some sort of a power that nearly had me? But I must read more to make sure, We have not yet opened that first book, perhaps now is the time, as we need to know if that is the source of this evil power and the curse. But not today.*

*Today I must go back to speak with my superiors and tell them my theory. Concerning auto suggestion as the cause. And then they may well close this investigation and allow the Coroner, issue a death certificate. Then you can all get on with your lives?"*

Before we could agree on this Mandy said.

*"What about the rest of the translations then?"* Mandy asked with some thought that I was leaving her, and

them? I managed to remember her invitation to be her lodger  and  then I would no longer be needed.

*"Well as to that, I believe that You are expecting the lady from Ireland? if she can read the text , then I am no longer needed."*

I saw the look in Mandy's eyes, were bright with a tear? As I decided I wanted to see her again I said.

*"But I also want to know what Leofric has written in these books. So perhaps I have a solution if you agree. You see I have two weeks leave due me and perhaps I could come back on my own time, and we could finish this task together. Mandy here has been so kind to offer me a place to stay,  and I would be delighted to accept her offer of a bed and breakfast stay?*

*And when i finish these translations perhaps Then we can decide if we should  tell the world what you have found here?"*

Then, I saw the look in these woman's face and their eyes, change then to one of surprise and hope.

I realised that Susan was more than glad to get rid of me, as she intended to speak to one of the professors about what I had told her about the quantum world.

While Mandy realised that I was going to want to see her again!

*"Ho yes! That will be a good idea, and a good plan Jake Rutter. And after work, I will go home and stock up my larder. My cottage is On Pennsylvania Road ,It is called Jasmine cottage, I will expect your call?"*

As, I expected the authorities, and the police were more than willing to agree that Higgins had died from natural causes. As then the university and his wife, one Mary Higgins, could claim on the insurance, and the University avoid any scandal.

*But it was two days later that I went on leave, and to find Jasmine cottage…*

And when I presented myself with a suitcase, and after a visit to Boots, with a week's clothes, my newly bought pyjamas and wash kit and some new under clothes, some aftershave and a new body spay the assistant had recommended, and an afterthought, a supply of contraceptives.

*More in hope than expectation."*

I found that Jasmine cottage, was a small stone built two-bedroom, single story building, with a slate roof and small windows. It was surrounded by a wonderful cottage garden, and a thriving vegetable patch A home, that guessed had once been a gardener's home.

I had changed int my most comfortable blue jeans, and a blue tee shirt, which I wore under a lur denim open button-down shirt that would also serve as a hacking jacket? And with and my new blue trainers, I was hoping this double denim outfit would seem casual enough? But I was feeling far from casual .As I saw the storm clouds that had been forecast for the night, had come a lot earlier, I felt the first patter of raindrops on the slated porch roof, as I rang the doorbell.

Mandy must have seen me coming down her path, as she opened it almost immediately, as I saw she was also wearing casual clothes. a long lose fitting Multi coloured silk flowing Japanese or Chinese dress, Kaftan, no not a Kaftan, no it was a Kimone ?that was open at her neck, and just enough to show her ample cleavage and her round breasts. Which was very close fitting, as she raised her hand in greeting, it clung to her body, and I thought she was nearly naked underneath.?

*Good God what was I getting myself into here.*

Her long brown hair was tied up on her head and held with elaborate decorated hat pins

I had to stop myself looking at this incredible changed woman, I nearly fell over the stone doorstep, holding a wilting yellow rose, I had thought to steal from her garden, at the last moment! And, realising, I should have brought wine, and some sort of a present? As I stood like fool looking at the transformation that stood before me.

*Gone was the frumpy laboratory assistant, and here was a very different Mandy.*

As she had let some of her hair down, and to be set in curl, which fell around her neck and one shoulder. the rest was piled high on her head, and held there set in the in Japanese style, by a comb and elaborate silver pins that were finished by an ornate flying bird a crane?

The rest of her long hair to fall over her shoulders and now wore some of white make up, and what could only be long black false eyelashes? Her cheeks were now soft rose read from her blusher. As for her mouth and lips, she had used her red lipstick that only enhanced their luscious shape, and as I looked into her dark brown eyes, which were now so large and deep, I saw then how afraid I would disapprove of her and at this overt display of a Geisha woman, she had become? And what a transformation, as her eyes were enhanced with eye make-up. So much so that she looked like a different woman. A woman who was full of life and yes here was beautiful Geisha.

*I had to think then as I wondered if Mandy knew what a Geisha was. A woman who aims was to pleasure a man!?*

But then I realised she was not naked, but her undergarment was a long rose ping silk shift. And I could not see much of her body, as it was covered in the dark blue Chinese silk, body hugging Kimono, which was embroidered with red and gold, and even silver, swirling dragons, that shone in the soft light candles I could see, and smell, set on the table behind her. The room was also lit by an oil lamp, that illuminated her silver hair ornaments.

I could smell that there were Joss sticks burning, and one could think her cottage had been transformed into a Chinees home? I was so gobsmacked all I could do was stand there, and try to findthe right words to say, Eventually Isaid.

*"Well now Mandy Jones, I have brought you a simple garden rose, but I see It should be an orchid, or some apple blossoms Are we to be in Japan this night?"*

Then I felt incredibly stupid at these words, but she smiled not rise to her full height and speak.

*"Yes, indeed we are Jake Rutter. I hope you will like the surprise dinner; I have set for you.*

*You see I have recently been to Japan and one day I hope to live there, as they are a wonderful people. But It took all my courage to dress like this the evening. and I must hope you will understand and forgive me. for my surprise Japanese evening.*

*And if you wish to have your Welsh Mandy Jones back. I will go and change. Or you can decide this is two much a surprise for you to enjoy, and leave, and we will never speak of this night again.*

*But please stay? Please do come it and enjoy this experience."*

And yes, I was still trying to recover from my surprise and astonishment that she should want to give me such a wonderful evening, and the obvious trouble she had gone to. And while this was beyond anything I could have imagined. How could I refuse this incredible experience. As I said. Grasping to remember what little I could remember from the book Shogan I had just recently read and told Many she should read it?

*"Konban wa, that means Good evening, I thank you my lady, for such a gift. And I would humbly accept this*

*evening. But I am not worthy, and I am not correctly dressed"*

I bowed to her, with the Japanese greeting of pointed clasped hands.

Then she bowed back and laughed, clapping her hands with delight as her smile of relief was wonderful

*"Welcome ➔ Youkoso, Hello Jake Rutter. You see, I am going to ask you to pretend to be a Japanese Man, as I will be a lady this night.*

*I know how hard these last few days have been for you and I intend to make you forget those blasted books for a while. So, as you can see, I also have some Japanese clothes for you to wear if you will. But it is your choice.*

*And in case you have never used chop sticks? We will eat with a knife and fork and English food this night. If you will indulge me on this as I wanted to give you a gift and a surprise, that will delight you and we can forget we are In Engand for a few hours.*

*If you remember when we spoke, I promised you it would be a different evening! You can change in the bedroom. If you wish, or stay as you are?"*

What could I say or do but agree, and the idea of spending an evening with this incredible woman, who had gone to such trouble to give me a such a wonderful surprise evening. Was both interesting and amazing! As was the change in her appearance and demeanour was in itself an amazing transformation . was indeed an intriguing one.

*I had come expecting to find a Welsh Maid, and had found a Japanese jewel? So, I went into the small second bedroom, to see a single bed and on it was a set of Japanese clothes, laid out for me to use. And to my delight, these were with a photo of a Japanese man, and a description, of what they were for, and how to use them.*

The topcoat was a *Happi*. A grey and blue, short straight jacket, made of cotton, with wide sleeves ,and the description said this was to be worn as a day garment. It has the design of a white Crane, embroidered on its back .

A note said, It is put on like an ordinary jacket , usually leaving the front open for comfort and freedom and to show off one's undershirt, a *Jimbel. A fine body length undergarment and is a soft pink shade that could be satin? It is worn during the summer because of its lightness and be moveability?*

The Jimbel, is worn closed, buy crossing the front panel over the left side, and tried with the fitted cords. The ends were carving solid silver Cranes. This garment is very long and there would be no need of Trousers, and set pants were beside this Jimbel, were some silk underpants, the details called *Fundoshi?* They looked like some sort of a baby's nappy, and I decided to give them a miss, and keep to my Y fronts! Thank you very much!

There were also, some open toed sandals, called Geta that consisted, of a wooden board that serves as a sole which is topped by two wooden supports. The note said was some grip teeth. *The geta are held to the feet by leather straps*

And when I was dressed in all this, I thought my shoes and socks would look stupid if I kept them on *I though the least I could do was to change into these clothes for this evening dinner, and whatever it was going to bring about? I went back into the parlour with some difficulty and not a little trepidation.*

But when Mandy saw me, she was all smiles. As she held up her hand to escort me to the table, The rest of her kimono seemed to move and the dragons were alive in the candlelight, they hid her body as it fell to her naked feet.

*Was she naked under that inner kimono then?* But the truth was she looked incredible. She took the rose to smell it. to save my blushes, I saw her eyes glance to her garden, but she smiled to say. I managed to trip over a raised flagstone, as I almost fell into her arms.

"*Well met Jake, and please do come in, I have meant to get that flagstone fixed for ages .Here let me take that your hand, and those sandals are a real menace. Please take them off if you want to. but how fine you look now.*

"*Yes, please I half stammered will be better off without them, but you look divine my lady , what must I call you this evening?*" I nearly said night!*!"*

Seeing the candle lit room and the table set out for diner and some wine classes. Once again, I cursed my stupidity for not thinking of the wine or a proper gift for her! But the smells coming from the small lean-to kitchen was wonderful, Some sort of stew I thought?

She saw me looking at her with such admiration and renewed interest. As I felt my passion begin to rise in more than one place in my nether regions. It must have shown on my face as she blushed, and she shut the door to my room, which led straight off the fire lit parlour. As did the bathroom and her bedroom. The smells were coming from a small lean-to kitchen. And to move from this awkward moment, Mandy pulled her hand away as said to me.

" Tonight, I am the lady, Mandolin. as for the food I regret that it is a simple Lamb stew with dumplings, simple food. I was going to bring some sushi as a started but then that would not be suitable dish until you have tried it. So, it is all English food my lord Jake. I hope you will like it. I know you are not a vegetarian, and there is a cheese board if you wish it?"

And before I could say anything to break the fear and the ice im my limbs, she said."

"Come Jake I do not bite. will you sit by the fire, and we can have a brandy to break the Ice? But before we start, I must insist no shop tonight! or while you stay here Rutter. can you leave the policeman at the door if you can as this is my weeks holiday as well?

I hope this can be A holiday, and a new start for us both. I want to use to get to know the real you Jake Rutter. You see, I want to be your friend during your stay. But I can be your companion and assistant at work. Can you do that Jake."

Somehow, I managed to smile at what she was not saying, but her eyes were full of emotion and passion.

And then, as I took the brandy goblet, she was holding for me to take. I looked into her mind, to see nothing, but her kindness and warmth in them and then as our hand *touched, it was something else, the, beginning of something promised deep in their dark brown depths, and her warm smile ,if I wanted to see it? Or was that my imagination and need? But I knew then, that if this new relationship was going to have Gods chance of working, I was going to have to stop looking into her motives, and thoughts, or I would spoil this incredible moment as I had done so many times before. I heard myself say.*

*"Yes, please Mandy, that all sounds wonderful, and I promise and cross my heart. No shop talk for our week here then. And Jake is so English? perhaps I could be called* **Aika***. I read it in a fortune cookie once It means a singer of songs.*

She was smiling from head to toe now, as she said,

*"Ho yes, that would be grand, but you are wrong , you see, I speak some Japanese's leant it for my holiday.* **Aika** *it is the name of A singer of love songs! But no matter. Then I will be Aia Mandolin, one who is the keeper of a house. What say you Aika?"*

*"I say I see a very beautiful woman, who is the keeper of this house, Aia. And I am honoured to be here with you."*

Again, she was all smiles as I had agreed to enter into her games this night. But then she became very serious, as she said to me, looking straight into my eyes.

*But I have a request of my own, If this is a dual holiday, I want you to have a long break from those blasted books Jake. So, I want you to stay here for a few days? I mean as a friend of course and perhaps we could take a look at this wonderful countryside?"*

I said nothing then as my heart was pumping so fast as this wonderful woman said what Was just about to ask her if it could be possible? But she took my silence as a rejection. As she went on to say? "

*" You see, I have not yet managed to explore much of Devon, and to do so with a companion would be so much more fun? I wonder if you have been to East Devon .I hear it is a very unspoilt place to explore. Perhaps We can use the cottage as a base. What say you?"*

I smiled to say

*"Yes, I would like that. But I do not drive, Not since my accident?"*

I realised she knew about that. As she was ready for that question.

*"Well, that is true, but we can take a bus or a coach It will be a part of the new experience for me. and one I want to share with a friend. And there are trains to*

*Honiton and taxis. I am sure we can manage if you are willing to let me be your guide.*

I said to her holding her hand now and looking into her eyes to see what she really meant. *Then I stopped myself from delving her, just in time!*

As I said.

*"Well then, my Aia Mandolin, I would like that very much, and then to be able to get to know a little more about my charming host. And now, I would like another large brandy, you see I am such a coward, with women that I like, and You see I need some Dutch courage, to say what is in my heart and mind Mandy my darling Aia You see, the truth is that I really want to become your friend and a companion, for this holiday, and so much more, if you will allow it?"*

*Would she see my true intent, hidden in these words or did she really mean me to be her holiday companion? As all I wanted then was to kiss her and take her to bed! I knew I was taking a big chance, to use such terms of endearment, and waited for her reaction.*

But she got up to go to the sofa, and placed our refills on a side table, as she put her hand down beside her, inviting me to join her there. *Or so I hoped?*

And once we were seated on the two-seater sofa, which was opposite the large stone-built fire hearth that held the open log fire. Mandy was silent for a long time, as I also was mesmerised by the flickering flames. But before she could speak to me there was rumble of thunder, Which was just a little two close, as the storm was about to break.

*And then, Mandy, virtually jumped with fright, and came so close, to me as I realised, I could put my arm around her, which I did. But then, and despite this comforting gesture, I realised that Mandy goes still rigid with fear, as her face had gone white with fright, and hands were trembling.*

As she said with some fear in her voice.

*"I am so sorry Jake; I know it is silly of me to be frightened of lightning and thunder! but I am terrified of storms and lightening. I have been so all my life. Ever since I was foolish enough to take shelter under a tree. You see, it was struck down, and I was nearly electrocuted. But I like to feel you are close to me now? Can you hold me tighter?"*

What could Isay or do but obey. I had managed to put one hand on her left breast. As she said.

*"Yes Jake ,how strong you are? But that is quite tight enough thank you. and I am feeling such a silly, and stupid woman now. So perhaps we should eat our supper while we can still do so?"*

So, our Tait de Tate, was cut short, and we got up and went to the table to eat the meal, to the sound of the now distant rolling thunder and rain. And when we had finished and back on the sofa, we had another brandy, Mandy said.

*"Look, it Is no good! I cannot try to pretend to be a good host now the storm has come Jake. I am sorry, that we must cut our first evening so short, But I am going to bed and hide under the covers! So will you turn out the lights and deal with the fire. There is a fireguard in that log cupboard.*

As another crash of thunder cracked virtually overhead as Mandy almost jumped out of her skin, and knocked what was left of our drinks, went flying, and we were covered. Then as we both tried to mop up the mess I was dapping at her dress with a napkin, so hard, that her kimono was pulled away, leaving one deliciously rounded breast exposed. Then I stupidly tried to pull the satin 'material closed and found her warm Breast in the palm of my land.

> We both stopped stone dead then. Frozen in the horror of this moment of intimacy, as I felt as if I had on electric

shock run up my arm and I knew then how much I wanted to keep a hold this wonderful breast

*But then a Bolt of real listening lit up the room and now Mandy was in my arms her head and hair now all wry as the hair tumbled to her shoulders, I hear her cry out in fear as I held her tight to my chest Try to think of the words to comfort her, and then feeling her terror, as she tried to bury her face onto my chest.* I became very aware of fact has then these Japanese garments were so thin, and here and now my hand was on her naked back. And now my own Body was reacting to the warm flesh and as I held her to me, I managed to whisper, my voice full of passion and wanting, I managed to say,

*"Mandy my darling, you are safe with me. Please look at me, let me kiss those fears away. it is only a storm you silly thing. It will pass soon. there is no need to be afraid while I am here."*

All she heard was that I called her a silly thing!

So, instead of staying cradled in my arms, I felt her trying to pull away, offended to be called a silly woman and, she managed to get to her feet, and the moment was gone. She was once again, the competent laboratory technician, and fully in charge of her feelings now. As she pushed me away and jumped up, to put as much distance between us as she could. And now I saw just how angry she was at my words and embarrassed at my clumsy attempt to console her! But she would not look at me as she said in as calm and hard a voice, as she could muster?

*"I am so sorry for my stupidity Jake, but I really am scared of this storm, and I hope you will forgive my schoolgirl fears. But I must thank you for a wonderful evening, Jake. And for joining in with my fantasy so well.*

*And this is not the end I led planned for us my darling man. But I am going to bed before we ruin this wonderful evening, and doing something we will both regret in the morning*

*So, I would ask you to be a gentleman now, and go to your Room, while I still have the courage, and will, to ask it.*

*Please let me thank you for this night, and how you have made me a very happy geisha?"*

I smiled and said to hide my disappointment,

*"Yes of course and I can only hope that there will be other such nights my Aia Mandolin?"*

Then she turned. and gathering what was left of her torn clothes, and dignity, she went to her room, shutting the door as firmly as she could. Leaving me to deal with the candles and the fire guard. I went back to my room and single bed, a very disappointed and confused man, and now my only release was to let out my frustrations in the normal way, that was my only sex act that night!

*As I tried to think of what might have been.*

However, It was much later that night, I heard the crash of Thunder overhead, and saw the forked lightening fill the small window in my room. So then, was my bedroom door flung open, and Mandy was there, but this time she was wrapped up in her duvet, but as far as I could see, she was naked under it?

Then there was more lightening, and before I could say or do anything, she was in my bed shivering with fright and seeking the warm of my side of the bed and my body.

And now I was wide awake, in every sense of the word! As my whole body was tingling with surprise with my pent-up passion, and I knew my stupid cock, was not going to obey my will and behave itself. As Mandy said in a voice that was also deep with passion.

*"Just hold me, Jake. just hold me tight as you can. I am so frightened. Please hold me safe!"*.

*And that was what I triedto do at first,* As then, she curled her body against my back, I tried to put my arm around her naked body I tried to ignore her warm naked flesh, and the bulge of her breast in my hand, so then did my erection manage to brush against her bottom.

*But this page is not the right place to speak of our love making in such detail. Suffice it to say that the first time was just pure passion and need ,so wonderful and complete as we found a way to fulfil all our desires, to enjoy every moment of our first lovemaking. It was only later, we were able to kiss and talk, and try to discover each of our likes, and dislikes and leave it at that.*

It was later that we were ready to try agin, then we showered and slept, until Mandies alarm went off in her bedroom.

She turned over to say,

*"Let it ring, We are both on holiday remember. I was stupid not to turn it off... And now you know what a great lover you are. What say you that we do not leave this bedroom today?"*

So, it was instead of touring the East Devon, we spent our days hidden away in Jasmine cottage, until the real world came looking for us. The day, I got a call from the office, and to learn that the rest of my holiday was cancelled. And they needed someone with my special talents. As I was required to track down a child molester, who had taken a young girl from her school playground! A call that I could not ignore, and I told Mandy so giving her a promise I would ring her, to let her know when we could meet again.

But then my life became so hectic and impossible, I found it was a week later, that I was in any state of mind to think about Mandy. But when I rang the cottage I only managed to speak to her answerphone. I know now, I should have gone to her, but that was not possible then! And when the University, I was to hear that she was gone away and there was a letter waiting for me at reception. It was then I awoke from this incredible dream, to find Mandy had left me a note.

*Jake.*

*When You did not Ring, I rang your office to be told you were still away on leave and you had left a message, that you were not to be disturbed. Not for any reason?*

*So, I know you do not wish to see me again, Not out of work anyway.*

*So, I have gone back home for a few days to see my parents. But I love you*

*Jake Rutter and this week has been wonderful, and special for me.*

*But I know I tricked you into agreeing to do all this that night of the storm and go along with my fantasy dream!*

*And you can walk away now if that is your wish, and with no hard feelings. I know now you lied to me about having another case to deal with.*

*But If you want me to come back to the books, then all you need to do is ring and I will come running.*

*PS I promise you that I never slept with Higgins.*

It took me a long time to decide what I wanted to do about her letter! *All I knew was that I wanted to see her again and tell her what was in my heart and how much she meant to me. And every time I re-read her letter, I cursed myself for a stupid fool, not to ring her that next day and explain that I was needed on a case and there was no telephone or mobile I could use.*

*Some say that Duty can be the death of love. But I am in love with Mandy Jones and love can also be the death of duty. And now I had allowed my duty to destroy my one chance of a life with thewoman I love?*

But that day, I had been called back to work and Barton and I, were evolved in the kidnapping of a young girl of only eight, and when Jasper and I had found, the barn, we saw how she had been raped and then then murdered. So, then any thought of Mandy, went out of the window, as all I wanted to do was to help catch the evil Bastard. That desire had consumed me for three days, as I had to put aside these wonderful day and evening with Mandy. As the reality of this case, had managed to sweep her from my mind.

But once we caught the man who had committed this evil deed. A school caretaker! So then was I was caught up in another case and the Next.

*Even so. Each night I would read her letter, to think of my promise, and promised myself, I would Ring for the next day.*

But, the next day, was four weeks past, and then when I rang the number of the Jones household, I was to find I was four weeks to late! As her mother assured me, in no uncertain terms, that I had broken Mandy heart.

*."Jake is it. are you the Bastard who broke my girl's heart. Well, she has gone away see. She is in America my boyo. And thank god for it! And from what she told me about what you do, poking into people's lives all the time. That aint no proper job if you ask me"*

*I can only hope you are satisfied. A policeman are yus. Well, yus' are not fit to lick her shoes ..so you are.*

*An' I only hope she can find a proper man, and someone who will love he see. An' not an English git like you, Jake Rutter. And you can put that in your policeman's helmet, and go to hell, For all I care. And if you come here, we know how to deal with a dirty rat like you!"*

With that the phone went dead, and I had lost my only contact with Mandy? Well, If I was down, but not out, as far as Mandey's family were concerned? I knew that the university would have her details and they would know if she was still in the country, or in America?

*And now, I was going to find her and try to tell her why I could not call and at least try to apologise in person.*

But when I want to enquire at the university office, and not the History department, I found they were not going to give me any such personal Information, and when I made a fuss, asking to speak to Susan, I was directed to the Vice Principals office and I knew just how much they disliked me, and my unwanted investigations.

So, I asked if I could at least speak to Susan who at least knew that I was staying with Mandy and was still expected to continue helping them with the books.

It was then the receptionist told me Susan also was on holiday, Somewhere in Spain! And then she had the pleasure in telling me that Miss Jones, had now resigned her position in the History department, and she was on her way to America, to accept, a long-standing appointment, at Harvard!

On seeing that I was not intending to go away, she thanked me for my help, but now they had found someone who was a professional, to do the translators. She said she had been told that I had to return to my police duties. And my day pass had been revoked"

So, I was just about to leave the building when Susan game running after me, and out of breath, she was blocking the doorway. she was very tanned, and she was holding a suitcase, with a Virgin Airways sticker attached. Evidently, she was back. As she grabbed my arm. She said to me, while gasping for breath.

*"Stop Jake, I saw you from my taxi. I thought it was you! So, please come inside we need to talk.*

So, I went back in after her , and as we sat in the reception hall, Susan told me the why and when where and when Mandy had gone to America, And now she was delayed at the Exeter airport for some reason. and it was later this very day, the connecting flight to Heathrow was fog bound! from a flight from Exeter airport!

As she said, she had spoken to Mandy to say her goodbyes, only this morning. Susan took my hand to say. Her words full of hope and excitement.

*"Look Jake, Mandy told me everything, about the night of the storm, everything about the lost Holiday. She waited and waited for you to ring her.*

*So, after two weeks, she knew you were not going to want to see her again! Then there was her stupid letter! And then the call come from America!*

*So, she decided she must make a clean break with us all.*

*You see, you broke her Heart Jake Rutter and now she is trying to forget you. But she is taking a plane from the Airport. It leaves at four this afternoon for Heath Row! But why here you come today, all days? Do you want to see her? Well then it is not too late?"*

My mind was working frantically to take all this in, and I knew now that I do still love her, and that I must at least tell that. Then what Susan was saying, broke into my confused mind.

*If you are quick, we can still catch her the airport? But I warn you Jake rutter , I will only help you, if you really mean what you said on the answerphone?"*

The look of hope that was filling my heart, must have shown on my face as |Susan said then.

*Look I have my car in the Carpark here, if you want to see Mandy again, I will drive you there it is only a short half hours' drive, we can catch her before she boards the flight.*

*But before you say another word, be sure you want this, as I do not want you to break her heart all over !"* I said, with as much feeling as I could muster.

"Yes, I am sure, and if she will let me explain, You see Susan, I am going to ask her to marry me!"

We said little as we drove to the airport , perhaps because I did not know what sort of reception to expect from Mandy, if and when we met?

*I was remembering what her mother had said to me on the phone, and the deep bitterness of her words. And perhaps Mandy would feel the same?*

As for Susan, she realised just how much this means to us, and she was willing to respect my privacy, as we drove into the airport car park, she said.

*"Get out here Jake and find the departure lounge. I will park up, and wait in the car for you both? Or take you back to Exeter!"*

As I looked around the departure lounge, and at first, there was no sign of a woman who could be Mandy , and then, I saw her standing in the check in queue.

*She was just about to pick up her heavy luggage bag, and put it onto the trolly, when I managed to get beside her and say into her ear But using my police voice.*

*"Well Miss Mandy Jones, where do you think you are going with that suitcase?"*

Then in a much lighter tone and my words full of hope. *"Look miss I think that It is far too heavy for you, I will have to take care of that Miss jones.*

*Then Come, with me Miss as you are under arrest for fraud my darling. Will you let me carry it for you? Will you come and sit with me and let me tell you how much I love you?"*

So it was, that we had coffee, and watched her plane leave without her, and to my everlasting delight, I found the courage to explain why I had not called her, and then I managed to propose to her, and to my joy and delight she said yes, and we kissed, not caring who was looking.

*So it was, that Susan drove us back to the cottage and left us to make up for lost time.*

It was after we had managed to make love, this time it was indeed a loving embrace and as we lay beside each other. I was still lost in the memory of our love making, but I realised that Mandy had been silent for such a long time, looking at the ceiling of her bedroom?

Just lying on her back with a sheet pulled up under her neck. A defence against a further amorous moves on my part?

But the truth was we were both trying to think about what we had done now, and what she had said to each other in the airport. *And now we were engaged to be married, although we had no ring as yet?* Both silent for a while as we tried to come to terms with the idea of a marriage, and a new life together.

For my part, I was delighted just to have her beside me, as I was so in love with her, I was still finding it amazing that she had said yes please Inspector .

I was trying to think of a way that I could allow her to have second thoughts, thinking that no woman in her right mind, would want to spend the rest of her life with a geek like me. Finally, I said, what was on my mind

*"A penny for your thoughts  Mandy, my love, I see you are not here with me in your bed. Where are you now my darling?*

Then I bit the bullet, to sit up on my left arm and elbow and to look at her in a very serious way, and to say to her something about our future, while I had the courage.

*"Mandy darling, I want to say something, and you must keep looking at the ceiling,  because if I see your face, I will see a lie. But the truth is that I trapped you at the airport. And I caught you at a weak moment, and the truth is that we both have been caught up with our feelings, and now we are lovers.!* I almost choked at that thought, and how freely she had given herself to me then

*But as for marriage, well that is for life as far as I am concerned, And that is different matter. And I think I should  ask you again if that is what you want? But not now. But when you have time to consider the life I live as a Police officer, and the things I must do .*

*You see I know from experience, that when one must put duty before love, well it destroys them both.*

*But I want you  to know this Mandy Jones, I love you with all my heart and I will try to put you before my duty to the police. As it was my duty that drove us apart…When I left you before.*

*No please do not say anything now, But I have thought hard about this, and I see I must resign from the force if we are to be married. There I have said it."*

Again, I knew that she was finding hard to speak.

Then she turned to throw the full weight of her naked her body at me ,wrapping her arms around my neck as we both crashed back onto the bed, it gowned with the force of the impact.

Then she was kissing me, and I felt her tears on my face. But then she managed to get up to stand by the bed now naked and full of fury, or so I thought. As she said.

*"What sort of woman do you take me for Jake Rutter. Do you think I sleep with just anyone who asks me to marry them. I was brought up to be a good chapel girl, so I was. And save myself for the right man, so I was! I always knew I would know the right man when I met him. A man who I could love and be loved. both as a wife and as a lover and friend. I do not care a toss about what you do for a living you silly wonderful man. All I see is the caring and intelligent man that would want to give up everything he has built in life for me!*

*But If you are having second thoughts, Jake! Well, you had best leave this place while you can still walk. Or we could make love again Booyah, and. Husband to be. So there."*

So, it was we had a late breakfast, and over coffee, Mandy told me what had been troubling her that morning. It was my intention to give up job. Then as we held each other so close, we were realising just what this new life would mean for us both, as Mandy would want to go back to the university, or even to her new position in America?

That was indeed a possibility , and I knew, I could not fit in there! As my job in the canine unit, was one I had come to enjoy and even love? *Perhaps not the occasional the horror of it , not so much. But any thought of being parted from Jasper was almost too much to bear?*

So, I ask her what was really troubling her this morning, and finally, she told me she had an answer.

*"Well Jake my darling, You have said we could have a problem with it is your life in the police force! But I know how much you love your work in the canine unit, and especially Jasper. 1. But when I think of your other work, and when you are expected to look into the evil world that you see then?"*

Here then was the crux of her hesitation to set a date for our wedding.

*" Well, my dear man, I know you will say you can keep that horror away from our home, and children. But I have seen what that can do to the other policeman, and their wives. So how can I ask you to give it up for me my*

*darling? So, in the light of day, I am sorry Jake I see we should not be married quite yet. That does not mean we cannot stay engaged and wait for a year or so, and until we are free of these blasted Books? Can you do that my love?"*

Before I could answer she went on to say to me, almost in a reverent whisper.

*"You see, I will only love one man, and I will never wish to be divorced. as that is against everything, I was brought up to believe in by my mother who stuck buy my Da,' through thick and thin*

*Yus must see that I do believe that. the act of marriage, is a sacred bond. any wedding vows are made to God and are sacred. You see I am just a simple Welsh maid after all."*

I saw then, how hard that was for her to say all this then, as she turned away, so that I would not see the tear in her eyes, at this declaration of her love and beliefs. That any marriage is for life! A belief that was not such a common promise these days! And now I knew what I must do and speak. I took her hand, and she turned back to face me, and now I saw how determined she was about this marriage.

*" Well now we have it my darling, and I see how important marriage vows are to you. and so, it should be for everyone!*

*But we do not live in the Welsh hill my darling. ,so yes, I will agree to a long engagement. We will wait until we are both sure of our feelings and willing to commit to each other and have a family.*

*But I cannot bear to be parted from you and I want to be able to love you in every way possible. So, we will have a modern engagement living together and with no fear of conceiving children. We could live together here in your cottage, or we will but a home. You see, I am quite well off financially, and we could have a good life together. If you can live with that .And perhaps we need not tell the stuffy University about that part?*

Mandy pulled away to reach for a handkerchief, to hide her face, and the tears on her cheek, and as we were both still naked, she lay down beside me to say.

*"Yes, my lover! I can do that, and we should make love now! As for children, these days I can take a pill see!""*

Then it came to me, I would not have to give up the police force altogether, and perhaps they would let me leave taking Jasper with me? It was going to be wrench, but if it allowed us to have a life together? I was going to give it a try! Ad I was glad to have this settled between us. But I was wrong.

As it was the next morning that we were due back to our task at the university, as Mandy told me of another idea, she had thought of about our work situation that would suit us both .

*"Jake my darling does you think you could work for the police part time And not become a part of these horrible investigations, could you just work with Jasper and leave the gruesome bits, to someone else?*

*You see, I am revolted by that part! And to think of the horrible things you have to deal with then. As I fear we will also become a part of that evil, and it will drive a big wedge between us. And yes, I know all too well from my father and mother that that duty to our farm was the very think that killed their love, as I saw my mother became his servant and work slave .*

*You see there is an opportunity for a senior man to head the security division at the University. And I think if you were to apply it would suit you. I know it would mean giving up the Police force, And it is a lot to ask of you, but I have been awake all night worrying about this, and I am sorry Jake, but I could not marry a policeman after all! Especially one who could read my mind!"*

I was stunned to hear this admission and so disappointed as she pulled the rug from under my hopes and dreams and she saw this reflected on my face as could not look into my eyes, Looking at the floor. But now I realised that she was right in that.

*"Well then, Mandy my love I hear what you are telling me now. But what does it matter what job I have, as that still leaves the mind melding and my ability to read what a person, has done or intends to do.*

*And with all this talk about love and marriage, I had forgotten that you see. And I know now I could never live with you, and see what you were thinking's we made love? So that is a very big problem for us?*

Mandy had been thing about this, as she said.

*"Yes, that is a very big problem, are you telling me that all the time we were making love in bed you were reading my mind. How could you?"*

My answer came out without me thinking of a reply. *"Noo of course not Sometimes I can section off that part of my brain. I had to learn how to do that when my emotions were so strong or go mad, with what I had seen and was feeling. I learnt how to do that with the help of a hypnotist. So, I promise you that I never tried to delve you then.*

She said,"

"Then you can shut that part of your brain down Can you do that when we are together?

So now it was possible we had a solution if I could shut her thoughts away like that.

*Well as for that problem my love, there is a simple solution.* then come the lie. *-what if I can shut off that part of my mind to you. And there is a way you, see? I was taught how to shut away this part of my brain at the mental hospital. It was the only way I was able to shut out the madness. so, there, we are a way to live together if you want to do that still? As for the police and the canine unit I could ask for a transfer to the normal branch.*

*So perhaps we should wait before…Before we buy a ring. And as for the job at the University. We could ask for an application form as the truth is I have only continued on with the canine unit because of Jasper. But he is due for retirement and perhaps we could adopt him?"*

She said with her eyes full of her tears

*"Would you do that for me Jake. What a wonderful man you are, and that will allow you sometime to work with us on the History books again I have spoken to Susan and the Principles, it seems the person they found for the translation work was not suitable and she had failed to do anything with Leofric's books.*

*So, they want us back to work as soon as we can and this time. I will be at your side and make bloody sure everything we do with them will not harm you.*

*And that will allow you sometime to work with us on the History books again I have spoken to Susan and the Principles, it seems the person they found was not suitable and she had failed to do anything with Leofric's books.!*

Isaid,

*So, they want us back as soon as we come back from our Holiday. We will not speak of our engagement. As Ido does not want that lot prying into our private affairs and in that way, we can go on living here.*

*As long as we are careful not to be seen, coming, and going together?"*

Mandy said she was not sure we could do that for very long and she said she wanted to tell Susan at least as it was going to be hard enough to maintain our silence in the History department, and she was sure to slip up. So , I had to agree to go along with that condition.

*"And as for the Security Job, I will look into it. I promise."*

*"Ho yes please! And I want to kiss you again, and never stop!"*

\*

It was our first day, of our holiday we went back to work at the University, we had spent our week's honeymoon touring East Devon, being based at the Grand hotel in Sidmouth, and were to find just how wonderful; and interesting was this part of East Devon, as we had now brought a car that was an new Ford Focas, an automatic that Mandy was willing drive, and we set about finding such treasures that East Devon would offer us. The belated holiday we had planned before the storm came.

At first, we stayed in Lyme Regis, a looking at the Jurassic coastline, and the inland countryside, touring the Blackdown Hills, that were a line between Devon and Somerset. To see its fossil beds and , seeking our own fossils, on the crumbling cliffs, at Lyme.

Then, on to Beer, and enjoying a crab lunch, and cream tea right on its pebble beach. As Beer a lovely unspoilt fishing village near Seaton. and then to enjoy guided tour of the Beer Quarry caves and to learn something about stone quarrying, and how hard it was. But it had kept the village alive, over the years. As the stone was sent all over Britain for our grand buildings. Then to learn these other small villages by the sea, was also used by the Devon smugglers of old.

Then To go to Exmouth, and take a ferry boat up the River Exe, back to Exeter, and then to return to Jasmine cottage refreshed, and ready for a new life, and to plan our marriage .

But to my surprise, *and not a little relief,* Mandy said she was willing to wait for that. To become engaged and wait until we were both sure that that was indeed the right move. And to give us time, to settle into my new job.

*The post advertised, as head of security at the university. And I had applied with excellent references from the police I was successful. A nominal position, and as I had an excellent team and deputy, they agreed to allow me also to work on the books, most of my time. Knowing that when the translations were to be published, they would be an incredible source of revenue for the University and bring worldwide recognition to Exeter.*

As for the police, I had been allowed to take early retirement. With a secret promise that I would be available for *special duty* when asked. Then I could keep Jasper as my own dog, and I had also said I would allow him to be used by Barton from time to time.

*What I had not told Mandy was a part of this arrangement as she knew that I was going to be his handler then and we were not going to have to deal with any of the murders or serious crimes. So, in a way, she* saw that I was still a part of the Canine unit, but as an advisor.

\*\*\*

*Back to work.*

And now this was our first Monday, and we were going to meet Susan again in the History department, as she was now the head of that department, and there was a new vice chancellor, who was going to give us all the help and assistance we needed.

*So, things were looking up in every way. And we had taken Jasper for a long walk in the grounds that morning, and now he had his own kennel in the car park where he was safe and warm, and we could visit when we should break time. But even that, had a draw back as I had to stop the other guards spoiling him with treats…*

And once we were once again all together in the reading room, it was Susan, who said that she wanted me to take a different approach to the reading of these books, as she said.

"*As you know Jake, We have not been able to read anything more of book four since you left them. And while we were about to learn something more about the blessing and the curse that you think was responsible for poor Professor Higgins heart attack*

*And if that is the case, I do not want you to risk doing the same. Moreover, I have had time to look deeper into the histories of the Godwinsons, and even the man Wulfnoth Child, who was Godwins father!*

*And what I have found out is both amazing, and interesting. So much so, I want you to take a look at Book one, and to see if what I have discovered can be true?"*

I said nothing, as I also, was concerned at the bad vibes coming from that book, as I waited for her to say more.

*"You see Jake it was Godwin, and his father Wulfnoth, were the family of Saxon shipwrights at the time of King Aethelred, with a yard at Bosham. It Wulfnoth was made the kings master of ship by King Aethelred and given some gold and men, to build him a fleet of longships that he could use to fend of the Danish raiders, as he was tired of paying them the* **Danegeld**, *to stay away from the English shores!"*

I told her that I had read something of this, at my collage, and that that was when there had been great falling out, and Godwin was forced to leave Engaland and that is why he went to hide in Denmark in the first place.

It was then that Susan said,

*" Well then you should know that there was a lot more to his story, and one that involved one of the evillest people of these times Eadric ,The earl of Mercia Eadric Streona, and he was both a traitor, and jealous of the powers that the Godwinson clan were gaining in the land.*

*And that it was this man who conspired to bring the Godwinsons down. But these are the bare facts as we can hope that these books can reveal so much more to us."*

So, I went to pick up this first book, was titled The Story of Wulfnoth Cild? And indeed, I felt it was completely different feel to the other books. Where they were warm to the touch, the was quite cold, and I wanted to put it down unopened. And then I remembered that Jasper, had not wanted to touch it. Susan saw my reaction and said,

"But there is another reason to take a look at this book, you see, It is a family secret known too few at Jelling. A very old family legend, that said that Wulfnoth was one of the Fey race of theVolva people, and he had the use of blood magic! So that is another reason to start with book One now, and try to see what we can find in it? And before we go blundering into further trouble with the rest of these books. What say You Jake?

I was thinking that we needed to take a lot of care now and some extra precautions ,if and when I managed to read what Leofric handwritten here?

But first we must see if I can do anything with this fist book. Indeed, I also was intrigued to do that, as Jasper had indicated that this was going to show us something that had upset him, when he had smelt it. So, I asked Susan what more she had found out about this man Wulfnoth, and the early years of his Son Godwin, who was to become so powerful, and famous, in these Saxon times. She looked at her notes to say,

*"Well, he is still something of a mystery, and the answers only have, are to be found Bishop Stigand records. as he lived when Leofric, became involved with The Godwinsons. We do not for sure who Wulfnoth parents were. We must hope Leofric can tell us? And that the ring will be able to help with him and his son Godwin, and some more about his Danish wife Gytha. And their incredible children?"*

I knew all this, but now I knew what it may cost me and now I had to think about Mandy and my new life with her. So, I said to them both.

*"But if Leofric wrote this book, we should try. As I now know that the sword we found, once belonged to Wulfnoth Child. That is the name on Book One is it not?"*

It was Susan who answered that question.

*"Yes, it is, And As you know Jake, you told me that my family came from Jelling in Denmark. But I have looked them up to find that we have a legend about the burning of the first Christian Kirk there! The time, when Gytha came there with Godwin. We saw some of this in Book Four, and the mention of a curse, did we not?"*

It was Mandy who had become ever more concerned at what was said now, and she said to us her fears showing on her words and face.

*"Look Jake Rutter, If this is going to be dangerous, I think we should consider just how this is going to work!*

*So far, we have brought you out by the removal of the ring. But what if that does not work this time. I do not want to lose you my darling, and perhaps we should stick to what we know works?"*

*"Yes, and that was such a strong vision, and one that was not complete before I was pulled back to this room. So, you are right to be concerned about what we are going to read about the blessings Mandy.*

*But I agree with Susan here, that we must look at Book One, and make sure you can pull me back from any danger. I suggest we have code word that we could use and one that works both ways.*

*If you hear, or see, it typed on a page, you must do everything you can to bring me back and conscious.*

*It must work in reverse to tell me to break the link . will use and you will know, I am in trouble. Then you must bring me out."*

Mandy said, *"Well then, it must be a word that could not possibly used in Saxon times as we will not recognise it as being a cry for help?"*

*Yes, I see that, but it must be short and sweet, Will Mandy suffice?" "No, there could be a Mandy then, how about Rocket?*

*"No, they had fireworks that were seen as a rocket! Blast it how hard can this be. What about a person name No that will not work. We need a modern name. Like Wikipedia. Surly that will serve?"*

*"Too long. But Wiki could do? So, we can hope that there are no people called Wiki in the past then.*

*Mandy said no that will not work. It is a Japanese word No that is too risky. I have it.*

**Television***. It is a little long, but surely no one will have used it in Saxon times."*

*"Television, it is then. And I know how we can be sure it will work no matter what. You know I can be self-hypnotised. As that was how Simon Robinson, was able to heal my illness. Now I can send myself into a semi*

state and then you Mandy, must implant this word in my subconscious and then no one can alter or erase it."

So, when this was done and tested, we were ready. We know need is the key and I will seek to find the first reference to this search WUlfnoth Cild….

\*\*\*

*Flash, Flash, Flash*

*. The Kirk at Jelling.*

So, it was that Jake was able to send his consciousness to the Jelling Kirke. And this time he was going to try to speak to Leofric and warn him about the Battle at Hastings.

But Gytha said that she had seen the sense in Godwins words, and then, even more surprised to learn that it was to conduct the ceremony was Father Godfrey, the very priest, that Emma had brought with her from Normandy and one of the

Streona clan? When she had asked Godwin about him, he had said.

*" Yes, I know that is not what we would wish But Leofric, is very sick and he lies in his bed, as he has eaten some bad oysters.*

*And now, Oswald is the only Christian ordained priest here, and Canute will not brook any further delay as he and Emma are to leav for Engaland in the morning.*

*But Emma, has vouched for this this man. But I think he had something to do with Aleric, and possibly the death of Edmund in some way? So, I have allowed him to perform the blessing that will keep him this, as here in Demark, So that I can have the chance to question him, about that time, and his service to Emma. So, I fear we must allow this my dear. He is a man of god, and he cannot harm us here?"*

*

And This Is What Gytha Said To Her Confessor As She Told Leofric About The Christening!

*

*"So now Bishop Leofric, you will see why we had agreed to do this, even though most of us were not baptised Christians. But he had said that we must agree to his*

leaving two of his acolytes, Simon, and Petar, who had agreed to stay here in Hedeby, to look after the chapel, and be the first priests there.

"They were two young acolyte priests, that Leofric had brought with him from Winchester, and they had agreed to become Godparents to my son and see that he would be baptised and taken into the Christian world, as Sweyn was to stay here in Demark with my uncles, until he was Five.

Another precaution that my brothers had asked for, so that Sweyn would become a Danish prince, as well as an English Lord. and to ensure he was to be brought up as a Dane?

As for this ceremony, Of course, Godwin had wanted us to wait for Sweyn to be told about your Christain God, until he was older and could make up his mind about the gods.

But Godfrey had told me that if my son is not baptised, his soul will go to Hell, and not heaven! That fateful day I spoke to Simon, and Petar, who confirmed what Godfrey had said and they had said we could come to no harm in Gods house!

So, it was agreed that Godfrey would not do any harm to his benefactor Emma of Normandy and now Sweyn, like Godwin, Sweyn, would have two religions and wear both a Cross and Thor's hammer, as his dual protection.

It was when I told all this to Godwin had relented; it was agreed the ceremonies would take place this day.

*But it transpired that the chapel, would only hold twenty people at the most, and that was without any benches for sitting. And as my people, would need space for myself and my baby, we had to agree to the suggestion that the door of the chapel should be left open, so that our guests could see and hear the service.*

With Canute and his party, Godwin and our bodyguard, the man Fin, were to line the walls of this small Saxon chapel, along with our Saxon house curl Fin. Who was to stand in for Leofric, as Godwins best man, and another to serve as our Saxon Guard. that had come with Godfrey.

Also stationed outside, were the only armed warriors, each with a shield and spear, to be able to deal with any trouble and to serve as the ten named men of our honour Guards. So it was that both Saxon and Danish honour guards were permitted to be with us for protection from any attack on the chapel, as Godwin and Canute were unarmed, as Godfrey had said that this was the house of God, and no weapons can be brought into this holy place.

*But I knew that Godin had a thin piece of waxed butchers' cord with Ivory handles, which was wound up beneath his tunic? A garrotting line was also a deadly weapon in the right hands!*

And our huscarl Fin, had a long thick staff that he said was his staff of office, as it ended in a thick iron knot that was carved to be our new emblem that were two clenched hands.

*But Godwin, had said it would serve as both a staff and a weapon when needed.*

*Moreover, Godwin had insisted that he should have this after I had told him of the warning from Rachel and Rosa; I had said we must be guarded at all times.*

And to get Godwin to agree that our party was not to sit on the front benches, and It was Rachel who was to have charge of baby Sweyn. We were sitting behind her and so to be seated at the front, and ready to hand him over at the right time.

*But sitting there she was ready to be our protector, and look out for any evil presence? And now she was to be at the front of our group, and near to the Font. Furthermore, she had asked that Rosa must be my companion and another of our protectors.*

Another of Canute's warrior, Anlan, had been told to select ten men, who were to be posted outside the door to this chapel could be called on at any time. And while they had no obvious weapons because, they were named as a guard of honour, each man had a standard that flew the Kings pennant, and that had a pointed metal end. And we had agreed that they would line the walls of the Chapel.

*So, when Godwin, heard of this, he said that he must be allowed to do the same. And I had been forced to agree to all this, because of a dream that Rachel, had the previous night that there would be blood spilt here this day – But she could not say whose it was.*

This left room for my two brothers and their bodyguards, and little room for Emma and Canute and his party.

`So, the compromise was, that all the guards would have to wait outside the chapel, and after they had made sure that no Ninja could be hiding in it, And now they were to guard at the only door, but from outside and with their lives.

That left Father Godfrey and his two assistants' priests. Who was to be ready at the chapel.

*But one secret addition to my party was now dressed as a Nursemaid, and Rosa, was holding Sweyn, who was covered in his swaddling clothes. and wonder of wonders, she had stopped him demanding to be fed. Content to be sucking on a finger Rachel had dipped in honey?*

But Godwin had also given me his amulet, that was once his mother's most precious possession and an amulet she had worn at his christening?

*I did not want to think about how I felt about the Amulet around my neck he had given me, but as he put it over my head, so did a feeling of peace and calm descend on my heart and mind.*

Then, as Godwin came to take my hand and squeeze it, I knew he would be there at my side during this ceremony was over and the danger passed?

Yet another precaution was, that Godwin insisted that our family stand away from Emma's men, who were stationed on the opposite isle from us and were there to protect Canute and Emma, and their party. and to we were told leave a space down the middle so that we could make our escape if this turned into a fight between Ulf and Godwin,

As my brothers had been forced to agree to this marriage and this Christian blessing, saying Sweyn should stay a baptised son of Odin, and a Dane and worship their gods.

So, it was thar Ulf had made sure that he and his men were free to get to an enemy, should the need arise.

So here then Bishop was afoul pot of soup that was more than ready to boil over at the slightest opportunity. and we were soon to discover that Oswald was about to set fie to this tinder box!

*As it turns out, we should have looked under the wooden Altar.*

However, Godfrey had come forward to begin the ceremony, as he and his assistant came out of an alcove and stood before us all. He wore his priest's robes, and a silver cross at his chest. He had a prayer book and a candle in his hands and spoke to us all.

*" So did God say let there be light, and there was light. So, I ask that these doors be held open so that all here can listen to my words this day! And so that the one true God, can see only the light of this single candle and know that he is with us."*

With his words there was a low murmur from my brothers then. But they did nothing, as Godfrey's two assistants had placed two candelabra onto the wooden Alta and lit the five candles that were placed ready in each. So now Godfrey was backlit by the candlelight, so his form seemed to grow in size in our imagination?

Then, as he came to stand before Godwin and our child, he placed the Candle he was holding and the book on the stone font. He led an Upside-down candle and an upside-down Cross .As he smashed the light and the candle flame into the Bible, it seemed for a moment, he had stolen the light from the Church as he was mumbling some sort of an incantation, which could defile it protection.

But as no one else had seen anything or made a move to stop him. But in my soul, and as a black hand seemed to grip my heart, I knew then he was intending to curse us with the dreaded Bell book and candle spell. Such a strong curse that was of Satan and not our God.

*But now I was bound up in his power and I could not speak or move, as the amulet, was no Icey cold on my skin*

Godfrey saw my distress and smiled as he took up a jug of what I thought was water, Godfrey filled the font below the rim. Then turning to us, he held the five candle stick up High and to light Godwin and me in its soft flickering Light as he began the ceremony.

*But not with a prayer! As he said, in a booming voice that everyone would hear?*

*"I See You, Godwin, Son Of Wulfnoth And You Gytha, Daughter Of Thorgil Sprakling. I See You, Cnut, Son Of Forkbeard, And I See You, Emma Of Normandy. So Do You Come Here Seeking God's Forgiveness For Your Many Sins?"*

*I heard Godwin growl at this strange beginning, but the priest was speaking the truth in a way, as he went on to say.*

*"The Question Is, Who We Are All Who Dare To Come Here This Day, as we And Stand Before The Lord Jesus. As I only sinners all and even This Child Sweyn, Is An Innocent soul Here. As he was born out of wedlock.*

*Yet Jesus said, come unto me and ask for forgiveness, and so shall it be given. But first, I must tell you a story and a long-forgotten secret. !"*

*Now he pointed at us and then Canute as he was almost shouting now, Spittal, coming with his words of hatred, and lies.*

*"So, it is my secret and yours, Godwin of Comptene! So, this day, I must tell everyone that you Godwin, are a liar and a murderer.*

*Then Let All Here Know That I Come Not To Bless You But To Tell Of The Evil You Have Done To The Earl Of, Mercia, The Rightful King Of Engaland, Eadric Streona!"*

*I thought I heard Godwin growl again, and he had made me let go of his hand as I sensed he wanted to be free to get to this priest. As he had long believed that this man was an evil force and involved with the death of Edmund. A liar and a murderer! But I held his arm, as Godfrey said.*

"As we have seen in these chronicles, it was on this day in 1016, and the kingdom of Engaland that the Witan chose Edmund at Lundune to be their rightful king and not Canute.

But this was done when Alaric, the son of the Queen of Ethelred, had a better claim to the throne.

 So then, did Eadric Streona, try to tell them that Godwin was in league with the devil! But so did Godwin here decide to support the bastard, Edmund, and he forced the men of Lundune to obey his wishes."

*Now, A low murmur of dissent, was growing in the chapel, but somehow Godfrey's words held them spellbound, as he went off with this rant against Godwin.*

"It was after his father's death on St George's Day 1016, Edmund had inherited a kingdom, *that was half overrun by a Danish army. And he spent most of his time trying to defeat the Danes led by Cnut and his Jarls, and so regain control of Engaland.*

*So was this man Godwin, to be seen at the last battle at Gloucester. Where, Edmund said that Godwin, was a foul traitor and a declared outlaw! A man that anyone could kill on sight.*

*But with the aid of his evil witch Gytha , he was pardoned for his crimes and Eadric Streona, was to be blamed for trying to overthrow this false king!*

*The man Edmund Ironside who Godwin was to have murder so that Canute can become king her in our beloved Saxon lands.*

*So must I tell of This was foul act, took place on the 18th of October, and he agreed to divide the kingdom of Wessex. But once again, Godwin engaged in all this, as he contrived with the Danes and Cnut to have Streona killed."*

Now I had to hope that Canute, and anyone close could see the madness that was to be seen flickering in Godfrey eyes, and on his twisted face. As he declared so loudly even those outside must hear his lies and half-truths, as now theywere blocking the doorway,

*I wanted to shout out against this lie and half-truth, but the words would not come. As the rant came to a climax.*

"So Now They Are Here This Day, Asking Our God's Forgiveness As I Say They Were Both Guilty Of Edmund's Death.

*But as for Edmund's death in Lundune, the bishops have tried to hide the actual cause of his death and avoid further bloodshed. But I tell you this, that their records say that it may well have been from his wounds .That our Saxon King Edmund, died at the end of a year of almost continuous warfare and his wounds he had received in battle.*

But I Can Prove That Streona Was In The Right All The Time, And Emma Her Can Speak Of It. But She Also Sees That She Can Become A Queen Again."

*But now I saw that many people were trying to get to Godfrey from both sides of the Chapel, but they could not get their limbs to obey their will. All except Rachel, as she came to me to say.*

"Gytha, you must see that cross, he wears. It is upside down. I fear he is a Mage, and he is using the black magic here this day to mask his evil intent, and to hold us in his power. So, You must use the Amulet Gytha. I can do nothing, as he holds us both in a Compulsion field."

*I looked to see that the cross was now hanging free from his bare skin and now touching his body, as Godfrey looked at it and smiled at me, I felt his evil power envelope me, and then Godwin, and our child, as he went on to say.*

*"So it was that day, and despite Streona's attempts to get justice for King Aethelred, Eadric Streona was unlawfully killed without a trial. So do I name, Godwin, son of the declared outlaw, Wulfnoth Cild, also known to have been A traitor and a murderer.*

*But it is Godwin here who is he is guilty of two murder's now and so many more who were so foolish to believe his foul lies.*

*So do I am priest of the lord God, a man who has told me to come here this day, and to demand justice from you our new King sire! So is it said so shall it be done!"*

*But, while we knew that this rant was full of lies and half-truths, and It was his arch-enemy Godwin of Comptene, who the cause of Streona's death at the hands of Cnut was… As so many times before, Godwin had tried to blacken his already pitch-black name by crediting him with a whole range of extra crimes by his foul lies! And realised that If they could have found some way to blame the dearth of the holy Bishop Lyfing on the Earl of Mercia, they would have. May God rest their souls! So, they would have done so, But I was there, and I could tell it was true!"*

But now, Godfrey was shouting, and spit came from his mouth as he shouted out his vile accusations for all to hear. And then, realising he was near to madness, he calmed down to say.

*"But I Will End His Lies And Attempts Of Deception Concerning The Death Of Our Beloved King Edmund As I Can Bear Witness To What Happened That Day.*

*I can prove this and bring forth a man will say what really happened as Godwin wanted you Canute to come here as our king."*

He was pointing at Canute now., as Oswald went on to say and almost shouting now, as his Spittal fell from his mouth, the madness went on.

"Godwin will say that Aelfric Streona did the deed by hiding in the king's Privy!

Content to sit among the shit and piss, waiting for Edmund to use it and then stab upwards into his vitals, twice with a sharp knife in the private parts and leaving a little bit as a reward for your excellent service.

But once again, this is a lie, as Godwin and Canute well know. And they will listen to the lies That Godwin has told of the murder of a man who was one of the Circus folk. A strong man and a father to an Innocent boy, Tom Brier, who told me of this murderous act! And it is also true, that Alaine was one of the men who had said he wanted to kill the king. But it as Godwin here, who ordered it done.

But all this was known to it Edmunds Danish enemy Cnut, the very man who stands over there, and he has changed his name to Canute. So that he had said was to be his target. But what little evidence that was sufficient to point a false finger at the innocent Circus folk that was when they were speaking against Edmund and when they were half drunk and in a tavern!"

So, here then were more half-truths, but some people were now looking daggers at us, but there was worse to come!

"But I can say that Godwin had Alaine and some of his drunken men arrested, and charged with Edmund's murder., but this was not done in a court of law!

I know now that he crushed this man's skull in his bare hands. So, we will never know if this man was guilty. But is true that our Lord God said Justice is mine sayeth the lord. And This Was An Execution."

Pointing to Godwin, Godfrey said.

"Stand and deny it here in God's house, and you will be forever dammed as a liar and a murderer, Godwin of Wessex."

I saw Godwin had gone deathly white now, and he groaned in anguish and looked to the ground. So, I knew that Godfrey had spoken some of the truth? As he went on to say.

"But Godwin will say that it was an execution that was ordered by the son of Eadric Streona, the man Aelfric has also been accused of this crime of Regicide! But as some say, king Edmund was killed in his privy by a thrust into his guts from the confines of his privacy? I ask you, is it even possible. No Edmund was killed by a red-hot sword thrust into his Arse and entered his heart.

 I Know This Because I also know who also wanted Edmund dead And that woman sits at your side King!"

*Now, there was dead silence in the church, as we all had to understand what this madman said.*

 "You see, It is a truth, that while I am the priest Godfrey. So was baptised with a different name. It Was Aelfric, I Am The Half-Brother Of Godwin, And My Father Was Wulfnoth Cild. The Man Who Sired On My Mother Was The Lady Estrid!

But I see you will not wish to hear that name Godwin brother! As It was Hugh of Winchester, brought me up. And to hate my mother and father, who abandoned me to the foul ministrations and horrors of the priests in this false Gods church!

So, I can prove to you all that I am Aelfric the son of, Wulfnoth Child And the lady Estrid and Godwin is my half-brother, **And I hate him for it."**

Now he had stopped to raise the upside cross and to point at Godwin, Aelfric-Godfrey said, in a more reasonable voice.

"It was thought that the child of lady Estrid and Wulfnoth was supposed to have been stillborn, But that is not true. Because I am the son of Estrid, and my father was not named as the earl Eadric Streona came to my rescue and told me the story of the kings eat hall and how Wulfnoth Cild came to rape my mother.

So, now, I can tell you all that Hugh of Winchester saved me that day. And it was he who told my parents had been told a lie that day to protect the bastard boy from Streona's wrath at being duped and chuckled.

.And it is also the truth, that Estrid had been told he had not survived his birthing, as was Wulfnoth Cild.

And so were we innocent babes swopped over! So, I was taken by Hugh, and the midwife was given another dead child, to show the world, and so that Lady Estrid would believe her son had been stillborn."

Now no one was moving or saying anything like this man who was now to be seen as Godfrey - Aelfric, who went on to tell more of his incredible tale and spread his lies and half-truths.

"But this deception was to unravel when Streona found out, and he had ordered that I should be murdered. But Hugh could not do this to an innocent, so he smuggled me away. He took me away to a hidden church, a monastery, and to find a breast mother who became my surrogate mother until Streona came for me there. I was now ten years of age. It was then that Eadric came to see that this boy was being ill-treated by the monks there, who saw him as someone who had no family. Moreover, those who *looked to have sex with boys would come to his bed.*

*So then did Hugh come to rescue him from the horrors of the Monastery. As Eadric had told him that his real son was such a sickly youth and a bastard, born of a whore, so did Streona, and his wife decided that I was to be raised in secret as his son with Eadgyth was sickly, and it was said he would not live very long? As we shall prove the truth of it Here and now!"*

*Now we were still entranced in the spell that The priest was using, and as we tried to make some sense of his tale of evil and his foul accusations, he pointed at Godwin as he turned the knife in Godwin's heart.*

*"Moreover, Eadric had done this so that the boy could be used against Wulfnoth when the time comes to punish him for sleeping with Estrid?*

*So, I was brought up in secret until Streona can marry the King's sister. Eadgyth But she is so afraid of her new husband, and because of the terrible stories she had heard about what he had done to the people her father needed to kill. Eadgyth had pleaded with AEthelred and her mother. that she did not wish this marriage.*

*But this was in the year 1009, and she is Fourteen years old, and still plays with dolls!*

*So, to her relief, she was allowed to remain in a nunnery, and stay a virgin until she was eighteen. The day that she was taken to the Home of Streona as his mistress, a lady Grace and to live at Kings Llyn with her son."*

*I heard Godwin gasp at these revelations as Wulfnoth had married this woman. Grace. But she and her son died of the plague, as had Wulfnoth! As Godfrey went on to say.*

*"But it was the priest Hugh of Chichester knew of who Aelfric really was! And he had been told to ensure that the boy would be taken from the Monastery, and then he would learn to hate his father. What if he was told every day that he must hate a Man*

called Godwin of Comptene. And he will one day have to kill him?

So, when that boy became a man who had learnt so many secrets as he became the clerk to Bishops. What If I was to find out their secrets and store them away in my heart and soul so that they can destroy the Godwinson.

But I had to bide my time until Godwin had a son that I could destroy and his family and reputation. But As a priest, I was not free to act against them. Not until today and after Godwin had become a murderer.

 So, after the killing Edmund, I made sure that it was said that Godwin had planned Edmund's death so that Canute would become their king. And that this was Godwin's plan all along. What if he goes to Emma in Normandy and tells her his lies? And that it was Godwin who killed Streona at Gloucester?"

What then, if Emma of Normandy had been Eadric's lover, and that was their secret. And that she had intended to marry Streona once her husband was dead and Edmund was to be put aside, and that was why she had raised the question of Edmund's legitimacy. So, then shall Emma be forced to hide Aelfric in Normandy? But here is what Godwin was to discover at Lundune about his new wife and Cnut that day when they were at Wareham?"

I tried to shout out against these lies, but I could not, and the Gods had said she had not killed Edmund, and there was no mention of Streona? Was this true or another lie?

As Godfrey then went on to say.

"So now we are to believe that this newborn baby is the son of the Earl of Wessex. But I heard a different tale from those who were at Wareham at the time of the Hostages', and it was Gytha who was to spend that night with Cnut.

Is that your dark secret, Gytha Godwinson? Is that why you rode to the hunt that day and were to lose this baby, a bastard that was the firstborn of Cnut?"

*Again, I tried to stand, and this time I managed to make the amulet touch my flesh, and its power flooded through me, and then I was free of his enchantments at last!*

 I handed Sweyn to Rosa and threw myself at Aelfric, intending to knock him down. But I crashed into the pedestal, and the font knocked it over, its contents were splashed over my clothes and the robe of this evil man. It was then I realised it was not water, but holy oil!

 *Now my hands were so slippery that my hold on Godfrey's robe was lost, and seeing that I was going to harm him, so did he slide away to go to the altar, and kick at it, sending it crashing to the ground and then all hell was let loose, as the others were now free to move. And they were all trying to escape from this horror!*

But my gaze was centred on the boy or man that was dressed in black, and who had been hidden beneath the altar all this time, as I heard Godwin shout out something about Tom, and Firesticks?

*Then Godfrey or Aelfric took the firesticks from the boy Tom, who scuttled away into the shadows, and lighting one of these dreaded fireworks, he held it up to the roof and with a burst of flame, this red firestick struck the wooden roof, and it logged there spreading smoke and flames its wake.*

Now Godfrey had another, and he pointed this one at Godwin and me, and ours. And as it exploded, it was one of the white ones, and not full of the Greek fire in the red Firestick, but full of sparks and flames.

*Just how Godfrey had these must wait for another day? If we had another day, Bishop!*

Godwin had said that this was a flame and fire; and nothing could extinguish or stop one; it was alight! But this was just as dangerous, and I saw our death coming at us.

*Except that Rachel was there in front of us all, and she had made some sort of magical barrier around herself, and we and the flame hit it its force was spread in all directions.*

I realised that they were not harmed, but the oil had been splashed onto my cloak and hood that I tried to use to protect myself but that was also alight now and I felt the flames on my face, as Rosa was there with bucket of piss. She saved my life then, But I did not feel a thing. As now all our side of the chapel was in flame, and Flames burning embers were now falling from the roof.

*But now Godwin was close enough to Aelfric, and he was picking up a flaming piece of wood, and he threw it at the evil man, who caught it in his hand, and at first, Godfrey laughed as he held out a red Firestick to fire at us again.*

*But then the holy oil caught fire, and he was consumed in a sheet of flame.*

So did Oswald, drop the Firestick, and tried to beat out the flames, but now his face and hair were burning, and he ran along the gangway towards the doors. But Now Ulf was there with a staff, and he used it to knock Godfrey down and then to beat Godfrey to a pulp.

*But now, the chapel was full of smoke, and we were all choking and bumping into each other, as we tried to get to the now unlocked door.*

*We could hear those outside shouting about the fire and trying to open the swollen door, But I, Rachel, Rosa, and my baby were still in the bubble, but our breaths became difficult as we needed fresh air.*

*So, did we hear Godwin shouting for everyone to lay down on the floor? I knew this was a way to get good air in a fire that would beat a low level, as the smoke rises above it. But Godwin had another Idea.*

*He was standing propped up against one of the upright beams, as I saw the roof collapse around Godwin. As I shouted for him to run, so was I forced to leave the chapel, as he kicked up in the arms of my brother Ulf and he carried me away along with Rachel and Rosa?*

Once we were outside, so did Rachel collapse in a heap. The bubble of protection was gone along with the chapel's roof as flame and smoke came from the doorway; I knew nothing could have survived inside it. I looked where

Emma was, looking at me, and her face changed to one of deep sorrow to realise that Godwin was not here. Then Canute came to say.

"By all the Gods, Gytha! What was that all about? I do not know about you, but we could not hear a fucking thing that madman said. And, then he fucking tries to kill us all with those bloody Firesticks!?"

Then he looked for Godwin, and his face went a deathly white.

" So where is Godwin? By the Gods Please do not say he is still in that Hell hole?"

Now there was a wall of flame at the Doorway. But I had no time to talk as I used my amulet to call for help. To call that came from out of the air as a distant voice said.

*"I come, Gytha my name is Jake. I come to tell you that you and all your family are in dire peril. That you will all perish unless*

*you do as I say, and I can help Godwin to escape this fire.*

*But to do that, you must throw the amulet into the fire. It will steal these flames and the air in there. Do it now, or you will be too late to save Godwin and all of yur family will be lost in time. As I shall be.*

* "

Then the voice was gone, and I knew that it was Odin who spoken to me.

I do not know why or how I managed to hear his words as I knew no one called Jak>

But somehow, I got to the door of the Chapel, and I must have been given super strength to run so fast. and push away anyone who tried to stop me or was trying  get in my way.

*All I knew was I was standing at the entrance, and the hairs on my arms began to sizzle and curl up as a voice from the depths of hell said, on the winds of the fire and flame.*

'*NOOOOO. He must die!* ' *It was the voice of Godfrey.*

Then there was wind, but unlike any wind I had ever heard of, as it was so cold and black and then the flames were gone — the heat was gone, and I saw only blackened timbers that would speak of the fire, and the remains of the amulet lying among the ashes The cord was gone but the jewel was still shining and glowing.

*But these ashes were strange and Icey cold. Then I saw Godwin standing there still alive and black with soot, but protected, hiding behind the post. Some of his hair was gone, and I realised that flesh on my bear arms, was now burning, and my face was beginning to hurt me. But Godwin had been spared. his arms were badly burnt.*

But Godwin held the amulet, and he turned to see me, he staggered to my open arms...

*Later, I looked for the amulet or any signs of the evil men, who had ruined the christening! But there was nothing to be seen of any bodies except A smear in the blackened dirt.*

And I had told Godwin that we must be thankful for what Rachel had done that day as it had been her powers, that no one else had heard a word of what Godfrey had said in the chapel. And Godwin refused to believe his lies about me and that Aelfric was his half-brother.

*But one day, I would ask this Hugh of Chichester about this tale.*

As for the christening and blessings of my son Sweyn and the future Danish sons, I decided they would be allowed to choose which they would serve.

And now we have Sweyn and Tostig, and I fear that they will forever remain a Danish Viking, in their hearts and souls, and they will never be able to turn the other cheek or wish to become a Christian. But speaking of my children is risking the fates, and the prophecy may not come to pass.

*As for Godwin, I fear he was changed that day in the chapel. As was I as my face had been so badly burnt, And now I would look like a burnt hag, for the rest of my life But that was a small price to pay and I must thank the Gods for sending their help that day, and that voice which saved us all especially my beloved Godwin when he seemed to be lost to us?*

But then did his burns which took a long time to heal, despite all that Rosa and Rachel could do with their medicine and creams. But they did save his life, as with their Romany skills Godwins burns never turned septic, as so often happens. And they helped him grow some new skin. But his hands and back will never be the same.

*For, in his heart and soul, he had been mortified at what Godfrey had said and done.*

So, I will never see him as Aelfric. But Godwin thinks he was cursed that day, and now he has lost his spark and thirst for life. But eventually, with my help, he healed his body and soul, and we began a new life that was to be in Denmark and a New Engaland as Canute came to deem, and he helped him win over the people there.

And that is why we did not get to the Coronation of Canute and Emma held in St Pauls Church in Lundune, as the burns on Godwin's back and arms had not to healed well enough for him to travel. *And then I was pregnant with our child once again!*

*"So, Bishop, do you ask me to tell you more of my eight children? But the truth is that I shall only tell of their birthing because they are part of the prophecy and the foretelling, and to say more, may prevent the prophecies from becoming true?*

So, I will allow them to speak for themselves when they are older or wish to do so. And for now, I will start with my son Harold...

It was in the year 1020 that Harold, our second son, was born and the year that Canute came to Hedeby in person to see that Godwin was now fit and well, and he needed him and his Sea-

Hawks, for war in his lands here in the North. And ask him to help him deal with those Danes in England, who would not accept his new laws and demands?!

*To help him discover who were now plotting against the crown, send some to their graves, and return home.*

But Canute had severely misjudged my husband, if he thought Godwin would become his spy, and I could see Emma's hand in that request. She wanted Godwin to have to enforce these new taxes and laws for both Danes and Saxons, and then he would find he was not such a popular overlord in this land?

*But Godwin had not seen through her plans, and he had agreed to enforce the new laws and taxes. But, first, he was to enforce the Danegeld, allowing the Danes to leave Engaland and return to Denmark and Norway.*

So now Godwin was to be a Kings Tax collector, as well as a Shipwright! And Canute's enforcer, as he hoped that by using Godwin, a Saxon noble, to enforce the taxes and the Danegeld payments, he would be able to divert the blame away from himself.

*At the same time, I was to stay with my two sons and try not to be so angry with Canute. But now, my brothers were going to be another problem, and I would have to try to save them from siding with Thorkell the Tall! Who was so angry at being sidelined in Denmark that he planned to overthrow Canute...*

*"And now Leofric, I need another drink of that mead wine if you please, As I am as dry as a woodchip. And if we are to speak of my wild sons, I will need something stronger than that! We will stop for some food, and I need to empty my bladder. I will send my husband to you."*

And then, did Godwin and some servants had returned to the chapel with some food and wine and some fresh drinking water, and I was told that Godwin would be free to resume his account of what happened when Godwin,

and Cnut, went to Trondheim, to put down yet another rebellion there...

So, *when Godwin was fed and watered, he put down his jug of ale and asked me what I wanted to know about his sons.*

*"So, what do you need to know now, priest? It seems to me that we are writing my life story here. And I have agreed with my wife that it is a story worthy of telling, and one day perhaps I will be as famous as King Arthur Pendragon. What say you?"*

I said nothing as now my mind was full of the stories of the Knights of the round table.

*"But my friend, if we are to continue with my tale of my life with Gytha in Denmark, I must also speak of the problems we had in the ten years that followed that abortive christening….*

As you know, It was In the year 1020. the year that Sweyn was born, and we have spoken of the horrors that would transpire at his so-called baptism ceremony. Of how my Saxons and I were to be called back into the service of our new King Canute.

But there is so much more that happened to us besides the birthing of our children in the following years, as we were once again heavily embroiled in state affairs. As we both were caught up in Canute's service during these early years of this reign, *That shall be seen as the birth of a new Engaland?*

A time when Gytha was to fulfil the Prophecy which was given to her by the Romany people, and to fulfil the foretelling. That was given to us concerning our children and their fates? A foretelling, that I would have for me to have the eight children, who were to play their part in the histories of both Denmark and Engaland!

First came Sweyn, In that fateful year of 1022 and then a second son Harold nine months later. As being laid up and recovering from the fire, had allowed us both some time to be together, and we made good use of it, to make love, and not war!

So it was that we were granted a healthy girl child, when Edith was born, that spring of 1026!

But still we saw that the gods were not finished with growing our family, as in the winter of 1932, we had our third son and in Demark this time.

A strong Danish child we named |Tostig. I saw even then how much he grew up to love the life of a Viking raider, and looked a lot like Cnut? Not that I dared to say so then!

Two years had passed, when a son that looked like me and we named him Gyrth, 1n that year of 1035. now we had five offspring!

*And Gytha said she was going to live away from me as she was sick and tired of being pregnant.*

*But she had not done so for very long and two years later, we had our Fith son Leofwine, and the next summer along came our last child, a boy Wulfnoth.*

It was the midwife said my beloved Gytha, had been so badly damaged by his birth ,that to have any more children, was going to kill her.

That the truth was that Gytha was now forty years of age, and many birthing's, they had indeed taken its toll on her strength. So, it was just as well that she went back to Demark, to visit Swyen, and Tostig there, with instructions, to bring them both to Engaland to live with us at Bosham

I remember then what the prophecy had said about eight or nine children? but then I had not known about the miscarriage of the first girl child. The daughter of Cnut! Conceived wham he had taken Gyth's maidenhood! *A foul deed of a rape, two years before we were married.*

*But Gytha had used some medicine to end that baby in her womb, and that had brought down the wrath of the Gods on our heads, and the curse that the amulet now carried!*

*But all that was to come to haunt us all so much later.*

But while the future would bring us good fortune, sorrow, and even heartache, which is always our fate.

*But the Yorns of fate had not finished interfering in our lives, as the Girl Edith was to fulfil her chosen destiny . The very child that the Gods had said would one day be a Queen in Engaland, And A secret that I had never told anyone.*

However, in the year 1032, Gytha was to fall for another child, and so was another Girl Gunhilda, her ninth child, was safely brought into this world, Named after my cousin.

*So, the prophecy was true, and who then are we, to go against the wishes of the Gods!*

But I have drifted away from my story and my service to Canute? Of how we Saxon bondsman came to serve a King? So, ask your next question Bishop, and let us be done with all the sty telling."

*** 

*Television. Television .Help me, Mandy. I cannot get back. Television. The ring it is so hot it burns so.*

*The Fires of Hell.*

In the hall, Jake, was still touching the books, as a burst of flame spread across the dry pages, as the ring became so hot, it welded itself to his finger as he tried to use it to speak across time and change the history of the Godwinson timeline!

Jake did so, then all of the four books burst into flame and soon the whole room was full of flame and smoke.

A fire so strong that no one in that room had a chance to escape and died where they stood. burnt in the fierce blaze that was to destroy everything and everyone in the room, and before the sprinklers could operate.

But somehow, Mandy was in the tearoom, and she managed to raise the alarm, and then to be able to hide behind the heavy fire doors, that were to save her life. And taking with her, what was left of the print outs and Jakes diary.

*\*\*\**

## A NEW UNDERSTANDING.

Professor Simon Robinson had finished the pages that Mandy had brought to him that incredible day when she came to see him from the hospital and to tell him how Jake had been lost to her.

*Lost in time?*

And then reading of book four had not been complete as Jake Rutter had been so caught up in this book, and its power Mandy had tried to explain how he had tried to alter their history and then about the fire that was to destroy him and the books.

Moreover, she had also brought his diary and the printed pages that she had said was the transcripts of what Jake had seen in the books, and those few, he had managed to look at.

Now It was three months since her first visit, So now was Jake Rutter was consumed in the fire, or as Mandy believed, still trapped in his timeline, and once the reading room had been restored, they knew that they must give him up as dead or lost, as without the books or the ring, they no longer had a link to the past

And now Mandy had come to him for help, once again and when she had recovered enough from her injuries from the fires, She had come to his Office, bringing with her the diary and the printed pages of these books. Which also were incomplete.

And seeing just how long the reading of these incredible documents were going to take Simon, had cleared his desk and read long into the night and to learn what was at the bottom of jakes and Mandy's troubles. To read some more of their reading of the secret books, the Bishop LEOFRIC, had written and hidden away, only to be found when the History department was renovated.

So then was Simon and Mandy, able to study the saved printouts and read, the how, and why, Jake had tried to use the ring to cross over into the Godwinson timeline !

and manage to speak to Gytha at the church fire. Such an incredible family, that was then, to grow up with Gytha, and Godwin.

But now, he had the photocopies of the four books that Susan had made ,and kept in the fireproof safe, as well as the sword that Godwin had from his father.

And now they were still the origional test ad codex, now Simon also had the translations Jake had made, and these could be used as a Rosetta stone, that he could use to translate these copied book pages.

And to read all four books and to realise that Jake had travelled in time, and changed history, losing his life and those of the people killed in the |university blaze in his own timeline! So now he had a revelation that may be away to get Jake back.

*What If the sword was still linked to this story?*

But he had touched it many times, and he had seen no power coming from it, But Wendy had said that she must have it back as she felt she could reach back to her memories of Jake, when she held it.

*So, was she also linked to these books through her love for her dead husband?*

*But now he also was getting caught up in this mystery and the powers of the Quantum worlds, And before he could speak to Mandy and get her hopes up, he knew he had to find out a lot more about this Multiverse?*

So now Simon, and Mandy, had come to realise that the only proof of all this where the documents and his diary. And Mandy of course. But she was still so traumatised with her loss and grief, she had gone away to hide from the media.

And now he led an idea of what had happened to fate. And if Jake was lost in time. lost in a different timeline, another part of the Quantum world, that was a branch from his and their Golden timeline, and now unless they could find a way to break the bond with that alternative timeline, and Quantum physics, Jake was lost to them.

But things had moved on a lot since he had tried to make sense of that part of physics.

As, only this week there was an article that would explain the latest thinking about the existence of Dark matter, and now, he would have to look it up, and try to find something to help them in its pages, which would throw a light on these terrible events, and if there was anything that could be done to change them in this here and now?

*So, Simon was to discover a possible answer, in a new study, which said that a particle of space time, that links to a fifth dimension, can explain dark matter.*

*And how the previous article has been updated. Concerning the current theories concerning what they called* **"warped extra dimensions"**

*This is an update of a popular physics model that was first introduced in 1999.*

*This Research, Which Was Published In The European Physical Journal C, Is The First To Use The Theory To Explain The Long-Standing Dark Matter Problem In Particle Physics.*

*It tells of The idea of dark matter, which makes up most of the matter in the universe and is the basis for what we know about how the universe works. Dark Matter is like a way that helps scientists figure out how gravity works.*

*And without a "x factor" of dark matter, many things would dissolve or fall apart. even so, dark matter doesn't change the particles we can see and "feel," so it must have other special qualities as well. Jake called this a matrix.*

*So then, here are still some questions which do not have an answer within the standard model of physics, so do some scientists, from Spain and Germany, set down their ideas to explain in their study.*

*one of the most significant examples is the so-called* **Hierarchy Problem,** *the question why the* **Higgs Boson** *is much lighter than the characteristic scale of gravity?*

*This went on to say that the standard model of physics, cannot accommodate some other observed phenomena. one of the most striking examples is the existence of dark matter.*

*So now a new model is being used in the new study to try to figure out why there is dark matter everywhere?*

*Some scientists looked at* **Fermion Masses,** *which they think could be sent through portals into the fifth dimension to make dark matter relics and* **"fermionic dark matter."** *could allow dimension-traveling!*

*These* **fermions** *explain at least some of the dark matter scientists have so far not been able to observe.*

*However as yet we know that there is no viable dark matter candidate, in the standard model of physics!*

*And now, these scientists say, by accepting this idea so have they discovered already this as a fact, that asks for the investigation of Dark Matter as the basis for the presence of new physics."*

*Basically, A Key Piece Of Math Makes Bulk Masses Of Fermions, Which Show Up In The So-Called "Warped Space" Of The Fifth Dimension. This Pocket "Dark Sector"*

*And that one possible explanation for the huge amount of dark matter that hasn't been found yet with any of the* standard model of physics measurements. Is because these fermions that get stuck in a portal to a twisted fifth dimension.

So, Then The Fith Dimension, Could Be "Acting As" A Matrix That Holds The Dark Matter Together?

The question is. how would we be able to see this type of dark matter to prove it? this is the biggest problem with many theories of dark matter right now?

But what if all that would be needed to find fermionic dark matter, in a twisted fifth dimension, is the right kind of gravitational wave detector? So now this type of research is which are becoming ever more common, all over the world. So, We Must See That The Answer To The Mystery Of Dark Matter Might Be Right Around The Corner.

*** 

And now the latest telescopes sent into space are sending back some new information about the newly discovered universes and ancient galaxies, that they are constantly having to revise their ideas about the age and time of the so-called Big bang as they now have come to think there has been many such cosmic events and before the one, we know of. And they are beginning to question the existence of Dark matter. because as yet it has not been found"

And now once again, I found myself lost in the many theories about space and time, and these Multiple Universes, I had to think Jack Rutter, was lost in an alternative reality.

But his body had not been found in the ashes? Had he done so much more than mind meld then? But I knew now that it was possible that Jake had been involved with some sort of inter dimensional timeslip?

And then to discover, that these books, existed in an alternative dimension, and different section of the quantum world. A very different golden timeline to his, and even That of Mandy and Jake Rutter and even myself!

Moreover, it was then I had an incredible thought! Jake had not returned to our timeline and his spirit and body could still exist in the Quantum world? it was possible that Leofric, had indeed set down the true history of his life and times, but as he knew it! And that of the Godwinson s. But it was not a branch line that they were to live and follow!

And now I must certain, of what I was going to say to Mandy. As now I had to think that Jake was lost to us, along with any proof that he was a Time traveller.

And if he could not recover from to this time slip event, because he also is lost in the Leofric story! and one that is very different to theirs!

But what if the sword did still hold some of the rings Quantum energy, perhaps they could use it to bring Jake home?

*Flash, Flash Fash.*

*Jake, Rutter,*

I saw Gytha, throw the amulet into the fire at the very moment I heard the recall from my own timeline!

But I knew then I was not finished with the Godwinsons as I needed to know that I had risked everything and my life with Mandy, here this day, and I needed to know my sacrifice had not been in vain. **Need is the key**

*Ring take me to the battle on Senlac hill.*

*Flash, Flash, Flash. At Hastings.*

*Leofric,*

However, reader, to tell you some more about the Fight at Senlac Hill, I must come back to the life and times of Harold Godwinson.

Be that as it may, in 1065, things were to be taken out of Edwards's hands, as in the month of May, Tostig had come South with those of the North Burghs, who still hated the thought of Edward and his Norman ways, being on the throne of a Saxon Engaland.

*And they had not forgotten or forgiven what king Edmund had done to force the Danes out of their lands.* So then was Harold forced to abandon his plan to wait for Duke William to come to Engand in the South, and go North, to fight Tostig and these men of Norway.

***

## The Road To Senlac,

Harold had not stayed long in Lundune, just long enough to collect his mother, his Saxon family, and his new queen. Leaving five hundred warriors, and ten of his best captains, there to prepare the Lundune guards, should William, get past him at the Coldbec Hills.

*They were to try to defend Lundune and send for help from the ealdorman Thorkell of east Anglia. And pray he will answer their cry for assistance against a very weakened force of Normandy knights, and soldiers.*

But the earl Thorkell, had said he must stay in his holdfasts and protect the Eastern shores in case this attack in the West was just a ruse, and the main attack was to be mounted against him? and Harold had seen that this was indeed a possibility

*So, Harold had told Thorkell to stay put, as the latest reports had said how small Williams's army was now greatly reduced, after the storms had decimated a third of his ships.*

But as fate would have it, the woman and Gytha's convoy were stopped just before Hastings held on Dere Street and at a place called Telham Farm.

A parting of the ways and where Harold and his escort were to go to the battle site only a mile away, leaving the women to go onto Rye?

But it was then that Gytha had asked him to show her this place where they were going to fight. And she would like to thank these brave men who were willing to throw down their lives for a Saxon England, so should the Bishop

*Leofric go there to bless his men who were to be there the next day? And Harold's scouts had not returned, or they had not seen or heard any news of the movements of the Normans.*

*And Harold had agreed to this request, thinking the Normans, were still fighting his brother Leofine and his force, who were trying to delay their progress up The Dere.*

*As Duke William was still making their way up from Pevensey. But knowing his brother would be sure to give them any warning of trouble?*

*Thinking that his men would welcome the sight of his Mother and the lady Edith coming to bless them before a battle, so did Harold agree that they could do this!*

*But the size of his own force, was giving Harold some concern, as he had expected to find fresh troops at Lundune. But fearing that Harold would take them his prisoners for their lack of support at Stamford Bridge, the Ealdorman and the City fathers had shut him out!*

*It was at Lundune that he waited for the promised help from Leofric of Mercia and Godwine of Hereford, all of whom had promised his mother they would get their forces together and Come to Wessex.*

*So, he waited five days in vain for the fyrd of the southern region and their Thegns to assemble at Mitcham. There to be mixed with Harold's husguards, much to their anger and amusement as these folk were no longer used to thing and in the years since Godwin had trained their fathers, they had grown fat and lazy.*

And all this was to change on the first night's camp at the bridge, and a village called Tun-Wells, that also had a holy well and Harold had Leofric bless it, and then to demand that every man must bring its holt waters and to prove it was pure he and his brothers were the first to do as then they would be protected. from harm, or any evil spirits, and if they died, they would die shriven.

*So then did the Queen and her women do the same, and the last was Gytha Godwinson.*

I was told to make sure that I was to be a part of the entourage to take Gytha and the Queen to Exeter, as Harold had to hope that any bandits or traitors, would see the Cross of our lord and they would not risk excommunication by attacking a man of God.

Moreover, Gytha had also come to say that she needed my consul about the coming battle with Normandy.

Along with their considerable baggage and took up three carts while the ladies had a new four Wheeled style carriage that Harold had seen in use in Normandy.

*It had a canvas roof and a back and front with canvas roll-up sheeting that could be used closed or open. They had a mounted escort of fifty huscarls who would be at the rear and front of this convoy.*

*The passengers and the handmaidens were in one cart. as the noble ladies were separate.*

And Gytha, her daughter, the lady Edith, her handmaidens Hilde, and Agatha rode together as it had not seemed suitable to put the new Queen Ealdgyth with them on this long journey, and she sat in the second carriage with her attendants who were from Wales.

The lady Cynethryth, her housemaid Rocola, and Hildy, who was a long-time companion to the queen, were also Mildrith, her body servant. And no one seemed to mind how often Ealgyth was to complain about the lack of springs to her carriage and that it was far too crowded. Or try to do something about it?

I knew that they were not pleased to see the lady Edith, was to be set aside like this? As They were going down Dere Street as far as the turn-off at the road junction that was the port of Rye and then to board the Sea Hawk that was to take them to Exeter.

The captain was her faithful captain Roland of Lundune, who had taken her to Denmark and back, and we knew then that they all would be in safe hands.

But I was called away from my meeting with Gytha, who had asked me to come to eat with her in her tent by a messenger that we both were to come to the king's tent that first night and to give a blessing to his captains and generals and this first council he was to call as our King.

Harold, had drawn a map of the south downs on a hide skin, using charcoal from the fire, showing the Roman road and the towns and *ports, that they, and William could use to take our towns and lands. A skill few people possessed and one he had learnt from his father.*

*There was Ermine street that led from Lundune to York and beyond. The Portway from Chichester to Lundune. The Fosse way is the way west and to Exeter by road. And Portway to Dorchester, as well as the vital link road to Gloucester, Ackerman Street. Watling Street to Dover, and not least Dere street that we are to use to get to the North Trade routes over the downs and then onward to Chichester. While these roads were a great boon for our traders, they were also a route that any invader could use this great network of roads to traverse our lands and take it all piecemeal.*

*Once we joined this meeting, I saw that the Earls and Thegns and their captains were arranged around a trestle table, with some jugs of ale and a barrel set up to one side. Some platters of bread and cheese had been provided for these soldiers to eat, but only the ale had been used so far. Harold was standing at the head with an empty chair beside him, and the*

*Brothers and the earls were seated on his left in order of rank, and the captains and thegns were on the right. I was about to count them when Harold told his mother and me.*

*"I see you, mother, and you, Bishop, And I know you must know most of the people here but not all, so please let me introduce them to you as these are our new generals and captains. And then I want to tell you how we will throw William and his Normans back into the sea?"*

We were still looking at the map of Senlac Hill and the High Ridgeway that would run across the South Downs with the marks that Harold had set down that showed us the valley of Powder Mill Fields, the farm at Telham and the roads from the mill stream and the two hills there. He had marked the woods and marshes, and the battlefield was to be seen between the roads from, the Coldbec, Sedlescombe and Ninfield hamlets.

There was another cattle path behind Coldbec hill that the drovers would use to take their cattle to the Bridge at Tun. A cross was marked on the top of the two hills, and some wavey lines were drawn in the valley with an arrow showing the route William would have to take from Rich Burg. It leads from Ninfield and then onto Sedlescombe.

*And to do that, William must avoid the marshes that skirted Senlac Hill.*

*But now Harold was speaking to one of his captains Adulf of Tamworth.*

*"So, you see how we can trap William here at these crossroads. But perhaps I would ask you, Adulf of Tamworth, if you will go outside and ensure that our guards are not asleep as we can have no ear droppers here this night. Or any traitors. Perhaps you should ensure no one comes in or near this tent, my lord?"*

*Was Howard saying that he thought Adulf was a spy? Well, someone had told William Harold was at York. And Adolf-s sister was one of the handmaidens to lady Godiva of Mercia. And her husband Leofric was not our friend in all this? But Adulf just got up and gave a breast salute and spoke.*

*"It is my honour, my king, and I will be a dead man if I fail you here this day. But I would ask a boon of you when we come to fight if I may?"*

*"Speak it then," Harold said, looking at Gyrth.*

"I would ask to be your bannerman and hold your banner safe from the enemy in this coming fight, and then you will know my worth."

I saw Harold look at Gyrth again, but he said.

"Yes, I shall see you that day, and I will know the worth of the lord Adulf of Tamworth as this is a lord's duty and not a thegn. So, shall you be seen as a King's Thegn? As it is said, so shall it be done."

Then he was gone, and I saw Gyrth and Harold look at each other and shrug as Harold said.

"Here is what we are to do at The valley of Coldbec, and you must pay careful note of what I have to tell you as this is a battle that I knew was coming for three months now, and since William's forces came to the coasts. It is a plan that must stop William from gaining the road to Lundune and the rest of our lands using these Roman-built roads that will be our downfall.

So, we must stop him here on Dere Road. We must stop him between these two hills that I have marked on this map. So, we will form up on the top of these two hills and force William's forces to come from the Ashen brook that I have shown here. Then he will be trapped by the marshes and the woodland between Powder ham in this lush valley here at Senlac.

As to how we are to ensure that he will have to come there and by that route, I intend to lure him there by letting him see a small part of our scouts who shall lead his scouts to find a section of the Wessex Fyrd, they must make it seem as if they are running away to the hill here that is marked here as Coldbec hill. A road skirts the hill, which will call the Lundune pathway so that the herds and sheep can be brought to market. It is a good cattle pathway and joins the Dere again. So, this will be an escape route for the people of the fyrd if needed. And it is there on Coldbec hill they will seem to be going to make a stand and allowing the Norman the time to set up their forces in that Valley, as William must believe that he only faces the Wessex fyrd and a few thegns who shall be seen to be digging ditches and forming a shield wall. And it is you, my brother Leofwine who shall command this third of our forces and the men you have brought from the coast and then you must make William see your banners. Furthermore, you shall also have mine with the crown and the three lions of Engaland so that William will believe I am there also?

And now we come to the crux of it? And a great gamble for us all, as William may not take the bait, we have shown him and not follow the fyrd and go on the Dere and onto Lundune.

Or he will not stop to challenge you on that Hill? Instead, he may want to take the other high ground, Senlac Hill.

If he does that, Leofwine, You must abandon your position and use the Lundune path to come to our side of the valley. But the timing will be a critical moment when it would seem that you can hit William where it will hurt him the most. But do not try to come through the woodland as it is full of brambles and thick thickets, and it will trap you there.

But if William comes against Senlac. So shall we be waiting for him to do that as we shall have the bulk of our warriors and the fyrd of the Southdowns' men hidden in these woods and hiding behind the hilltop, and as The Normans try to ascend the hill, we will show ourselves. So, shall we crush these Normans between our two forces as they will be faced with a tidal wave of Pikes spears and shields that will smash and crush this pitiful Norman army that this Duke has brought from Pevensey?

So that is my plan, and these are my orders to you all.

I want my Brother Gyrth to have control of the Huscarls at Senlac. I want the Ealdorman Walthnof of Huntingdon to command my left with all his thegns and the Fyrd he has brought here. And that is our weakest spot as it borders the woodland and the hard ground where William will want to use his cavalry and try to get behind our lines and drive from the hill.

So Walthnof, my friend, your people must hold and not run away. I know it will be hard to ask of them, so keep your best fighter ready to fill any gaps you may have. But you are the end of the line. No matter what, You must stay put until the day is done. Can you do that?"

The ealdorman gave the breast salute and spoke.

"Have no fear as The men of Huntingdon will see it done, my king."

Then Harold turned to look at the earl Godwine of Hereford.

"I see you, Godwine of Hereford, and you bear a great name and task. You must hold the right flank, and your task will only be easier as the marshes protect you. But you also must hold the high ground and not move off it until the battle is won. You also must stand no matter what, or William will be able to send his archers to that mound and hit us from the side of that slope. Can you be my right arm, Godwine of Hereford?"

*"I will, my lord And king."*

*"Then I will give you five of my best captains to see it done! They are the lords AElfgar, and Beorn Cynric. Dudda and each will bring fifty shields and warriors to*

*make another shield wall behind the ditches you must dig and line with stakes to stop William from coming at you with his cavalry. He will try to do so along that dirt road from Pow Ham mill.*

*So, you must station some of your best men at Telham farm, and they must give warning of Williams's approach from Ninfield?*

*I shall hold the centre of our forces with the rest of our best warriors and some of the Wessex thegns and their men. I see you Ulf of Crawley, and you Odda of Horley, and you Hundred from Fareham and not last or least Sweyn from The Thegns of Maidenhead.*

*All of you are the best of men, and these I have chosen to stand with me at my side and my standard. And now Adulf will be there with his hundred good fighting men from London. A worthy company all, and I must hope and pray that some will live through this day, and so shall our names ring through the land, and we shall go down in History as the men who won the battle of Senlac Vale. A battle that was to save our Saxon Engaland, that day of days.*

*But my friends, I have seen some of us are not yet fit to sit in a shield wall. Let alone stand in one, and we must look at our men and ensure that they will know how to fight and lose some weight.*

*And the bishop here will pray that is so and for our souls? Then, as the next time, we shall be on Senlac Hill?" Then Gytha,*

*"Well, mother, I hope you see this plan worthy of my father. But by then, you must be on your way to Exeter?"*

*She smiled and spoke.*

*"Godwin would say until the first arrow flies, my son."*

\*

*But that was to change on the march south, as The force that arrived on the south downs had been welded into something of a fighting force who could obey an order and we their left arm from their right and how to use a long pike and stand in a shield wall. So then, when the chance came, they were given a belt knife to slice the hamstring of a man or beast, And when they were ready, were they given enough weapons and food for the journey to take them along Dere Street and assemble at Coldbec Hill? And now they would be an unpleasant surprise for these Norman bastards.*

But it was Harold and his Saxons who were to find that the Normans had come to Coldbec vale, and Harold's war plan had been betrayed as the Normans had managed to get there a day before the Saxons and they had already taken up their battle positions! And even worse, was there no sign of the earl of Sussex or Leofwine men?

So then, Harold and his generals realised he could not take William by surprise. He also saw that William had positioned his forces between the hills Harold had hoped to hold against Williams's soldiers and thwart his Calvary. And now his force had been split in half with most of the Wessex fyrd hiding behind Coldbec, and he was left with placing his standard on Senlac hill. So, Harold selected a site protected on each side by some marshes. And to his rear was some thick woodland and the hillside. And then he put his Saxon huscarls in front of his standard, and they were to provide a shield wall that would stop Williams soldiers from breaching his defences.

*

As For The Duke William, Here Is What Was Recorded To Occur In His Camp That Day.

*But in Norman's camp, William and his generals were waiting to see what the Saxons would do next. And Williams plan was to send out a section of his crossbowmen who were to be seen as an attack on the Saxon shield wall.*

*They were told to stay out of range of the Saxon archers and their spear throwers as this force was to test the Saxon line and draw the fire of Harold's archers so that Williams' generals could pinpoint their position as, yet they were not to be seen as part of Harold's battle line.*

*These Norman archers were to do as much damage as they could and fire into the Saxon line until they ran short of arrows, and then they were to make a disorderly retreat. They were hoping that the men of the fyrd would see this as an easy victory and charge them.*

*If they did this, he had two sections of his knights hidden and ready to charge at the Saxons. One section was hiding in the Telham farm and a hollow, and they were to charge these stupid Saxons and kill them using their war horses and lances. And hidden to the Right* of Harold's line and concealed in the light woodlands were three troops of knights and their heavy horses that were there overnight so that Harold's men would not know of them. These men were dismounted and hidden behind cut branches waiting for the signal to charge the Saxons as soon as they were foolish enough to break ranks."

But to William's regret, the Saxons did nothing then. As William's generals, had hoped they would break ranks and charge after their archers, who, once they were safe from the harm they had been told to, make it look like they were running away In disarray.

But now they can see, The Saxon lines stood firm, and we must do it the hard way and use our foot soldiers!"

Then looking at his generals, Roger de Beaumont, and, then to Eustace of Boulogne, William took the hand of Robert Le Blount, and said to him.

"So, our spy with Harold has told us the truth. Look there at his line and the disposition of his men. He has the Ealdorman Walthnof of Huntingdon to command his left with all his *thegns and the Fyrd he has brought here. And that is his weakest spot as it borders the woodland and the hard ground where we must break the line to allow our cavalry their chance and try to get behind our lines and drive from the hill, Sire."*

*William said.*

*"I also see Godwine of Hereford has the right flank, and your task Beaumont will be to take and hold that high ground? And it is there we will break his line. And I want the Bretons to hit the Earl on the left, the French lot, and the Flemish soldiers to attack Walthnof of Huntingdon on his right flank. And my Norman soldiers with be at the head of this first massive attack. But we must not press it home, as I what we want the Saxons to believe and to think we do not have the stomach for this battle.*

*Moreover, we must also see that while They can afford to lose some of their men as we must preserve ours until reinforcements can come from Pevensey.*

*So, we will stand our ground until the second bugle sounds, the strident blasts three times and then we must all try to disengage from the* line, and some shall even be seen to turn and run for it. But then we shall regroup and see if Harold takes the bait. If not? We must wait and find our dead and injured and be ready for a second and even a third attack. Surely then, the fyrd men will want to break ranks and chase after us. And if they do so, we will bring up the knights and their heavy horses.

I want those mercenaries and the Welsh archers that are also hidden in those woods to stay hidden until the time comes to rein arrows from the sky!

And then we shall see Harold's line break as we send death and destruction from these woods that must seem impenetrable to Harold and his generals. And so they are, but one man and a long bow with a quiver full of arrows will not need much space. And when they are ordered to fire at the Saxons, they must fire almost vertically, and this time, it will be the Saxons who are killed by arrows from the shy. And then we will make a last charge to win the day.

Come to my lords, and this is a manoeuvre we have practised, so you must keep your people in line with no gaps, and we shall advance *information until the last moment, and then we shall sound the charge and hit the shield wall from three directions, and it must bend or break. But with God's help, we will have Harold Godwinson and his men in this nutcracker. So let us be about it as we have our God on our side.*

\*

*But in Harold's camp,*

*It was Gyrth and his force that were the first of our commanders to come to the brow of the hill at first light. And on the next day, to see that their best laid plans were going to be for nothing! And the grim discovery that awaited us in the valley below. And we knew we had been betrayed this day as William had come with all his force during the night.*

*The Normans were in force and lined up in three sections of William's army. And while our men had a mixture of weapons and hardly any battle armour, helmets, or protection.*

*These men were some of Williams's elite force of trained soldiers. As they had insisted that each of their lords must pay for them to have a uniform.*

*Comprising a chain mail vest, solid boots and an over tabard that held his Sigel and that of their lord. And with their long-tapered shields all in a line, they had come ready for battle wearing their metal helmets with their distinctive nose guard, shining brightly in the early morning sunlight, carrying their hooked knife spears, and most had short stabbing knives at their belts.*

*But the truth was that These were no fully trained fighting men, as were the bulk of our battle horde and the men of the fyrd.*

*So, the only men in our force who would have a chance against this infantry force were our three thousand husguards, who were similarly equipped.*

*But they were going to be outnumbered two to one. As Harold said to Gyrth.*

*"Just look at those bastards in the centre with Williams standard. These were trained killers who would move and*

*fight as a unit and would be deadly fighting machines today. But so, few mounted knights, brother. I wonder if our scouts were wrong. If so, we may win this fight this day.*

*Fucking pretty bastards, so they are but will they fight on a hill like this, and we hold the high ground? And I do not need to count them as our spies had told us of their numbers. So, brother, he is hiding the rest to be his reserve. But where?"*

Leofric…

*We knew that William had brought to Engaland Five thousand of his Infantry, bedside the men from Flanders, France, and Picardy.*

*But only a third of his army, that we could see placed either side of his Normans. and Three Thousand Mounted Knights with their war horses, Who I knew, would be his greatest weapon today.*

*And while our men were well used to fighting hand to hand in a shield wall. But, although most of our army were the men of the Fyrd, who had not fought in a battle for years.*

*So, we could not know how they would perform this day. And this yeoman and villagers that were our weakest point here today?*

*I knew in my heart that they would not stand when these mounted knights came at them at speed. They would drop their pikes and be mowed down and killed by the slashing swords and lances of the knights who would be impervious to arrows and spears dressed in their chain mail and body armour, as were their horses.*

*But their horses were vulnerable to our pikes, and the long-sharpened staffs would be a line of deadly spikes to piece a side or underbelly, and these pikes had a hook and blade to sever tendons and gut a man or horse.*

*And that was how we had trained our men to use them. But I knew these men of the fyrd would not stand a second charge.*

*So we were on the hill, and I saw only two ranks of horse and knights in the valley below? Half the number that had been reported.*

*But I had told Harold so and now he said that he did not intend to allow them to get anywhere near our shield wall.*

And soon, our mounted warriors would be here from Lewis if the ealdorman Leofric of Mercia had promised me he would be here with his force of five hundred battle knights? And they would be a nasty surprise for these Normans. But five hundred will never be enough here this day. But I had the two thousand Husguards who were my men of Wessex, and they would be the backbone of my shield wall. And we had the high ground."

*As the sun rose in the East, it was behind our Saxon battle horde, and I had come to stand with Harold Gyrth and the lady Gytha, who was standing on the top of Senlac hill, looking down into the valley to see just how hard this day was going to be for us now.*

*Because William was there before us, we could see his army was set out in battle formation, and as the sun shone onto their small Army, it lit up the bottom of the valley, to show how he had set out his forces and heard Harold groan and swear such an oath.*

"Who is that fucking cunt who has betrayed us again."

Then he looked to Coldbec hill and the standards there; turning to Gytha and her escort, he said to her and them.

"Well, mother, it seems you were correct to warn me about this day. Godwin would say until the first arrow flies my son, and how right he would be, mother, And this is no place for you now. I see that you must return to your waggons, and you all must leave this place while you still can. So, you must Do it now!"

I thought Gytha would argue with her son for a moment. But, still, two of her escort picked her up in their arms as she was carried away, kicking, and shouting about being with her sons as Gyrth and the Ealdormen stood aghast as this sight was laid out before us, as Godwine of Hereford said.

"So, we have a spy, my King, and now William knows our plans, and we are all dead men. Because, if my eyes serve me right, those are not your banners flying on Coldbec Hill but his. How is this possible? Where are your brother and his men? What are those stakes that are planted there?"

Harold said nothing as he shielded his eyes; he asked a younger man Agar, to ride across our *hill and to say what he saw. Agar went to find his horse and cantered away to get a closer look, and then he came back; the look on his face was as grim as can be.*

*"I fear They are the standards of Guy of Ponthieu, my King, And the stakes hold the heads of Leofwine, and his commanders and captains and the hillside is covered in bodies, my King. How can that be? Where are the Wessex men? Where is the rest of the Wessex fyrd Sire?"*

Gyrth swore a foul oath and spoke

*"Where indeed and how could the Normans know to do this and when? How long has the Norman host been waiting for us to enter their trap?"*

Then it was as if Harold had been reading my thoughts, As he said.

*"If we can find that traitor who has told William of our plans. I will be fucking good skin the treacherous cunt alive. But I questioned that man, and he swore a holy oath, he was loyal to our cause?"*

*Then, turning to face his commanders, Harold had some control of his anger as he said to them.*

"But we must see this as God's will. And we must not let this setback, cause us to abandon our battle plans, as William is still greatly outnumbered."

Then, as he turned to me, the look in his eyes was grim indeed, as if he was remembering his mother's warnings and perhaps my dreams that told of his death here this day? By all I held to be holy, I knew then, I must find out some more, about this Jake Rutter, Was an evil spirit or a messenger from God?

"Leo, my old friend, I fear that we will need your Christian words here today, and your best payers, to your Christain God But as this is going to be also Viking battle with no quarter given or asked. I will also pray to Thor, to ask him to hear my prayers as the son of a Viking mother.

So go back to my mother and tell her what you have seen. But, no, do not speak of Leofwine has not joined us yet. I will do that later." He had paused to take out the Amulet she had given in remembrance of his father's God Thor.

"Give her this amulet, which is a gift from my grandfather Wulfnoth Cild, it is Thors hammer. Tell she must wear it this day, and if she can indeed speak to the *old Gods, ask her to pray for us. Go now while you still can find her and t ell her guards to keep her out of harm's way! Tell her I love her!"*

However, I did not get far as the bugles began to blare from Norman's camp, and I saw a group of Riders coming from William's encampment. One of these Riders wore a bishop's white gown, and held high the cross of Jesus, which was glittering in the sun. There was red cross emblazoned on his chest.

*Another held Williams standard and another banner that was that of our Pontif, in Rome! So then did my heart sink to my boots, as I knew who's side our god was on this day. That was pope Leo's banner, and William had sent to Rome for help. And now he was going to kill us all as excommunicated heretics!*

A steward also carried a living branch of a tree, the universal signal, that William, wanted to talk. But as this Steward, came closer to the shield wall we could all that he was so brightly clothed?

*My thought was that he could be, a jester or a minstrel. As he had a lute strapped across his back ? And now as my path to Gytha was* blocked by our warriors. I waited to be able to look and see what was about to happen.

And when they got close enough for Harold, and his men, to hear them, they stopped in front of the Saxon line, and the minstrel started singing and strumming his lute. I heard Harold say to Gyrth.

"I know this man. I met him in Falaise; he is Williams Minstrel, his name is Taillefer, and the standard bearer is the Count Guy of Ponthieu. The man with the tree branch is a bishop. He is Odo, a half-brother to William, So, We must speak with him if that idiot will shut up?"

It was then realised that the minstrel was singing the 'Death Song of Roland':

But Taillefer stopped singing when Harold got onto his horse, and instead, he began juggling with his belt knife twisting it over and over between his fingers, and we saw the blade spinning and shining in the sunlight, it became a blur of flashing steel, and we waited to see who, and where, it would strike?

But then, Taillefer, on seeing Harold approaching, he turned his horse and calmly rode back down to his side to sing another verse of the Song of

Roland. And all this time we could hear the Normans were cheering and clapping his act of bravado.

As now, the rank of our Saxons horde, were no longer silent as they were pointing at the Norman camp, and the many fires thar were now to be seen on Coldbec Hill!

And to realise that these were funeral fires that were to tell us of the massacre on Coldbec hill, And then we heard the pitiful cries of our Saxon warriors, that told us of a massacre there.

and now there was a foul wind which brought the smell of Burning flesh and we knew what that meant for the fate of Harolds brother, The earl Leofwine and his men who had been stationed there! As the smell of so many dead bodies began to come to us on the breeze that had sprung up with the early morning sun.

So, Harold rode alone to meet this group who he hoped had come to parley, but Wido spoke first.

"I see you, Harold Godwinson. And I bring you some entertainment and sweet music to calm *your men. If music is the last thing they hear, it will be Duke William's last gift to them all!"*

Harold said nothing that I could hear, but he never stopped staring at the Count of Ponthieu all the time. Who said as loudly as he could in his thin, squeaky high, pitched voice.

*"I see you come prepared for a battle here this day. But you come late to this hillside this day!"*

Still Harold said nothing but pulled his horse alongside that of the count to look him in the eye; Wido backed away as he signalled for the Standard bearer to come forward so that this man could speak to Harold.

*"I am Bastian of Beaurain, and I am the high steward to Duke William of Normandy. And this man is the Commander of the forces of Ponthieu. A man, you know of I believe and after your time in his castle? castle? Earl Godwinson.*

*But now he is the Count Guy of Ponthieu. You should know that it was his men, who captured your brother and his scouts during this night. But it was this brave Count, who Your brother was to mistake as a friend! So then could our men infiltrate your camp and then we found your people asleep As we cut off Leofwine head, and placed it on a spike on that hill, last evening.*

*This man led his men of Ponthieu, on this nighttime raid, as he led the assault on that hill, using the Lundune way, and we caught your Saxons sleeping. And as the count came to parley with your brother at first? But it seems that Leofwine was in no mood to surrender the hill. so, as you can see, it was hardly a fight? More of an execution, Once their lookouts were silenced.*

*Why do I tell you this, I do so, so that you will know that you have lost almost half of your Saxons warriors, Harold Godwinson.*

*But you should know that our Duke William, wants you to know just how hopeless your position is he this day.*

*But, as he is also a generous and Christian man, and I am instructed to say if you will honour your oath given to him at Falaise, That is to be his liege man, and to see him wear the crown of Engaland here this day.*

*To do so here and now in front of this Bishop and the Pontiff standard. You must bend the knee and lose your head as a traitor. Do that and we will spare your battle herd if they do that as well? That is the only offer. What say you? Harold Godwinson of Wessex?"*

Harold still said nothing, but he was biting his lip, as he realised this man was trying to get him to lose his temper and do something foolish here. As Bastian, went on to declare.

*"And that was how we found the camp where your scouts were hiding and asleep! And to find that your brother was foolish enough to want to be with them. You should know he took a long time to die. I am sorry to say he was tortured before he told us of your battle plans. And now his head and those of his men decorate that hill yonder. And soon your heads will match his on this hill called Senlac."*

Harold said to this man. Ignoring count Wido. A man he knew from his capture in Picardy!

*"I see you herald and you, lord Bastin. And I say this to every Norman invader who has come to my lands.*

*I spit on these false words you speak and your offer.*

*Do you not know that William dares do not leave a good Saxon alive in Engaland, should we lose this battle of Senlac. But we still stand on it.*

*So now shall my Saxon battle horde win out this day.*

*And your Normans ill you all suffer a defat here, as did the men of Norway who thought to steal our land from it lawful king.*

*But these are just words. So come to my shield wall that you can see on that hill, and we will talk some more!"*

And then, turning to the Bishop, he said to Odo.

*"I see you, Bishop Odo; what are you, a man of God and god sworn, never to do harm, and these priests doing here this day?"*

Odo rose in his stirrups and to declare

*"I come not to fight but on a mission of mercy.*

*I see that your Bishop Leofric, are among your numbers? and also your mother the Lady Gytha, and her people.*

*I come to offer sanctuary to them all. so must our beloved Duke William, wish to offer her his clemency this day, as he would spare her life and that of those in her baggage train.*

*And as you can see, we have; you Saxons, trapped here, and we have now destroyed half your army, you cannot win this battle. I see that You all are caught in our trap, Held on that hi waiting to die! Like the rat and oath breaker you are.*

*So, I see that there can be no escape for your men or Gytha, once the fighting starts.*

But I am instructed to offer your mother and her entourage, safe passage away from this place! As I am sure you do not want there to be any unfortunate accidents with her person?

So, if you take a moment to send her back with me and you have my holy oath, she will not be harmed this day."

I saw that Harold was torn as to what he should do, as it was possible that Gytha could be caught up in the fighting, and then, some men would be sure to try to take their chances to harm or rob her then. Harold nodded to the Bishop and to say to him.

"That is well said Bishop, and I thank you for such consideration. And you should know I have sent Leofric to do this very thing So he and my mother are in Gods *hands and if they come to harm, our God will know of it, and those responsible will pay a terrible price. But yes, You should pass on my thanks to the duke, for this act of kindness. But know this and before these witnesses, I do not hand them to you as William's hostages! We will wait until the battlefield is clear of your party before we begin this battle.*

*God with God Odo."*

*And so, I got on a spare horse, galloped down the hill, as a part Of the bishop's party and was almost thrown to the ground as we reached the side of this hill and the safety of the farmhouse, I tried to maintain my feet, as I needed to tell Odo, that I was in the service of lady Gytha and her confessor. As I said to Odo.*

*"You must know me, my lord Odo; we met at Falaise if you remember. I am Leofric, the Bishop of Exeter. And I am about to take the lady Gytha to Rye harbour, and then to Exeter. But I fear that is no longer possible as the whole area is full of your soldiers.*

*I fear that we may have come out of the field of this battle, but this is not a safe haven for any of us this day. But I know this farmstead. It is called Telham, we should go there my lord*

Bishop, as they are good honest people who will have run away by now, lord?

Odo was looking at the valley and the road to the farm and he said to us all.

"Yes, that may serve, so we will ask you Leofric to bring the Lady Gytha there, and I will follow with some guards to keep us all safe, until the outcome of this battle is known, and for its duration? But first I will bless this house and make it holy ground so there will be no fighting as it will be a place of Sanctuary. What say you all?"

By now, the Lady Gytha and her party had arrived with her escort, and she was told of what was going to happen, I saw her bridle at first! Until the captain spoke to her of Harolds wishes, and the agreement, he had brokered, with this Norman Lord and Bishop. I saw Gytha, give me a look, that said thank you, and then Odo said.

"Yes, we could do that, and As it is said, so shall it be done, and I will go with this Bishop to make sure it is a safe refuge. Come, Bishop Leofric, I am starving, and we have some fine *food and wine. See you my lady and your people are also frightened and hungry.*

*So, I ask you to join us if you can manage to eat and share in our Norman Lunch. Then, we will leave these men to do what must be said and done here this terrible day. And may Gods will be done."*

However, and Once we were about to head for the farm so did the *Count Guy of Ponthieu.* As Wido, feel emboldened to place his horse in front of the carriage , looking at Gytha we all saw his face and eyes were full of anger and resentment, concerning this bargain. he said as loudly as he could manage , almost spitting out his words and anger at the thought that Odo, had stolen his prize.

"So, Harold Godwinson, liar, and oath breaker, I see you send your mother away, and I know you to be such a man with no honour Oath breaker. A man we now also known as someone we thought you had intended to hide behind her skirts.

But now she has escaped my wrath for what you did to me and my family! So be it and until you are dead at my feet oath breaker!

And now I must see that it is thanks to our Duke and the rightful king of Engaland we see that she may live another day.

But she was promised to me as a part of the spoils of war. So now I shall speak for our Duke and our God this day and see who wears that crown of yours on the morrow.

 Then you have my promise that I will find your mother,  and then she will pay the price for your betrayals."

I do not know to this day  just how Harold said nothing as he looked to the farm where his mother was to be held under Williams's protection. As Guy said, pointing at Williams camp.

"But if you have eyes to see as far as our standards, you will see the cross of God and the standard of Pope Leo, God's servant on earth, And the Bishop of Amiens. It is he who guards the holy relics brought here today.

The very relics on which you swore a holy oath, that you would supports Williams claim to this kingdom Did you not!

*And, now all our soldiers, will know that God is on our side and not yours! And to Remind them that you swore to uphold your promise to our Duke William and their rightful King of Engaland."*

Harold said nothing, but his face was thunderous, knowing Guy had come to confront this man, as he was trying to make Harold strike him here when they were under the bounds of a truce? We all saw just how much the count hated the man who had destroyed his life at his castle, and he would have his moment of triumph.

*"So, I have asked William to allow me to give you this last chance to give up Alfred's crown to him here and now, And we can end this bloodshed. So then can your people leave this place and live. Refuse and William has decreed that this is a fight to the death, with no hostages taken, and no mercy given.*

*But you, Harold, must live so William can spit on you or your live body, and call you a liar and the oath breaker you are. So, what say you, Godwinson will you come back with me here* and now, and I will get the Bishop to hear your last confession?"

But Harold was not going to say anything as he was silent for a long time as he looked at Williams's small army. Then he said.

*"You count your chickens to soon Wido. And yes, I have agreed to Williams's offer to spare my mother, and the women with her. I will allow the Bishop Odo, to send her to that farmhouse for safe keeping, along with Bishop Leofric. But if she is harmed in any way, I will find you Wido, here or in heaven or hell. And I will destroy your very soul and any hope of redemption and rebirth he may hope for in the hereafter.*

*As for you, Wido, for what you are a, just a fucking cock sucker? I will end you, the so-called count of Ponthieu, and I pray that we will meet in this battle. I see that your Duke does not have enough men . And yes, many men will die on this hill today. Wido, you evil bastard to threaten my mother so! And I will win this day. As I call on the Norse gods to hear my call to arms.*

*So, leave this place while you still have a hand to pleasure yourself, Get out of the way you fool."*

Then before anyone could stop him, Harold reached for this count's head and struck him on his nose, sending him flying from his horse, and so was the first blow struck, and the battle was to begin as both parties turned away and rode back to their lines.

But before they reached their lines, a man came forth from the Saxon side and was dressed in the Duke William clothes and a paper made crown. Wearing a black and gold cloak that had Williams Sigel.

He waited to face the Normans until Harold was safe from their arrows. Then this joker began riding this mock hobby horse with a broom for a head.

Trying vainly to keep On his head, the wonky crown, as this buffoon character, began riding up and down the Saxon lines. All the while shouting a ditty that he had heard about the Duke falling off his horse at Pevensey and having to be helped up the Stoney beach. It went like this.

"I am a Duke who had to vomit on England's shores, and I am the Duke who was so weak to walk on Engaland shores.

*I am the Duke who cannot Ride a horse on England shores, and I am the man who king Harold will soon kill here on Egeland's shores."*

And now, as this jester turned his bare arse to the retreating Normandy. The rider gave a great fart from his bare backside, and now the whole of Harold's army was shouting and banging weapons on shields and then began singing this song to Williams's army and his fury.

*I am a Duke who had to vomit on England's shores.*

*I am the Duke who was so weak to walk on Engaland shores.*

*I am the Duke who cannot Ride a horse on England shores.*

*I am the man who king Harold will soon kill here on Egeland's shores.*

Then Harold came to meet with this jester, and he raised his sword to his shoulders and said as loudly as he could.

"So, I Dub thee my Knight of Senlac Hill, my good man! And I thank you for this fun this day, As I fear we will need some jollity here this day, Come to my good Knight of Senlac hill, and you will be well rewarded for these valiant deeds  But perhaps we could have one last verse? As it is known that the Duke did take a tumble that day.

**And that is a good omen for us, is it not?!"**

And this time, Harold was leading the singing!

"I Am A Duke Who Had To Vomit On England's Shores.

I Am The Duke Who Was So Weak To Walk On Engaland Shores.

I Am The Duke Who Cannot Ride A Horse On England Shores.

I Am The Man Who King Harold Will Soon Kill Here On Egeland's Shores."

So then was this joker and Harold both to be welcomed back with a round of loud cheers, as they took up their allotted  position beside his standard.

 So, did Gyrth, shout out the first of his battle orders. as he saw a section of Norman crossbowmen begin to march slowly up the hill.

As Gyrth said to his captains,

*

*So then did Harold ride off to war! And As we will take up his story in this part of this battle, this is what I was told happened next. As Gyrth strode ,forward to face the shield wall.*

"See, the enemy comes! We need to form a shield wall! Come lads form up as we have practised. These men come with crossbows. So, we need interlocking shields; we must make the three shield walls and be ready to receive their fucking crossbow bolts. Have courage, lads and know your friends are with you! They are counting on you. We must stand firm, lads. Do it, do it now!"

To do that, they would form up in the manner of a Roman Testudo with locked shields overlapping and the first man kneeling. The second standing and the third rank were protecting everyone's heads. And while these bolts were fast and would breach a single shield, they would get stuck in the overlapping section of this shield defence. Moreover, the Norman archers would have to come to twenty yards to make them effective. Then they would be exposed to the horned beast manoeuvre that would allow these archers to be enveloped on each side by another wall that would try to trap them in the arm of the moving head of this bull. as the order went out for the whole of the Saxon to advance, a one step from the Saxon shield wall and each step would bring Harrods Saxons closer to their line and then these crossbowmen had to avoid coming in the range of the Saxon pikemen.

But now, Gyrth ordered his Saxon archers to bring down these crossbowmen who were firing over the shield wall, and many of the crossbowmen were falling to their arrows from the sky.

So now did the Norman bugles ring out to announce a retreat back to their lines, leaving many of their comrades dead and wounded behind them lying on the hillside? So now were the Saxons cheering at this retreat and a small victory?

*But some of the Fyrd had begun to move only to be shouted at and told to stay put as their captains knew this was only the start of the battle. And Judging by the sun's position, it was past mid-morning and halfway to noon.*

 *As Gyrth had come to stand with his brother to say,*

*"I would ask you brother, just what you have agreed with that Bishop and that piece of shit from Ponthieu, later, brother.*

*But I thank our Gods that our mother has left the field as she was always a worry for me.*

 *And now I can clear my mind and concentrate on killing Normans. As for that Git Guy, I saw you hit him, and hope you broke his nose well and properly because he has had it up William s arse for sure!*

 *But see there, where the Normans are on the move at last. But those crossbows mean business, and they cannot be allowed to get too close. So, we need our archers forward now...."*

\*

*But in Norman's camp, William and his generals were waiting to see what the Saxons would do next, as they hoped they would break ranks and charge after their archers, who had been told to make it look like they were running away, In disarray?*

*But now William's commanders could see, the Saxon lines stood firm, and they must do it the hard way, and now to use their foot soldiers!*

*Then William, looking at his generals, Roger de Beaumont, and Eustace of Boulogne. William took the hand of Robert Le Blount to say.*

*"So, we are going to force the Saxons off that hill. Well, so be It as we can see, He has the Ealdorman Walthnof of Huntingdon, to command his left with all his thegns and the Fyrd he has brought here. And we know now that is his weakest spot. as it borders the woodland and the hard ground, where we must break the line to allow our cavalry their chance and try to get behind our lines and drive from the hill.*

*"If Godwine of Hereford has the right flank, and now it is your task Beaumont will be to take*

and hold that high ground? And it is there we will break his line.

I want the Bretons to hit the Earl on the left, the French lot, and the Flemish soldiers to attack Walthnof of Huntingdon on his right flank. And my Norman soldiers with be at the head of this first massive attack.

For that is what we want the Saxons to believe and to think we do not have the stomach for this battle.

So, we will stand with our original plan. We must stand our ground until the second bugle sounds, the strident blasts three times and then we must all try to disengage from the line, and some shall even be seen to turn and run for it.

But then we shall regroup and see if Harold takes the bait. If not? We must wait and find our dead and injured and be ready for a second and even a third attack.

Surely then, the fyrd men will want to break ranks and chase after us.

And if they do so, we will bring up the knights and their heavy horse's Welsh archers. And then we will make a last charge to win the day.

*Come to my lords, and this is a mounted manoeuvre we have practised, so you must keep your people in line with no gaps, and we shall advance information until the last moment, and then we shall sound the charge and hit the shield wall from three directions, and it must bend or break. But with God's help, we will have Harold Godwinson and his men in this nutcracker. So let us be about it as we have our God on our side."*

\*

## On the hill,

*It transpired that it was the Earl Gyrth, had command of this section of the shield wall, and managed to secure some long-handled danish battle axes, which could be used to slice away a head or leg. Should an enemy come in range, and these five hundred warriors were his fiercest fighters! Placed on either side of the shield wall was the Fyrd of Lundune.*

*And some who had served with Godwin, and they knew how to fight. And on the other side of his shield wall was the Fyrd from the South Lands that had joined could do was to wait and watch what the Normans intended now?*

*As all he and Harold waited for the battle to begin.*

But it was late in the morning, that William decided to start this battle, and did so with his Norman Archers, which had the deadly crossbows. But they were wrong to think had to be used at close range?

*And when Gerth had time to look at what was left of the fyrd, after a considerable number of cross bow volleys and now so many gaps in the line, and far too many of desertions! He was forced to plug the gaps with his trained warriors, who had instructions to bolster the line And now these fighting husguards had managed to stop the retreat, placed on either side of the Saxon-poorly trained warriors.*

As Gerth, shouted at his own guards to keep the line and fill any gaps and to force the Leaders of the fyrd to stand firm. Despite that they had been told to keep their men in line and wait for them the orders that would tell them to stand to move back or attack?

The Three simple orders that Gyrth hoped would serve his purpose. And these farmers, townspeople butchers, bakers, forge smiths, and all sorts of sizes and ages had been given some javelins or long pikes, or they had their own shield and knife, and some had a sword of some sort? And some basic training by the Reave or their lord.

*However, the rest of the men were inexperienced fighters, such weapons as iron-studded clubs, even a lead-weighted cosh and their reaping hooks. And these people's task was to seek an exposed neck or shin and cut a tendon or slice open a neck leaving the main fighting to their warriors. So now, these men must make peace with their maker and prepare for battle according to their custom.*

*As we have heard, the Saxons spent their last night of peace as best they could, either night while sleeping or drinking and seeing the dawn come with dread or false courage that would soon disappear at the first moment of the fighting. But this day, they knew their Saxon way of life was at stake, as were their women and children that would become serfs to these Normans and no longer free men. And in the morning, as the Norman crossbowmen proceed toward the enemy. They raised their weapons to the sky to cheer King Harold, who had just knocked a Norman knight to the ground.*

*As their King went to stand with his brother near the standard, all shared equal danger. And none might think of retreating.*

*

*William,*

*On the other side, the Normans passed the whole lot in confessing their sins, as they received the sacraments in the morning. As did the Saxons, When Bishop Leofric was to do so before the battle began, but the word was that he was missing and had left the Hill with Harold's mother. So, one of his priests came to bless this Saxon battle horde.*

*As for the Norman infantry, They were in front of a single row of Welsh archers ready with their long bows and iron-tipped arrows. And they would have spent soundly kept their bow stings dry and tied around their bodies. It was not yet time for them to be deployed. But Harold looked at the cluster of mounted knights and realised they also seemed depleted in numbers.*

Gyrth, on seeing this remarked.

"Only twenty long bows then. I was told there were at least a hundred that William paid to fight us. Well, my King, we need not have worried about them after all. But we must keep one eye on them all the same if they get in range of you, my King, as I hear that William has promised a bag of gold to the archer that can bring you down." Harold grunted, then to say,

"Then Brother, I will be sure to keep my helmet and my eyes on the ground, and we shall see who will win gold this day!"

So, then to one of his eagled-eyed thegns one Cynric, and to ask him how many men he saw and where. And as the Norman bugles began to sound, the advance Cynric came back to stand before his King.

"I am so sorry, my lords, but I could not accurately count the number of soldiers to part in this battle his day. Some say that William had about five thousand infantry. And three thousand mounted Knights?"

Cynric waited to let these numbers sink into the hearts and minds of these noblemen as five hundred mounted knights could quickly sweep

Harold's army off these hills. As Harold said nothing, Cynric said,

"But I see only fifty, my King, And I see a phalanx of the Bretons trying to use the smoke from their brasiers to get before the forces of lord Godwine of Hereford, my lord. And there are French and Flemish standards with that five hundred that have the right flank, Williams's standards are in the centre with his main force of Norman foot solders my King. But I saw no large force of mounted knights, my King, and once the crossbowmen move aside, I fear they will be upon us soon. So that is what I saw, my King?"

Gyrth grunted his derision at this puny force that William was using as he said.

"Let them come then. We are ready. What is the time do you think, my King?"

"I would judge it to be about Nine candle rings?"

The battle begins, as now Harold,

was to see the battle opened, after the parley was over, with the playing of trumpets as the Norman archers then walked up the hill?

*But then to stop about one hundred yards away from the Saxon army, they began the fight with their crossbow bolts, which soon began to hit the Saxon shield wall.*

*And then Their shields began to look more like a Hedgehog than a line of wooden shields, and of course, some of the bolts found a way through this defence wall and those that were aimed high also found their mark back in the Saxon line of warriors.*

But as men fell, the line did not move or break. Saxons. But they continued this barrage unmolested until they were nearly out of missiles. Then they stood up and began to withdraw, calling out to the Saxons that they were not men and cowards who would not come to fight them man to man.

*But the Saxon shield wall and their line remained unbroken. Until around 10:30 hours in the morning. The Norman bugles recalled these archers back to their own lines.*

But, As their main force of foot, soldiers began to move forward in three main groups. On the left were the men of Brittany, in the middle were the most significant section of Normans, and to the Right were the men of Flanders. The latter were mercenaries, paid men, and Williams's force comprised paid only a few true fighting men, from Flanders and France.

*At the centre with the main Norman contingent was the Duke William himself, who had. So, he closed himself to the church's relics and around his neck. And beside him was the better man with the paper banner high above his head. But still, the English line held firm, and eventually, the Norman losses, were so heavy, William's generals were forced to order the retreat. Still, the Saxons could afford to lose a few warriors and men of the Fyrd, while William could not."*

And then came the second wave of Normans, and now they had only sent a small force against the centre to reinforce the sides of their line, hoping the Fyrd would give way. Some men tried to run, but fresh men quickly filled their place. Members of the third on the Right came from the other hill as the Norman captains were waiting for the fyrd to break the line as they made a fake retreat waiting for the Saxons to chase after them.

*But then, a rumour went around the Norman line that William was among their own casualties. And William, afraid of what this would do to his men, pushed back his helmet, and went to a high mound of ground, and rising himself as high as he could on his stirrups, the Duke of Normandy began shouting that he was still alive.*

*But this attack had faltered as his men feared they had lost this fight, and far too many pulled back as William was taken to his command tent for treatment. The truth was that he had been knocked from a third horse, and he needed some healing.*

So It Was That It Was About Noon. The Norman Bugles Sounded A Retreat As A Rider Came Forward With A High White Flag.

*As Gyrth came to see if Harold was uninjured, we saw a herald approaching with a white flag, and he shouted to them.*

*"I see you still live, Harold Godwinson. But This has been a gruelling day. And you Saxons have lost half your warriors. But our Duke does not wish your Saxons who are only wounded to suffer more than necessary. So, we give you two*

hours to surrender this hill at noon. And two hours to attend to your wounded, as we will for our fallen. But At Two Past Midday, We Shall Come Again And Kill You All.

But know this, if you fight, it will be to the death and with no hostages taken. We will kill every last man we find here. So is it said, and so must it be.

**My name is Robert de Beaumont, and we will meet again Oath breaker."**

Then he returned to his lines, and the trumpets sounded the recall, a peace for two hours. So, there was to be a break in the fighting for an hour so that both sides had a chance to remove the dead and injured from the battlefield.

*

As for William and his generals, who were to discuss this day's fighting, William saw that he had to change his tactics if he could get the Saxons to leave their hill.

All that morning, he had hoped that his trained soldiers would turn the tide here this day. But alas, he could not get them close enough to Harold's husguards, and his standard still flew *on the highest point of the hill for all to see! and then to see that it was the Saxons who were now winning this battle.*

*And to see that after three attempts to break the Saxon line and get off the top of this hill, his Army had failed to break the shield wall, and his warriors alone were never going to be effective.*

*Moreover, he felt that one more retreat would make his men lose heart, and he had seen how they reacted to the rumour of his death! So, the first question in his mind was would they go again and not break? So now, the question was how to bring his three hundred knights into the fray. And they had asked him why they were not in the fight.*

But William knew they would not charge the Saxon line of pikes, and the line of ditches, that Harold's men had managed to construct at either side of the hill. And this charge would have to be made up the hill?

*No, that would be madness, and he would lose most of the knights, this battle, and this kingdom! But Perhaps they could use these two hours to their advantage and send his mounted knights to go around the Coldbec hill and take the Saxons from behind these two hills?*

*And yes, that was the beginning of a plan, as he had fifty knights with him. So perhaps they could swing around the woodland and do this. And then Harold must turn to face them.*

*But what if this was another ruse and not the main attack?* What if this attack from Coldbec hill was coordinated by an attack by the Welsh bowman in the woods? Could they launch their arrows from these woods, and if so, they would take Harold and his men by surprise, and they would have no protection from these arrows falling on them from the sky?

*William could almost see the carnage they would wreak on the Saxons then.*

*And then Harold would be attacked on both sides of the Senlac hill, and then shall he send his soldiers in a fourth assault on the hill.*

*But they must again be seen to break and run away from the fighting, another false retreat this time,* Such A well-known tactic that Harold would be aware of, and he was never going to fall for it for a second time as he had prevented his men chasing away the crossbow men!

*Or would he? When these men of the fyrd, shall see his men throwing down the shields and weapons to make this false retreat as realistic as possible. While his left and right sections stayed firm and ready to close the trap on these Saxons?*

Surely then, the Saxon peasant army will want to chase them, and if not, the main force of his knights must charge the line regardless of how many are brought down. as long as they get to Harold Godwinson.

*But someone had told Harold not to wear his kings body armour thisday and now he was not such an easy target for his Welsh archers, Dammn him!*

*But it was thanks to the traitor, Adulf of Tamworth, as his task was to raise the king's standard at the right time and then they would know where Harold was to be found in the shield wall!*

*So now he had another plan that must work, or he would lose this last fight, and he also made* sure that he would not be taken alive by these poxy Godwinson's.

So Now He Must Call A Captain's Meeting And Put All This Into Action?

*

But now Harold, always about to gall a council of war, or his brother and his captains.

*As the morning truce ended, he could see what William intended with all the false retreats and now he knew that William must play his last card and try to use his knights to get behind his shield wall. As he would soon lose the daylight, He must withdraw, or to make a final charge against his shield wall But the truth was this was late afternoon and theywere all exhausted from this waiting. And his captain was having a hard time maintaining their position, and the fighting spirit of their men.*

**They needed another plan and soon.**

As Harold and Gyrth judged it was about two past six hours since the fight had begun. So then did William decide that the time had come to mount an assault the whole line.

*It was as the Normans began this battle with trumpet playing, and the whole of this Norman Army began to move towards us with Williams standard in the centre; they came forward in three groups.*

*On the left, were the standards of the Breton fighting men, and some of their auxiliaries, who were not their best fighters.*

*On the Right, were the standards and men from Poitou, Burgundy, Brittany, and some from Flanders? In the centre was the bulk of Williams Normans.*

*But the Saxons were soon to realise that was not to be another half-hearted attack.*

*They saw that the Duke had committed his whole army with no reserves left behind, and then it became clear. Harold, realised that William was aiming his best troops at their side wings, who were now heavily engaged with hand to hand, shield to shield, as their largest fighters were trying to break the line and Harold saw the* cavalry and mounted knights, were waiting for their chance to get thought any gaps.

And now the Normans were fully committed, testing the resolve of our line, and especially the men of the fyrd would they hold the line when fired upon?

And so far, our men of the Fyrd had not moved, and these brave Normans had risked death for no gain as they began to test the strength of our shield wall. As their attacks became ever more ferocious, they had some pike men waiting to exploit a fallen man and even ready to pull away their own dead and injured as yet another section of Normans and their captains filled their lines. So then Harold saw the shield wall buckle at its left end.

As the knights were now standing their ground swinging their great broad swords that would be able to take down any shield they were now fighting back to back and protected by some of their best hand to hand fighters and behind these terror squads were their crossbow men fighting and firing into the fallen and now this phalanx were making headway as the Saxon s died by the hindered as their shield were smashed and their short swords were no match for these long two handed Norman knights heavy swords. sword So was the shield wall breached in at least ten places.

using the shield wall remained intact; as a few found their targets, so did some of our men fall and could not be replaced.

Then Gyrth was there with his best warriors had formed on the right and left side of this latest phalanx of his soldiers. And they would become his spear thrust into our battle line once these men at the front had worn my men down, and we became exhausted?

It was then Harold realised how clever William had been to wait until his men were at the end of their strength, as this test would show him if we had any *mounted cavalry, we could use to come against this phalanx of archers who were now stationed behind this main attack.*

*And sweep them away or see where our archers were stationed so his knights could ride against them. But thanks to the betrayal of the Earl of Mercia, we had no calvary, and I had far too few archers to waste their arrows on these crossbowmen. And after what I judged to be an hour and a half, The Norman trumpets sounded the charge as Williams advanced against us, and this time, Harold saw these Normans were better trained and had better weapons and armour and this battle was all but lost and the new men, were still fresh, and eager to fight and they were not going to stop until he had the hill!*

*And now they had changed formation, and these hardened warriors on the left and right were in a wedge shape, with their best warriors as the point of a spear that was going to punch a hole in our shield wall and then we would lose this battle almost before it had begun!*

As out of nowhere fifty of their knights had come to force the gap wider. And all would be lost. So, would you have a tough time as they came to charge us?

But now, our bugles and the Celtic Carthic horns were sounding the Alarm, and we knew our time had run out. And that we had been betrayed by the Earls Lundune and had not come in time, That Leofric of Mercia had not come to this battle with his men, they had stayed in Lundune, hoping we would both be destroyed today?

So Now We Men Of Wessex Were Going To See If We Could Save Our Saxon Engaland This Day?

So now that these archers were out of range did Gyrth come to stand with me and our standard? So, this is what my brother was to see from the hill and his report of what happened to him and his half of the Husguards. And From our position on the platform, we had made using two lashed carts so that we could see everything on the battlefield Tower, the first er saw looking West were the storm clouds and the dark, ominous signs of an approaching storm or rain that was filling the sky from the West.

And if this were going to be a wet end to this day, then so be it as we held the high ground, and the Normans would be fighting in the mud and marshland that lay before them.

But when we turned East, we saw a cloud of dust a hundred yards wide, coming down the road from the hamlet of Coldbec. But this was no natural dust storm; it was hooves whipping up the earth ground, and the air was full of dust.

They were some Norman horses, and their riders were not dressed as knights in armour, but they were the Norman hustlers and stable hands riding bareback! And they were driving a small herd of cattle before them and using horses and mounted men swinging what could be flaming pig skins on a rope full of oil-soaked straw; the bullocks and bulls were now trying to escape this fire monster; who was chasing them!

It was then we realised they were heading for our baggage train, and our reserves. And now, they would get behind our lines and crash into the rear of our shield wall. Harold looked at Gyrth and told him to stand Fast.

"Well, brother, it would seem that this fight will be full of surprises. First, William sends his crossbowmen to be killed, and now these cattle, I wonder what he will do next?"

Gyrth pointed at fifty of his best hand-to-hand fighters and said to the king.

"Well, now we know. And You must deal with those knights, and I shall go and swat those Flemish flies away from our line. It will not take long, and I will be back."

If Harold was caught in that brief moment of fear and horror at this strange attack and then the clarity and calm that sometimes comes at a time of great stress and danger. So, now he saw that nothing was going to stop these enormous knights from smashing their way deep into their shield wall, that he had managed to form up on a slight mound on his side of the hill. And he knew this fight would be over unless we did something to stop this charge. But he also had a surprise ready for these knights.

So, Harold sent Beorn to tell their men to form a second shield wall, but on our side of this hill that would entice these Normans to attack them with these mounted knights who were going to be caught in the hidden, spiked Fosse.

And then he saw the standard raised on the high ground at the scrub; it was that of the Clenched fist that was the Sigel of Guy of Ponthieu.

So here was my enemy and the man who would kill us all now. But he still had his mounted messengers and another battle plan to change our formation. But It took ages before he could see if things were changing, as each section became a square that could make a Holdfast!

And now Gyrth had also brought a section of our archers who soon set to work picking their target: the leaders in this group from Ponthieu as he saw that their Count Guy was one of the knights who rode away!

But now, these surviving knights, had formed up in a phalanx that was about to cut a path towards Harold and Gyrth, and now the crossbowman had long pikes; as They were also fighting for their lives, They managed to *clear a path towards the king's standard that was now to be seen high above the melee.*

*The very place where he and Gyrth, stood at the centre of his square. Where they could see the Saxon king was also fighting a losing battle with three of the biggest of the Norman knights.*

*But it was Gyrth who held the shield wall now, as Harold had pulled away and to ride back to the centre of their line so they could see this new frontal attack.*

*And now Gyrth was winning this fight with these Norman knights and at his side was Thomas the Strong, who the Normans believed was Harold this day. But Gyrth would also be a victory for these knights as they saw he was wearing the horned helmet and Gyrth s Sigel on the shield. And if they could bring him down, the Saxons would lose their greatest general.*

*And now another section of Williams's best fighters was about to join this fight, and soon Gyrth and his would-be surrounded.*

*But Gyrth had seen them, and he had a way to deal with this diamond attack. This was to order the hedgehog defence, a Roman legion* attack formation. But then, the spearhead was being attacked on three sides, as this new section of Knights had ridden past and sought another way to attack these Saxons! So now the Normans Knights had to fight on foot and the Saxon warriors were dying all over the battlefield.

But when Harold looked at the battlefield, he saw that there was nothing more he could do up here. as more warriors were coming from the woods behind Gyrth's defence line that we had formed at the ravine, he was killing the Normans who had to survive the crash into the ravine?

And they had formed up with some Norman Knights hiding in the woods? Perhaps Harold should have realised then that they would be the real threat, but he was also engaged with Williams's army, who had managed to get over the shock of seeing the knights from Colbeck running away and the others burnt alive.

Then there was a shout from their ranks from a man with a booming voice that everyone could hear, and it stopped the fighting for a moment.

"*Harold has fallen. See, his horse runs free.*" And another shouted,

"*Our King Is Dead! We Have Lost This Fight! Run Men Run While You Can!*" *But knew that second voice. It was that of Adulf the traitor*

*But now William knights came charging out of his line, and they were mounted on the biggest war horse we have ever seen.*

But seeing Gyrth and Harold were standing back-to-back, And that Harold was standing there bareheaded. It was Guy who pointed to him telling his phalanx of crossbow men to fire into the square, and so were they all killed, pieced by so many bolts, as one hit Harold Godwinson in his Unprotected eye so died King Harold Godwinson, destined to be the Last of the Saxon kings of Engaland"

***

*Leofric, Story,*

*And so it was that Gytha, and I were to witness the massacre at Senlac and be there when Williams's captain came to find Harold's mother, hid first and wife, at their baggage train and drag them to the field of Senlac, and they were forced to find Harold's body for them*

But it is here that I must ask my God for his forgiveness, as I was forced to swear an oath that day that these men, who had found were Harold was to lie under a pole of his men. I could do that because he lay beside the dead bodies of his brother, Gyrth Whose bodies were peppered with Norman arrows, as was the head of Harold, with an arrow in the left eye, and his head was so mutilated it was no wonder no one of his Saxon subjects could tell him from the others but as Gyrth was near they saw his and mutilated head. As Harold's body had been trampled beneath a charging horse, smashed, and battered so badly?

*So was this body put on a cart as it and Gytha and Edith, were taken to see the victorious Duke William so that we all could swear on the cross that this was indeed the body of our king.*

But even then, William was not sure we were speaking the truth until Edith pointed to a birthmark on the man's inner thigh. And to say

"If you will open his broken legs a little wider, lord Oda, you will see a mark that only a woman who has been him naked can know off? Or a wife and his mother have seen. See there it is a red birthmark on the inside by his privates. A strawberry mark that says this the body of our King Harold Godwinson. But we would pay you any sum you want to have him. So that he can have a Christian burial."

But the bishop Odo, was looking to William for his instructions` as Gytha said,

"Will you allow this William of Normandy As my daughter in law is correct to say it is you who are the victor here and we are at your mercy, And I also ask that you allow us to bury my sons. As I only have Wulfnoth, to care for me now my last male heir that you hold your prisoner in Falaise. As I need time to morn my three sons who have died here on this Hill. Do this and I will trouble you no more I will retire to a monastery if you can grant this my last request. I will pay you his weight in gold to be allowed to do this for my sons?"

For a moment we looked at the duke and for a moment we could hope he would let Gytha do as she had asked, but then we saw him harden his heart and we were refused as William was determined that no one would know where Harold Godwinson was to be buried or any of his kin. Saying to us all.

"No that cannot be, there can be no grave for people to find and try to say here lies. And I want to hear you all say that Harold Godwinson, was not true of king of the Saxons.

We will burn his and his brother and no one will know where we scatter his ashes to the winds. We will do so out at sea Gytha Godwinson.

But as for you and yours I was told by Leofric here, that you were on your way To Exeter . But I cannot agree to that as you have lands there, Nor can you go home to Denmark where you are loved. I will send you to Flanders then,

So, I will allow this if you will for fill your promise to go to live in a monastery of my choice and remain there for the rest of your life.

Furthermore, I demand that you must give up your Saxon name and titles and lands here in my kingdom. to revert to your maiden's name as must all your kin.

*That is my mercy this day lady. Can you do that .If so you and your bishop may leave here unharmed?"*

*But as we all listened to Duke Williams words, that would let Gytha leave this place alive, so did I see Gytha's back stiffen and now she was staring straight at William, standing strong and with her old fire in her eyes.*

She stood proud and Tall Gytha Godwinson *mother of a king.*

*"So, then it is true that To the victor goes the spoils, Duke. And yes, I will go to Flanders and into banishment But as for giving up my name or bending the knee to you as the King of Engaland Godwin and Harold would not wish that.*

*So, No, I will not do that. So, you had best slit my throat and burn me with my king . You see I have lived far too long as it is, and I do not fear death or the judgement of the Norse Gods. But you are said to be a committed Christian must know how you tricked Harold that day.*

*And you also, will be judged for it. As for the poor Engaland. It was never my home, and I am well rid of it, and you! But I fear for these poor Saxons who will have to suffer your so-called mercy now!"*

As William heard and saw this wonderful women who was never going to see him as anything as a usurper, he managed to give us a wry smile, and then to say.

"Well now woman, I see the real you at last Gytha of Denmark A true Viking warrior to the last. and Yes, I have decided to let you live to regret your angry words as we all must stand before our maker soon and our Gods. So, I charge you Leofric, to take their woman and her

people to the port at Hastings, where you will all take ship to Flanders. Leave us now, before I change my mind."

***

Back in twentieth century Exeter, Doctor Simon Robinson, put down the printed sections that was to describe the battle of hastings , and put them aside as he tried to come to terms with what he had read there, But the truth was there was a lot more unread about the aftermath of this battle and how the Duke William was to take the Crown and force his will and his people on what was once a Saxon nation. Turning his anger, on anyone who opposed him as he forced the whole country to bend its knee to him and his Norman noblemen and their new way of life.

And now he had to see that Jake had failed in his attempt to change all this. At least in his and their timeline.

*So Simon can now see Est evidence that fake am not only the slip across the matrix and enter , workers live and make contact with the alternate dimensions and time lines that there and now he must once again as the experts how this could be possible for a human mind of without any credence of these Dark matter on the amount of particle energy, that is required so then can he talk to one of the minerals at CERN and what he is told outed their experiments leads him to be necessarily alarmed and concerned as this sacrist Belarus that it is their experiments*

*then search for the Higgs- Boson particle which ray here well opened a rift in aw space time and that is that fake can use. But then it gets much worse when he is told of the alert developers of battered intelligence a) QUANTUM computer. A tensing feed of study and a. store where the fitters of the film-the TERMINATOR to a*

*led by monitors could not pass. Come AND INFO HERE, Reading blot fate has tried to do in the past and that*

someone has merged to thwart his efforts to mountains these time love Soren realises that he must suppress

these "Rutter notes and the Diary Before they are published end, even worse, the fake news that must remain lost in the post-so that no one Eres con use them to cargo their history. for the worse bus now there was the protean if the Al and Quorum computers that were about to charge avg.la they knew to be possible? THER m i N top D used a time machine to destroy the putout going a foothold in their fantasy world, but now severe fibres was about to come true? What then if the Senor Roberson could send fate Beats to stop this research before it. got a food held in our world. perhaps then fate would not love been lost without a good Reason. But fist then must shut this rift on time and close down EEE RAV, But how? Is it possible for Jake to do all this as he was just a normal man?

A man lost in time. And now Simon was going to make it the rest his life's work, to find out. Not just for his own sake and peace of mind but to fine some answers for Mandy, and her new son. Even If that meant going back to school, to learn about Quantum time and the new work being done at Cern and this question of multiple dimensions. So be it. As for this Dark matter, and all that *it involves for them all he would start at Exeter University, and with Professor Paul Foster.*

*But before he could make contact with Foster, he had a very unusual letter from him, and one that was to change everything he thought he knew about the Jake Rutter mystery.*

***

The Memory Stick.

It came, the morning that he was to go to the Exeter university science department at Ten am. Sharp, to meet Paul Foster, who was going to show him their laboratories and also meet with some of the other experts in this field of Quantum Mechanics ,and particle physics. And to make sure that Simon would have the answers to his questions, Simon had sent them a list. That would cover the gaps in his studies.

He had previously sent Paul his comments, and his theory about the Time slipping into the past, and an extract of the Leofric books. And then Paul had told him to come the very next day.

But before he left his office, his secretary Jane, came into his office clutching a stuffed brown envelope to her chest and she was holding it, as if her life depended on it as she said all in a hurry.

"I am sorry Sir, but I think you should see this package before you leave the office. I think it has something to do with that man Rutter. It was handed to me by a young student in Sainsburys. He asked me who I was and if I was going to work. I was about to tell him to sod off when he gave me this and said.so softly I had to listen hard to hear him. *This is for Doctor Robinson see, from a well-wisher, and it contains Some vital Information he will need to have before today's meeting. But he must not open it in his office or home. Do not fear lady it is only a memory stick. But his life depends on this so you will do as you are told.* Then he was gone leaving me standing in the soup isle., So I came right here Sir. See there is some strange writing on the envelope. I do hope I did the right think Sir. I do hope it is not a letter bomb Sir. Should I ring the police?"

She asked, as she passed over this mysterious package, Simon saw the strange writing on it and knew it was that of the Bishop Leofric, and written in his codex that only he and Jake, could read? So how could this be possible.

But when Simon looked at the message, he realised he would need his primer to read it? but there were some initials at the bottom of this handwritten note. They were P.F?

So then was this package from Paul and then he was to read the message to know it was.

Dear Simon, I write this to tell you that we both are in terrible danger now. And I if you have received this memory stick, you must keep it safe and not try to open it on any of your electronic devices, in your office or your home. So, find a safe place to read what is on it and soon.

When you know what I know you will know what you need to do.

PS.

You will need your private computer code to open the files.

## PF

Simon read his translation three times, to make sure he had not made any mistakes, and when he opened the envelope, inside was a single memory stick, that one could insert into a suitable reading device.

And realising this must be important, and just how urgent this was he went out to the reception, to speak to Jane, and to ask her a big favour.

*"Look Jane, you should know that inside the letter, is this memory stick but the note said I should not open it here or at home. You see, it is from Professor Foster , the very man I am expecting to meet this morning.*

*As yet I cannot think, why he has gone to such lengths to send me this the very day of our meeting. Or why all this cloak and dagger stuff is necessary. But I know him well enough now, to trust what he tells me.*

*So, I need a favour, I know you have a personal lab top in your Office, that you use sometimes to be able to work at home? So, you see I wonder if I could borrow it for the morning. You see Paul, has sent me a memory stick, and to read these files. But I fear there could be a problem* with this memory stick as it may contain a virus. And I do not want it to corrupt our computer and our files!

But if that is the case, I would understand that you also would not want to risk that. If you could back your files, I was hoping to use your laptop and if there are any problems, we could buy a new one to use.

She said,

"Good heavens how mysterious Simon but yes of course I understand we must be so careful with our computers these days! I have it in my car give me ten minutes to fetch it. Do you want me to open the Document section. I will do a backup and I know I can trust you not to look at anything else on it?

And that was happened and when, Simon was alone in his office, he inserted the memory stick, it opened to an icon, that said insert password. And he thought long and hard, before he typed his own most secret, and difficult password.

The file opened to a picture of Paul Foster, and once again some typing, which used the Leofric codex.

*This is for the eyes of Doctor Simon Robinson only. And if you cannot reinsert his password within five minutes the files will be deleted.*

Reading this dire warning, Simon did as he was told and he had to wonder, just what he was getting himself into now.

*Here is what he was to read and discover…*

*I see you have the stick Simon, and now you should know that I am possibly dead, or missing, and I can never meet you again. And once you have read the attachments, I would ask you also to be very careful as to what you decide to do next!*

*You see, by sending you these files, I am breaking the law, and the official secrets act.*

*A document that we all had to sign to work on the University labourites that deal with the research into the fields of Quantum Mechanics, Quantum computers and now the search for Dark matter.*

*Our Work here at Exeter is located in a secret separate building on the campus and is funded by our Government, Nasa and more especially Cern in Geneva.*

*But you need to know our work is so secret and important, that we are monitored by MI6 and the American CIA. And That Is Why Your Home And Office Has Been Bugged, the moment you began looking into the death of Richard Higgings, and the Leofric Books and then to listen to what Jake Rutter, Could do!*

*So perhaps now you will see why the people at Exeter were horrified to learn of the police investigations!*

When You Are Finished, You Will Understand Just What We Are Dealing With, As Both Higgings And Jake And Even Susan Were Murder, To Prevent The Publication Of

What They Had Discovered About The Possibility Of Time Travel.

*And now Mandy Jones is missing!*

But as yet you have slipped their nett. So, I leave it to you to decide what you should do with this memory stick You see I was about to send it to someone in the media, who could expose these murderess for what they are! But I made the mistake of speaking to someone in MI6

*So now you could be next to be made to disappear so. Do not make my mistake…*

Simon stopped reading then, as he knew about Cern, and the work at the Haldon Collider and he had been there to see it when he had been on holiday in Switzerland. so then did Simon open his I pad, to look up what google said about Cern…

\*\*\*

**Cern.**

*Founded in 1954, the CERN laboratory sits astride the Franco-Swiss border near Geneva. It was one of Europe's first joint ventures and now has Twenty-Two, member states…*

*How did it start? Physicists at CERN are seeking answers, to their questions to how the Universes were created and why>*

*They do this by using some of the world's most powerful particle accelerators*

*At CERN, The European Organization For Nuclear Research, and their physicists and engineers, are probing the fundamental structure of the universe.*

*They use the world's largest and most complex scientific instruments to study the basic constituents of matter – the fundamental particles. The particles are made to collide together at close to the speed of light. The process gives the physicists clues about how the particles interact and provides insights into the fundamental laws of nature.*

*The instruments used at CERN are purpose-built* **particle accelerators** *and* **detectors. Accelerators,** *that can boost beams of particles to high energies before the beams are made to collide with each other or with stationary targets.*

*These Detectors, observe and record the results of these collisions...*

As Simon read more of the Cern files and reports he was looking for something that would explain why Paul had sent them to him, but theywere mainly reports of their experiments and routines.

*While he found them incredibly interesting, he* could not see anything to through a light on their problems with the Quantum world Well that was not quite true, as at the end there was a note that said.

There may be a problem with our Safety of particle collisions.

*Main article: Safety of high-energy particle collision experiments*

The experiments at the Large Hadron Collider sparked fears that the particle collisions might produce doomsday phenomena, involving the production of stable microscopic black holes or the creation of hypothetical particles called strangelets.

And Two CERN-commissioned safety reviews examined these concerns and concluded that the experiments at the LHC present no danger and that there is no reason for concern, a conclusion endorsed by the American Physical Society.

HERE THEN WAS A POSSIBLE RIFT IN TIME?

*** 

*A Rift In Time.*

*However, as Simon saw no difference or any problems with what Cern was doing, and he returned to Pauls files, to look at the headings*

*Early Days. The Search For The Shield.*

**The Accident.**

**Quantum Time experiments.**

**Dark Matter.**

**Quantum Computers.**

**Artificial Intelligence.**

*Looking at this list Simon, realised just what Paul was about to show him in these files, and that he would need a lot longer to study them. so, he removed the memory stick and left his office, to go back to find Jane and speak to her. Knowing now, that someone was listening to what* was said! and now they knew about the memory stick He handed over a note he had written, that would tell Jane what they must do. It said,

*Jane my dear we both are in deep trouble .here this day! Do not speak to me now, as everything we say is being overheard and recorded.*

*Just believe me and do as I ask, and with no comment.*

Then as she looked up in some alarm Simon said for the listener's benefit. If Paul could ask him to take great care here today, he was going to do just that.

"Look Jane my dear. I do not feel very well, and I want you to cancel all my appointments today.

I must hope that It will pass. And you must shut up the office and go home. No do not do that. Look I will not need you to keep the office open for a while. Take a weeks paid holiday Go to your sisters in Brighton. Do it now."

Jane was looking at him as if he had gone stark staring mad, as she knew, Simon also knew she had no sister in

Brighton, Helen, was in Eastbourne. Then the penny dropped, and after what Simon had said about listeners! This was his way of telling her to leave the office and do so in secret.

She spoke out as loud as it would be proper, and in such circumstances for those listeners to hear her words.

*"My sister Sir. Yes, I could do with a holiday Sir. I need to visit my sister in Brighton. She is always asking me to drop in anytime. It will be a nice surprise for her! and if you are sure, it will be alright. Then, I will tidy up here and go down in the morning. my sister will like that Sir. And I hope you feel better soon. You know how to find me in Brighton then"*

*Good girl Simon thought,* and then he left the office, to find an hotel and a new lab top and a suitcase and a week's clothes as well as some toiletries.

*He would have liked to go home to get his things.*

He lived in a fist floor flat, in a new block of apartments, that was beside the River Exe, and opposite Exe Island. It was his choice he had never married. Not after Rachel had tricked him by saying she was pregnant.

*She was a staff Nurse at the Royal Devon Hospital, and they had met there when he needed to see some of his sick patients. And it was true that he had found her incredibly attractive, But there was no way he was going to become involved with anyone at the hospital where he was a consultant.*

That was until that fateful Christmas staff party, and they both had drunk far too much at the free bar, It was then, she had shown him just how much she wanted him to fuck her, and that had been all too easy to be caught up in her incredible body as the kissing and groping become so much more, as they found an empty room and bed.

*But on his part their love making had been pure lust, and he had never been in love with her. Even so he was about to stop their affair, not wanting her to get pregnant, And people were beginning to talk about them at work!*

*That was when she told him that she was barren, and they need not worry about any consequences.*

It was later that he was to learn, that she was a well know easy lay, and he was one of her ticks on her long list of doctors, and consultants ,and anyone she thought would help her want to marry her and help her to climb up the social ladder. She said, she was thirty-five years then but like some women she had lied, and he had discovered that she was nearer Forty. But it when he said they must take precautions to avoid having a child, she had said she was barren, and the doctors had told her she could not have children

*And then and once he had tasted her incredible body and her unusual, and fantastic ways of love making, he had found that he could not give her up.*

But their affair, was to begin to break apart when she suggested they should marry! He had baulked at that and told her they must stop meeting At their rendezvous which was the Devon motel. But it was then that Rachel, told him she was with child! His first thought was could she say it was his?

*but then he knew he also wanted a child. And then they were living together in his house on St Leonards Road in his father's large Edwardian Villa.*

And as time went on And he had thought he would grow to love her, and their child! But he was wrong to hope that, and when the baby was still born, she simply went complete off from having any sort of sexual relationships. Then as his work became so difficult when she took a Matrons job in Bristol and then, they drifted apart and stopped seeing each other.

*And now, he was content to be a single man of Forty-Five and content to live the life of a Batchelor for a while.*

But, Looking in a mirror anyone would see a tall man of just under six foot and well-built and fit. As he went to the Gym once a week to keep himself in reasonable trim. And he was of medium build, but now his once blonde hair, was thinning and he could see that he was become grey at his sideburns and thin on top. And he now needed his glasses to read any fine print?

*And while his craggy face was not handsome, as his nose was a little twisted after a broken nose playing Rugby at university, but he still had a strong wide mouth and firm chin. Rachel had said she thought he looked like Richard Gear, and he had started to think of Richard as a role model. Not really handsome but quite respectable. and a man who had no trouble attracting the more mature women he liked to date.*

But that's as far as he wanted it to go, As he had found he was far too busy to have much of a social life, as he found it hard to trust a woman after his affair with Rachel the hussy! It was a case of once burnt , twice shy was his motto. Love them and leave them. Or pay for their services.

*He knew that the truth was that he was seen as a little hard hearted, but he was never going to love a woman who could trick or hurt him again. But now as he got older, and his work was becoming a routine task? He was finding that this was a lonely life.*

And then, Jake Rutter, had come into his life, and he had been caught up in his incredible life story!

*A life that read like a science fiction novel! and now he knew he had a Tiger by its tail and that was both frightening and exciting.*

It was time to get back to the files on the memory stick , he would start at the beginning

*But Paul had said he was next on the list! And if Paul had been so careful, and if he was missing, well he was not going to play their game. And this was some sort of a game alright!*

## The Early Days. The Search For The Shield.

Simon was on full alert now and not a little paranoid about being watched or in danger, as he let two taxies pass, before he hailed one, and then changed his mind, as to what hotel he asked the driver to take him to. Even then he looked to see if he had been followed but of course he saw no one, as he went into the lobby of the hotel and out the back door to find another cab a Third hotel.

*All very James Bond!*

As for a car, well he would leave the Jag in the garage He would call an uber when he needed one and the truth was, he was more than a little excited, at this new game of cloak and dagger.

*Perhaps that was a bad simile*

And now he was going to take his time looking at the files on the memory stick and then to decide what he must do with it.

*And besides, it was getting late evening, and he needed a shower and a change of clothes. So, he unpacked his new clothes underwear and showed and wearing the blue jeans and a printed blue sweatshirt, that said he was from Nike and a pair of sneakers, he had to hope he looked less like the professional doctor, that had registered at the desk.*

As he went down to the dining room for an early dinner of Stake and chips with a mushroom sauce. Then, another indulgence, as he never usually had afters, a cream caramel, and a large brandy.

Much fortified, he went to his room on the top floor, and it has a balcony, one could use to took across Exeter and down the River, to Topsham. *One of his favourite eating and sailing places.* But he had no time for the view today! As he poured himself out another small brandy from the curtsy fridge and inserted the memory stick. into his brand-new laptop and remembering to change his password he was ready to begin reading these secret files.

## Early Days. The Search For The Shield.

*The first thing he saw was another message from Paul.*

Well then, I will start at the beginning when I was requited by Richard Higgings, to help him to understand something of the Quantum world, as he told me that he needed to find a way to research the past and find a way to read some old books he had found in the Exeter archives.

I was more than a little surprised, when I was approached by the Historian Richard Higgings, a professor of History and not a scientist...

But then, he told me that History, was his second interest, and his real love was for mathematics, and the new revelations and advances in computers.

*That he had heard of what we were doing to help the people at Cern, and then he showed me some calculations* he had made about the work of Albert Einstein, of all people.

The paper Richard had given me was all And about worm holes black holes that could change time, and swallow space and light.it said that a black hole could form a rift in the fabric of the matrix. or the dark matter we saw as the binding glue of the Universes.

*Even to be responsible for the formation of alternative dimensions that could exist in the Quantum world .Just how Richard had managed to work all this out was quite astonishing!*

And it was then I agreed to try to help him look into our experiments with Quantum time. But that is putting the preverbal cart before the Horse, I expect you know about the Hadron Collider and the work at Geneva.

*But before that One Must Open The Files On*

**The Accident. and the Quantum Time experiments.**

What you don't know is that theywere having a problem with their shielding and their control of the Lazer beam and they had to shut it all down, until they could fix it.

And it was then they came to us here at Exeter, to meet with Professor Hendric .I expect you know of him as he is an old man now, but he has an incredible mend and a compatriot of Reinstein and Oppenheim. and it was the people at Cern thought he could help with their shielding problems.

*As Professor Martin Henrick, was one of the leading people in the field of Electromagnetism, having work for the Americans at Los Alamos, and working on the shield that was a part their nuclear programme and the Thermo-nuclear bomb.*

He also built a collider in America, and he was just about to begin using it when the Yanks joined with Europe at Geneva, and he came her to England and Exeter. A , he was here to study the new field of Dark matter and his lives in a cave deep underground waiting for his computers to register this phenomenon of Dark matter.

*However, that is something you will read about elsewhere.*

What you need to know Simon, is that Martin agreed to build a testing facility, and a small collider similar to the one he shut down in the USA, as early as the 1950/60 period. As, it was thought to be too dangerous to use at that time, and it was draining money that was needed elsewhere for the space programme.

Furthermore, Martin was able to test its shielding, here in Exeter, and we were more than delighted to become involved in his new project.

*So, with the help of the Americans at Nasa, and our own scientist, who were a part of the European project, we call Cern. We built a small model of the collider at the Military base out at Lympstone, here in Devon. A secret secure base, that was also deep underground.*

It was there, that we did manage to combine the Cern research, with that of what Martin had found, and my team were convinced now Martin Henrick, was right and that our different construction of the magnetic shied would hold, when we fired our twin lasers.

*But, while his shield was working at first our engineers had made a terrible error in the fitting of one of the magnets as the shielding worked at first, until one of the magnets failed, and buckled. As it released a sort burst and for a microsecond, we shot a particle beam of energy out into the base. And the countryside.*

As you know, our collider, was not to be a full scale working a particle accelerator, all we needed to do was to

test our shielding. As our laser brings two
opposing particle beams together, and with such force ,
these particles collide.

*As you may or not know, In particle physics, colliders,
though harder to construct, are a powerful research tool
because they reach a much higher centre energy
than fixed target setups.*

Even so, Martain had had proved, his new design would
work at Cern! As our analysis of the results of the byproducts of these collisions, so then would they give us a
good evidence concerning the structure of
the subatomic world, and the laws of nature that are seen
to be governing it!

Many of these byproducts are produced only by high-
energy collisions, and they decay after very short periods
of time. Thus, many of them are hard or nearly
impossible to study in other ways.

*]But the strength of one of the magnets was out of line,
and when the magnet failed, it allowed a minute breach to
occur in the wall lining.*

It Killed A Lot Of The Marines, And Some Of The
Local Fishermen At Lympstone Harbour.

*There was an enquiry, But the real cause was hushed up and blamed on a computer glitch and an explosion of some out-of-date ammunition and a fire caused by Sunspot activity . As by a coincidence or not there was indeed a reported discharge from the sun that wiped out so many computers then.*

**It Was Later That We Were To Discover That The Accident Had Some Side Effects, On The People In The Area.**

And one such victim was Richard Higgins, and now I believe another, was your Jake Rutter

*As like Jake, who I know now he was taking his parents in his car to have lunch at The Globe. I know now that that was the day of the so called ancient. What if Jake had blacked out at the wheel at Lympstone that day.*

I know now that Higgins was to develop what you will now as a dual personality disorder, and also suffer black outs and have terrible dreams. But what we did not know then, was that Richard Higgings, was wearing that ring that was to be charged with negative ions, and in the right conditions, it could be used to open a rift in **Quantum space and even time.**

*And we know now that Jake was using his metal walking frame then it was that which took a blast from the experiment and started his blackouts.*

*So now Simon you see what I am trying to tell you, is I have come to believe that Jake also can open a wormhole or an opening into the quantum space and an alternative dimension of space time where he can make contact with a different past? when he wears the ring.*

But I made the mistake of telling my fellow scientist, about my suspicions, and they told the CIA man, and our secret service at MI6. And I believe now some of our people went to the reading room to confront Higgings that day about his claims for the Leofric books, are from a different dimension, and an alternative timeline.

*And having read Jakes account about the battle between the Normans and the Saxons, as set down by Leofric, one where the outcome of the battle at Hasting, had a very different outcome, as the Bishop tells us that Harold survives this fight. But He is wounded, and taken to Exeter, where Gytha and his surviving family will continue the fight against the Norman Invaders.*

That in itself is an incredible seed change in their history if William is eventually defeated and the Saxon way of life is maintained. Who could know what incredible changes in that timeline this change would bring about.

*And that is why we need to try to find a way to bring Rutter back to our time if it is possible and prove that it is possible to Time slip.*

But before you decide what you must do next, I urge you to read the rest of these files. As only then, can you make an informed opinion. Good luck.

*Moreover, Richard was being very vocal about the dangers of our research and the development of the Quantum computers and how we wee using the new science of artificial intelligence to do this. I saw a paper he wrote that spoke of a great threat to or lies and jobs, and even our National security.*

I see now that it was that paper that brought him to the attention of the equity people, and perhaps they went these to the reading room, possibly, to question him about this paper. You will see a copy in the files.

*But what if it was these people at the CIA who were to cause Richard to have a heart attack? What if he resisted their questioning take him their prisoner and bring him here for questioning about what had happened at Lympstone and about what he had found in the Leofric books and his claim to be able to time travel!*

But that went all badly wrong when the taser started a heart attack, and they were forced to cover up his accidental death. And I think the CIA managed to alter the records and recordings to do that.

*However, that is not why you and I are now at risk. That is because of my own research, into the building of these new Quantum Commuters, that is our current aim.*

Moreover, you will need to open the next set of files, that will tell you all we know about Dark matter!

*And how we are using the new advances with artificial intelligence machines and programs, we can use to find the elusive elemental forces of the universes, and how dangerous the use of Artificial Intelligence computers is and can be for our future development!*

I expect you have seen the Science fiction Films about it called Terminator. Well, they are only the beginning of a new age, and soon no *one or country, will be secure from their touch.*

But I was foolish enough to tell all this to our government and MI6, and now I am a wanted man and on the run.

*\*\*\*

*It was the next day, Simon was ready to go on with the story of these incredible advances in science and to read some more about the Quantum Time experiments, Dark Matter, and these Quantum Computers and about the use of .Artificial Intelligence To build them.*

### *This File Is Called, The Alternative Dimensions Of Space And Time.

It was when our scientists opened the door to the previously unknown dimensions, and their incredible potential for reaching across our dimension of space time, and enter this magical threshold was to be found a new theory, that was previously only a possibility.

*It was the work of Peter Hicks, who saw the possible existence of this energy field entire universe as early as 1964*

As he worked with Albert Einstein, Higgs realised that Albert, was both right and wrong, to say that the speed of light was a fixed constant. and Higgs said it was a beam that could be bent like any wave of energy, and changed, by a great mass of Gravity like a Black Hole.

And now, we see that Elementary particles, reacts completely differently to the field just as a streamline this is the discovery of scientific achievements 125 which is around 133 times is real!

*And elementary particles, must also obey the laws of particle physics. and to move incredibly fast. That we ca can describe this unpredictability exist for around 10 to the power of -22/2*

But this does not make it so easy for scientists to prove outside a particle accelerator. as if we are getting further and further away. indeed, it is particularly exciting this process is about 6.6% of the time calculation.

*Nevertheless, any previously discovered experiments, provide us with the keys to understanding and the universe and the deviations from these theoretical predictions.*

It was Higgs who was to understand the fundamental forces in the 1970s, that describes these fundamental particles, and forces are universe as well as force transmitters 125 minutes,

And their ability to give practically impossible calculation has proven to be extraordinarily precise, and now to open the door to develop a Quantum time computer. Using the power of this new field of artificial intelligence and thanks to the film industry and its writer's fantastic imagination. The 'Terminator films' for instance.

But we also know just how this work will be viewed by the public. Who will see it as a dangerous field to explore, or build, such an incredible artificial mind, a machine that can build a Quantum computer and we need it to use one?

But we cannot put that Genie back in its bottle and with the discovery of the new particles that form from an atom and compose the very building blocks of all life and matter, everywhere. When something like the electron appears to be stronger than physics and natural science could have imagined or subscribe to!

And now we have developed the quantum computers, we are on the brink of another revolution difficult to calculate.

Especially when combined with artificial intelligence and machine soon take control of everything, so must we devise a way to ave some additional security that can give us the control over these new computers.

As they will have the control of almost everything we need and use.

*From online banking to government secrets, the switches on our weapons and machines.*

*It Is These Advanced Electronic Brains That We Can Use Calculations That Is Beyond A Human Brain And Do Something That Makes A Big Difference This Is Really Strange Computers And Superposition Or Predict The Weather.*

*It is a bit like having a super emergency madness galaxies hundred percent confidential information technologies for national security.*

A potential threat of security the accuracy of information, But now as we come to rely on these extremely expensive quantum computers, that will probably be available get to grips with the problems of computers supercomputers

*It is they who have only the result of the calculation temperature and the nature of reality disappear exist*

*seems to be the case is very unstable nevertheless is that a possibility we can just about to get to the bottom of the new fields of the Quantum space and time, that we cannot see, or reach as yet.*

If You Are Such A Computer At The Entrance To A Completely New Physical Dimension Of The Distance Between Them To Communicate With Each Other And To Share Information.

The most famous example of the quantum experience is when a living entity, is considered to be alive and dead at the same time. To be able think about the Schroeder cat who existed side-by-side until it made the Quantum choice to use the death switch. It was alive as it could never do anything, but die in the box?

*It is these recent experience every day because we experience them every day trips this reality is reality but it's true*

 I probably never be able to fully describe the true nature of the universe, and the reality this is a never-ending process.

That is how we use the Alfred Nobel prizes, in the categories of physics chemistry physiology and peace exclamation receive the prize has been awarded it subscribe to advances in all science and technology.

*But now we should tell you a story about quantum computers, as we are on the brink of another difficult leap over a cliff.*

As we use these new Quantum machines that are not really a part of this world, to calculate especially when combined with artificial intelligence.

*We have made A monster that soon we allow to take control of everything we ask of it. A brain, with the ability to perform calculation everything cryptography additional security and everything from online banking to government secrets it switches calculations.*

*As, they can do something that makes a big difference different from normal PC computer computers*

*But we have a manual control of these as they can to calculate much faster computers thana human brain.*

*But now a Quantum computer, can predict the weather it's a bit like having a super reproduce the dynamics of galaxies, and enter Quantum space.*

But we cannot control them or be use what they learn is kept confidential. As they can use this information technologies to breach our national security data, of any the security of national and international space projects computer systems.

*Even Nasa Is Worried About This That They Have Put A Stop On Their Development, Until They Are Sure, They Are Safe To Use*

To halt the new computer technology opportunities complex molecular structures and develop new potential threat computers mechanism, is created, at the same time we also didn't really know less the accuracy of information generated by AI systems

But as we are on the brink of another revolution binarily world to open the door by the public are dangerous masterpiece of engineering which is something like the electron appears to be stronger than physics and natural science subscribe now tell you a story about quantum computers.

*We are on the brink of another revolution difficult to calculate especially when combined with artificial intelligence and machine soon take control of everything.*

**You are probably wondering if we are a little too late to be worried about all these artificial brains?**

The answer is yes because this area has not been well thought out.

But now at last our governments have seen how a foreign power can use this new technologies to our disadvantage, and they have become both alarmed and frightened about national security issues!

Hence the enrolment at Exeter and other places with MI6 and the CIA.

They are also the problems on how to get to grips with the problems of these computers, and supercomputers in order to verify the result of the calculations, temperature, and the nature of reality, do not seem to exist in real time?

*Nevertheless, this is that a possibility we can just about to get to the bottom if you are a quantum computer.*

So now, are we at the entrance to a completely new physical dimension, that will apply to the distance between them, and their ability to communicate with each other. Sharing any information.

*We know that NASA was using this computer technology, as an opportunity to study these complex molecular* structures and develop new trucks potential threat computers mechanism is created at the same time, we also didn't really know less the accuracy of information generated by AI systems, but we are on the brink of another revolution.

*** 

*And while Simon was having more than a little difficulty in understanding all this 'Mumbo Jumbo; but even he could see some of the dangers these Quantum computers were going to pose to the security industry and how and why they would wish to put a stop to the artificial brains taking over the world!*

And they would not wish to believe in alternative realities into which someone could time slip to be able to alter the past. Or the present!

*And why, they had tried to prevent Foster sharing these files!*

And now the people at Cern were finding that their origional ideas, about the Higgs Boson molecule were going to be modified, as well as the Dark matter theories.

***

So, having finished what was on the memory disc, Simon was left with more questions than answers. And what he should do about all this as while Foster had said Higgings may had been killed, Susan had been killed in the fire along with Jake?

*That left Mandy, and this memory stick? but what was on it as far as he could tell, is also to be found in the public domain. And it is only Paul Foster who has said that a crime had been committed and he was missing.*

*It was true he could send the stick to the police or the media but that would not bring Jake back.*

In the end Simon decided to hide the memory stick and return to his normal life. As he came to realise that he was not only risking his own life by continuing with his investigations into the life and times of Jake Rutter.

*He was also putting everyone else he had spoken to about this in danger Especially as Paul was still missing.*

*And try to forget Jake Rutter, and time travel.*

*The End*

***

*Epilogue,*

Mandy was sitting by the fire looking into the flames, and she had the old sword on her lap, as it was all she had left of her beloved Jake.

She had not realised that she was stroking it, thinking, and wishing her Jake, had managed to hear the recall home that day .

*Remembering that Simon had said he was lost in time, and she had to get on with her life, and care for her new son.*

As her grief became too much to bear! As she shouted out.

*Blast you Jake rutter did you not hear me call you back What was the word Television. Please Come back Jake!*

*Flash, Flash, Flash!*

With that the sword, became too hot to hold, as the air shimmered, and Jake was there beside her.

*As he had heard the recall this time, and he knew then that I was no longer back the University reading room. I knew this place and those smells; They were those of my beloved Mandy and this was her home! He was alive and unharmed!*

Printed in Great Britain
by Amazon